Copyright © 2021
Podium Publishing, ULC
All rights reserved.

No part of this publication may be reproduced, stored in a retrieval system, or transmitted in any form or by any means electronic, mechanical, photocopying, recording, or otherwise without the prior written permission from Podium Publishing.

Shadowplay Copyright © 2021 by Terry Mancour and Emily Burch Harris
Book Design and Layout Copyright © 2021 by Podium Publishing

This novel is a work of fiction. Names, characters, places, and incidents are either products of the author's imagination or used fictitiously. Any resemblance to actual events, locales, or persons, living, dead, or undead, is entirely coincidental.

Website: www.podiumaudio.com
Series Website: www.spellmongerseries.com
Newsletter: www.spellmongernewsletter.com

SHADOWPLAY

SPELLMONGER - LEGACY AND SECRETS, BOOK 1

TERRY MANCOUR

EMILY BURCH HARRIS

Sign up for Terry's newsletter for the latest musings, updates, and release information from the Archmage himself!

Head to the link below and enter your email to stay connected.

http://spellmongernewsletter.com/

CONNECT WITH TERRY MANCOUR

Get updates
http://spellmongernewsletter.com/

Check out the Spellmonger series
https://spellmongerseries.com/

Join the Spellmonger Discord
https://discord.gg/68txXKR

Follow him on Amazon
https://www.amazon.com/Terry-Mancour/e/B004QTNFOO

Like his Facebook page
https://www.facebook.com/spellmongerseries/

CONNECT WITH EMILY BURCH HARRIS

Visit her website

https://emilyburchharris.com

Follow her on Amazon

https://www.amazon.com/Emily-Burch-Harris/e/B017Y87Q7U

Like her Facebook page

https://www.facebook.com/avalonschoice/

Follow her on Instagram

https://www.instagram.com/emilyburchharris

Follow her on Twitter

https://www.twitter.com/emilydbharris

MORE TALES FROM THE WORLD OF SPELLMONGER

SPELLMONGER SERIES

Spellmonger, Book 1

Warmage, Book 2

The Spellmonger's Honeymoon: A Spellmonger Novella, Book 2.5

Magelord, Book 3

Knights Magi, Book 4

High Mage, Book 5

Journeymage, Book 6

Enchanter, Book 7

Court Wizard, Book 8

Shadowmage, Book 9

Necromancer, Book 10

Thaumaturge, Book 11

The Road to Sevendor: A Spellmonger Anthology, Book 11.5

Arcanist, Book 12

The Wizards of Sevendor, Book 12.5

Footwizard, Book 13

SPELLMONGER CADET SERIES

Hawkmaiden, Book 1

Hawklady, Book 2

Sky Rider, Book 3

SPELLMONGER: LEGACY AND SECRETS

Shadowplay, Book 1

This book is dedicated with gratitude to my family – my husband, Doug, and our son, Connor, and my parents, Pat and Bobbie. I want to thank the Spellmonger, Terry, for pushing me to do this. I also want to thank Laurin for sitting on my books back at Githens – S/B/S.

– Emily

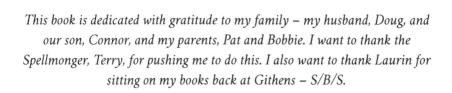

Dedicated to Emily Burch Harris, who has put up with my writing as my editor for a decade, now, and who has been my wife's best friend since she was 12. Ever grateful for your help. Composition isn't as easy as it looks, is it? Welcome to the Dark Side.

– Terry

CONTENTS

Map of Falas	xvii
Chapter One *Forbidden Territory*	1
Chapter Two *Family Secrets*	15
Chapter Three *Apprentice Kitten*	27
Chapter Four *Playing In The Shadows*	41
Chapter Five *Politics Is Exhausting*	57
Chapter Six *Becoming Lissa*	81
Chapter Seven *Lissa The Mouse*	99
Chapter Eight *From Nit To Rat*	117
Chapter Nine *Into The Rat's Den*	133
Chapter Ten *A Ruckus On Parchment Street*	145
Chapter Eleven *Whispers In The Dark*	159
Chapter Twelve *A Reckoning Of Shadows*	169
Chapter Thirteen *An Unusual Errand*	181
Chapter Fourteen *The Streets Of Falas*	193
Chapter Fifteen *Occupation*	205
Chapter Sixteen *The Broken Fountain Riot*	217
Chapter Seventeen *Lady Isadra*	231

Chapter Eighteen *Codes And Ciphers*	241
Chapter Nineteen *Lissa's Last Run*	253
Chapter Twenty *An Unexpected Problem*	265
Chapter Twenty-One *The Mouse No More*	277
Chapter Twenty-Two *Shadow Blade*	289
Chapter Twenty-Three *The Docks*	299
Chapter Twenty-Four *Escape!*	311
Chapter Twenty-Five *Safe House*	323
Chapter Twenty-Six *A Reckoning*	335
Chapter Twenty-Seven *The House Of Shadow*	347
Chapter Twenty-Eight *The Conspiracy of Shadows*	359
Connect With Terry Mancour	369
Connect With Emily Burch Harris	371
About the Creators	373
More Tales from the World of Spellmonger	375

MAP OF FALAS

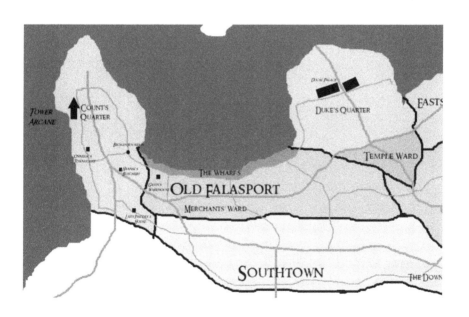

"Don't get caught. The gods help those who help themselves."

– Rule of House Furtius

Cysgodol Hall has been a possession of House Furtius for over two centuries. Situated on the southern bank of the Laris River, a tributary of the great River Mandros, it was originally constructed by Sir Alsonus of Solic, for his new wife and large family, just before the Narasi Conquest. Built in the graceful period style of local stone and enjoying a commanding view of the Laris River, it has a generous mixture of wood, field, and meadow. With its distinctive violet shutters and beautiful gardens, it is considered one of the more picturesque estates in the Solic domain, though it is quiet and secluded. As one of the House's longest-held estates, it has been carefully cultivated over the years to ensure that it is of ideal use in the raising and training of the children of House Furtius for their particular vocation.

– from **The Shield of Darkness**,
Secret Family History of House Furtius

CHAPTER ONE
FORBIDDEN TERRITORY

Move as quiet as a shadow, as light as a breeze.

Her mother's words echoed in Gatina's head as she moved silently into the forbidden territory, her slipper-clad feet seeking the spots on the floor she hoped would not squeak under her light frame and betray her. Any sound could attract attention, she knew, and she did not want to get caught. The big wooden door to the chamber loomed in the darkness, and Gatina swallowed as she prepared to transgress. She barely breathed, though her heart pounded in her chest with the excitement of the unknown. She had to be careful, she knew. She stretched out her hearing between careful steps, listening to every noise she could identify as she slipped through the door, her nimble fingers opening the catch without a single click or thud. Thankfully, the iron hinges did not squeak in the slightest when she pushed the door open just enough to get through. She pulled the imposing door silently closed behind her. She didn't realize she had been holding her breath until the catch was set.

Success! She praised herself. She had done it, and without attracting attention. Not even her brother Atopol could move that quietly, she suspected. Nor would he have been so audacious as to use his skills to assault their parents' quarters.

Gatina was in her parents' chambers, a suite of rooms normally off-limits to her and her brother. A week ago she would not have dared to trespass there. But she had a mission, one her mother, Lady Minnureal, had herself set for her. *Mother said to look everywhere,* Gatina thought, seeking a rationalization for her transgression into forbidden territory. *This is everywhere.*

As she turned, she startled at some motion across the room, only to realize that it was her own reflection in her mother's large silver looking glass. She did not gasp or squeak – she was better than that – but it did take her by surprise to see another girl with long white hair and violet eyes staring back at her. Gatina realized how anxious she really was, and took a moment to steel herself before beginning her search by using a breathing technique she had been practicing in lessons.

Like her older brother Atopol, Gatina had started her search for the coins outside, in the chicken coop near the stables, but she had felt somehow drawn to the house while her big brother ransacked the hayloft.

She had found the first of four hidden coins, ancient and worn bits of silver minted in Vore, long ago, in a bookcase in the family's library, hidden behind a richly illustrated volume of Gilmoran fables. She'd detected it by studying the dust in the room. The bookcase had been cleaned a week prior, she knew, and the thin layer of dust had not been disturbed when the coin was hidden by her mother – she was far too careful to be that obvious. But there was the barest difference in the dust in front of that volume, when she observed it. What drew Gatina to it, she guessed, was that nothing had been hidden behind a book yet. It was a new hiding place. Mother had said to broaden her mind in the hunt. So, she had.

Her brother was still looking in the stables, she saw his pale shock of white hair catch the late-afternoon sunlight from a window, when she felt the tug to their parents' chambers upstairs, pulling her away from the library and sending her up the steps as fast as her slippered feet could carry her. She couldn't explain the pull or why it affected her. It didn't always happen, but when it did, it got her attention. It was as if the metal called to her, saying *I'm here for you. Come find me.*

So, she had.

She stood in front of her mother's wardrobe, the one that contained her everyday clothes and hosiery, the smell of sweet herbs hanging in sachets washing over her from within. She was nervous about opening the cabinets and drawers, wondering what she might find inside. One's parents' secrets were always problematic to discover, she reflected.

While Gatina was excited to be on an adventure, even admitting to herself a secret thrill at the risk of being caught, she also knew that doing so would invite great shame. Still, the risk was worth it. She knew she was on the right path to finding the metal coins her mother had hidden. It was her mission to locate four specific coins somewhere in the house.

It was a part of a family game, the kind she and her brother had played for as long as she could remember. There were rules. The first one of the children to find at least three of the coins would win. Gatina also knew she would be in a heap of trouble if her mother found her in her chambers without the coins. That was also part of the game. Gatina could not disturb one single thing in her hunt. And in her private quarters, her mother had plenty of things that could easily be disturbed.

Gatina's fingers worked quickly and carefully as she opened the cabinet doors and began searching, nimbly feeling for the coins, her mind racing with excuses if she were to be discovered. Proclaiming ignorance was right out, she knew. So was acting as if she were looking for something innocuous or pretending to borrow some piece of clothing from her mother.

No, she knew she had to be forthright. Gatina thought maybe she could explain away her presence here as if she were expected to rise to the challenge of a coin being hidden in an off-limits location. Or, to use her mother's own words: anywhere is *any*where, she reasoned, as she moved on to the next drawer, carefully closing the cabinet first once she was satisfied it looked precisely the way it had when she opened it.

This was no childish game, either, though it seemed simple enough. Her parents had played these special kinds of games with her and her brother since they were little. Each one came with lessons and lectures, based on their performance. Often, the games revolved around the subject of *risk*. Risk was exposure to danger. Risk was to be avoided, or minimized. Risk was vitally important to her family, it was clear. She wasn't sure why, but it was.

Gatina knew that these games were getting progressively more challenging of late, and this challenge was a fine example of risk. For one thing, she barely knew her way around, in here. Lady Minnureal and Lord Hance rarely allowed the children into their chambers unattended, or for very long. It was their haven from the cares of the world, her parents had often declared, where they could discuss the problems of life in privacy . . . and the one place they could find respite from child-rearing. They said that with laughter, though, Gatina reasoned, so it must be safe.

She turned her attention to the bottom drawer. She did not think it would be in there, but she forced herself to be thorough. This game demanded it.

There were so many things in their rooms, yet they were uncluttered. Little knick-knacks and intriguing objects they'd picked up from all over Alshar were displayed on tables and shelves. Her parents' suite was large, the windows overlooking the river that ran along the back of the estate. There was a bedroom and a dressing room, a bathing room and a sitting room where Mother took tea each day with Father, when he was home. The sitting room, which opened out onto a balcony overlooking the river, was also the main entry into the suite. Gatina started to look there, searching under her mother's stationery paper and quills without disturbing them. The coin wasn't there, she knew after a brief few minutes of searching, nor was it on the table by the door, she realized. The balcony took seconds to search until she was certain it hid no coin. She even checked under the potted plants, as Mother had used the plants in the garden as hiding spots before.

She turned away from the balcony and walked through their bedroom, into the dressing room, and prepared to search her mother's linen chest.

That's when she heard it again – no, she felt it as much as heard it, as there was no real noise in her ears. Not really. But it was *similar*. The noise that wasn't a noise started as a buzz in her head, a kind of background sound that got louder as she got closer. She realized the buzzing was louder in here than in the sitting room. It was almost as if her body could feel it.

Gatina walked around the room, past her father's chest of drawers and his wardrobe, her left arm raised with her palm facing away from her on impulse. To her surprise she found that this helped her to feel her way toward what she supposed was the coin, providing guidance like a candle if she were walking in the dark.

She stopped in front of her mother's other wardrobe, the one containing her fanciest gowns. The sound in her mind was so loud she wondered if her brother would hear it outside. She pulled the heavy, ornately-carved wooden doors open and her mother's gowns fluttered with the disturbance. The noise jumped in her head. The pull was so strong she nearly fell forward. The wardrobe had space to hang dozens of gowns, a shelf above covered with neatly-folded wimples and hats, and two drawers within for undergarments and corsets. But the buzz persisted, like a scourge of mosquitoes.

Gatina pushed aside the gowns, the noise pulsing, strumming in her head. She was prepared for victory as she felt along the back wall of the wardrobe but . . . *nothing*. She opened the first drawer, which contained the finely-boned corsets that Mother called torture devices. But it wasn't there, either.

Between two corsets, she found a pale dusty rose-colored silk bag the size of a small book. The bag wasn't heavy, she noted, but it was firm. Compelled by curiosity, she untied the drawstring and looked inside, unsure what treasure this small bag might contain. She knew it was not metals, but maybe love letters from her father, or perhaps earrings. Instead of anything of value, Gatina found a deck of cards. She pulled one from the bag and felt the smooth cool parchment on her palm. She remembered these cards! These weren't cards for parlour games. These were a tradition for the wizards in her Mother's house, House Sardanz. Before she could investigate further, the noise in her head persisted.

With a start she realized that this might actually be *magic,* this phantom sound in her head that seemed to lead her to the coins. Both of her parents were magi, after all, so it wasn't as if that was impossible, she reasoned. Gatina knew that if she was so blessed her *rajira,* or the precious Talent to do magic, had not yet arrived. It would not for a few years, her mother had explained, probably not until after her first moon cycle.

But the way she could suddenly feel and hear metals like the silver coins made her feel special, she realized, and might be part of her *rajira* somehow. It was a gift, or that's what she told herself. She hadn't even told her mother about it. It was her secret, for now; hers *only.* And she didn't want her mother to think she was cheating at these games. But the gift was new, a *recent, noteworthy development,* as her father would say.

She slid the cards back into their bag and returned it to the drawer. Her fingers nimbly sorted her mother's folded undergarments in the second drawer, following the pull of silver, not recognizing the soft fabric she touched in the hunt. Then her fingers discovered something solid. Only instead of the coin, they found a small silver box.

Snorting quietly, she pushed it aside and delved deeper in the drawer, fingers probing until her index finger finally touched the source of the pull, a cool, lumpy coin. She recognized it at once. With a satisfied smile, she slid it out. But the coin hit the metal box, creating the slightest clink, and she froze. When her ears detected no signs of discovery, she reached her other hand into the drawer and lifted the box, and her coin, out. Only one more, and she would beat Atopol!

Gatina slid the coin into the pocket of the leggings she wore, where it joined the first she had found. She could wear comfortable leggings here at the estate, but never in public. In public, she dressed as fashion dictated. Her mother was raising her to be *a lady,* after all, among other things.

But dresses did not afford the movement Gatina needed, craved, especially on these little missions. Lady Minnureal wore leggings when riding, exercising, too, as did many of the female tutors their family employed; but when she was out in society, she dressed in the full regal clothing that befit her station as a noblewoman.

She expected Gatina to do the same and Gatina *hated it*. Skirts and gowns might be pretty, objectively speaking, but they were damnably uncomfortable and impractical for climbing trees or other important tasks. While magi weren't technically allowed to be nobles, she knew, thanks to the Royal Bans on Magic, Gatina also knew that her parents' arcane powers were a closely-held family secret. They pretended to be nobility, though they were a family of magi.

It was normal, she thought as she replaced her mothers' undergarments where they belonged, for women to embrace comfort over fashion as needs dictated. It was not comfortable to ride a horse in a dress. When she expressed this opinion to her mother, Minnureal reminded her that keeping up appearances is what allowed House Furtius to remain prosperous and maintain its position in a world that seemed to despise those who could do magic. Gatina had only a vague idea of what that encompassed, but based on little games like this she was starting to guess.

The ornate silver box that had obstructed the coin drew her attention and fascination. Gatina lifted it for closer inspection.

She noticed tiny sigils carved into the box along the lid, symbols she recognized as magical, not mere letters. She'd actually learned what a few of them were, when she asked her father or mother about them when she'd encountered them on other things. These sigils were used for protection or security or safe-keeping, from what she remembered from her general lessons about magic. Someday she would have to learn them all, if the Shadows blessed her with *rajira*. She weighed the box in her hands. It was fairly light. She shook it. There was a soft thud inside.

Gatina suddenly wanted to know what it held. *Desperately.* Was it a present for her? A magical box with a wonder inside? Her imagination took over as she studied it. Her name day was coming up in a few months, when she would turn eleven years old. Maybe it was jewelry? If it was, she wasn't terribly excited about that prospect. A dagger would be far more practical, she decided, but this box was far too small for that. Still, a gift was a gift and a lady always accepted one with grace, her mother had often lectured. Gatina became convinced that was what this box held, for no good reason. More, she was determined to open it and see. Curiosity and Gatina were old friends.

She turned the box over and righted it, inspecting it for a clasp or button to open it. The hinges were there, she saw, but she couldn't find a clasp. Nor would it open of its own accord, as if the lid was welded onto it. That only intrigued her more.

She balanced the box on the dresser drawer and steadied it with her left hand so she could use her fingernail to feel along the lid crevice for a spring or trigger to open it. Her parents had a few boxes and chests with secret openings. She'd played with them, occasionally. Sometimes opening locked boxes became a game, but always under the watchful eyes of Mother or Father. But she found nothing on this box. Challenged but not frustrated, she set the box down and walked to her mother's desk. She took her mother's pen knife from her desk, unsheathed it, and tried to pry along the edge of the box. The box did not yield.

"By the blessed Darkness, why won't you *open?*" she muttered under her breath, staring at the little box accusingly. She sat down, placing the box, which was no larger than her little fist, sideways between her knees. She tried again to open it by prying hard, careful with the letter knife. It still would not open. *"Darkness!"* she swore again, louder this time as she tried twisting the little knife to gain more leverage.

She was so focused on her illicit task that she did not hear her parents enter the chamber, at first. When she did, she nearly panicked. Discovery, here, would amount to being caught – the worst possible outcome.

"Parents!" her mind screamed. She cursed by the darkness a third time and dove into her mother's wardrobe, bringing the little box with her, and closed the door behind her to avoid being discovered.

She was doubly surprised as her father, Lord Hance, who had been absent from the estate for over a month, due to his attendance of the Summer court in far Vorone, and wasn't expected home for weeks, yet. Gatina found that disturbing, but that wasn't what worried her. Getting caught was.

Her parents did not notice, she hoped as she silently curled up in the bottom of the wardrobe, silk and taffeta tickling her face. She could still hear them even through the thick wardrobe door. She decided to try to see them, as well, and risked opening the door back up the barest crack as she peered outside. She saw the two talking quietly to each other as they entered the sitting room. Her father's white hair, like hers and her brother's, was covered with a dark wig. Mother had her arm around Father's shoulder, and she looked distraught. So did her father. That was even more concerning to Gatina. Her parents almost never looked distraught.

"It will be alright, somehow, Hance," Lady Minnureal said quietly in an assuring tone. Her father's face was stoic and weary, and bore a very somber expression as he stripped off the dark wig. "The news is terrible, the worst. But it will be alright," she insisted.

"Lenguin and Enora are dead," her father said, shaking his head with a despairing finality. "This will inevitably spark a political crisis," he warned, as he hung his traveling cloak on a peg and took a seat in his favorite chair. "We both know who's waiting for his chance. This will provide it," he reasoned, gloomily.

Gatina didn't really have an idea of who they were referring to, unless...

Then she stifled a gasp as the realization hit her. Lenguin and Enora were the Duke and Duchess of Alshar, she recalled from her lessons. The supreme sovereigns of the duchy of Alshar. Her father had even met them, she knew. He'd gone to Vorone as part of the court. Inadvertently, she gasped.

As Lord Hance nodded his head, Lady Minnureal suddenly and swiftly pounced on the wardrobe door, opening it in a flash, allowing Gatina to be caught off-guard. The girl tumbled into the room as her father's eyes fell on her.

"I *thought* I heard a gasp!" her mother said, her eyes narrowing and her smile triumphant. "And I thought my letter desk looked out-of-place! An intruder, my husband, in our very chambers!" Her mother picked up the letter-opening knife, which in her haste, Gatina had left on the floor.

"Gatina, what trouble is my little kitten getting herself into?" her father asked gently, with a heavy sigh. The question hit Gatina like an anvil thrown across the room. The last thing she wanted to do was disturb her already-disturbed sire.

Hance wore his riding clothes, leather trousers, boots, and a woolen tunic, all in black, as was his cloak. His clothing was covered in road dust. Her father looked strange, and not because he had been wearing a wig. Gatina realized that he was not his normal, happy self. He was sad, she realized, and worried, and she knew instantly that something was dreadfully wrong. He had been gone for months and was usually very happy to be home after such trips. But if what she'd heard him say was true, she could imagine that the disturbing news might be the cause, somehow.

That suddenly seemed secondary to her discovery. Gatina knew that she had been *caught*. All she could do was explain herself to avoid punishment . . . or maybe she could use her parents' state of mind to her advantage without having to explain exactly why she was in their room, in her mother's wardrobe, holding the mysterious box in her lap.

But then she saw the look in her mother's eyes and knew an honest – and brief – explanation would be best.

"I found my coin, mother!" she fished it from her pocket and held it up. "And I found *this*. It's my name day gift, isn't it? I know it is!" She lifted the silver box triumphantly to show it to her. Her mother gasped, putting a hand over her mouth in shock and surprise. But her father knelt down to her and gently took it from her hands. He kissed her on the top of her head and her mother lifted her up to her feet.

"That, my darling, is *not* your name day present. That is actually a very special item I am keeping safe for . . . for an old friend," Hance said, choking a bit on his words as he spoke. There was a hint of sadness in his voice.

"In Mother's *undergarment drawer?*" Gatina asked, indicating her disbelief.

"Yes, in your mother's undergarment drawer," he chuckled. "I felt it was safe enough, entrusted to her care. Though I agree, it is an odd hiding place. I will do better," he promised as he cradled the box protectively. Gatina saw that his normally clear violet eyes were red. He often obscured them with magic when he went out in public, she knew, just as he wore a wig to hide his distinctive white hair. But this was not magic, she realized. She suspected he'd been . . . crying.

"Father, why are your eyes so red?" she asked, suddenly concerned. "Was the road dust that bad?" Gatina asked, suspecting that it was not, in fact, the dust that was responsible. She looked closer as Hance looked away. Her father's eyes were puffy and his face was, too. She was suddenly certain.

He *had* been crying.

That shook the young girl. Her father was the most stoic, even-tempered man she'd ever met. She could not imagine himself crying. *Not if all the world were on fire.*

"Are you *well*, Father?" she asked, a note of apprehension in her voice.

"I'm fine, Kitten," he assured her with a deep sigh. "Just very tired and dusty. It was a long journey from Vorone. But . . . I am fine," he assured.

"I am not!" Minnureal said, putting her hands on Gatina's narrow shoulders. "I seem to have kittens where kittens *should not be*." Her mother began ushering her out. "Excellent job in finding the coins, Gatina. But the game is over, for now. Please find Atopol and ask Sister Karia to begin the afternoon's reading lesson. Your father and I *must* have some time to catch up before supper." Before Gatina knew what was happening, she was gently nudged out of her parents' room and the door was closed in her face with unusual brusqueness. And, to make it worse, Gatina heard her mother slide the lock into place. That was highly unusual. Mother and Father never kept their door locked.

Gatina stifled the protest she felt welling up in her throat, as she stared at the thick door. This was not the time for a childish outburst, she knew from her mother's tone and her father's face. There was something important going on. And Gatina was suddenly determined to learn what it was.

There were secrets about. And no self-respecting kitten would allow that to pass without investigation, she knew.

"Secrets protect us, just as Darkness conceals. But unworthy secret-keepers may cost dearly. Place your trust in your family and House, who have a sacred duty to maintain it. Likewise protect the secrets with which you are entrusted as if they were your own."

– Rule of House Furtius

CHAPTER TWO
FAMILY SECRETS

Mother was never *that* rushed. Father was never *that* emotional. And her escape from even token punishment for being in a forbidden area told her all that she needed to know. It was so odd, she decided, that Gatina was determined to learn what was happening, and made the ill-considered plan to listen in on her parents' private conversations – a clear violation of trust, a cornerstone of House Furtius. But something in her father's red eyes compelled her. A few moments later, her brother Atopol found her with her ear pressed against the door concentrating intently on what was being said within.

Her older brother was out of breath and excited, his violet eyes flashing under his stark white hair.

"I ran all the way from the stables! Look what I found, Gat!" he held his hand out to show her the other two coins from their game. He was overly triumphant. He usually only found one coin, unless she was with him. "What about you?"

Gatina didn't have time to worry about the coins and the game. She was too focused on what she could hear, and too concerned that her brother would disturb her spying.

"Shhh! Attie, *quiet!* Father came home unexpectedly, and Mother is acting strangely. I need to *hear* this!" she whispered, harshly.

"I thought I heard a horse come up the lane!" he nodded, his eyes narrowing. "Father's home from Vorone? Early? Why—"

Gatina ended his questions with a glance and a sharply raised finger. "*Listen!*" she encouraged, breathlessly.

Though she was two years younger than Atopol, Gatina acted older – and bossier, according to his complaints. But apparently Atopol realized that if *she* needed to hear what their parents were discussing, then he probably did, too. He crowded beside her against the door frame where the hinges met, which allowed a sliver of unmuffled words to slip through the crack. But what they heard seemed out of place from their parents' usually measured tones. Even with the louder voices, it was difficult to hear through the thick door . . . especially with her big brother breathing in her ear.

Gatina elbowed Atopol and mouthed *"move!"* He rolled his eyes, but obliged, standing on his toes to give her a better angle to get her ear against the door, instead of standing with his elbow in her face.

Why were boys so predictably inconsiderate? she wondered, annoyed. *And smelly?* She caught a whiff of sweat and decided to breathe through her mouth.

"*Sorry!*" he mouthed back, silently, and they returned to their eavesdropping.

They held their breath as their father paced nearer to the door; she prayed he wouldn't hear them but that they could hear *him*. Gatina wished she did have her *rajira,* already. There were spells for listening in, in situations like this, she knew.

"I can't believe she did it," she could hear her father explain, an anguished tone in his voice. "After all these years, we thought she was finally, safely, out of the duchy. But that . . . awful woman has won. She ordered his . . . his *murder.*" Hance's voice shook as he pronounced the word. He was angry, angrier than Gatina had ever heard him. He was upset. And he was crying.

"Oh, Hance, are you certain?" her mother asked, her own voice wavering.

"Completely," he agreed, grimly. "I cast the spells myself. And Master Thinradel passed along his suspicions as well. Darkness, take her!

Lenguin was my *friend*. And she always hated him, bitterly. Was a new throne and her husband not enough to soothe her venom? How did I not see this coming? I did not like him going to Vorone in the first place. I knew I should have gone into battle with him." His voice grew quiet, as Gatina imagined him struggling with his emotions. That shook her. The sadness seemed to be washing over him like a wave on the shore.

She heard the rustle of their mother's skirts, as she rushed to comfort their father, and despite her curiosity Gatina felt guilty at overhearing a deeply personal moment.

"Hance, you most certainly could *not* have known this would happen!" Mother insisted, her voice clear as she faced the door. "Nor are you a warrior or a knight. No one could have predicted this! I did not see it coming, myself," she admitted, "not after *she* was so cordial during the Farisian affair. I thought she had put her enmity behind her, too, but I suppose she merely tended it. Grendine ordering the assassination of her brother and her sister-in-law . . . and succeeding?" she asked, incredulously. "That is beyond propriety, even for someone like her!"

"She has plotted for years," Hance answered, miserably. "Especially when she was a maiden. And all of her attempts were stopped or prevented," Hance told her. "Until now. Now, it appears as if Lenguin died in battle, and Enora, Trygg's grace be with her, was killed by the Brotherhood of the Rat. Only . . . only it was not they who struck," he assured her. "And now rumor says that Rard intends to make himself king over three of the Five Duchies. With that awful woman as his queen."

Gatina looked at her brother with horror. Lenguin and Enora were the Duke and Duchess of Alshar, revered figures that ruled the country from the shoals of Enultramar in the south to the great forests of the north. She was gratified that her brother looked equally shocked and troubled by the news. But she spared him no more than a meaningful glance – they were continuing to speak.

Mother grew quiet, her voice choking. "Dear gods, what does it mean for the duchy? Do they really mean to rule as king and queen? The people will not stand for that. There will be a rebellion!" she predicted.

"More than one," Hance agreed. "Rard sent men to . . . to take care of little Anguin and his sisters. They're being escorted to Castal for 'their own safety,' according to the Castali. Father Amus has gone with them. But they are essentially hostages to Alshar's good behavior."

"That *will not* stand!" her mother insisted. "The people of Alshar will never allow . . . oh," she said, stopping her thought in the face of some new one.

"Exactly," Hance agreed. "Who will ride to war against Castal for Anguin and his sisters? Count Vichetral is the next most senior noble, and he hates the ducal family and wants to replace it. The other counts . . . they will not stand for a Castali duke to rule over Alshar as king," he warned.

"Nor will they fight against Vichetral's behest," Mother said. "Yet he simply must do nothing, save protest Rard and Grendine's actions and rule in Lenguin's stead!" her mother said, her voice pregnant with despair.

"They will frame it as a rebellion," Hance agreed. "Yet it will not be the only one. In the days after the assassinations, I met with Lenguin's closest supporters in the court – the ones who actually have the interests of the duchy at heart, not the courtiers. We have an agreement. People I trust," he insisted.

"Who?" Mother demanded. "And what kind of agreement?"

"A peace-keeping, duchy-preserving agreement, I hope. Father Amus will stay with the children in Castal. Viscountess Threanas will stay in Vorone and preserve the rule there. Master Thinradel, the Court Wizard, had a very interesting conversation with me. He's asked me to call the old council to order, to help preserve the realm. He pledged to stay close to the Spellmonger—"

"Spellmonger? What spellmonger?" her mother asked, confused.

"Some back-country bumpkin wizard from the Wilderlands," her father explained. "But he has irionite. And he persuaded Lenguin to follow Rard into battle against the gurvani. To his doom."

Gatina looked up at her brother and saw the worried look on his face, and she shared his anxiety. She knew, even at ten years old, that the duke and duchess were very important to their father and to their family. Their parents had long been friends with the royal couple. In fact, their father had played a large role in Duke Lenguin's courtship of Duchess Enora, according to family lore.

"The official report is that Lenguin died from injuries sustained in battle," her father continued. "He died a hero. But Master Thinradel and other magi think that the *Family* used the battlefield injury as a cover story. I tend to agree."

There was something in the way her father said the word 'family' that immediately caught Gatina's attention. She tapped Atopol and mouthed "Who are the family?" He shrugged and ignored her, as he soaked up everything he could.

"But why would Grendine want to paint her brother as a hero? She hated him!" Mother asked. "She took every opportunity to mock or undermine him."

"Part of her scheme, I suppose. It makes sense, if she wants to unite the duchies and build support for Rard, who has publicly hailed Lenguin as a hero." He paused a moment, just long enough to make Gatina anxious. "There's more. After the battle, the two dukes knighted the spellmonger and the warmagi. Despite the Censorate. They're lifting the Bans, at least somewhat. Another part of her scheme."

"*Lifting* the Bans?" her mother asked in disbelief. "This news gets stranger and stranger . . ." she said, as her voice faded. Gatina guessed that their parents were no longer within hearing range. They had moved to the outside balcony.

Gatina again looked up at her brother. Atopol had a grave look on his face, and his brow was furrowed with worry. He moved away from the door and took her hand, pulling her behind him toward their quarters. When they were in his room, he let go of her hand and motioned for her to sit down. He closed the door. And opened the window.

"What does all of that mean?" she asked him, confused. "The Duke? The Duchess? Rebellion? What does—"

"It's a mess," Atopol said, shaking his head. "Like someone tipped over a chamber pot in the middle of a temple sanctuary. I only understood part of it, but *that* much was clear. Politics," he said, with a shrug of resignation.

Gatina was more concerned with her parents than politics. What did this mean for them? For her family? She knew they were wealthy and a lot of that stemmed from business her father did in the duchy. But she also knew that they weren't like other families. In a lot of ways. Their odd white hair and violet eyes, for one. They covered the hair with wigs, often, when they were in public. But that was just one of the things that set House Furtius apart from the other families she knew. The rest was more subtle.

"Yes, Attie, but what does it mean? For us?" she asked again as she flung herself onto his feather-filled tick in frustration. "I am worried about Father. He seems so sad. And Mother was livid – and frightened! She *never* gets frightened!"

Atopol did not respond immediately. Like their parents' room, each of their rooms had balconies. Their views overlooked the garden, on the side of the house. Atopol walked to his balcony door, opened it and stepped outside.

"I'll be right back. Stay here, Gat." Then he hopped over the railing toward the side of the house.

Gatina flung herself off the bed to watch. Atopol's daredevil feats of climbing were legendary on the manor, and she loved to watch him. He nimbly hugged the stone wall as he effortlessly descended to the ground floor, where the library was. He did not miss a step, she saw, as he deftly pulled something wedged into a crack above the library window. In moments he'd returned to the balcony his prize in hand.

"Gat, I guess they'll tell you soon enough, but they only told me last year," he began explaining, as he unwrapped the leather-bound package. "There are things you will soon learn about our family that are important. Things about our history and heritage," he said as he removed a small book from the package.

"I already know we're magi," she pointed out.

"There's more to it than that. First, we are not what we seem. And it's not just the white hair and purple eyes. Our family has many, many secrets."

"Like what?" she asked, intrigued. Gatina loved secrets.

"Our family . . . *steals* things," he explained.

"We . . . steal?" she asked, mystified.

"Not like a petty criminal. We don't take stuff from just anyone. Nor just any stuff. And we've been doing it for years. Centuries," he corrected. "House Furtius have been thieves of the highest rank for hundreds of years. Our entire family," he emphasized.

"That can't be . . . I don't think . . ." Gatina mumbled, as she tried to understand what Atopol was telling her. The idea that her father went about pilfering from other people's pockets was both appalling and intriguing. But as unlikely as it sounded, it also explained a few things that had always mystified her.

"The stories about our ancestor Keira the Great you love so much? They are not simple stories. She really did steal things back in Vore . . . including those coins we keep searching for in those games we play. But she didn't stop stealing once she came to Alshar. She got better at it. She passed the craft down to her children. Those games we play, like finding those same coins and hide and seek? Those are more than children's games. Those are lessons, first taught by Kiera the Great, to teach us how to disappear and how to find and retrieve objects without disturbing the things around them," he said, authoritatively.

"But . . . but I thought Mother and Father were just wizards! Magi!" she corrected herself. "Sure, we have to be quiet about it—"

"Oh, we're wizards," Atopol agreed. "But not regular adepts. Father uses magic to *steal*. Shadowmagic. So does Mother, sometimes. They're training me to do it, too," he said, proudly. "I'm certain that they will teach you, too. And when you do begin your apprenticeship in earnest, you will start writing down what you learn in a book like this one," he said, holding it up for her to see. "It's called a *heist journal*."

She looked at the mostly-blank journal with interest, noting that only a dozen or so pages were filled with Atopol's messy script. She let the information work its way through her imagination, as she tested it in her mind.

"That . . . that's unbelievable," she finally managed.

"It's the unbelievable things that are often true, Father says," Atopol grinned. "We've stolen things for centuries. But there are rules," he cautioned. "Acres and acres of rules you have to learn to do it right. And *not get caught*," he emphasized. "We aren't common footpads, after all, we're highly skilled adepts in the art of . . . acquiring things," he explained. "And it's high time Mother and Father told you." Attie was serious, otherwise Gatina would have laughed at the idea. "I knew by the time I was your age, after all," he said, in all seriousness.

"And you kept this a secret from me?" she demanded. Gatina realized that he was excited to know something she didn't know; that annoyed her. *She* was usually the one who figured things out first. It's not that he wasn't smart; Atopol was brilliant, all of his tutors said so . . . but she was a *genius*. She was convinced of it.

Of course Gatina had explored the family's history a long time ago, once she had mastered reading. Her parents had read some of the simpler stories to her when she was young, fanciful tales about her great-great-great-great-great grandparents, and she loved them. When she learned to read she'd pillaged the family library, once she realized all the interesting stories about her noble house it contained.

For six hundred years House Furtius had left a legacy of adventure and history, and it captivated her. While her tutors encouraged her to read about the gods or history or other ladylike material, she was far more interested in the small section of books and scrolls featuring her ancestors' legacies. She had found both the material deemed "appropriate" for her as well as the more illicit stories of her house.

She'd learned all about the great wizards in her family tree, Magelords and Coastlords, and the daring things that they'd done in ages past . . . and she now realized, after Atopol's revelation, that many of their adventures were actually *attempts to steal things*. Which did, indeed, make a lot more sense, now that she knew the secret. Gatina was good at history, especially family history. She'd often mention some obscure piece of it when in lessons, just to prove her superior memory over her brother's to their tutors.

But, in this situation, Attie *did* know more than she did. And she did not like it.

"Of course I suspected some of this," she said, softly but with an air of superiority. "At least, I knew *something* was missing from the histories. And this explains it. But what do the duke and duchess have to do with us, though?" she asked, before Atopol could challenge her on that. "Why is Father so upset?"

She watched his facial expressions shift from neutral, likely weighing her sincerity, to animated as he engaged in the conversation. Atopol's eyes lit up as he began to talk, explaining what he knew of the ducal court and what he had seen first-hand the season prior.

"He is upset because our father and Duke Lenguin have been friends since they were young men, before they married. In fact, from what I have overheard Father say to Mother, Lenguin relied on our Father for intelligence and advice, in an unofficial capacity. He was a kind of private counselor to Duke Lenguin."

That certainly explained why their father would often head off to Falas or Vorone for 'business' involving the ducal court. And, perhaps, some of his other travels. Gatina always hated that he would leave, as the journeys pulled Hance away from their family for weeks and months at a time. But it was exciting to think that her parents had such a secretive life and a high connection to royalty.

"The Duchess of Castal is Grendine, sister to Lenguin," her brother lectured her. "They grew up here in Alshar. But, Grendine always plotted to take the throne, because she's older. So they married her off to Rard of Castal, and hoped she'd leave Lenguin alone. Instead, it sounds like she continued her plotting. If the duke and duchess are dead, most likely by his sister's hand," Attie continued, "even if no one knows it's her, then it could get bad in Alshar. I am sure we will find out," he said, with more confidence than she felt was warranted. "My money is on assassination. I would bet you all of the coins from our game that Duchess Enora's death is connected to Duchess Grendine."

"How could she do that? She's in Castal!" Gatina pointed out.

"Duchess Grendine runs a secret network of spies called the Family. And one of my last tasks with Father when I was in Falas with him last spring was to observe Duke Lenguin's court for those who seemed oddly out of place."

Gatina blew out her breath, which she hadn't realized she had been holding. Gatina was no child, for her age. But all of this seemed a bit confusing. "Can we prove that?" she added, wondering.

"It will do little good," her brother said, matter of fact. "From what Father told me, they want to become the king and queen and unite the duchies under their rule. From what Mother has said, that's what Duchess Grendine has always desired – full and absolute sovereignty."

"Mother knows her?" Gatina asked, surprised.

"Oh, yes, from years ago," Atopol affirmed, grimly. "They weren't friends. And it's terrifying to hear her talk about Grendine's history, you know, from when they were younger. Those stories would even scare *you*," he teased, shuddering at the memory.

Gatina did not ask Attie what the stories were about. She didn't get the chance before their parents suddenly opened the door and came into Attie's bedroom. Both looked sad, their eyes puffy and red from crying. They also looked furious. Gatina's blood went cold. Atopol froze.

"Just what are you doing, Apprentice?" their father said in icy tones, as he gestured toward Atopol's journal. "Sharing secrets that aren't yours to tell?"

"Let each master in our sacred vocation find for a wife the most skilled of thieves, and each mistress seek the most adept of magi for their husband to ensure the line is strong, and thus the House. For in each generation, take among you the children with which Trygg has blessed you and have the wit and ability Blessed Darkness provides, and teach them the secret ways of our House and all the skills of our Craft, both arcane and mundane. Make them your true apprentices, father to son, mother to daughter, and instruct them to the limits of their ability. Spare no vigorous lesson out of love nor relent in the harshness of the exercise due to gentle affection. For the blessed Darkness demands our House produce strong Furtiusi in the pursuit of our Art, and it is our duty to faithfully relay this legacy to future generations, lest it be lost."

– Institution of Kiera the Thief, Founder of House Furtius, from **The Shield of Darkness**

CHAPTER THREE
APPRENTICE KITTEN

Mother opened and closed her hands into fists while breathing deeply from her belly and exhaling through her nose, like a bull about to charge. That was never a good sign. The children were familiar with the breath exercise, as they had given their mother plenty of reason to use it over the years. Gatina, herself, was a cause of nearly daily chaos in her constant quest to best her brother, which sent him into fits of frustration and set Mother on edge.

But this was different, she knew. There was a somber air in her mother's attitude, a seriousness that made Gatina take her parents' demeanor as significant.

"I . . . I'm sorry, Master!" Atopol babbled. "I just thought—"

"Thinking was clearly entirely absent from your reasoning," their mother chided him. "Honestly, Atopol, you *must* learn the importance of keeping secrets. It could mean your life, one day!"

"This news was not yours to tell," Father agreed, sternly. "We would have told Gatina in her own time . . . as is our prerogative *as her parents*. But the damage is done," he sighed. "And the time has, indeed, come to inform her. And to discuss a great many things that will change about all of our lives, now."

They each made space on Atopol's bed and pulled the children in close. Hance cleared his throat in an effort to choke back frustration, Gatina guessed, or maybe tears before speaking.

"Children, I am certain that your ears have already heard the news I shared with your mother a few moments ago. My friend and patron, Duke Lenguin, died as a result of his battlefield injuries fighting against the goblins up in the Wilderlands. His wife, Duchess Enora, also died the same day. She was killed. I also suspect he was killed, but the death was made to look like an accident. The children were taken to Castal where they will be kept 'safe' by their aunt and uncle, the Duke and Duchess of Castal, Rard and Grendine."

"You mean hostages!" Gatina pointed out.

"I do," he nodded, sadly. Father paused to steady himself and Mother reached across Gatina to put her hand on his shoulder in a show of support. He breathed and nodded, reaching up to squeeze her hand.

"The Duke's enemies won't hesitate to use this opportunity to seize power," Hance explained, somberly. "Count Vichetral, in particular, will move against the court the moment he hears the news. He has coveted the ducal coronet all of his life, and he is preparing to challenge the Prime Minister. That could lead to . . . well, a good many things, all of which are bad. In such times, families who were closely allied to the old order will be . . . in danger," he said, hoarsely. "We must take action to protect ourselves and the rest of the family. And we must do what we can to stop Vichetral and his cronies from ruining the duchy. It is our duty," he pronounced, solemnly.

Gatina glanced at her brother for his reaction. Attie did not show a reaction, so she decided to sit up straight and not show one, either.

"Will we have to fight, Father?" he asked, instead.

"If it comes to fighting," their father conceded. "But as you are learning, House Furtius has other ways of contending with our adversaries. We are not knights," he declared. "We are magi."

"And thieves," Gatina added, earning a sharp look from her mother for her impertinence. The novel admission hung in the air like a thundercloud, and it took her parents a moment to reply.

"Yes, we are magi *and* thieves, Kitten," their mother said, soothingly with a measured tone, "and while we traditionally try not to get involved in politics, in this case we have no choice. Things in the duchy have suddenly gotten complicated. We pray they do not get violent. We must be particularly careful, now. We hope it won't last for terribly long, my dears. A season, perhaps. Maybe a year. Not to worry, it will fly by quickly." From the look on Hance's face, Gatina doubted that.

"Our House must act, from the protection of the shadows," Hance agreed. "For our own safety, as well as the security of the realm. All of us," he said, picking out each of them with an intent stare. "Atopol, your lessons will be advanced accordingly. Kitten, you will begin yours in earnest, now."

"So we truly *are* thieves!" Gatina burst out, excitedly.

"Exceptional thieves," her mother agreed, a small smile on her lips. "And it's time you learned the truth of that – *properly*," she emphasized, glaring at Atopol. "Your father and I will accelerate your training, beginning with a look into our family's rather storied history. Our *private* history," she added. "The one you haven't found out about, yet. It's known as *The Shield of Darkness*. Only four copies exist, in the keeping of acknowledged masters of our Art. The book contains the Institutions of the House, which are guides to the successful practice of magical theft."

Gatina couldn't contain her excitement. "Do you mean about Kiera the Great, Mother? I want to know everything about *her!*" The illustrious ancestor had captivated Gatina's imagination since she'd first heard the tales of the white-haired witch from Vore. She had romanticized their ancient matriarch's life to the point of creating her own adventures about stolen treasure and secret lovers the infamous mage might have had.

"Among many others," her mother nodded. "Indeed, she wrote the original Institutions, when she founded our House, but they have been added to over time as your ancestors refined her rules. You enjoy a long legacy of noble thieves and magi who have contributed their knowledge and wisdom to the book. It will reveal the truth behind many of the childhood stories you've read.

"More importantly, it contains the rules by which we conduct ourselves, and often guides how we pursue our vocation. You'll be expected to learn, understand, and practice all of those rules under your apprenticeship. And come to know your ancestors, their successes and failures, and what they learned from their experience. Kiera is your favorite, I know, and she was a brilliant adept, by all accounts. But there were many others whose abilities in both magic and theft were just as impressive."

"I already know about the magic part," she nodded. Gatina could not wait to be old enough for her *rajira* to arrive. Once it did, she knew she would be unstoppable; she didn't know how she knew it, but she did. "Could Kiera sense things, like I can?" she asked, not meaning to divulge her secret. She knew at once that she had alarmed her parents with the admission.

"What do you mean, Gatina?" Hance asked sharply, his attention suddenly on his daughter.

"Well . . . I can . . . kind of . . . feel metal, sometimes," she admitted, guiltily. "That's one reason I'm so good at finding the coins."

"You mean you are able to *sense* objects? Without your *rajira?*" her father asked, his brow furrowed under his white hair. He glanced at Minnureal meaningfully – one of *those* parental looks – before returning his attention to her. "How long has this been happening, Kitten?"

Gatina could not take back what she had said, she realized. Nor could she lie about it to her parents, she knew. "A few months, I guess. I mean that I kind of . . . hear the objects, usually the coins. Or smell them, or, or . . . I don't know," she confessed, "they just seem to call out to me to find them. And I do. Like that . . . that little box in your wardrobe," she reminded them. "I could feel that. There's metal inside it. I don't *mean* to cheat!" she promised.

She studied her parents' faces for some clue as to what they might be thinking, fearing she had admitted some horrible mistake. But their faces were their normal blank masks, with no indication of their thoughts. That was annoying. She continued to explain. "When it happens with the coins in our games, it's as if I am drawn to them. It's as if they are calling to me, saying *'Here I am.'* And that continues until I put my fingers on them."

Hance looked over at his wife, a faint smile on his lips. "Well, Kitten," he sighed, "I find that very interesting! It sounds like perhaps you are on a path similar to Kiera's. We'll see how this develops. We will, of course, check the extended family lore, but I do recall at least one story of her being drawn to certain metals. My wife, do you have any thoughts on this matter?" he asked, deferring to her arcane experience.

Gatina clapped her hands, genuinely excited. She always knew she was different, somehow.

Gatina's mother nodded, thoughtfully. "I do. It may be a form of magic starting to show up early, before full onset of *rajira* at maturity. It *has* been known to happen. Don't worry, Kitten, it shouldn't worry you. Indeed, I am certain more abilities will appear as you are closer to the full arrival of your *rajira*."

"Does this mean my *rajira* is coming soon?" she asked, excitedly. Atopol had, technically, begun to demonstrate his own magical Talent a few months prior, though it had yet to fully develop. He'd already begun training in the discipline, she knew. She hoped that she would get her *rajira* even earlier, and that it would be more potent than her brother's.

"Not quite, Kitten," her mother answered. "It will take a few more years, yet, but it is an encouraging sign. It just means one avenue of abilities has opened a window for you. We can work on it more in our lessons," she promised.

"Of which there will be a great many more," her father agreed. "Ordinarily, our family trains slowly and carefully for our . . . business. Our vocation requires a lot of instruction and practice even before you learn magic. But if things fall the way I suspect they will, you will both need to learn the skills more quickly, *rajira* or no. Our very lives may depend upon it," he said, grimly.

"You must learn how to hide in the shadows, move quietly, avoid attention and notice – or attract it, sometimes," he lectured. "You must learn how to get past doors and windows locked against you, and avoid encounters that imperil the mission. You must learn to disguise yourselves, to distract people from looking where you don't want them to, and to disappear from view without a sound. And you must learn to fight," he added, with a sigh, "when those other skills fail you."

"Magic lessons will come in good time," her mother added, quickly, as Atopol's eyes lit up at the mention of fighting. "Long before you cast your first spell, you must learn a *great* many other things. This is the true beginning of your apprenticeship, my kittens," she explained. "And it will be a great deal more challenging than I'd anticipated, now. So we will begin it in earnest . . . in the morning."

THE NEXT MORNING, JUST AS THE ROOSTERS WERE ANNOUNCING THE sunrise, Gatina was startled by the unexpected presence of her mother, not the maid, coming to wake her up.

"We have much to do today, Kitten," she said, energetically, as Gatina hurried to dress. "Today, you are my new apprentice. That alters our relationship," she explained, pacing back and forth in Gatina's small quarters. "For one thing, you will address me as your Mistress. You will be addressed by your name-of-art. It is a kind of code, to obscure our true meaning and purposes."

"What is my . . . name-of-art?" Gatina asked, confused, as she fastened her skirt.

"Kitten, of course," her mother smiled. "You've always been my precious Kitten. But that will not keep me from being hard, in your training," she continued. "Indeed, it is because I hold you so precious that I will be hard on you. Your father and I spoke, late into the night, about how to introduce you to the skills and knowledge you will need."

"To be a thief," Gatina reminded her.

"We are not common footpads, Kitten," her mother reproved. "House Furtius does not steal to enrich ourselves. We steal because it is high art," she said, philosophically. "We take what we do because we have a special need, or wish to acquire something of significance, to bring balance . . . or just because we can."

"That seems . . . wrong," Gatina frowned, as she ran a comb through her white hair. "The priestesses say so," she added.

"It is wrong . . . if it is done for evil purposes," agreed her mother. "Trust me, the moral consequences of theft are important – vital – for you to understand in fullness, if you are going to be able to help the family. It is not the act of stealing that is wrong, according to our family codes. It is what is being stolen from whom, and to what purpose, that is important. And that is for your father and I to decide right now, not you and Cat."

"That must be Attie's name-of-art," nodded Gatina.

"It is," she nodded. "Your father is attending to his training, now that he is home. I shall oversee yours, at least this first portion, beginning with learning our codes. Both those we perform our art by, and those used to obscure what we do. Let's walk through the garden, before you break your fast, and I'll explain."

As the household staff bustled about their busy day feeding the stock, gathering eggs, fetching water from the well and weeding the vegetable gardens, Minnureal led Gatina through the estate, explaining the long history of their family, beginning with her favorite ancestor, Kiera. She was the one, her mother told her, who began the tradition of pairing magic and thievery. House Furtius had kept it, ever since.

"Because her distinctive white hair made it difficult for her to escape attention, she cleverly employed wigs and disguises," her mother – and Mistress – explained. "A Furtiusi will steal to survive, if we need to, but if we steal from the poor at need, we repay that debt five-fold, later. We usually set our sights on something small, valuable, and easily portable . . . often belonging to terrible, rich old men. Kiera gave us those rules. And a good many more."

"You said stealing was an art?" Gatina asked.

"Address me as Mistress," her mother said, sharply.

"Mistress, you said stealing was an art?" Gatina repeated, blushing.

"Yes, a high art," Minnureal agreed. "But it isn't merely in the taking. Any idiot can steal, if they have the opportunity. The Furtiusi steal valuable things from secret places. We take them not because it is easy, but because it is hard. And we do it without getting caught," she said, with special emphasis. "Getting caught is against our code. And we have developed, with magic and trade craft, countless ways to avoid getting caught. You must learn them all."

It seemed a daunting task; learning her letters and numbers had seemed difficult enough, but all the things Gatina imagined she would need to know seemed intimidating.

"Mistress, what am I to learn first?" she asked, politely.

"Discretion, for a start," Minnureal decided. "You must *never* discuss our lessons, or any part of your training, with other people. Even the servants. Even your brother," she insisted. "The Furtiusi work in secret, and secrets can only protect us when they are kept." Gatina wasn't worried about that – she was good at keeping secrets. "No one must ever suspect us. Indeed, the very existence of our house is largely hidden, known in full by only a few other Coastlord families. Thus, we employ a number of fictions to disguise ourselves from society, even when we are not working. When you maintain a disguise over a long time, it's called an *alias*. We have several, and I'll teach you to create your own."

"An alias?" Gatina asked, intrigued.

"It's like assuming another name and story," Minnureal explained, patiently. "We live under one, now. To our neighbors, we are known as Lord Hansis and Lady Minway of Flanmar, two minor, unimportant petty nobles who prefer our own company, keep to our modest country estate of Cysgodol Hall, and are reluctant to engage in local society.

"But if we were in Falas, we might become Yeoman Amaran and Goodwife Lita, peasants visiting the city. Or Master Kireal and Mistress Manala, Certified Resident Adepts. Or Brother Klestan and Sister Furmatha, clergy of good standing. Or, if Father is visiting court, he becomes Lord Shatarly of Espreen, childhood friend of the Duke. Or any other name, with any other face and story. Keeping an alias is like keeping a cloak about you. You must know your new name, your new story, and be able to play the role convincingly. Break that secret only at the greatest need," she urged.

"So, I'll have different names? Mistress?" Gatina asked, pleased. She loved playing pretend.

"So many you will risk losing count," Minnureal assured her. "You will have to adjust your accent to reflect your class, breeding, education and region," she continued. "You will have to learn all the accents, from Enultramar to the Wilderlands, and be able to slip into them effortlessly.

Disguise is an art, itself, within our craft. And it begins with learning discretion."

As promised, Minnureal added additional assignments to Gatina's lessons, after they had eaten breakfast. Instead of reading with her tutors, her mother repeated the previous day's task: seeking four silver coins hidden around the estate. Only this time she wasn't competing with Atopol. She had to find them all herself.

She threw herself into the mission with confidence. Her mother had avoided hiding them in the house, this time, and Gatina found herself probing the perimeter of the estate in her search. Each coin seemed to lure her to it directly, though, and she was able to find them far more quickly than her brother ever did.

She smugly walked into the kitchen at luncheon, as her brother viciously tore into a heel of bread.

"You already gave up?" he asked, surprised. "Mother must've hidden them well, this time."

Gatina dropped all four coins on the table in front of him with a satisfying clatter.

"No. It was *too* easy," she said, as she reached for an apple. "It's like they wanted to be found. Mother says I have a unique talent, apparently," she bragged as Drella, the cook, rolled her eyes and clucked her tongue at her.

"Those are cooking apples, not eating apples!" she scolded, flicking at Gatina's fingers with her long wooden spoon.

Drella had been with House Furtius since their father was a child. Gatina suddenly wondered if the old cook knew about her family's secret lives as thieves. Whether she did or not, it was clear that the old woman had detected a change in the household. Her wrinkled face was unusually grim as she served them each a bowl of soup.

"Sorry, Drella!" Gatina said . . . but it didn't stop her from taking a bite of the sweet fruit.

"Foul news your sire brought from the Northlands," the old cook growled as she ladled a serving into each bowl. "I know not what it is, but it will bring no good. Him sending away Sister Karia and the others," she said, shaking her head, ruefully. "More work for me, now."

"*What?*" Atopol asked, sharply, his mouth full of bread.

"Aye, the Master has ordered them to prepare to leave. This very day," she said, disapprovingly. "As if they'd stolen the silver!"

"Sister Karia is leaving?" Gatina asked, shocked and distressed. Suddenly, her soup didn't matter, anymore. The nun who had served as her tutor for years was leaving!

"This very day!" old Drella assured them. "They're packing their bags in their rooms even now!"

Gatina sprang from her stool before she knew what she was doing, and in moments she was flying down the wooden stairs that led to the back of the house, where the senior servants and hired clergy were quartered. She pushed open the narrow wooden door to find not just Sister Karia, but the other priestesses and servants her mother used to run the household at Cysgodal Hall packing their few belongings into satchels and cloth bags. Most of the house staff seemed to be leaving!

"No!" she cried, and plunged into the dark room. Gatina ran between the nuns, removing items from their bags as soon as they were packed, flinging them back into their chests and presses, desperately trying to halt them leaving.

"Gatina, you must stop this!" Sister Karia said, kneeling down and holding out her hand for Gatina to return a small tablet. "We must leave and if we cannot pack, we cannot leave!"

"Which was entirely my purpose!" Gatina said, tossing the tablet instead back into the chest it had come from. "Then you will miss your boat and must stay with us," Gatina said, angrily. "Why would Father send you away?" A note of desperate sadness filled her voice as she stared angrily at the nun.

Sister Karia had always been her favorite tutor. A Birthsister of Trygg, she had been with the family since Atopol had been born, but she had always doted on Gatina. Though she professed that she had no favorites, Gatina guessed that the priestess favored her over her brother. They had spent hours, apart from lessons, just talking about the world. Sister Karia was the closest thing Gatina had to a friend.

Sister Karia sat down on her simple bed with a deep sigh, and motioned for Gatina to do the same. She took Gatina's hands in both of hers, and stared into her violet eyes with her kind brown ones.

"Your father has his reasons for sending us away," she explained. "It wasn't anything I did. He has a need for us elsewhere. But, though our time here is done, I will *always* be with you. No matter what. The lessons you have learned are yours for life. And, by Trygg's holy grace, you will always be with *me*, little Kitten. Right *here*," she said, pulling her hand to her heart. "I've known you since the day you were born. You are the little sister I did not know I wanted. You are so curious and kind and intelligent. I've taught you so many things, and you have been such an impressive student. Promise me that nobody will take that from you. Those are your gifts. I merely added the education you need to use them. They are part of who you are."

"I promise," she said, sullenly, as she began to cry. "But I don't *want* you to leave! Can I go with you, on the adventure?"

"No, Kitten," she sighed. "You have to complete your education. But I have not left the service of your House. I have been instructed to go on a pilgrimage."

She explained that the nuns employed by House Furtius were being sent as pilgrims to a Temple of Ifnia, goddess of luck and fortune, in the duchy of Castal. But though they would be there for religious and educational purposes, Sister Karia had another mission: to monitor the health and safety of the late Duke Lenguin's children.

"Your father explained what happened to us," the nun said, hoarsely, at the thought. "How the Duke's heirs are held hostage in Castal. He thinks the frontier between the two duchies will be closed, soon. But the clergy have special privilege of travel, even in war time. If we can make the journey quickly, we can be well within Castal before the frontier is closed."

Gatina knew from her long talk with her mother that morning that House Furtius had always been a supporter of both fortune and education, and had arrangements with several temples to aid their work. A generous and silent supporter.

Gatina later learned that the Temple of Ifnia had long ago struck a bargain with the House to protect itself from being looted by the

Furtiusi. The games of chance the temple ran brought great riches to it, and many a merchant used its strong houses and vaults to secure their valuables. In return for a pledge to avoid raiding their sacred vaults, House Furtius enjoyed several quiet benefits of the alliance, including housing a household of nuns on pilgrimage. The house also traditionally donated to the temple, after a significant heist. After all, sometimes even thieves needed a bit of fortune. Bad luck got you caught, her mother explained.

Despite her weeping, Gatina saw the reasoning behind the assignment. If the hated Castali were holding the heirs captive, then knowing where and how could be important. The nuns were all loyal to Alshari, and personally loyal to Hance and Minnureal and the children. Clearly, her father trusted them with the task. They were safe, trustworthy, and they were part of the extended House Furtius.

"I promise that we will meet again, Kitten," Sister Karia assured her young charge. "Perhaps sooner than you think. There is much happening, right now, and I imagine all of us must do our parts. Trygg alone knows what they might be." With that, Sister Karia opened her bag, and gestured. Gatina reluctantly picked up her tablet and handed it to the nun, who packed it away.

"And when we do meet again, you'd best be prepared to demonstrate how much farther you've come in your lessons," she teased as she made her way down the stairs. "I didn't spend two years teaching you to read and write to see you forget it all the moment I left!"

"Keep your life and your feet balanced. Shadow is the child of light and the blessed Darkness. It is within the equilibrium of this twilight that our House thrives."

—*Rule of House Furtius*

CHAPTER FOUR
PLAYING IN THE SHADOWS

THE ENTIRE CHARACTER OF THE HOUSEHOLD CHANGED, AFTER FATHER HAD returned and the nuns left. Every day was filled with lessons, now, but not lessons on history or philosophy. During the mornings, if the weather permitted, Gatina and her mother would retire to the gardens where Minnureal taught her a thousand different things about disguises and aliases, the differences between the classes and the various roles she might have to play in the course of her career.

Some games were simple, like the one where her mother presented her with a covered basket. Gatina would have but a brief moment to look at what it contained – which could be any number of random objects – and then report back precisely what she had seen a few moments later. Gatina was good at that game. She had an excellent memory and a sharp eye for detail.

Other games seemed more tedious and pointless, like learning to balance her feet on the top of a narrow fence well enough to walk across it. She fell several times during that one, her mother sympathetic but unrelenting on her returning to the exercise. Indeed, there were daily excursions to practice her balance. Other times, her mother taught her simple games to improve her dexterity and reflexes. Snatching pebbles from her hand before she could close it, or pulling a ribbon from under a cup without tipping it, or taking feathers wound in her mother's braids without her realizing it. When she was caught, there was always a lecture from her.

While Gatina enjoyed the attention and even the challenge of some of the lessons, she couldn't help but note that the estate seemed far more somber, after Sister Karia and the other clergy had departed. The few servants who remained still chattered at mealtimes, but they were far more subdued than before. Her mother and father were clearly trying to maintain their composure, but a steady stream of messengers and mysterious passers-by who brought news to Cysgodal Hall seemed to leave them increasingly despondent. Every trip to the village on Market Day added to the burden, as more reports filtered into the countryside.

Gatina had begun accompanying her mother and the cook to the local market every week, now, and along the way her Mistress would lecture her or quiz her or test her in other ways. Observing the local peasants and tradesmen, listening to their accents, and learning their mannerisms became as much a part of the trip as purchasing flour or bargaining for butter.

Each week Gatina watched as her mother listened to the gossip from the merchants from the cities for more news. Occasionally, when she didn't think Gatina would notice, some of these men passed her notes. She never mentioned them, and Gatina had quickly learned that asking questions about such things was *highly* discouraged in a newly-minted apprentice.

Their parents tried to keep their mood from affecting the children, but Gatina and Atopol were subtle enough to pick up stray bits of news and fit it to their parents' anxieties. The announcement of the deaths of the Duke and Duchess was shocking, when it was announced, for the villagers. Lenguin and his wife, Enora, were popular with the people, and there was genuine grief and outrage in the market in response to the news.

A week later, as Gatina was helping her mother purchase a bolt of new cloth, even more troublesome news came: the Counts of Rhemes, Roen, and Erona were riding toward the capital . . . each with a small army behind them. The rumor was they were to discuss the crisis, and perhaps form an emergency Council of State to rule until Lenguin's heirs were returned from Castal.

That had troubled her parents. Before the next Market Day, a rider brought news that the three counts had suspended the Prime Minister, Vrenn of Darlake, without authority. But there was one man who all held responsible. The one who was calling for the formation of a ruling council to contend with the crisis.

"Vichetral!" Gatina heard her mother say under her breath at dinner, that night.

"Count Vichetral? What's he done?" Atopol asked. After exchanging glances with her mother, their father sighed.

"It is as we feared. He's gone to Falas to raise support amongst the other high nobles," he answered. "The news is he's brought a personal guard of two thousand men. Three other counts have joined him in removing the Prime Minister from office, despite his protests. If Vichetral has his way, then he will make himself duke in all but name," he said, sadly. "Perhaps even seize the coronet. Which is what we were afraid would happen."

"Can he *do* that?" Gatina asked, confused.

"If no one stops him," her mother replied, a dark look on her face. "Consider it a lesson in power, children, one every thief should understand: political power grows from the hilt of a sword. Right now, he's the strongest noble in the south. Only Falas is a stronger land than Rhemes, and without the duke there is no legitimate leadership here, now. The Prime Minister does not have the power to call Lenguin's vassals to fight. If Vichetral and some of the other counts decide to take power, there's little anyone could do about it. Too many are angry at Castal for taking the heirs hostage, and blame Duke Rard for Duke Lenguin's death. There are plenty who will back Count Vichetral simply because he rails so loudly at Rard."

"Is there nothing that can be done?" Atopol asked, hopefully.

"Not without a lot more knowledge of what is truly going on. Alas, we only hear a tithe of the news, and half of that is untrue. I will be riding to the capital tonight," agreed her father. "I will likely be gone for a few days. I need to know what is happening in Falas," he explained.

"What if he does do it?" Atopol prompted. "What if he makes himself duke?"

"It isn't his assumption of the throne that will be the trouble," their father said with a heavy sigh. "It's the policies Vichetral intends to pursue. Quite apart from my loyalty to Lenguin, Vichetral has cultivated some *unsavory* allies as he's plotted against Lenguin over the years. Allies who wish for him to reverse a number of good policies Duke Lenguin championed. Like slavery," he added, quietly.

Gatina winced at the word. She knew that once the great bay of Enultramar had been a thriving hub of the sale of human slaves taken overseas and sold to the great estates and manors. Under the infamous Black Duke, the practice had thrived, and enriched the wealthy landholders while impoverishing the peasantry who competed with the unpaid labor. But upon Lenguin's ascension to the throne, he had boldly forbidden the brutal trade. While Alshar had prospered as a result, the former slave traders resented the change. That had been long before Gatina had been born, but she was quite aware of how repugnant her parents thought slavery was.

"Well, he couldn't *do* that, could he?" she asked, frowning.

"He can and will, if we don't stop him," Hance nodded. "But I don't think we'll be able to. His . . . supporters are eager to return to piracy and slavery. He has other allies amongst the Vale Lords, as well as Coastlords, he's cultivated. Many barons simply seek strong leadership, now that the Duke is dead. Allowing slavery is not too high a price for it, in their minds. And those who are furious with Castal will ignore the change in policy. Or welcome it," he added. "No, we must do something, but first we need to know what is happening . . . beginning with discovering just who will now sit on this council he wants to form."

Her father was gone when Gatina arose the next morning, but she had little time to think about it. Mother was waiting for her in the kitchen and began her lessons at once. After breakfast, they retired to the garden, where Gatina figured they'd play more games with feathers or coins.

Instead, her mother pulled two smooth, straight wooden sticks from a planting bed and handed one to Gatina.

"Mistress? Are we weeding today?" she asked, confused, as she stared at the stick as long as her arm.

"No, Kitten. Your father and I decided that it was time to accelerate certain parts of your training. Today," she said, flicking her wrist, sending the stick over Gatina's head and nimbly down her back until she lightly spanked her behind with it, "we learn swordplay!" As Gatina yelped in surprise at the sudden strike, her mother took a position with the stick that she seemed very familiar with.

"We are not warriors, Kitten," Minnureal lectured her as she held the mock blade steadily in her hand. "We use the shadows to conceal our movements. But there are times when the shadows fail, and we are forced to fight, rather than get caught. If we *must* fight, we fight to *win*," she said, encouraging Gatina to assume a similar position. "Winning means getting away without getting caught. Not killing a man, unless there is no other choice. Not showing how adept you are at swordplay. You fight just long enough to run away. Now, adjust your grip," she said, pushing Gatina's fingers into the proper position on the stick. "And *always* know precisely where the tip of your weapon is. Now, come at me!" she invited, resuming her pose.

Gatina did, though hesitant at first. Her mother was much taller than she was, and had much longer arms and legs. But Gatina was determined, and though she knew she was doing it poorly, she leapt at her mother as she imagined a knight would in battle.

A moment later, her backside was stinging from a well-placed strike as her mother easily evaded her attack and responded.

"Good!" she praised, unexpectedly. "That was aggressive! If you are ever in a fight, aggression is *important*. Your size and age already make it difficult for a full-grown man to strike you. But if you charge him, and threaten a dangerous attack, he's even more likely to make a mistake. Now, again . . . and this time, keep your wrist and elbow up."

By the fourth pass, Gatina was starting to enjoy the challenge and excitement of the exercise, even though her mother successfully tapped her each bout without Gatina landing a single blow. She made corrections to Gatina's stance and her grip each time, giving her advice about how to improve. It wasn't until the tenth or eleven pass that Gatina finally poked her mother lightly in the wrist.

"So when did you learn how to sword fight, Mistress?" Gatina asked, as they walked back to the hall.

"Oh, your father insisted I learn, once we were married. House Furtius has a swordmaster in the family, over in Rhemes. I studied with him for two years. Eventually, you and Cat will take proper lessons, but under the circumstances I thought it best you get an introduction. Just remember that swordplay is a last resort," she lectured. "If you have to draw a blade, it means something went horribly wrong."

"Have you ever had to . . . to stab someone?" Gatina asked, thrilled and horrified at the thought.

"Only a few. But they required stabbing," she said, with a chuckle. "We might be seen as criminals, in the eyes of the lawbrothers, but there are proper criminals out there. Entire organizations of thugs and brigands. The Sons of the Sea, the Iris, the Poor Fellows . . . but the largest and worst of them is known as the Brotherhood of the Rat. They infest the docks and tenements of Enultramar in every city along the Great Bay. Once, before you were born, I was stealing something from them and . . . something went horribly wrong."

"What? What happened?" Gatina asked, intrigued.

"There were two sentries assigned as guards that night, not the one I had spotted. The other surprised me. My mistake," she said, guiltily. "The Rats are brutal, but they are careful with their loot. I had to fight both of them. For the first time in my life, I had to fight for my life. I ended up stabbing both of them before I got away."

"Did they . . . did they die?" Gatina asked, almost afraid to hear the answer.

"Not from my blows," her mother admitted. "I wasn't trying to slay them. I was just trying to get away. A few slashes on arms, legs and faces allowed me to do so. Had I tried to kill them, they would have likely slain me, instead."

Gatina tried to imagine her mother fighting with a real steel sword against two big ruffians, and an involuntary shiver shook her spine.

From then on, fencing with sticks in the garden became a regular part of her education. Atopol, too, joined them when their father was away. But it was just one part of their schooling, now, albeit a part that Gatina grew to genuinely enjoy.

The art of disguise was also an important portion of Gatina's apprenticeship. The simple dark wig her mother made her wear to conceal her white hair on their weekly trips to the market was elementary, compared to the extensive lessons in cosmetics, costume, and mannerisms Lady Minnureal gave her. Gatina discovered that there was an entire room concealed in her parents' chambers where all manner of costumes and modes of dress were stored.

"We speak of the shadows concealing and protecting us in this family," she said, as she introduced Gatina to the stuffy little room. "In truth, much of our work does happen in daylight, not the darkness. That doesn't mean we cannot obscure ourselves from notice. Each costume here was assembled to allow us to pass through the streets without attracting attention. Some have hidden pockets and secret attachments, to aid in our work. One of our kin is a talented wigmaker, which can truly change your appearance. Props, too, assist in that; a woman carrying a milking bucket or a book communicates much about herself and her station.

"And I will soon teach you how to use cosmetics to subtly change your face to achieve a desired goal. Most young girls your age learn some of that to make themselves more attractive, to stand out from their peers like a priestess of Ishi. You will learn to use it to make yourself less noticeable, not more.

"But disguise is about attitude, more than attire," she pointed out. "The same woman in the same dress can appear as several different people, if she but changes her attitude and bearing. The shadows of obfuscation protect us in our work as much as the shadows of darkness. Speaking of which," she said, taking a wicker hamper from atop a shelf, and setting it on the dressing chair, "this arrived yesterday. I had them made for you."

"Clothes? Mistress?" Gatina asked, curious.

"These are very special clothes," her mother said, removing a neatly folded parcel from the basket. "I had them made for *you*," she emphasized, repeating herself so that Gatina understood the importance. "Your first set of *working blacks*, as we call them in the family," she explained, with a fond smile on her face. "They are the working wardrobe of the thief. Note the color," she said.

"Black," Gatina nodded. "Like shadows!"

"Not just black," her mother corrected, "*matte* black. Even black clothing can still reflect light. These are made so that they don't. Trousers," she said, unfolding the top of the parcel, "because stealing things in skirts might be ladylike, but they also get in the way when you're climbing a building or diving through an open window. These are designed with gussets so that you have the most mobility possible. There are pockets here, at the waist, and two here at the ankles. The trousers tuck into your boots, which we'll get to in a moment.

"The tunic is also matte black cotton, with a black woolen waistcoat," she continued, as if she were demonstrating a ball gown. "The wool is for padding, warmth, and flexibility. The tunic is tight-fitting, but also has gussets to allow an extended range of movement," she said, pantomiming climbing a rope, twisting at the waist, and other extreme gestures. "There are small pockets at each wrist. The waistcoat has two pockets in front and a large one behind the small of your back – a good place for carrying loot," she added. "There is also a stiffened piece of leather both on the back and the breast. It isn't armor, but it might keep you from scraping yourself if you're climbing something rough."

"It sounds like I'm going to be doing a lot of climbing," Gatina remarked.

"And running, and swinging yourself around, and skulking through sewers, and all manner of unladylike pursuits," smirked her mother. "Your wardrobe has to be built to accommodate that, and provide you with every possible advantage."

"I thought we had magic for that?" Gatina asked, curious.

"Magic is always a help," her mother conceded. "But House Furtius prides itself on mastery of the fundamentals of thievery; using magic to make up for one's lack of skill is beneath us," she sniffed, with pride. "Back to your blacks. Note that the tunic has an attached hood – more of a cowl," she explained, pulling the hood up. "Inside you can pull this mask down from here, and likewise up from here," she said, reaching into the collar. "Between the two you can conceal as much or as little of your face as necessary. The area around your ears is particularly thin, so as not to obstruct your hearing. Your ears are easily as valuable as your eyes on a heist. Your nose, as well."

"And it can hide my hair," Gatina nodded.

"Exactly. There have always been rumors of our family's unique looks, especially amongst the other Coastlord nobility, but we try to keep your pretty white hair a secret. Likewise your eyes. That's an easy enough spell to do," she assured her. "The belt," she continued, pulling a thick black leather belt from the basket, "has pouches built in all along the waist. Back here is a sheath for a working knife – not a dagger," she stressed, "but a special tool that can also be used as a pry-bar, a hook, and serve many other functions besides cutting. We'll provide a suitable one later. Note, as well, that this second strap runs from your left hip to your right shoulder. At some point you may carry a sword – but we'll get to that when the time comes."

"Which is why we're doing all of those exercises in the garden," nodded Gatina.

"Correct. Thieves carry their swords on their back, so as not to interfere with our legs while we're on the move. The strap is to provide secure support for it. Also note this hook, on the left side. You can carry a coil of rope or other devices there, within easy reach. The ring next to it allows you to secure yourself to a rope, if you're climbing over twenty feet or so. You can put five times your weight on it, and it will not part from the belt. The buckle," she said, turning the accessory over in her hand, "has a sharpened edge, to cut rope, and has this little compartment for hiding things. The back of the belt also has a piece of sharp steel concealed behind it. If your hands are ever bound behind you, you can use it to cut the ropes. We'll cover escaping from shackles later," she assured. "But I don't expect you to use them. My daughter will not be caught," she said, a statement of fact more than a hopeful wish.

"What are in the pouches?" Gatina asked.

"Whatever you need for the heist," her mother shrugged, "which could be any number of things: meatrolls, for instance—"

"They're to keep my lunch in?" she asked, confused.

"In case you run into dogs, silly!" her mother chuckled. "You should never eat on a heist, if you can help it. That can leave evidence behind. But if you run into a dog, having one or two on hand is helpful – particularly if they are drugged. A vial of bitch's urine can also be helpful, in the right circumstances."

"Eww!" Gatina said, wrinkling her nose. "What else do we carry?"

"It varies, from job to job, but I've carried all sorts of strange things to help out on a heist. Things like a vial of oil to lubricate a squeaky hinge, a coil of black string, lockpicks, a bit of flint for cutting glass, a bit of sharp glass for cutting things that shouldn't be cut with metal – there are a host of tools that a thief might need during a heist. Ink and parchment, or at least a charcoal pencil, can be helpful. A long brass tube for listening through a wall or under a door. A lodestone. A tiny mirror, to see around a corner before exposing yourself," she listed. "And a piece of chalk – white chalk. That can come in handy more than you might think," she nodded, recalling some old job, Gatina supposed.

"This is your thief's mantle," she continued, unrolling a black cape. "It's for hiding, not for stealing. And certainly not for warmth. Matte black silk, which is strong and less likely to catch or tear, which can be awkward on a heist. But the catch is specially made so that if someone grabs you by it, it will slip off and let you slip away."

"What about the boots?" Gatina asked, eagerly, searching through the basket. "You said there were boots?"

"Very special – and very expensive – boots," agreed, her mother, taking the basket away from her and withdrawing the boots. "They bind tightly to your ankles, once your trousers are tucked in. There are pockets in the calves. The upper is matte black, and the sole is made of sharkskin – a very special kind of shark. It will make your footsteps all but silent, and provide a tremendous grip while climbing. Note the pointed toe – once you learn how to use it, you'll be able to climb a brick wall as easily as you climb trees. As long as you also have these," she said, taking something else from the basket.

"Gloves!" Gatina said, taking the two leather garments from her.

"Very special gloves," her mother nodded. "The same sharkskin lines the palms and the fingertips for climbing, but the fingertips can be slipped off if you need the sensitivity of your own fingertips. These straps keep them secured to your wrists. And the knuckles have a strip of hard leather across them."

"For protection?" Gatina guessed.

"For punching," corrected her mother. "Bruises are unladylike." Then she sighed. "Don't get too used to these, though. The way you're growing, we'll have to have another set made within a year."

That night, Gatina experienced her first exercise involving actual darkness, when her mother awakened her after the moon had set.

"It's a fair night, tonight, no rain and no moon in the sky, Kitten," Minnureal explained to her. "I want you to go fetch my silver brooch from the milking shed. But I don't want to see you do it."

"Pardon? Mistress?" Gatina asked, tiredly.

"I will be observing from one of the balconies on the top floor," she said, "and Cat will be somewhere in the yard, hidden. I want you to fetch the brooch, but do it without being spotted by either of us. Now get into your working blacks."

It was a challenging trial, made more so by the lateness of the hour and Gatina's tiredness. Yet she was determined to succeed. As she pulled the dark cloak over her shoulders and secured her white hair under the hood, Gatina began forming a strategy to avoid her brother, knowing his habits from hundreds of games of hide-and-seek they'd played on the estate. As she slipped through the kitchen door and into the herb garden, she was fairly certain that Atopol would be stationed somewhere near the woodshed. It was centrally located on the estate, and would provide the best ground-level vantage point, she reasoned.

Glancing up to see if her mother was visible, Gatina silently padded across the garden and found a dark and shadowy nook under an oak tree where she could see the rest of the yard better, but could still remain hidden. Indeed, she could see the woodshed clearly, from that vantage . . . and just as she suspected, she saw an irregular lump of shadow near the peak. It wasn't moving, but then it wasn't supposed to be there. That *had* to be her brother!

Convinced, she changed her plan and skirted the eaves of the house as crickets sang and nightwebs darted through the darkness. It was a different world on the Cysgodol estate at night, as opposed to daytime. A world of shadows and sounds, with a distinct aroma to it. The river provided a constant growl, just as it did in the daytime, but it seemed somewhat muted by night, she noticed. By the time she reached the corner of the house her eyes had adjusted to the low illumination and she had a much better idea of how to proceed.

She went from the house to the chicken coop; from the chicken coop to a large and unkempt fig tree; from the fig tree to the well house; and from the well house to the smokehouse, so near to the woodshed that she was worried Atopol would hear her breathing. But the lumpy shadow on the roof did not move.

Feeling confident she hadn't been spotted, she checked her position by glancing back at the big hall, where she could see the silhouette of her mother standing on a balcony. There was no way to tell whether or not she could see her – her shadow gave no indication – but Gatina was certain she hadn't been seen, yet. Just to be sure, she slipped through the fence around the little pasture where the house cows were kept and used the cowshed's shadow to conceal her. The milking shed was close, now, only a few steps away from the byre. But there were no convenient shadows she could see, ones dark enough to keep her from being spotted. At least from the roof. Not from this approach.

Her heart beating wildly, Gatina sought to control her breath before deciding to retrace her steps and find a route from behind the shed, using it to obscure her mother's view. That meant skirting the edge of the great manure pile, and then taking a long excursion through the blueberry patch, but eventually she was directly behind the milking shed. From this approach, she reasoned, the shed obscured both the woodshed and most of the house from her sight.

Silently, she crept up to the side of the shed, knowing she'd have to slip around the side to get to the door. The drying rack where the milk buckets and washed cheesecloth were hung to dry provided a bit of cover, enough for her to make it to the front corner. But as she was preparing to slide around the edge of the shed and dive into the doorless opening, Atopol rolled out from underneath the drying rack and grabbed her ankle.

"*Caught!*" he called, triumphantly.

"Hey!" Gatina shouted, as she stumbled and fell to the ground, surprised and shocked by the sudden attack. "You're not supposed to be here!"

"That's what you were supposed to think," he agreed, grinning in the darkness. "I covered a couple of sticks of firewood with my cloak because I figured you'd think I'd hide up there. I saw you in the fig tree," he boasted, "and once again when you went through the cow yard. But not bad," he conceded, as he helped her up. "Those were the only two times. Until you fell into my trap," he added, with unnecessary drama.

"That's not fair!" she complained, as she finally snatched the simple silver brooch from the milking stool.

"There is no 'fair' in thieving," Atopol countered. "Father says you must assume everything is going to be unfair. That way you are rarely disappointed."

"Your brother is correct," Minnureal agreed when they returned to the hall and Gatina complained. She was waiting for them with two cups of hot tea in the hall. "Fairness is an expectation that rarely gets fulfilled. You can never assume that what you see or suspect is actually what is happening. Always assume that the odds are worse than you think, that the game your playing is rigged, and that there're two sentries guarding, not one," she reminded her daughter. "The shadows may protect us, but they also can obscure our own vision, and keep us from knowing what might be right next to us. I saw you five times, betwixt the house and the milking shed," she added. "I only lost track of you once, when you doubled back in the cow yard. But then I heard a single footfall, and managed to find you again. Tomorrow night you will do better, Kitten," she predicted.

"Yes, Mistress," Gatina agreed, dully. She was disappointed. She thought she had done much better than that.

"Don't lose heart, Kitten," her mother soothed. "Hiding in shadows is a skill that must be learned, and then refined. When your *rajira* comes, you can improve on that skill with magic. Your father is the best I've ever seen at it," she boasted. "It is said he can hide in the middle of an empty pasture on a sunny day."

"It's uncanny," Atopol agreed, nodding reverently. "If I *blink*, he can disappear!"

"When is Father coming home?" Gatina asked, suddenly missing him desperately. It had only been a week or so, but the murmurs in the market had impressed upon her how dangerous times were becoming. She worried that, despite his superlative skill at hiding, that he might get caught up in the political mess in the cities.

"Soon," her mother promised. "But not quite yet. I received a message from him this morning – in code – that said he will return once he completes his errand. In the meantime, we have an errand of our own. In two weeks Kitten and I will don disguises and go visit a cousin in the capital. Among other errands . . ." she said, a hint of mischief in her voice.

"This is about the new council, isn't it?" Atopol asked, uneasily.

"This is about a great many things, but yes, Count Vichetral's new council is of interest to our House," she said, carefully. "Your father's message confirmed it. Vichetral is consolidating power, he's placed the Prime Minister under house arrest, and he's using that power in terrible ways, undoing all the good Duke Lenguin's rule accomplished. But that is not your concern," she warned. "That is ours. You two should go back to bed, now. We have an early morning. Tomorrow, I will begin to teach you how to pick locks."

"Family service and loyalty. Pride and professionalism. Ethical action is what separates us from common thieves. Any man can merely take what is not his. Thus are tyrants and thugs alike made. There is honor within our House."

– Rule of House Furtius

CHAPTER FIVE
POLITICS IS EXHAUSTING

Though it was still high summer, the promise of autumn was in the air in earnest the morning the little barge conveyed Lady Minnureal and Gatina by river toward the mighty Mandros River, the one that stretched the length of the duchy from the Narrows in the north to the Great Bay of Enultramar. As they left the manor's dock under the fading cloak of darkness, Gatina heard the birds chirping, the lapping and sloshing of the water, the thump of the oars against the side of the barge. Gatina enjoyed the crispness and the color of the first turning leaves poking through the mists on either side of the river in the light of dawn. But before noon, the heat reminded her that summer was still reigning in Alshar.

She and her mother were both in disguise, technically, as a long brown wig obscured Gatina's white hair, and a simple spell had darkened her eyes. Both wore the clothing of the petty nobility, which was not far from the truth; though wizards were prohibited from owning property or bearing noble titles, the Royal Censorate of Magic was unaware of her family's *rajira*, or their clandestine magical practice. Her mother assured her that the parchment that "proved" their nobility was every bit as valid as any other noble's, though that was a challenge that was unlikely to arise during their trip up the river.

Gatina had watched the polemen push the barge away from the dock and into the misty river just as the sky was beginning to lighten in the east. The fog was thick that morning, hanging over the water like a mantle as the bargemen cast off their ropes and pushed the barge into the current of the river Laris. It struck her that she was really going away from Cysgodol Hall, her home and the only place she had ever lived, just as it had taken Sister Karia from her, and it had filled her with a mixture of sadness and excitement. She was on her own adventure, now.

The geography cut in and out, creating a serpentine pattern for the river to follow. This pattern was designed by landowners who had their workers cut into the land over the years, her mother quietly explained. The work was designed to encourage the flow into little canals, both as a means to provide water for their crops and their estates and to facilitate sending those crops to market by barge – far less expensive, she knew, than hiring carters to move it. Docks seemed to appear every few hundred feet. More than half of the commerce in southern Alshar was moved by river barges like this; she remembered as much from Sister Karia's lessons the year before. That seemed like a lifetime ago.

So much had changed, she reflected as the barge moved slowly through the fog. Her life, like the river, was moving from slow and relaxed to fast and dangerous, she realized, as she began to embrace her training and her future. It was exciting, but it was also . . . scary.

She had to admit that Sister Karia's geography lessons helped her better understand her father's maps of the region. Before those studies, Gatina couldn't imagine a river coming this far inland because it had seemed so far away on the map and because the river, as drawn, was a skinny line of indigo ink. The Great Bay had been at least two hands away from their home. That didn't seem like it was too far away. At the time, she'd imagined she could have hiked there in an afternoon. Alshar was much larger in reality than the map suggested. The nun had tried to explain the distance and scale, but Gatina was insistent. So much so that Sister Karia had gotten her parents involved.

She smiled at the memory of her innocence as she pulled her drab wool cloak tight around her shoulders against the chill of the early morning air. She remembered Father showing her the map after Mother had tired of her questioning where they lived, not just the name of the Cysgodol estate and the nearby village of Larisby, as well as the Laris River they lay upon . . . but also where everything else in the great big world was in relation to it. Gatina had struggled with that until Father had invited her and Attie into the library.

She had only been five at the time, before her lessons with Sister Karia had begun in earnest into areas far more challenging than penmanship and reading. She'd been excited that Father had taken an interest, and what he showed her delighted her. Nearly covering the top of his giant polished wood desk had been an unfurled map of the Duchy, with weights at its four corners holding it into place. Father had sat in his desk chair, pulled Gatina onto his lap and Attie to his side, and explained to them both that this map was their county, the County of Falas, and then explained what a county was and whereabouts in that region they lived.

The map was smooth linen paper, not parchment, she realized as Father pointed out key geographic areas – the ducal capital city of Falas, the Great Bay of Enultramar, the Alshari Coastlands, where they lived, and the vast Great Vale north of the city – explaining why each was important, the kinds of people who lived there, and what manner and type of business was conducted there.

Her mind had whirled at the idea of Coastlords like her family (though in ancient times they'd been called Magelords, he'd assured them) living on the fertile plains of the south, the Sea Lords of Enultramar sailing their mighty ships off from the havens around the Great Bay, the proud knights of the Vale Lords with their magnificent horses in their tournaments around the Great Vale, the industrious rivermen who plied the Mandros, and even the poor Ridge Lords who made their holdings high up in the mountains that circle southern Alshar. He spoke of the Cotton Lords of fertile Gilmora who now had the hated Castali as their sovereigns, and the dour but valiant Wilderlords of the distant north who fought in the forests of the Wilderlands against beasts, goblins, and mostly each other.

He also showed them distant Vorone on the map, the legendary

Summer Capital where the Duke and his court could spend the summer months hunting and hawking, not sweating and swearing. He had traced out the route he usually took with his finger, describing the desolate Land of Scars and the arid towns of the Westlands he had to pass through to get there.

It hadn't occurred to her as odd at the time, but Gatina and Attie knew that Father had been a close friend of the Duke and Duchess. Indeed, at five she didn't really understand who the Duke was or how important he was. She just knew that Father often traveled to see Duke Lenguin and his pretty wife. She'd imagined them as neighbors who lived just down the Laris River, not the sovereigns over more than five million people across five provinces.

She knew better now. But she also knew the days of Father setting out to visit his friends were over. Duke Lenguin and Duchess Enora were dead – murdered – and now things were in an uproar. Those trips were canceled. Hance had poured his grief into protecting his family and what was left of the Duke's legacy. Gatina sighed, her happy memory overtaken by sadness for her father. She knew he still mourned his friend, and she felt bad for him. But she was also haunted by a bit of worry for her family, and her future as an active member of House Furtius.

The change in Father since he'd returned had reflected the transformation in her quiet little family, not just in the servants leaving and the intensification of the games, but in the unspoken fear that her very House was threatened. The change in regime was a danger to them. The chaos and uncertainty was an unpredictable risk – and she had learned how her parents felt about risk. Gatina sighed, as she stared at the water, and she forced herself to be optimistic. She knew her parents would make things right. That's what parents do, she reasoned. There was nothing that Lord Hance and Lady Minnureal of House Furtius could not fix . . . at least in her experience.

She turned to find her mother talking quietly with the barge master. Lady Minnureal nodded and smiled at the man, then approached Gatina.

"Our captain was explaining that we'll stop off in a few miles to make a delivery. Then a few more after that," she explained. "It won't delay our arrival, much. We were lucky to even book passage, this time of year," she added, reminding Gatina. "Most of the barges are downriver. Finding one willing to go north was lucky. Best that we avoid travel overland as much as possible. Too many possible encounters with the wrong sort of people," she said, with an aristocratic sniff.

That was her way of reminding Gatina that they were traveling under aliases and in disguise to avoid the Censorate, among other unsavory people. Had they taken the family's yacht, the *Daydream*, they may have drawn attention to themselves as two women traveling – sailing – alone, which was rare in the country. Besides, the *Daydream* was at the coastal estate, Atopol had told her before they'd left.

Their disguises were simple, but efficient. They both wore well-made homespun dresses far beneath their station, more suited for artisans than Coastlords. The rough cotton fabric was itchy on Gatina's skin. The wig she wore, however, was far more problematic; the damp air and the heat that would arrive later in the day, and that would make her sweat and cause the wig to slip if she wasn't careful. The wimple she wore to keep that from happening was dark brown, like her dress, and it seemed to trap heat in, making her scalp warm and adding to her discomfort and heat. Mother had used a spell to darken her violet eyes to an unremarkable hazel, too. Mother wore a simple gown and habit in a lighter brown with a goodwife's woolen vest in a darker hue, and her wimple was starched white linen over her hair.

When she caught a glimpse of herself in the water, Gatina did not recognize the face that looked back at her. The very uncomfortable face, she noted. Hiding in plain sight was not as comfortable or as glamorous as she had thought it would be. Indeed, though it was still new to her it was already uncomfortable. Her family had done it for generations, as Mother had explained repeatedly before they left the manor while fussing at her for tugging at her wig. Gatina had no idea how they had contended with it.

She tried to focus on the wildlife around her on the river to distract herself from the discomfort of her disguise. A pair of robins playing an entertaining game of tag through the diminishing mists narrowly missed one of the polemen, who ducked out of their path just in time. The oblivious robins flew off toward the melody of other birds chirping their morning song through the trees on the shore. There seemed to be an entire symphony of them. The birds' songs made her happy, even in the early and still chilly morning hour. She was not a morning person – no one in her family was – but it was hard to be grouchy with the serenity of nature around her.

Besides, she reasoned, the prospect of adventure outweighed her grouchiness. She was out in the world, in disguise, and everything seemed strange and new in the glow of the dawn. Cysgodol Hall was now a dot behind her, as the barge rounded a gentle bend and she lost sight of it. A much larger estate came into view on the opposite shore, where the first stirrings of the daily chores were occurring as they floated by. The barge flowed with the current past a dock where lush and fragrant gardens sprawled behind it. The white stone house seemed to be glowing pink in the pale dawn light.

She wondered what the place was called, who lived there, and if her family knew them? Had she seen the residents at Market Day in the village?

Before she could ask her mother, the barge began to slow. In a moment, one of the pole men leapt to the dock with a rope and tied it fast. Two men from the estate were waiting for them.

"Our first stop," Mother said, nodding. "Just a regular delivery. Not to worry." She took Gatina by the hand and they found seats in the middle of the barge, where they could watch the happenings without getting in the way. The boat rocked under the weight of the men offloading crates and barrels.

"These are our neighbors?" Gatina asked.

"Yes, the Andiron manor. Sir Balmoral is the tenant lord there, has been for years. Coastlord," she added approvingly. "On his fourth wife. They keep dying, poor things."

"Is he murdering them?" Gatina asked in a whisper.

"Oh, no!" her mother giggled. "The first was an older widow he married when he was young, and she died of the flux. The second and third died in childbirth, Trygg bless them," she sighed. "Otherwise I might guess they died of exasperation. The man is a boor," she pronounced. "I danced with him once a few years ago at Larison Castle. After five minutes I would have chewed my arm off to escape. But other than that, he's harmless."

The process of unloading only took minutes and then they were back on their journey. The barge made three more stops in quick succession before the sun had fully risen. By the third, they were already miles away from Cysgodol Hall.

Gatina returned her focus to the landscape, which was more visible now that the fog had lifted from the river. Each mile was like looking at a new page in a book as the estates rolled by on the shore, a page bounded by fences of stone or woven hazel boughs, sometimes coming right to the riverbank.

The rural areas stretched from the river up the gentle slopes, all the way to town, perhaps, and certainly to the road leading to it. These were far larger manors than their small estate, she realized, manors with hundreds of peasants and workers trudging off to fields, orchards, or other duties. They paid the barge no heed as they went about their work. She could see crops and livestock dotting the property.

In fact, she heard all sorts of livestock and marveled at how much sound traveled across water – something, she realized, that she should keep in mind. If she strained her ears, she could hear the horses, cows, pigs, donkeys, turkeys, geese, ducks, hens, and other farm animals making an uproar as the morning feeding began. The air here was so fresh, she reflected. She smelled the water and the musky stink of manure and hay, but if she tilted her head up and away her nose picked up the scent of the wildflowers and honeysuckle that grew along the river. Honeysuckle, she decided, smelled *delicious*.

Mother provided lunch from a hamper, at noon, just before they reached the fork in the river. Over farmer's cheese, maislan bread, hard-boiled eggs, and a tiny mushroom pie (clearly Drella's work, she recognized), Mother quietly explained what to expect before they came to Falas.

"It's a huge city," Minnureal said, between bites. "Nearly a million people, all living under the great falls. It has been the seat of government of Alshar since the Coastlords came and claimed it, hundreds of years ago. The Ducal Palace is there – it's quite beautiful. So is the Tower of Sorcery. It has theaters, operas, taverns, wineshops, temples, libraries, schools . . . why, it's one of the most beautiful cities in Alshar, and one of the largest."

"And the Duke is also Count of Falas?" Gatina recalled.

"Yes," her mother said, suddenly sad. "The city and all the lands east of it. At least he was. I've spent quite a bit of time in the city, over the years. It's fertile ground for the kind of work we do," she said, purposefully ambiguous.

"So it's full of rich, wicked people?" Gatina prompted.

"It's full of opportunities," her mother corrected. "But we must be careful. It is not as safe as it was during Lenguin's reign. And I expect it will get even less safe, as time goes on. A consequence of the times, I'm afraid," she sighed.

While they were out of earshot of the boatmen, Minnureal lectured Gatina about history and politics, the family codes and ciphers, and the differences between village life and city life. She urged Gatina to study the mannerisms and customs of the places they would visit so that she could emulate them, at need. She said nothing about the goal of their errand, though it was clearly important, save they would be visiting some of their relatives.

"That part of our alias is true," her mother instructed. "We have plenty of kin in Falas. It's always best to cloak your lies in as much truth as possible. Except with your family," she corrected. "Because we must be regularly dishonest with the rest of the world, it is vital that we be absolutely honest within our House. Trust is the glue that binds House Furtius together."

"Where exactly are we going?" Gatina finally asked, after days of resisting the urge. She reasoned that information would not betray the purpose of their mission.

"Firstly, we will disembark at a dock at a village outside the city, under the Temple of Ifnia's protected banners."

"Ifnia? The goddess of luck?" Gatina asked, confused.

"Apart from the blessed Darkness, the Mistress of Fortune is often our patroness. We have a special arrangement with some of their clergy: they help us, and we don't steal from them. And they keep quiet about us. It's been a good arrangement: Ifnia's temple, among others, has often been important to our work, over the years. It's a private dock, at an estate a few miles downriver from Falas proper. It's owned by House Furtius, through an intermediary, but the dock and the estate are leased by the temple. In return, they provide us certain services and security. We have many such relationships."

"Mother?" she asked, suddenly concerned. "Just how wealthy *are* we?"

Minnureal smiled. "Enough that you should never want for anything. But wealth is not important, in and of itself. We can steal as much of it as we desire. It's what you *do* with that wealth that matters. Our holdings are an accumulation of generations of successful heists and careful investments. This particular dock and the warehouse attached to it was purchased by your grandfather after he looted a wealthy merchant's treasure room. The temple keeps a cloister there. It's nice, you'll like it."

By afternoon they had come to the conjunction with the Mandros River. It was only slow here, she knew from her studies, because it was so wide and deep for a river this far inland. The Mandros dwarfed the size of the Laris, more than four times wider than the tributary she lived upon. The other barges and boats she saw on the Mandros were far larger than the little barge they were on, too. They nearly looked like ocean ships.

But if the river was larger, it was also more difficult to manage, she quickly realized. The pole men who had mostly steered down the Laris, using its current to propel them, now had to use their poles in earnest as they began the journey upriver, against the current. The men on the boat strained as they fell into a rhythm, walking their poles along the sides in practiced succession. It was hard work, she could see.

As they neared Falas, Gatina felt the buzz of excitement around her as river activity increased. There were all manner of boats going laboriously up and easily down the river past the barge. Fishermen worked alongside the river and dotted the small docks, casting nets and lines for the day's catch. She also heard belly-shaking laughter before they passed a group of women washing clothes on the riverbank.

The birds were far more active, too, and she realized these were different types of birds than what was at home – and a lot more of them. Their legs and beaks were longer and their wings wider. She watched in fascination as they skimmed the water's surface and then scooped fish into their beaks.

Gatina realized everything was more crowded and busier near the city than the slower pace of the countryside. She could feel the change, as well as observe it. The houses along the bank were getting closer together and more frequent, only a few hundred yards apart, and each seemed to have its own dock, many with boats or even sloops tied to them. There were a lot more people on the shore as well.

"We are past midway, Kitten," Mother said, as she passed a skin of watered-down wine to Gatina late that afternoon. "That cluster of halls we're passing on the left is Andronipy. That's in Rhemes, across the river. The next village on the Falas side will be where we get off – Old Duke's Landing, it's called. We'll be taking a coach from there, instead of proceeding on to the harbor. It's where the Dukes disembarked, back when the Tower of Sorcery was their palace. It was once quite grand. It's just a sleepy little river village, now. Not much longer. Eyes open," she reminded Gatina.

She settled in, next to her mother, and tried to keep her eyes open. All of the late night, early morning, and overnight training combined with the warm sunshine, watered wine, gently-rocking barge, and the sound of the river lapping at the side of the barge conspired against her, and she dozed off for a few minutes in the late afternoon.

The stink of dead fish and briny water woke her. There was another smell, too, and it was godsawful. She couldn't place it. Not cow manure. Something far more foul.

Gatina shook off her sleep, rolled her neck and jostled Mother, who quietly asked, "Good nap?"

"Yes, it was, until the smell woke me," Gatina answered as she surveyed the landscape and realized they were nearly to Falas. She could tell by how close together the houses were now along the river – so close that you could lean out a window and touch the next building, sometimes.

The smell hit her again, like a slap in the face, and that coupled with the body odor of the barge crew, caused Gatina to gag before tucking her face toward her cloak, which smelled of lavender.

"What is that?" she demanded of her mother.

"The main sewer for the city runs through Old Duke's Landing," she explained with a grin. "They run more than half of the city's waste down here, downriver from the nicer neighborhoods. It used to just get dumped into the port, and that was just awful. But a city the size of Falas needs such efforts. Nearly a million people produce a lot of poop every day," she pointed out, as they passed the great masonry pipes that dumped an unrelenting torrent of brown into the Mandros.

Yes, this was the city, she thought.

As the barge got closer to the dock, Gatina reflected on the very obvious shifts in the landscape. The biggest difference was the lack of space. In the country, manors were spread out and seemed to be miles apart. Even cottages had space for small gardens and pens for livestock. But the nearer they got to Falas, the closer together the homesteads became – homes much smaller than the grand manors and estate halls to which she was accustomed. Nor were all of them in good condition. Some homesteads dotting the riverbank seemed to be barely held together, their thatched roofs rotting and their beams and walls dirty, broken, and in desperate need of a whitewashing. She saw a shift in livestock, too, from horses and cows to mules and goats. There were a lot more geese, she noted, and fewer chickens. But dogs and cats seemed to be everywhere.

"There's our dock," her mother finally announced. "We'll be able to get off, soon. We're landing at a temple's wharf. Ifnia, Goddess of Fortune," she reminded Gatina. "We'll meet our contact there."

One of the first things Gatina noted as they approached the village, with mild disgust, was the stench of firewood and smoke that hung in a pall over the houses and warehouses. She was used to that, in moderation, but here the smoke was pervasive. She realized just how many fires a city the size of Falas burned every day – it must be just as overwhelming as the amount of poop, she was sure. It even hung out over the river in defiance of the gentle breeze, invading every fiber of clothing and coating every brick, stone and bit of mortar with soot. And her hair, she realized. She could already smell it in her wig.

In the country, back at Cysgodol Hall, the fireplace in the kitchen was the only one that was stoked most of the time – for cooking. In the main house, though there were many fireplaces, they only used the fireplace in the Great Hall in the depths of winter when it was cold, as the manor had been designed for maximum sunlight and airflow. Here, there was barely room between buildings to allow either air or light to pass. The thought of that many fires crammed together made her shudder.

Gatina was both fascinated by and terrified of fire. Her parents were overly cautious around the large fireplaces at the manor, repeatedly and sternly warning both her and Attie to stay clear or give a wide berth. Indeed, at Cysgodol Hall the hearths were generous and made of slate, and covered with screens to avoid any accidental sparking which could lead to an unfortunate outcome. And, adding to that fear, Gatina had heard stories about how quickly a fire could spread in the city, the flames climbing walls and engulfing entire city blocks, destroying houses, businesses and families one after another. She could imagine, with horrific detail, just how quickly a fire could spread in a place this crowded together . . . and they weren't even in the town, yet!

She heard the shrill, urgent bark of dogs, which grew louder the closer they got to the docks. The dogs were upset about something and one pack of dogs' barking gave way to another, she reasoned, until there was a canine chorus sharing its disgruntled harmony. The closer they got to their dock, she giggled as she listened to the very inappropriate shanties being sung by several fishermen as they cast their nets into the river. Gatina turned away when her mother shot her a disapproving look.

Soon, the bargemen once again leapt to a dock under a sign like two circles joined, side by side, and tied off the barge. It only took them a few moments to unload their baggage with the same quick efficiency that they had shown with the barrels and crates downriver. A few more parcels destined for the temple's dock joined the pile of baggage quickly enough. Then her mother paid them, and they cast off again, leaving the two of them standing on the wooden planks of the dock next to their bags.

This was it, she thought, *I'm actually in the city!* Or, she corrected herself, a village very near the city. While she waited for her legs to get used to a solid surface again, she looked around and tried to absorb what was going on.

The Temple of Ifnia's private dock was abuzz with activity as temple workers rushed to unload crates of cargo so that boats could move along. Dock workers swore while lifting heavier parcels, passing each down the line until every barrel and box had been sorted and loaded onto the proper wagon or cart. Among them strode several monks and a few nuns, each dressed in a neat brown habit, who checked in shipments and directed each to its proper destination.

Gatina was so preoccupied absorbing the activity in the little river port that she almost missed a different kind of habit than the Ifnite clergy – and, to her surprise, seeing Sister Karia at the end of the dock, standing next to a strange but oddly familiar-looking man. She ran to embrace the nun with squeals and shouts, and she was pleased to see her affection returned.

"This is your father's cousin, Onnelik," Lady Minnureal introduced, when the squealing and excitement of Gatina's reunion subsided. "The relative I spoke to you about on the way here," she added, knowingly. "We'll be staying at his home for a few weeks."

Gatina nodded, curtsied properly to the older man, and introduced herself quietly and formally, remembering to use her alias. Onnelik looked a lot like her father, she realized, apart from the dark hair and normal-looking eyes; a slightly taller, heavier version, perhaps, but the shape of the face was similar. And he had kind eyes, she decided.

Cousin Onnelik was one of several relatives who Mother had told her about, members of the family who were not themselves wizards or thieves, but who aided the more active members of the House in their missions. In Cousin Onnelik's case, she learned, he was known as a master forger of documents and a facilitator of heists in the capital city, Falas.

"When did you get back from . . . Castal?" Gatina asked Sister Karia.

"Just today," the nun revealed, as she grabbed Gatina's satchel. It was full of traveling clothing, but it also contained Gatina's newly-gifted tools of the trade: some tools, her working blacks, and her brand new heist journal. Everything was concealed in a special compartment, safe from a casual search of the bag. Her mother had emphasized the importance of practicing secrecy as a discipline, even when there was no immediate threat to discovery. She had been also lectured about the need for secrecy, even in her journal. Avoid incriminating others in the House in word and in writing, a House Furtius Rule said. It seemed sensible advice, when your family stole expensive things as its vocation.

Gatina was particularly excited about the presence of those items in her baggage. It suggested adventure. She just didn't know what kind of adventure. *"I'll explain it in detail when we arrive,"* Lady Minnureal had promised when she presented Gatina with the gift of her journal the night before they left home. *"It is important. And it concerns your role in our family's fortunes; a role we think you are ready to fulfill."*

"Your trip was well, my dear cousin?" Onnelik asked, politely. "No rough water?"

Gatina thought it sounded odd, until she realized they spoke in a kind of ambiguous code. Lady Minnureal nodded.

"A little bumpy, as it always is this time of year," her mother replied casually. "A few stops along the way, to drop off supplies. Just preparing for winter." The little barge had, indeed, stopped three times, Gatina remembered, quickly offloading barrels and crates in a flurry of activity that took minutes before quickly returning to their journey. She hadn't thought anything of it at the time. Now she wondered what those barrels and crates contained. Perhaps illicit materials, perhaps artefacts, wine, or gold.

Then Gatina realized that each of those stops was likely one of the family's properties, like this one, probably kept by a distant cousin, aunt or uncle. *Safehouses*, she realized. Her mother had stressed the importance for a thief to have several places where they could lie low and avoid detection, recuperate from wounds, and enjoy some security. But so many? Her mind raced with the possibilities before Sister Karia distracted her and brought her back to reality.

"Kitten, you're so much taller!" Sister Karia said, noticing that Gatina had, indeed, grown a few inches in the time since she'd departed. "When did that happen?" The nun had not seen Gatina since she left Cysgodol Hall months ago. "You must be as tall as your brother now!"

Gatina laughed. "Sadly, no. He is still taller. Mother says I might reach five feet. Her side of the family tends to shortness. But I can now get things from the top of my wardrobe without a stool," she boasted.

Sister Karia laughed, took Gatina's hand and they fell in line behind Cousin Onnelik, who was now carrying both satchels as he led the women off the dock and to a waiting carriage bearing the temple's livery, complete with a coachman and a fine-looking team.

"You were unobserved?" Gatina overheard her mother asking Onnelik.

"Without a doubt. I have regular business here, so my presence would not raise suspicion. The Count's eyes are closer to the palace," he said, as he handed off the baggage to the coachman. "The rodents would never bother the temple of Ifnia," he said, indicating the temple's holy symbol, an infinity sign within a circle. "Most of them are too fond of gambling to tempt the ire of the Ifnites. We are safe. Hells, they even loaned me the carriage," he bragged.

She saw that while the dock workers showed respect to the clergy, the level of deference differed vastly from home, she noted to herself as the coachman began the journey north, away from the docks. At home, in the countryside, the clergy's carriage would have the right of passage in all instances; but here, as they jostled along the cobbled streets, they stopped abruptly several times as other carts and wagons frequently blocked the way. The carriage driver yelled angrily, his voice deeper, and she could feel his temper simmer.

His accent, despite his tone, was a lilting drawl, different to what she was used to at home. When she first heard him speak, as they loaded into the carriage, she found it reassuring and almost sleep-inducing. She was instantly intrigued by it and the other accents she heard around them as they left Old Duke's Landing. In the carriage, once the curtains were drawn, Gatina practiced the accent under her breath while listening to Mother, Cousin Onnelik and Sister Karia talk. Mostly about politics, betrayal, the future . . . and rodents.

Gatina knew the "rodents" to whom her mother referred were the Brotherhood of the Rat, the criminal organization her mother had told her about, the one that had been blamed for Duchess Enora's death. Indeed, she had gotten a few lectures about the gang in the last few months. There was a history there, a legacy of sorts.

Though House Furtius was descended from a long line of thieves, her parents had made it clear that it had high standards . . . and enemies. The Brotherhood had been a thorn in the family's side for decades, and House Furtius had been happy to return the antipathy. The Brotherhood, her mother had explained, did not want any unauthorized thieves around, as they demanded a portion of the profits from all such activities.

House Furtius not only refused, they had stolen from the Brotherhood repeatedly, and with impunity, over the years. But House Furtius was not the only house to have difficulty with the gang. Gatina had learned that her mother's side of the family, House Sardanz, had made much of its fortune since the Narasi Conquest through the clandestine use of magic. And while one would not expect them to have any problem with the crime organization, as their interests rarely overlapped, in fact the Brotherhood had a habit of trying to coerce and blackmail the houses of clandestine magi. While that irritated the Coastlords, they either paid the bribes or did what the Brotherhood asked.

But the union of Hance and Minnureal had changed that, however. It was a point of family history that, since they were wed, the Coastlords and clandestine magi had increasingly resisted the Rats' "requests." She was certain there was a story there, but her mother was tight-lipped about such things until she thought it was necessary for her to learn them.

It was frustrating, not knowing what was really going on, but Gatina was starting to get used to it. And that frustration was abated, to an extent, by her joy at seeing Sister Karia again. She hadn't realized how much she'd missed her tutor until she saw her once more.

"Where are we going?" the nun asked, once the carriage was underway.

"My home in Falas, for now," Cousin Onnelik supplied. "It's in the Count's Quarter, near the Tower of Sorcery. A small place, but there is plenty of room. You will be my guests for a few days. We can speak in candor, there; on the road, I'd be cautious about any casual ears overhearing important topics," he said, glancing up toward where the coachman was sitting.

"We're going right into the capital?" Sister Karia asked in surprise. "Isn't that . . . dangerous?"

"Things are chaotic, near the Duke's Palace," agreed Onnelik. "The rest of the city is in mourning for the Duke and Duchess, and things carry on as usual. We should be safe at my place. For now."

Gatina could not help but gawk at the houses, after they entered the great city gates that evening. It made the cramped streets of Old Duke's Landing seem almost roomy by comparison. They passed hundreds and hundreds of houses, all crammed together and stuffed full of people, more people than she had ever seen in her life.

Indeed, the streets were crowded even in the evening, she noted, with throngs of artisans and laborers returning home from their day's work. Instead of mere dirt, the roads that rumbled under the carriage's wheels were paved with cobbles well-worn with the daily passage of hooves and feet in the thousands. Lights seemed to sprout from every open window after dusk, more candles and tapers than she'd ever seen.

Gatina knew that Falas had been an important port since before there was a duchy to be capital of. It had been founded by Magelords, in the mists of time, and its location on the mighty Mandros River, above the Great Bay of Enultramar and below the great cliffs to the north, where the river formed an amazing twin waterfall that was legendary for its beauty (and which she desperately wanted to see), made it the natural capital of the province, and eventually the duchy.

It had nearly a million people within its walls and as many living in little towns and villages within sight of it. Gatina didn't think she even understood what a million people would have looked like. But her ride through the streets of Falas gave her a place to start.

Cousin Onnelik's quarters proved to be a tidy townhouse in a stately residential quarter of the city, near a grand old tower her mother informed her was the Tower of Sorcery, the traditional residence of the Alshari Court Wizard.

"That's the symbol of the Coastlords," she reminded her daughter. "It looms over the river and can be seen for a mile, in the city. Remember it, and it will help orient you. It's easy to get lost in Falas."

"If you do, find a canal, follow it to the river," suggested Onnelik, cheerfully, as the carriage finally came to a stop. "You'll see the Tower of Sorcery, eventually. From there, you can find my house again."

Onnelik graciously welcomed them in, apologizing for the lack of servants at this hour, and showed them to their rooms before dinner, which he'd arranged to procure from a nearby inn.

It was interesting food, Gatina decided, once they were seated in his kitchen at a broad table. It was rich and exotic fare – not the country fare she was used to – with strange seasonings and intriguing flavors. But she barely tasted the food as she listened in to the adults, trying to gain as much information as possible about why they were there. This was not a mere social gathering, she knew, this was family business.

The first order of that business was hearing Sister Karia's report from Castal.

"We made it into Gilmora without problem," the nun reported, "and they accepted our pilgrimage parchments without question. It did not take us long to find the Temple and establish our quarters there. I made some quiet inquiries and discovered, eventually, that Anguin is being held at an abbey of Huin, outside of Nion. His sisters are at a convent school near Barrowbell, close to Castal proper."

"I thought Gilmora was in Castal?" Gatina asked, confused. She knew they grew cotton there, but she knew little else about the land.

"It is now," Onnelik admitted, with a note of sorrow. "It used to be Alshari, but our duchy lost control of it about fifty years ago. Now the Castali rule it."

"I visited both abbeys, under the cover of visiting their chapels," the nun faithfully reported. "I was able to see the girls myself," she boasted. "They seem in good health and good spirits, and they are well cared for. And very well guarded. Each has an armed knight accompanying them wherever they go."

"And Anguin?" Minnureal asked, anxiously.

"I was able to meet Landfather Amus in the catacombs," the Birthsister said, blushing a bit. "I think the monks thought it was for a romantic encounter, but they were willing to arrange it. He tells me the heir is healthy, but genuinely inflicted with melancholy."

"Well, of course!" her mother fumed. "His parents were slain, and he lives in exile to a foreign power!"

"Well, from what I understand, he's being pressured to support a union of the duchies under one king," Sister Karia said, sourly. "The Duke of Castal wants to rule Alshar and Remere, as well. But Father Amus said that Lenguin was seriously considering the policy, before he died."

"Does he deny the legitimacy of Anguin's inheritance?" Onnelik asked, concerned.

"Not according to the Landfather," Sister Karia said, shaking her head. "Indeed, he is quite willing to see Anguin take his father's throne. Under a Castali king. He needs Anguin, and the Duke of Remere, to agree to his ambitions."

"*She's* behind that idea!" snorted her mother. Gatina knew very well who she was speaking of: Duchess Grendine. "She's always wanted to rule Alshar."

"There is some merit to the idea," Onnelik advised, cautiously. "A unified authority could do much to improve the lot of our people's lives. The Farisian campaign proved that. And Count Vichetral is dead set against it," he reminded them. "That itself suggests it might, indeed, be a good idea," he said, with undisguised disdain.

"What is the news from the palace?" her mother asked. "The *real* news, not the tavern gossip."

Onnelik looked thoughtful. "Duke Lenguin's death left a power vacuum. Count Vichetral is attempting to fill it. He removed the Prime Minister from office and put him under house arrest. He wants to proceed with the new Council of State, and he suggests ruling by decree in its name."

"And the people stand for that?" Minnureal asked, skeptically.

"With the Prime Minister under arrest, there are few who dare oppose it," Onnelik pointed out. "He has a plan, after all. Vichetral proposes that the emergency council should be made up of five counts, including the counts of Erona and Roen, with Vichetral as the leader. He wants the other two to rotate amongst the – dare I say it – 'loyal' counts. He is already choosing a new court and administrators. Vichetral has declared three months of official mourning for the Duke and Duchess, and he has issued a number of other interesting edicts under his own name, but with the endorsement of the other counts. Including an official demand to Rard to return the heirs to Alshar."

"Not into his hands, by Shadow!" her mother insisted, her nostrils flaring. That was not a good sign, Gatina knew from personal experience.

"The investigation into the Duke and Duchess's death has gone nowhere," Onnelik continued, "and besides the Prime Minister, several important palace officials have been removed from duty, quietly arrested or just . . . disappeared," he said, grimly. "Baron Jenerard has been overseeing that," he added, knowingly.

"Of course, that filthy sewer rat would be involved in that sort of thing," Minnureal sighed, her eyes narrowing.

"Which is why Shadow opposes it," their cousin agreed. Onnelik was about to continue, when he paused and glanced at Gatina. "My lady, I mean no offense, but is this matter really appropriate fare for the ears of a child?" he asked, concerned. He looked remarkably like her father when he did that, Gatina realized.

"Gatina has begun her apprenticeship," Minnureal pronounced. "Hance and I discussed it, and she's certainly bright enough. Under the circumstances, it seems best we instruct her now. Uncertain times," she added.

Onnelik bowed his head deferentially. "Of course. Then, welcome to the family business, little one," he said, in all seriousness. "May Darkness obscure you, and your heists be successful. Have you chosen a name-of-art, yet?" he asked, curious.

"Kitten," Gatina supplied, with a swallow. For some reason telling Onnelik made it feel official. Her cousin nodded, sagely.

"It fits you: small, nimble, enthusiastic . . . and curious," he added, with a grin. "People underestimate kittens," he continued, philosophically. "They can be unpredictable. They are utterly fearless. And they have claws. Your name is well-chosen," he approved.

"Back to the palace news, then," he said, pursing his lips, and what followed was a conversation filled with a dizzying number of names and places that Gatina had never heard before. Mostly her mother and Onnelik spoke, but Sister Karia broke in several times, revealing the nun's knowledge and familiarity with matters Gatina never would have suspected. Facts and news, and names and places flew across the dinner table like birds, and Gatina eagerly pounced on every one.

She learned much, during that revealing meal. The Brotherhood of the Rat apparently controlled or had an interest in nearly all the ports and seafaring activity in the Great Bay, legal and illegal. By coercion and corruption they controlled the men who sailed the ships, the men who loaded and unloaded the ships, and the men who traded their wares in dockside markets. But their corrupt reach stretched far inland, she realized.

From what Onnelik told them, by taking over the palace Vichetral's men controlled the land and agricultural economy of Alshar, now, as well as the legitimacy of business in the cities across the duchy. That rule undercut the officials appointed by Duke Lenguin, but by maintaining control of the capital, they had little recourse but to obey Vichetral's rule.

"There are many who would resist this," Onnelik reported. "Especially in Falas, the traditional enemy of Rhemes. Vichetral has many enemies. But in the absence of a greater legitimate authority, and the army to enforce it, they are scattered and unorganized, and most are willing to follow the lead of any strong man who seems to have a plan. For all his many faults, Vichetral has a plan," he admitted. "It's what he is planning that has me concerned."

For the Brotherhood had allied with the Count, Gatina learned, and was quietly supporting Vichetral's grab for power. In return, it was suspected, the council would change policies and regulations in ways that would benefit the Brotherhood of the Rat . . . and hurt the common people of Alshar. The Great Bay and its ring of port cities might be great hubs of trade and commerce, she knew, a place which provided the livings for hundreds of thousands, many of them desperately poor . . . but she learned that it was also the duchy's vast underbelly where the worst sort of people – criminals, pirates, thugs, gangs, and outcasts – preyed on the already-downtrodden citizens. Most of the people in the Great Bay were poor bondsmen or peasants, or laborers who got paid by the day. The rule of Duke Lenguin had given them some protections from abuse and unfair treatment, she realized. Count Vichetral was likely to take those away.

It was a fascinating and enlightening thing, to hear about the politics of the world from adults, unfiltered. Gatina drank in the complex web of associations and alliances until her head spun. There were a thousand questions she wanted answered, but she dared not interrupt such an intricate discussion. She reluctantly went to bed only when the adults did, and fell asleep contemplating the complicated world she'd barely realized was outside of her little country estate.

Politics is exhausting, she decided, before darkness finally took her.

"Disguise is high art, within House Furtius' vocation. Though the blessed Darkness conceals, to change our appearance with magic or craft allows us to pass by without notice, or deceive others about our intentions. Disguise begins with learning discretion."

– Rule of House Furtius

CHAPTER SIX
BECOMING LISSA

THE NEXT MORNING GATINA AND HER MOTHER TOURED THE EASTERN wards of the capital city with Cousin Onnelik serving as a guide. She was relieved to have worn comfortable shoes, walking shoes recently handed down from her mother once her feet grew into them. They were made of supple leather with a hard sole. While well-worn, they were suitable for rough cobblestone.

"Kitten, pay attention to your surroundings," her mother said, quietly, as they left Cousin Onnelik's townhouse in the Count's Quarter.

"Yes, Mistress," Gatina replied automatically. She was paying attention – how could she not? This was really the first time she was actually seeing things up close, in the light of day. It was one thing, she reasoned, to see out of a covered carriage, but this was immersion, in her mind, as if she had been dropped inside of her parents' many conversations about Falas.

Her head stayed straight and her posture tall while her eyes scanned both sides of the street, taking in all of the sights. Her wimple did not move. Mother had insisted that she work to maintain proper posture, which was far less memorable than that of a fidgety young lady gawking at everything and everyone she saw.

Strategy requires planning. Tactics require observation, she recalled from one of the many rules of House Furtius.

They walked slowly away from Onnelik's townhome and headed into the heart of the merchant district while he explained the class distinctions, which wasn't terribly difficult to grasp despite the number of titles and positions and occupations involved. There were two – the ruling class and the working class. The wealthier, however, fell in a gray area between those two groups. The wealthiest tended to cluster in mansions near the palace, or in idyllic estates in the newer, western portion of the city. Here in the older, but still distinguished Count's Quarter, well-to-do commoners and less-wealthy nobles mixed without regard to title or position.

"Nobody really cares. The coin spends the same," Onnelik assured her when she asked.

The homes they passed on their walk were similar to his – narrow brick structures of three floors, with small gardens in front and behind – but as they neared the merchant district of Old Falasport, they came to a stretch of wider townhomes with four floors and lavish front gardens where, Onnelik explained, the wealthiest of the merchants lived. Those were still white-washed stone with slate roofs, but they often had elaborate balconies or wooden porches, and sometimes even more ornate structures.

"Minister's Row," Onnelik announced. "When the Tower of Sorcery was the palace of the count, this was where his ministers lived. Now it's where the merchant princes make their homes. It's pretty," he acknowledged, "but from here the streets get worse and worse until you get to the docks."

Gatina noticed a narrow street behind the luxurious townhomes large enough for a wain and realized it was the same alley that ran behind her cousin's home. She determined the alley must be used for deliveries, as there was no place to stop for such a time on the main street and the kitchens were in the back of each townhome. As in the Count's Quarter, each block backed up to another, with the alley dividing property. His townhome's alley was buffered by a small but lavish year-round garden and a well-made wooden fence, she recalled.

She tried to see the street as a thief should, observing every detail that might be important. She saw that each group of houses was set into six townhomes with street lanterns at the first and last residence, on the corner of a more narrow road, for alley and delivery access, she reasoned. She counted five blocks on both sides of the street, compared to the ten blocks in her cousin's neighborhood. Onnelik's neighborhood also had lanterns, but these were placed either side of the street.

The lush greenery and vibrant summer flowers did not prepare her for what awaited on the other side of a short bridge crossing the canal to the Old Falasport merchant district.

"Many of these families are old Coastlord houses," he explained as they walked. "Some are friends, or acquaintances, and some are my best clients." Gatina knew that the man did both professional scribing as well as forgery. She didn't bother asking which category of clientele, as that would have been rude. And unprofessional. *Keep your secrets, and let others keep their own*, read another rule of House Furtius.

She saw younger children playing in the front gardens as tutors and nannies watched them like hawks tracking prey. She counted children playing in four houses to her left and two to her right, their squeals and shouts full of excitement and joy, not threats and fear. She smiled, wondering what they would say if they learned who she really was, then immediately erased such a thought from her mind, lest the Darkness bring it to light.

But those weren't the only children she saw. Skulking between the houses were a few raggedy-looking kids even younger than she was . . . and there was no one watching them. Indeed, they stared at her as if she were prey.

"Why are those children –" she began.

"We'll take a shortcut through the port district," Onnelik suggested, glancing at the filthy children. "We can avoid the road repairs they're doing ahead."

The port district, Old Falasport, was a few blocks past the merchant district. It was here that Gatina felt a rush of excitement, different from the Market Day crowd. This was a more rough and dangerous place, teeming with an energy that sent a jolt of excitement down her spine.

This was the heart of commercial activity in Falas, she realized, where cargo came in and went out from the city, where the ships, barges, docks and wharfmen were. And they were a colorful lot, she could see at once. She'd heard that most of the bargemen were descended from the Sea Lords, and a few looked the part.

There were bare-chested porters and stevedores hurrying back and forth from the docks with great loads on their shoulders or in wheelbarrows. Drovers with teams of four were being cursed by all as they tried to lead their horses pulling heavy loads through the crowded lanes; angry captains and dour counting men, all shouting and yelling as great wooden cranes swung huge rope nets full of cargo from wharf to wagon overhead. There were plenty of street vendors, pushcarts hawking ale or food, and scores of beggars, some horribly maimed.

Warehouses stretched from the waterfront back several blocks, with dozens of smaller shops catering to the needs of the bargemen. There were shrines to a dozen gods or more, most squeezed in between warehouses. Of course there were clergy in plentiful supply, though they did not look like the serene priests and priestesses Gatina was used to. Most carried ledger books and heavy purses, or just reams of parchment. They were here not to preach and pray, but to pay and be paid. Many temples, after all, indulged in money-lending or commerce of one sort or another. This port was far busier, vastly larger and much rougher than where she and Mother arrived, at the temple's private dock in Old Duke's Landing.

She recalled from her father's map why Falas was so politically important: it lay on the river between the fruitful Coastlands and the broad, fertile fields of the Great Vale, where the Narasi had largely settled. From here, trade could only ascend the escarpment down which the twin waterfalls descended by land. The great grain barges from the Great Vale had to unload upriver, and send down their cargoes to be reloaded in downstream barges. Wine and sea fish from Enultramar had to be unloaded here, and then taken up the escarpment by wagons. Upriver or downriver, whoever controlled Falas controlled the commerce of all Alshar. And Old Falasport was where trade began in Falas.

But it had a dingy feel, an element of danger underlying the chaos of the docks. The canals they crossed over were thick with garbage and flotsam. There were stains and broken plaster, and many of the buildings were growing mold in places. A few places were streaked with soot. It smelled ... colorful.

Gatina imagined it was also where a lot of thievery was conducted. It was easy for things to go missing from the dock, she reasoned. She noticed that Onnelik and her mother had lengthened their strides while also tightening around her. She matched their pace while watching and listening to the various profane shouts from the dockworkers.

The happy, musical chirps of morning birds vanished and the din of commerce came alive as they crossed through an open gate separating residential quarters from the purely commercial. The state of the neighborhood immediately became more shabby, she noticed. The large, white-washed stone townhomes gave way to sun-bleached row houses made of common wood beams and plaster. Much of the plaster was broken and in need of a good whitewash. There were still tile roofs but they seemed more chipped and eroded than the ones along Minister's Row. Haphazard drainage pipes and old fountains, some broken, were set between shops made of the same materials.

It seemed each building supported the other and everything was stuffed together like an overfull bookcase, she realized. She also noted that these would be much easier to climb, should she find a need. There were lots of places on the old bricks and beams to gain a grip and footing.

Then they passed a market. It was not the airy, spacious Market Day she had imagined, like in the country – it was frenetic. Everyone, it seemed, was shouting. Vendors were arranged on corners, streets, sidewalks – anywhere they could find purchase – yelling over one another to gain the attention of shoppers. They jostled with each other for customers.

If her ears weren't overloaded, her sense of smell was. She could well imagine a fight breaking out over the sale of sausages or pies, both of which smelled heavenly, but the roasting chestnuts and the vendors grilling river fish and eels overwhelmed her nostrils and she choked back a cough as they hurried by those carts.

Most of the merchants' carts had brightly-colored fabric bearing their symbols. She saw produce, meats, cheeses and milk, vinegar, fruits, fish and fowl, all laid out atop crates and barrels or in the back of carts before smelling fresh-baked breads and sweets, then roses, lavender, and honeysuckle. The mixture of scents was confusingly intoxicating.

She noted the litter lining the streets and in the sewer, and wondered if anyone ever cleaned it. She skirted a fresh few piles of horse manure. And, she counted ten City Watch members, milling around the edges of the market, near enough to the merchants to intervene if called to pursue a thief.

As they pressed through the crowds, she watched Mother scan the crowds, as if seeking out a person or some important object. She was clearly on some secret errand of her own, Gatina realized.

But Gatina's eyes were drawn away by a cluster of children her age and younger, boys and girls alike, begging for alms or food at a dilapidated, soot-stained stone fountain that looked centuries old. The children were as pitiful as the fountain. She wondered, as she considered their bare feet and tattered rags, where they lived in the vast city and where they fell in the class system. They were clearly below the working class. Had she a coin to give, she would. She did see Onnelik give each a small coin as he guided them around the children and they continued their walk.

They pressed past the cart vendors and she observed shops – wineshops, butchers, bakers, grocers, tea shops, taverns, potters, chandlers, seamstresses, cobblers, storefront shrines, spice merchants – a dizzying array of merchants and artisans lining both sides of the street. Then she noticed the pavement beneath her feet was smoother. Ahead of them was a vast, open iron gate and cleaner streets and lots more City Watch and soldiers.

Gatina quickly recalled the conversation from the night before and guessed they were approaching a far more affluent neighborhood. She counted two fountains, both in good repair, four upscale wineshops, and two coinsisters' shrines in the first block alone.

"The Temple Quarter," Onnelik announced, as they walked through the gate. "Abode of the gods and those with godlike coin in their purses."

Among them were a number of guildhalls. It seemed each guild was represented here, from what she saw, and they were as richly appointed as the shrines. She noted that instead of tile, all of the roofs were made of handsome gray slate, which may prove tricky to silently climb onto, especially in wet weather, she noted to herself.

That first block gave way to two additional blocks of elegant shops and artisans, where the keepers and their families lived comfortably above. It was far better appointed than the shabby streets of Old Falasport's neighborhood. There seemed to be a pair of City Watchmen on every corner. And there were far fewer shabby children begging. She saw merchants and their wives milling about, plying their trade to the well-to-do without the shouting and barking of the market. These shops were clean whitewashed stone, like the townhomes in Onnelik's neighborhood, and to her quickly-educated mind, indicated a wealthier station of merchant. Despite the name, there was only a modest increase in shrines along the route.

And then they came to the grand Street of Temples, and she saw the houses of dozens of gods in splendid glory.

The greatest were to Orvatas, the King of the Gods, and to Trygg Allmother, whose impressive gold-leafed dome sparkled in the morning sun. The tall spire of Duin's temple contended with the huge scroll symbol of his brother Luin the Lawgiver's impressively elegant temple. A massive gilded sickle told out the temple of Huin the Sower, next door to the shrine of the Maiden of the Havens, one of the more popular Sea Lord deities; and the highly suggestive double domes of Ishi, the popular Narasi goddess of love and beauty dominated an entire quarter block. Apparently, Ishi had a devoted congregation.

Between the major temples were shrines to a plethora of gods and goddesses Gatina had never heard of before. Cousin Onnelik helpfully named them.

"That one is to Briga, a Narasi goddess, and that one belongs to Ferum, god of blacksmiths and ironworkers. That one over there is to the Maiden of the Havens, right next to the Fairtrader – those are Sea

Lord divinities," he explained. "Colleita was the goddess of grain, back in the old Magocracy. That's when this shrine was built. She's not very popular, now, though some in the lower classes still follow her rather than Huin. Oh, and that's the shrine to Antyr, the old Imperial sea god. A lot nicer fellow than the Stormlord of the Sea Lords. Not very popular, anymore. That shrine to the Monkey God of Farise gets more visitors," he said, amused.

"Where is the shrine to Darkness?" she asked, curious.

"There are a few divinities that might qualify," her mother replied in a murmur. "Perduna was the Cormeeran goddess of the night sky. She has a gloomy reputation though. Sagan was an old Imperial god of the night sky and the stars. But we need no shrine, Kitten. Our temple opens at every dusk, and closes every dawn," she said, with a smile.

The street led to a much wealthier neighborhood of small city estates; each stood by itself and had extensive gardens, almost yards, all the way around them. They had gloriously tall trees, which were rare in other districts of the city. It reminded her of Cysgodol Hall, her country home, and made her a little homesick. She noted that each property was grouped with three others, all sharing a modest-sized but ornate fountain.

Onnelik led them on, pressing through the crowd of carters, artisans and servants headed to market, not slowing his pace. As they climbed a small hill, Gatina saw the ducal residence for the first time. The palace was everything she had imagined – grand, large, and towering, with turrets and towers and the roofs of many halls – but it looked more somber, somehow, with the black mourning banners hung to honor the deaths of the Duke and Duchess. In fact, she reflected, several houses nearby also flew mourning banners, publicly demonstrating their grief.

She knew her father had broken into the ducal palace once, in his youth. Gatina wondered how he'd done it. The smooth stone construction offered little room for error should she be tasked with scaling it. Yes, ropes would be needed, she realized. Of course, Hance may have chosen a different way. She realized there was a lot about thieving she did not know, yet.

Finally, Onnelik found the shop he'd been seeking, and with a triumphant smile he ushered them inside. The smell of tea was overpowering, but Gatina got used to it quickly. Her cousin led them to a table near the open window, where they could watch the street.

"You'll love this place," he assured them, proudly, as he held the chair for her mother. "They have tea from all over the world – from Vore to the Wilderlands, from Merwyn and Remere, even from the Shattered Isles, where the men ride the waves on planks, and Unstara, where the men have skin as dark as night," he said, proudly. "Any sort of tea you can imagine!" Then he took great delight in recommending a few, before placing their order with the teamaster.

"Now, you were asking about those children," he said, his face turning somber. "Down along the Bay they call them 'barnacles;' in Falas they're often called 'nits,' because they're as common as fleas. There are *thousands* of them in the city," he said, shaking his head sadly. "They're children who have been either orphaned or turned out by parents too poor to afford their care. They sleep in alleys and hedges, or under bridges or wherever they can find a place. They beg or steal to survive."

"That's terrible!" Gatina said, genuinely shocked. Even the poorest village children she knew had parents and a place to live. "Why aren't they in a temple orphanage?"

"There are far too many of them, and too few orphanages," her mother said, sadly. "Many don't survive to adulthood. It has always been a problem in the cities. But where we see a problem with the nits, others see opportunity."

"Those children became tools of the rodents," Onnelik agreed. "They are trained to steal for their dinner, so to speak. The most vicious they recruit into their ranks. Others are taken and sold illegally. But the rest act as spies and lookouts for them. For a penny they will do just about anything the Rats want."

"The . . . the Rats?" Gatina frowned. She'd learned a few things about the infamous criminal gang. Very unsavory things.

"Where else?" Onnelik shrugged. "The strong among the boys might get some work on the docks or as laborers, eventually. The weaker ones die early. Some do deliveries all over the city, and some run messages. It's all they can do. The guilds and the city keep them from taking up much honest work. Some of the girls take piece-work, doing sewing or cooking until someone hires them. Others . . . are not so lucky," he frowned. "Those unable or unwilling to destroy their bodies for a few coppers a week oftentimes continue begging. So to a nit, the life the Rats offer is enviable. To the Rats, they have an endless – and disposable – reservoir of young recruits."

"They think it safe to do so," her mother said. "The children can't read, they don't have parents to challenge them, and the City Watch doesn't ask too many questions of the nits. For if anything goes awry, they can . . . deal with the matter. Another nit shows up dead in a canal, and they can move on to the next. But where some see safety, others see opportunity," she observed.

"That's why it was agreed to include you in this mission, Kitten. Your job," her mother said after the teamaster brought their order to the table and poured the tea with great ceremony, "is to *infiltrate* the nits. Learn to blend in with these children. Gain what little trust they have. You cannot do that by revealing your true nature. You must be able to act, speak, and look like one of those orphans.

"Then comes the hard part. Once you gain their trust, you must find a way to get inside one of the local Brotherhood headquarters. They are highly suspicious and take their security very seriously to protect their criminal enterprises. The Rats won't let anyone who isn't sworn to them inside. Any *adult*," she emphasized. "Onnelik tells me there are often nits coming and going on various errands, however. They are allowed in without question."

"That means trading that pretty gown for rags, and mastering the Falas accent," Onnelik agreed. "As well as learning how the nits talk to each other."

"A disguise," Gatina nodded, letting the idea take root in her imagination.

"Much more than a disguise. An alias. You will have to change your entire person," her mother nodded. "You must *blend in*, make some friends, use the things I taught you. You must be subtle. You must observe, and be constantly aware of your surroundings. You must understand their lives well enough to live in the streets, *yourself*.

And you must curb your boldness. It is one thing, Gatina, to be bossy; it is another to manipulate the players like a puppet master. You must not be obvious. For you must *not* be caught," Lady Minnureal emphasized.

"Is it dangerous?" she asked. Gatina knew she looked confused; her mother was prepared.

"Of course it's dangerous," she said, patiently. "Such things always are. But you have been well-prepared for this. All of the games we have played? That was training for this sort of thing. All the finding of marks, coins, documents? Training. The disguises, the accents, the mannerisms? You learned those things to prepare you for this. This is the first of many missions you will undertake for the House. We would use Atopol, but he is too old to pass for a nit."

"So what's he doing?" Gatina asked, suddenly suspicious.

"Nothing you need to concern yourself with, Kitten," her mother said firmly. "Your attention needs to be here, on this mission, not on him and his mission. It should be a relatively simple task. But it is not unimportant," she emphasized. "There is much going on, in the shadows of Alshar. Knowing what the rodents are up to could prove vital. Many forces are stirring in the absence of the Duke. Indeed, much rides on your success or failure, else I would not risk my only daughter."

That stirred a bubble of fear and excitement deep inside Gatina, and stoked a fire in her heart. Gatina always wanted to be the absolute best. At everything.

And if that included besting her brother, it was even better. She wasn't as sloppy, and she was twice as confident.

Onnelik cleared his throat, after taking a long sip of his steaming cup. "You were also chosen, in part, because of your emerging magical Talent. Your affinity with metals is something I have only heard of in passing. It has not been recorded in House Furtius' history. There are suggestions that your ancestor Kiera had a similar skill, however."

"There were also rumors that it had been seen in my family," her mother agreed. "One of my grandfathers could sense the difference between silver and copper without touching them. I suspect that as your *rajira* develops, it will be something extraordinary. You never know how that sort of thing will come in handy," she said, cryptically. "Do you feel confident that you can do this?"

"Yes, Mother," Gatina said as she sipped her own tea, sweetened with honey and tasting of some exotic, far-off land. "When do I start?"

"Today. We will begin with changing your appearance, once we return to Onnelik's house after our walk. But I want you to start studying how the nits act and talk. We'll toss them a few pennies so that you can see that. Then we'll start easing you into their society."

Her mother and Onnelik continued their discussion – mostly in coded language – while Gatina sipped and stared out the open window of the tea shop. There were three or four of the homeless orphans in sight, clustered around a rain barrel across the cobbled street. Their clothes were mere rags, cast-offs and repurposed flour sacks. None of them had shoes. She began dissecting how they stood, how they carried themselves, and their mannerisms. She was so enrapt in the process that she didn't realize that she had finished her tea.

This is going to be fun, she decided.

"It is absolutely disgusting, but for your purposes, my dear, it is the best way to go," Cousin Huguenin said, as he smeared the mixture he had carefully prepared into her hair. "Such a shame to sully your pretty white tresses, but all of those poor children have dirty hair. A wig would be too obvious in this situation and may fall off. We need truly disgusting, sticky, *dirty* hair to work with," Cousin Huguenin assured her, as Lady Minnureal watched him work.

"But does it have to smell so bad?" complained Gatina, as the aroma of the mixture hit her.

"Most of those children have never had a bath in their lives," her mother chuckled. "I can assure you that they smell worse."

Cousin Huguenin was a first cousin of her mother's, Gatina had learned that morning when he arrived, a scion of House Sardanz. He was a small, slender man with a lovely voice, and did resemble Lady Minnureal in the face a bit, Gatina decided. He had been an actor in one of the capital's many theaters, in his youth, and his artistry with dyes and cosmetics was impressive. He certainly didn't look like a mage, to Gatina. While he now worked as a highly-sought-after hypnotist for the upper classes, Minnureal revealed that he had other talents that could prove useful to them.

Before Gatina sat down, Cousin Onnelik managed to drape a drop cloth over the settee, in an effort to preserve the pale, yellow silk fabric from the goop on her scalp.

"I will buy you your first wig, Gatina. It would be my honor and pleasure," Cousin Huguenin had promised, gushing as he sank on to a padded stool, setting his satchel of theatrical wares beside him on the floor when he first arrived. "I haven't seen you since you were a baby, without any hair. I'm here to introduce you to your first real disguise. I am going to have such a good time teaching you the tricks of the trade. A delightful change from my usual profession."

As a mentalist, he explained, he spent hours working with fat old noblewomen or merchants' daughters to help ease their various anxieties. He had *rajira*, and had even studied at a magical academy, but he kept a very low profile in regard to the hated Royal Censorate of Magic. As it was, he managed to maintain a wealthy client base, using his subtle abilities to aid his patrons in their struggles.

But he was also a master of disguise. Huguenin had brought a heavy satchel of cosmetics and wigs, as well as other items that could change a person's appearance. The costumes allowed him to remain anonymous when he wished to go into taverns and shops, he explained. Gatina suspected there was far more to the story than that, but she had learned not to ask too many questions about such things.

He taught her how to mix soot and henna and then how to compound it with leeches to create a long-lasting hair color. She found the process both very distasteful and fascinating. But she also knew that her bright white hair would stand out if it were not colored.

He'd instructed her in how to make the salve, standing behind her as she ground the leeches in an old, stained mortar and pestle, their essence gushing out and coating the soot. Now those pulverized leeches were in her hair, and she felt a little sick.

"The leeches are for color and aroma," he said, sipping wine while she worked the disgusting mixture into her scalp. "You want the maximum coverage, no suspicious spots. This is *such* a shame! Your hair is so beautiful! What I could do with your natural hair, honestly!"

Her mother laughed. "You're jealous, too? We were both given the family's barley-colored hair. It's exciting as hay, I tell you," Lady Minnureal said, shaking her head and fingering one of her long tresses. "Hance's hair and eyes are so amazing. One of the things I found alluring about him."

"Yes, they are," Cousin Huguenin teased, his voice dreamy. "He is a very handsome man, when he's not all made-up to not be."

Lady Minnureal, who had already had her second cup of wine, squealed and feigned shock. "That is *my husband* you are admiring!" she teased, then added more seriously, "I am delighted both Atopol and Gatina got his hair, even if it does make things a little difficult. And they say that no Furtiusi born with the distinctive hair and eyes has failed to get their *rajira*."

"Oh, it's nothing I cannot contend with," Huguenin clucked as Gatina followed his instructions with the nauseating glop in the bowl. "Work from the scalp out," he advised. "And comb it through! It must be allowed to dry for the color to take and soak into your hair. There's a complicated alchemical explanation, but the basic is that it must be allowed to adhere to your hair."

Gatina watched the transformation in the looking glass. She had to, as she was the one applying the goopy and smelly dye to her head. She sighed loudly as she worked. "It is *vile*. Why can't I wear a wig?" She didn't normally complain, but this was absolutely distasteful. "How long until it is done?"

"Until it's done," her mother said, unhelpfully. "Darling Kitten, this requires patience and perseverance. And kittens have very little patience." Gatina snorted and rolled her eyes, which were still violet. "We will dirty your face, of course, and use a spell to change your eye color. And Onnelik has some very filthy rags for you to consider for your wardrobe."

"Have you picked a name yet? For your alias?" Huguenin asked her, curious.

"Uh, no," she admitted. "I suppose I need one."

"Street orphans usually have nicknames, as well, but regardless you must commit the name to memory and respond to it the same way you'd respond to your own," he advised. "Perhaps Lissa? Manda? Laldine? All actresses I used to know."

"I like Lissa," she decided, as she watched her hair start to turn darker under the mixture. But she couldn't help but feel the name needed something . . . *more*. "I could be a Lissa. Lissa the . . . . *Mouse*," she decided. It was opposite from Gatina the Kitten, after all. And she was trying to infiltrate rats. It seemed completely appropriate, she decided. "What happened to my parents?" she asked, suddenly, as the imaginary person she was to become began to form in her mind.

"You don't know," her mother said, firmly. "You don't remember them. But you know they came from the countryside."

"Street orphans rarely have much in the way of family history," chuckled Huguenin, sadly. "They often invent wild stories to fill in. Half of them claim to be the bastards of some important noble family. I suppose every homeless orphan is entitled to do so. It's human nature," he proclaimed. "All right, Lissa the Mouse," he said, as he checked her hair. "I think we've achieved our purpose. Let's rinse this out and I will give you your properties for this mission."

"Properties?" she asked, confused. "I thought the nits were poor!"

"A technical term, from the theater," Huguenin explained, loftily. "A property is an item you have or hold or wear that convinces people you are who you say you are. Prop, for short. Like a pilgrim's staff, or a spellmonger's hat. If you appear with an apron and a cleaver, people will usually assume that you are a butcher.

"And while the nits are, indeed, the poorest of the poor, they do cling to a few treasures. Here is a bag," he said, pulling a small, ragged cloth bag from his satchel. "Within are a broken comb, a wooden cup, and a shard of a knife blade."

"To protect yourself," her mother added, earnestly. "Street girls must be able to defend themselves. And every girl tries to get a bit of comb for their hair. It will help explain why yours isn't in complete tatters. It would be Lissa's most prized possession," she counseled.

After rinsing the nastier parts of the salve from her hair, Gatina saw it was transformed. No trace of the bright white was left under the dye after she toweled it dry. The image of her face in the looking glass was startlingly different, especially with the smudges left from the dye.

"Lissa the Mouse," she said, as she stared at her strange reflection. Then she repeated the name in the Falas accent, which was tighter and quicker than the way folk spoke in the countryside. "My name is *Lissa the Mouse.*"

"Much of our sacred vocation relies on deception and manipulation, of convincing the unwary and gullible of our motives while concealing our true intentions under Shadow's cloak. Be not concerned with the falsehoods you utter or the methods you use to achieve the ends of the House; for every man is deceived a dozen times a day and suffers no harm from it, but can be sent into anguish with one word of truth. Therefore choose your words wisely and deliver them with all due sincerity. Only among House Furtius should you be overly concerned with truthfulness."

– *from* **The Shield of Darkness**

CHAPTER SEVEN
LISSA THE MOUSE

It was exciting and scary to leave the security of Cousin Onnelik's townhouse and take her first barefooted steps as Lissa, and Gatina was very self-conscious, at first, before she shook off the feeling. Her mother had advised her to begin her work nearby, at first, before she tried to blend in with the gangs of nits in the less-wealthy part of town.

She quickly learned that people in Onnelik's neighborhood were not particularly happy with her presence. Women on their way to shops or markets looked scornful or sympathetic, but often even their sympathy was colored by a scowl. Gatina kept to herself, walking hesitantly down to the corner and around the block, trying to shed her old identity and adopt the new with every step. Her little bag of treasures was tucked into the rope belt that held her ragged skirt in place, all save the slip of knife blade. That was in the filthy sleeve of her tattered dress.

The farther she got from Onnelik's house, the more confident she became in her disguise. She looked longingly at the baker's cart delivering bread, but the driver ignored her. Street children were always hungry, she knew. Securing food was always the highest order of their day.

She waited until she was three blocks away before she started begging. The tradesmen and artisans hurrying on their errands ignored her, too, a look of distaste on their faces as they strode by. Gatina felt invisible to their gaze.

No, she realized, *Lissa* felt invisible. Lissa was a castaway child to be ignored by good people, who had better things to do with their hard-earned coin than spend it on the likes of her. It was easier to give her a grimace and pass by as if she wasn't there. As soon as she realized that, her entire approach to her alias changed. Her shoulders slumped, her feet began to shuffle, her chin dropped of its own accord. When you are invisible like that, she realized, the whole world seems against you.

Gatina kept walking, practicing her new persona and trying to perfect it. The cobbles were hard under her feet, which were soon aching and then nearly numb. She skirted the edges of alleys and found streets that led to poorer and poorer parts of town.

Soon she discovered a few of the street children gathered atop a broken fountain, watching the passersby and occasionally begging for alms, if they thought the person might feel sorry enough for them to spare a coin. She approached cautiously – timidly, as Lissa the Mouse would. The children, three boys and two girls, waved at her to join them.

"Haven't seen you around before," one of the girls began. She was skinny – not slender, but scrawny, maybe a year younger than Gatina. "What's your name?"

"I'm Lissa," she said, the lie springing casually to her lips. "They call me Lissa the Mouse."

"Who calls you that?" one of the boys, a redheaded fellow whose face was covered in freckles, asked mischievously.

"You do, now," Gatina shot back. "I just got here," she admitted. "They said things might be better in this part of town."

"If 'they' told you that, 'they' were lying to you," a dark-haired boy laughed, humorlessly. "I haven't eaten in two days. Except for a carrot," he added.

"It's not that bad," the second girl insisted. "There's a shrine to Trygg up the street where you can get a bowl of soup, if you're willing to chop some wood. The nun who tends it is nice," she assured her. "These fellows are just lazy." She looked Gatina up and down, then scooted over and patted the seat beside her. "I'm Marga," she added. "This is Liddy. Those guys are Toscar, Twopenny, and Gan. He's the red-head," she added.

"Why do they call you 'mouse'?" Gan, the ginger boy, asked.

"I don't know," Gatina shrugged. "Probably because I'm quiet. People don't notice me. And I don't eat much."

"None of us eat much," chuckled Toscar, without much humor in his voice. "People here are stingy with the alms. No matter how miserable you look." To demonstrate, the boy's expression turned from smiling to one of sorrowful destitution. Gatina was impressed. She would have tossed him a penny, she decided, based on that face, alone.

"You know, you could just try to work," Liddy criticized. "Marga and I work, sometimes, when the seamstress on Torch Street needs us. Toscar really is lazy, Lissa. You can find stuff to do, if you're clever. And willing to work!"

"Where do you sleep?" Gatina asked, genuinely curious, but her tone indifferent. She did not want to be invited to a sleepover. She had to report back to her Mistress nightly. That was the rule.

"At night?" Toscar said. "Mostly in the hayloft behind the shoemaker's place. Or the one over on Parchment Street; that used to be an inn. The back corner is broken," he informed her. "You can squeeze through even if they do lock the door."

"Best place is at that old shrine to Herus near the mermaid fountain," advised Marga. "It's a little windy, because the roof is caved in in spots, but no one will mess with you there. Except the bloody Watch," she added, disgusted. Everyone present agreed with that sentiment, Gatina noted. The City Watch, she quickly learned, was one of the forces of nature that the children – the nits, she corrected herself – built their lives around.

Gatina spent hours at the fountain, talking and listening to the street orphans that day, though she listened more than she talked. She discovered the children had a very different perspective on the world than she'd developed growing up in Cysgodol Hall. Several times during the day other orphans would stop by and chat with her new friends, exchanging information, jokes, jibes, and occasionally some surplus loot from their begging or stealing.

It was fascinating, Gatina realized, listening to their tales of life in the streets of Falas. All of them really were orphans, save for Marga, whose mother was locked away in a temple somewhere – or so she said. Gatina quickly developed a healthy skepticism of every tale the nits told her. But that willingness to toy with the truth did not mean that the nits were ignorant. Or useless.

Toscar proved as knowledgeable about the geography of the neighborhood as he was determined to avoid any actual labor. Twopenny, while quiet most of the time, had some insights on the best places and times to "find" certain items. Marga seemed to know where one might find cast-off clothing, and she was willing to trade or even give it away, when she acquired it and it didn't fit her. And, she and Liddy could mend things if needed. They each had a needle, thimble, and thread in their bundles.

Indeed, within a few hours, Lissa the Mouse learned a great deal about the life of the street orphans. Most of it was hopelessly depressing. She discovered that the dilapidated two-tiered fountain still worked, which was one way they all earned small bits of food. The old, pitted stone-carved basin was long past its prime, she knew, but Gatina imagined the fountain was a center of activity and entertainment when the palace was still located in this part of the city, and Falas was much smaller than it was now. The three open-mouthed limestone fish whose tails supported the upper tier were entertainingly cartoonish, goofy characters that would have attracted folk to the basin. Those days were long gone, now.

She could also imagine, despite its crumbling, that it had been a symbol of the growing duchy's wealth, once. The ornate carvings were still intact, though they were coated in soot and street dust. The covered cisterns that once fed it contained clean water, piped from the river, but they had to be opened by hand. Back in its prime, she learned, water would push through the pipes and spout up and out, pouring down the first tier, then the second, before filling the five-foot wide basin, which was now bone dry and served as the nits' safety zone in this part of the city. But if a goodwife didn't want to go another three blocks to a working fountain, for an iron penny or a bit of food one of the boys would helpfully open the stone lids of the cisterns and fill their water jugs. For another, or the promise of more food, they would haul it back to her flat for her.

By the time the group broke up in late afternoon to go scrounge individually for some morsel for supper, Gatina had a much better idea of how to speak and act like a street orphan. They took a practical approach to their desperate lives, she realized, along with a healthy dose of fatalism. None of them had any particular plans for their future. None of them had much hope for a better life. And few of them thought beyond the absolute basic necessities of life.

She explained as much to her mother, after she carefully returned to the townhouse that evening, being cautious she wasn't spotted by her new friends.

"They're just kids, like me," she explained. "Just hungry and desperate and afraid, all the time. Twopenny got beat up just last week, when someone caught him trying to steal a pair of shoes. But they're all still pretty cheerful about it," Gatina said, shaking her head. "It's just what happens sometimes."

"Children are nearly always optimistic," her mother agreed, as she filled a bowl of bean soup for Gatina. "They rarely have experienced the real horrors of the world, at that age. But it sounds as if you did well. They accepted you as one of them?"

"I looked the part," Gatina agreed, as she greedily wolfed down the soup. Talking about being hungry all day had made her ravenous . . . and grateful. "Now I can sound like one of them, too. Another few days and I should be ready," she said, confidently.

"It all sounds hopelessly depressing to me," Cousin Huguenin said, with a sigh. He had lingered at Onnelik's for the day, to ensure Gatina's first disguise was adequate. "They are everywhere, in Falas. Poor things. No house, no family, no food . . . it's depressing," he pronounced. "Say, Cousin Minnureal, while I'm here, it might be a good time to . . . play a little game?" he suggested, setting a deck of cards on the table. "Do you remember these?" he asked, with a smile.

"Are those *grandmother's?*" Lady Minnureal asked, with an eager gasp, as she sank onto a chair beside him. "Oh, Gatina, we played with these for hours as children."

"Is it a game?" Gatina asked, interested. Cousin Huguenin began to shuffle the cards. She remembered the deck she'd found hidden in her mother's wardrobe, back at Cysgodol Hall, and was intrigued.

"It can be," her mother agreed. "But they have other uses, as well. We used them to learn family history and lore, among other things. Many Coastlord families do. From back in the days when the Censorate was raiding our homes and burning our secret books – but they mostly ignored the cards. The deck looks similar to ordinary game playing cards, but—"

"But each card has notations on it," Cousin Huguenin interrupted, holding up a card to show her. "It's a tool to teach not just history and lore, but the elements of our family magic. Including my specialty: Blue magic," he explained. "The magic of the mind and the psyche. That's where the Sardanz family excels. Each card represents something our side of the family has accomplished, discovered or endured. Each has a story, and a hidden meaning. This one here, for example," he pointed to a small rose drawn onto the elegantly illustrated representation of a noblewoman overseeing a garden, "represents family loyalty and duty. Powerful forces in anyone's life, but it has especial meaning for us."

Gatina realized she *had* seen those cards before – not this particular deck, but one just like it. Her mother's, long before she found them during the coin hunt.

"Mother, you taught me these cards and told me these stories when I was little, did you not?"

"With my own deck," she agreed, with a small smile. "I painted them myself, like all magi of House Sardanz. Perhaps not the most beautifully done, but they have served me well. And now House Furtius has absorbed the tradition. Indeed, we've passed it along to some of the other magical houses we've married into. No matter how . . . *unpleasant* those unions might have been," she said, making a face.

"Now, Minny," chided Cousin Huguenin, "not everyone falls in love with the perfect man and actually has a chance to marry him. Some of us were subjected to the traditional arranged marriages. You were favored by the gods. Not everyone is."

"In other words, most of the women in our lineage married for reasons other than love," her mother said. "Fortunately, your father and I managed both. But the rose on the cards became an important symbol for us. That was first drawn by our grandmother's great-grandmother, who came into her powers shortly before the Narasi came to Enultramar. Lady Amrosa. She prevented our family facing those horrid Censors by marrying a Narasi knight she did not love. But it spared House Sardanz much grief. She did her duty," Minnureal said with a resolute sigh. "As must we all."

"But it also represents *determination*," Cousin Huguenin began, before noticing Gatina's questioning look. "Lady Amrosa was a talented Blue Mage," he explained. "She was able to keep her powers a secret, and used them to learn things about the Narasi that protected the entire family during those difficult times. Her own deck is simply stunning – oh, yes, there are many decks, all hand-painted by our ancestors during their apprentice phases. Perhaps you will receive a blank deck of cards for your name day, yes?"

Gatina nodded, swallowing the last spoonful of bean soup, glancing hopefully at her mother.

"They were supposed to be a surprise," Minnureal chided. "Just remember, when you paint the roses, they must always be red or white, never yellow," she insisted.

"You must paint them yourself," Huguenin explained. "It's really not hard to keep track of. There are five suits of ten cards, each, and ten independent cards – the trumps. Sometimes more, sometimes less – it depends on the family. Each card represents your understanding of the concept it represents, as well as your experience of it. Now this one," he said, pulling another from the deck, "is the Ace of Lamps, and represents your magical will . . ."

Gatina watched and listened carefully, absorbing the novel lore of House Sardanz as both Cousin Huguenin and her mother recounted the lessons and stories their own ancestors had taught them through the cards, with Onnelik offering the perspectives of the secretive House

Furtius. Gatina was fascinated as she learned lessons and tales of family history that had been handed down by the magi of her mother's family since her great-great-great-*great* grandmother's time. One theme was clear in the tales: the women of House Sardanz tended to be more important as leaders than in most other Coastlord families.

The stories captured Gatina's imagination, leading her to wonder what happened to allow the family's women to have such a strong say in who they would marry, and why. They also introduced her to specific ideas associated, she was told, with the practice of Blue Magic – the magic of mind and memory, emotion and reason. Once Cousin Huguenin finished showing and elaborating on each card in the deck, her mind was spinning with all of the history and symbolism . . . and all of the concepts and symbols that intertwined with that history.

"Now, before bed, let's play one little game – a game of memory," her mother said, shuffling the cards and then laying some of them face-down on the table, after she'd cleared away the dishes. "Remember us doing this when you were sick, when you were little? Remember? We played a memory game. Then it was finding cards in similar suits." Her mother looked at Gatina expectantly. When Gatina nodded, she continued. "Good. Well, for a Blue Mage, memory is an *essential* skill. It's also vital for a thief, as a heist can fail or succeed on one little detail. We've explained the cards. Now we place them face down. This time, you'll flip them over and tell me what each card means."

Gatina smiled at the early childhood memory, but then frowned. She remembered that sickness – the fever, the sweating, the headache – but it had been one of the few times she'd had her mother all to herself, without Attie, so it seemed more pleasant than it was. "So, you've been teaching me about magic all along, Mother?"

"And our family, but yes, it will help with your understanding of our particular kind of magic, someday. Blue magic isn't like what a common spellmonger does," she explained. "It focuses on the mind: how we perceive and how we remember, among other things. Those can be very difficult concepts to understand, but it all begins with memory. You were very good at the game when you were little. Let's see if you have improved with age, shall we?" Lady Minnureal flipped the first card.

Holding it up for Gatina to see, she asked, "What does this card represent?"

"That's the Ace of Keys," Gatina responded, after a moment's thought. "The key to a door in our great-grandmother's manor house in Sarly. The door leads to the family's secrets, which are kept in fire-safe boxes. The meaning of the card is Secrecy. Because everyone has secrets to protect."

"And this one?" Minnureal asked, pleased at the direct answer, as she flipped over another card.

"The Three of Ships," Gatina responded, instantly. "The story of our first mageborn ancestors arriving in Enultramar. The meaning of the card is Hope, which every person carries. No matter how hopeless they are feeling," she added, thinking of her new orphan friends.

They went through all nine cards that Minnureal had laid out, and Gatina was pleased that she'd remembered all but two of them. So was her mother.

"Tomorrow night, we'll work on something a little more challenging," she promised as she swept the cards into a pile. "But you look tired, and I want you to be alert, tomorrow. I'd tell you to wash up, but . . ."

"Orphan kids don't have clean faces," Gatina agreed. "It's fine. It's disgusting, but it's fine. I don't even smell how bad my hair is, most times. I will endure, just like the Ace of Ships card suggests."

She fell asleep, that night, with the realization that her comfortable bed and warm room was a stark contrast to where and how her new friends were sleeping: in haylofts and well houses and decrepit shrines. It made her feel guilty, just as her supper had. It was hard to enjoy even a simple meal when you knew your friends went to sleep hungry.

She rose before dawn the next morning and slipped out of the kitchen door with her bundle . . . and the heel of leftover bread from the previous evening's meal. Carefully, she retraced her steps back to the broken fountain, where one by one the orphans began arriving. She waited until there were two of them there before offering the meager piece of bread to them.

"A servant gave it to me, when her mistress wasn't looking," Gatina said, the lie coming easy to her lips. "It's a bit old but—"

"It's *bread!*" Marga said, smiling. "And it's not stale, at all! Great find, Lissa!" she praised, as Gatina tore the bread in two. There was just enough for both Marga and Toscar to have a few bites. "Wait, aren't you going to have some?"

"I had my portion when I got it," Gatina assured them. "But I wanted to share."

"You don't want anything for it?" Toscar asked, suspiciously. Trading for food was common, among the nits.

Gatina shrugged. "I didn't pay anything for it," she reasoned. "Go ahead."

The two orphans devoured the bread in an instant, both enjoying a small bit of comfort as the day began on the busy street. The others joined them, one by one, only to hear how they missed out on the meal. That made Gatina feel even guiltier.

But she also learned the children had ways of getting what they needed. She watched as Twopenny fetched two great urns of water from the fountain for an old woman, who gave him an apple in return. Liddy showed her the shrine to some goddess Gatina had never heard of, where an hour's worth of carrying firewood earned her a small cup of watery soup from the nun in charge. But, most importantly, Marga began to explain the politics of the neighborhood to her.

"Most people will just ignore us nits," she said, as they sat on the edge of the fountain. "The ones that don't are usually mean. That tavern over there?" she said, indicating a small establishment crammed in between two other shops, where it looked out of place. "Stay away from it. That's where the drunks go, and they fight a lot. It's too easy to get involved in that. And the tavern keeper will *stare* at you. Like you're his dinner, or something. It's creepy," she shuddered. "This place is mostly safe, since the fountain's broken. But if one of the City Watch comes by, just try to look like you're doing something for someone, and they'll usually leave you alone.

"There's a grocer on Well Street that will sometimes give you scraps, if you're cute enough," Marga explained. "There's a barber on Sable Street who will sometimes pay you to sweep, if he's busy. But don't linger there, because the adult beggars will come after you," she warned. "That's their territory. They don't like us nits."

"Where should I stay away from?" Gatina asked.

"Down that lane and to the left, there's a burned-out building that some of the older kids hang around. Stay away from there, too. They're tough. They'll beat you just because they don't know you," she said, bitterly. "That's near the Butchers' Guildhall. Stay away from there. There's always something . . . ugly going on there," she said, her eyes narrowing. "It's said that it's full of the Rat gang. The Rats are the worst!" she declared.

"The Rats?" Gatina asked, feigning confusion.

"Criminals," Marga assured her. "Cutthroats. It's a gang. They force the local shopkeepers to pay them, or they'll mess up their shops. And they loan people money that they'd best pay back. They fight a lot. They're worse, down by the riverside, but they are everywhere, it is said. Like that guildhall. Sometimes, they will pay you to take a message somewhere, or carry a package. They pay good coin, too. But that's dangerous. A kid was late, one time, and the Rats threw him in the river. He couldn't swim," she said, sadly. "They're as bad as the City Watch, sometimes. I don't know why they're at the Butchers' Guild, but you don't want to go near it. Bad business," she frowned.

Of course, that was precisely where Gatina wanted to go, but she couldn't tell Marga that. Not without revealing who she really was. But she needed more information.

"You say they pay good coin?" she asked.

"*Lissa!* Don't even *think* about it!" Marga said. "It's bad enough that people don't care if we disappear. And we do," she said, shaking her head. "But getting involved with those people is just stupid. You'd get hurt. Or worse," she said, wrinkling up her nose.

"Maybe," shrugged Gatina. "I just wanted to know.

"You'd be better off staying away," her friend promised. "I've been thinking about heading over a few blocks tomorrow," she added. "Me and Liddy have a dressmaker that the boys don't know about."

"You're . . . you're buying a dress?" Gatina asked, confused.

"No! No!" laughed Marga. "But sometimes they'll have spinning work. Or errands to run. And sometimes you can grab a few scraps, or a needle or something, when someone isn't looking too hard. But they pay better than most, and sometimes you can get some food, too. And the dressmaker told me that I'm good with a needle."

"Maybe I will," Gatina lied. In fact, she knew she would not be joining her new friends, as much as she would like to. She would be investigating that Butchers' Guild. That was her mission.

She recalled the Ace of Keys from the deck of cards, last night. Secrecy. She was quickly realizing how important that was.

Twopenny returned from his walkabout, where he had scrounged for more food. "No luck. No pies or bread set out to cool," he said, dejectedly. "That apple left me wanting more." He patted his stomach, which the girls could hear grumbling.

Marga snorted. "Honest work for a meal. It is not that hard, Twopenny. Pick up a broom or carry some firewood to earn some coin and fill your belly." Marga had done that daily, either for shopkeepers or the seamstress, and she was proud of it.

Toscar, who overheard the exchange, affected the look of a stricken artist, hand to his heart and head bowed. "How could you think that we should work, Marga, when we have the gift of all of this?" his tone joking with a hint of seriousness. He swept his hand out to indicate the passersby who moved in a steady throng, passing the fountain nits with barely a glance. "We are performers. The street is our stage."

Gatina did not look convinced. She knew how artisans and nobility worked, and she also knew they paid no mind to a swarm of orphans in tattered clothing.

"I *do* work," he insisted, his tone firm. "Watch."

With that one word, issued as a command and not a suggestion, Toscar jumped down from the stone fountain's broken, uneven bench and shuffled to the cobbled street. His entire being changed, Gatina saw; she reasoned it was similar to how she imagined her own shift from her real self to Lissa the Mouse.

Toscar's self-assured attitude gave way to a new persona, a kid with slouched shoulders, a set jaw and eyes on the group of minor noblewomen walking his way. He stood, arms out, palms up and jaw set. As they grew closer, he lowered his eyes to the ground in front of them.

"Alms for a hungry child today, my ladies?" His voice was weak, not the self-assured boasting tone to which Gatina had grown accustomed. "The gods bless those who help others in need!" he assured them, pitifully.

The first group of three women did not slow their stride; they simply shuffled around him, as if he were a pile of horse manure, or worse, invisible. Gatina listened as they passed; they didn't alter their voice or pay him any notice. Yet, she saw each slip him a single coin. When they had passed, he returned to the fountain. Triumphantly, he held open his hand. "Tonight, we dine on fresh bread, maybe more apples," he declared.

"But what about tomorrow?" Gatina asked. "What if you have no luck then?"

He took the question as a challenge. He put his three coins inside a pouch tied to the inside of his trousers and returned, wordlessly, to the street. The next two women, who were not nobility from their dress, Gatina noted, ignored Toscar and walked past him. A man carrying a satchel and wearing the habit of a lawbrother gave a penny, stopping to encourage him to join a temple because anyone that industrious had both drive and spirit.

"I can't believe that act works so well," Marga said, shaking her head. "It's pitiful!"

"That's the point," Gan said, quietly. "They pity him."

The rest of the afternoon, Toscar stood his post, arms outstretched until he grew tired, then he would cup his hands in front of himself and firmly ask for alms, altering his speech by tone and wording to fit the potential donor, as he observed his likely patrons. He would venture back to the fountain to get out of the beating heat of the sun when foot traffic slowed.

Gatina did as she was trained: she observed. As she did so, she became both fascinated by his skill and ability to judge strangers and appalled by the sheer number – it had to be roughly one in twenty – who actually gave him a coin. How hard must it be, she reasoned, to part with a small coin? One small iron slug or copper penny? And how hard did Toscar – and all of her friends – work to only buy a chunk of day-old bread?

It also led her to wonder, which she admitted to herself that she hadn't considered, how do you look pitiful enough to gain coin without being struck down by passersby?

"Marga, does anyone ever hit him? Or any of you?" Gatina asked, her eyes still focused on Toscar. Gatina waited a few breaths, an eternity in her mind, then pulled her eyes away from Toscar to glance at Marga, who chewed her bottom lip, wondering, it seemed to Gatina, if she should divulge a huge secret. Gatina wanted to steer the conversation back to the butcher shop and the Rat gang she had mentioned before Toscar had returned to the fountain.

"Marga?" she asked, in a softer voice, "do you nits get beaten?" Marga looked anxious, so Gatina tried again. "I won't tell anyone, I promise. I just want to know that the fountain is a safer place." She hoped she sounded sincere, but her heart was beating so fast from excitement that she was sure Marga felt it.

Marga slowly exhaled, then said, "Who would you tell? Who would care? Sure, we get beaten. Sometimes badly. We used to get it a lot more, when we worked the streets and neighborhoods in Old Falasport, closer to the warehouses. That area belongs to the Rat Orphans. They'll kick you from here to Sinbar Shoals, if you cross into their territory. It's a shame. I've heard that area used to be really nice, as nice as this part, back when this fountain still worked."

She grabbed Gatina's wrist, jarring her focus from Toscar, who was still masterfully begging. "Lissa, never, *ever* go there. Avoid the Rat Orphans. Promise me? They're older than us and they are *mean*. The boys are bullies and the girls are meaner than you can imagine. They hang out at that burned-out inn like they own it. They say they . . . do things, there. Bad things. I think half the time they work for the Rats," she predicted. "Promise me. It's dangerous. You might never see another sunrise."

Gatina nodded her head, knowing she would not keep that promise. Those were the very sort of people she sought.

"Well, I couldn't avoid them until you told me where they were." She hoped Marga would tell her more about where to find them, but she merely shook her head as Toscar skipped back to the fountain.

"You seem awfully happy," she said.

He opened his hand and showed both of them his earnings.

"That's a lot!" Gatina admitted. "How did you get so good at begging?"

"I learned from one of the best," the boy admitted. "My older brother is high up in the Rat Orphans, but he's kept me out of it so far," he bragged, shooting a look at Marga. "At least, he says he's my brother. I am just a gifted minstrel," he boasted, boldly. "My brother taught me how to read the crowd," he said, "who to watch for, who looks kind. It's in their *eyes*."

"Your 'brother' just met you last year," Marga pointed out, skeptically.

"I don't see him except on colder nights. Haven't seen him in months, actually," he admitted, sadly. "But he always has a fire and room for me. He doesn't want me in that life. He says when he has enough, we'll go off to the countryside somewhere. Farm a bit, or at least have a few rods of garden. Wouldn't that be grand?" he asked, quietly desperate.

Gatina sat silently and regarded her new friend. Back in Cysgodol Hall, even the poorest peasants had at least twenty rods of garden, sometimes more. She was aware of how much those peasants strove to gain more and how hard they worked in that pursuit.

But for Twopenny and his friends, just the thought of a few kale plants or a row of peas and another of carrots was the promise of better times for kids who'd never seen better times. A roof you wouldn't be rousted out from under, food you didn't have to steal or beg for, but you grew yourself. That, Gatina realized, seemed like palace living when you made the streets of Falas your home.

It made her think. A lot.

"Theft is an art. Rat Orphans treat it like a thuggish sport. There is no craft in picking a sleeping drunk's pocket."

– *Gatina's Heist Journal*

CHAPTER EIGHT
FROM NIT TO RAT

AS MUCH AS SHE WANTED TO RETURN TO HER NEW FRIENDS THE NEXT DAY, she avoided them, instead. She turned right, instead of left, and went down Parchment Street and then crossed over two lanes to get to the place she sought.

The street was filled with shops, halls, workshops, and houses, all crammed together; indeed, it was so overbuilt in places that it seemed dangerous, like a too-tall house of cards. It was much different than the more stately homes and upscale shops in the Count's Quarter near the Tower of Sorcery. There were two taverns, a barber, a grocer, a blacksmith, three cloth merchants, a tinker's shop, and four merchants who sold general goods and second-hand merchandise. It was more commerce packed into a smaller space than the entire village of Solic had, back home, she realized.

She also noted that it smelled of stale spirits, body odor, horse dung, chimney smoke, and sewage. She wrinkled her nose at the distinctly musty and musky odors that hit her as she hurried past the taverns, hoping for better scents closer to the merchants' shops.

Many, if not most, of the shops had living quarters above the first floor, as many as four or five stories, in some cases. Gatina couldn't help mentally planning how she would climb each of them, thanks to her training, noting the roof material was not slate and that chunks of tile were missing in concentrated areas of the tallest buildings. But her observations of the Butchers' Guild were the focus of her study.

The hall contained an open-fronted shop on the first floor; the sign for it bore a bloody cleaver and a dead pig to demonstrate what trade it practiced, and for the literate it added, spelled out, *Hanik's Butchery*, along with the stylized jewel symbol that indicated that whoever Hanik was, he was an accepted master of his trade. Above that was a smaller, sloppily-written sign that declared the establishment certified by and accepted as a guild hall for the City Butchers' Guild. Men in long, darkly-stained aprons regularly came in and out of the place, often carrying baskets, bags or large pieces of recently-butchered animals. It was plagued by flies. There was an aroma of death and raw meat that was inescapable, when you walked by it.

Gatina made two passes of the place in her reconnaissance. She was able to learn a bit more about the establishment with each stroll by the shop, once in one direction and then the other. She committed as much to memory as possible. But she did not overstay and attract attention.

Instead, she did what everyone expected a nit to do: she begged.

Beginning with the tavern, she went from shop to shop offering her services to sweep, scrub, or fetch water from the fountain – or whatever other little chore the shop's keeper might need. She was surprised to be taken up on her offer on her second attempt.

"Well, then, I suppose I could use you for a bit, for a bite to eat," the frowning wife of the tinker said. "But keep your hands to yourself! If I'm missing anything, I'll thrash you!" she warned.

"Of course, Goody, of course. I'm honest! And a hard worker!" Lissa the Mouse declared, enthusiastically, just before she got a broom thrust in her hands.

"Then start with the front of the shop, then move back," the dour woman instructed. "After that, you can empty the chamber pots and fetch some more firewood. After that . . . we'll see," she said, suspiciously.

Gatina's unexpected work also gave her the opportunity to view the butcher shop for a few hours without suspicion. She observed a number of men and the occasional woman enter the place to transact business while she swept. But she soon realized that there was some distinction between the customers. Some seemed . . . out of place. They went in for far longer than one would think you would need to purchase something, and then left. And some of them looked threateningly mean, even for butchers. They bore scars, or crude anchor or sea axe tattoos she associated with mariners, and they seemed to scowl at the world.

All morning long, she counted who went in and who came out as she swept and carried. Regular customers came and purchased cuts of meat, likely taverners or innkeepers. A number of goodwives likewise came away with packages. All day long a string of delivery boys – nits, like Lissa the Mouse – delivered wrapped parcels of meat to nearby destinations. Twice, she noted, wagons arrived with fresh fare from the slaughterhouse. In each case, every butcher pitched in to get the carcasses brought inside, and the bones and other refuse hauled away to the renderers. Nine men came out in each case. Eight of them worked, while the ninth – apparently the master butcher – spoke to the drivers of the wains.

But when the driver passed something to the butcher, they exchanged a handshake that was . . . *off*, somehow, she noted. There was a significant glance between them that told Gatina that something greater than a mere delivery had just occurred. It was a subtle thing, but she was learning to pick up on the subtleties of life.

"Why are you staring at the butcher?" the tinker's wife demanded.

"I . . . I was just thinking about eating, Goodwife," Lissa confessed, a guilty expression on her face.

"Fine, fine, finish that load and we'll settle up," agreed the woman. "I've got a bit from last night's supper I was going to add to the slops, but you'd appreciate it more than the pigs, Trygg knows." She disappeared into the back, where the kitchen must lie, Gatina figured, and emerged a few moments later with her payment: half a potato pie and a wedge of peas porridge.

"The pie's a bit burnt on the bottom," the woman said, guiltily, "and my husband didn't eat it. The porridge is a bit dry – made it Market Day. But it's still edible. Now off with you!" she said. "You did a decent job," she added, looking around at the shop. "Nothing missing, as far as I can tell."

"Thank you, Goodwife!" Lissa the Mouse said, timidly accepting the praise and the food. "I told you I was honest! May I come back tomorrow?"

"We don't need an extra mouth around," warned the woman, "but perhaps. Might try down the lane, a bit. A couple of others might have chores. Tell them Goody Gavine said you were . . . acceptable," she added. "That might help. It might not," she admitted.

Gatina left and tried not to even look at the butcher's hall, as she wandered away from the shop. Instead she greedily ate the peas porridge, long settled into a dry cake. But her empty stomach didn't seem to care much. The pie she carefully wrapped in a scrap of cloth and tucked into her bundle.

She found her way to the old broken fountain and saw Marga, Toscar and Twopenny sitting with two new boys.

"The mouse is back!" squealed Toscar. "We thought you got lost."

"No, just scrounging," she said, removing the pie from her bundle triumphantly. "Who wants pie?"

There was just enough of the burnt pastry for each of them to get a bite. The two new boys insisted on paying her with a glass marble each – apparently a common token of trade, amongst the nits, she learned. Marbles and thimbles, she learned, were common items and nearly worthless to most, but they had some tiny value, here. She added them to her horde.

They begged and chatted through the noon hour, when traffic on the street was highest and there was a greater likelihood of receiving alms. It happened only occasionally, but there were, indeed, people who took pity on the nits and threw them a few miserable pennies. Enough so that, together, by early afternoon there was enough gathered to bargain for a head of cabbage and three apples at the grocers.

She got to know the nits who frequented the fountain a little better, too, as they chatted and gossiped. Twopenny had a wicked sense of humor, and was adept at mocking those who didn't fall for his begging routine with deadly accuracy. Toscar was extremely observant and tried his best to help out the other nits with advice and guidance.

But it was Marga who really seemed to like Gatina – or Lissa, she had to remind herself. And Gatina liked her. She was friendly, smart, and didn't say mean things about the other nits when they weren't around. Marga genuinely seemed to care about her friends, not merely use them for what she could get from them. Indeed, she warned Gatina about a few to steer clear of who didn't mind exploiting fellow orphans.

Marga seemed to have at least some good sense, which Gatina admired, and she had a knack for figuring things out. She explained how she knew the scribe who lived on the third floor of a nearby flat was visiting the wife of the chandler on the second floor of the next flat over twice a week when his own wife was at market, because they always gave each other a particular look those mornings when they both came down to buy pastries and tea from the morning cart vendors. And how the big red-bearded City Watchman who patrolled the ward with his partner was extorting ale and possibly money from two of the neighborhood taverns – and they weren't happy about it. She figured that out by watching how the tavern keepers followed him out of their shops and scowled after him as he strutted down the street.

Gatina also learned more about the neighborhood, and confirmed that the butcher's shop was, indeed, a place with a reputation for rough characters and suspicious criminal enterprises. A man could be hired to beat a business rival, there, she learned. Or even killed, if his purse was heavy enough. One of the boys had heard that you could tell the butchery was run by the Rats because no one was ever late on their bill to the place. And it was well known that there was always a game of dice going on up on the second floor. That explained a lot of the traffic, Gatina decided.

All in all, she felt it was a very productive day. She was tired and a bit hungry, but she'd learned a lot. And, perhaps, made a few new friends.

"That's the place," she assured her mother and the cousins, that night at the townhouse. "Or so the rumors say. When do I break in?" she asked, boldly.

"Oh, Kitten!" Minnureal said, shaking her head. "We haven't come to that part of the journey, yet. We're still surveilling. We need far more information before we even decide to act – Shadow has been very specific about this. The goal is to get you within, and without getting you caught. Just keep doing what you are doing," she urged. "Keep watching. Keep taking notes. Build on your alias. Make a few allies. Every day we get a little closer. If we rush it, we might get caught."

"And we don't get caught," Gatina nodded. "But I might have to be out of contact, for a day or so," she predicted.

"We'll see," Minnureal said, shaking her head.

Gatina was quiet for a moment, before she looked back at her mother.

"Mistress, who is Shadow?" she asked, cautiously.

Her mother started, then looked at her sharply.

"All you need to know is that he is leading us, right now. You don't need to know who he is, where he is, or what he is doing," she said, her voice deadly serious. "The less you know about him, the better. Just understand that he is in charge of our plan. And we always have a plan,' she stressed. "It may change, it may go awry, but we must always have a plan. You don't need to know more than you do, but know that Shadow is in charge of it."

That was the end of the matter, Gatina could tell. She tried to tuck the incomplete information away, as disappointing as it was.

Gatina returned to the street the next morning, but took a slightly different route. This one took her down a lane with a large patch of burnt timbers, the unfortunate remains of some fire. Though it was clear that the blaze had happened years ago, no one had done much to clear the lot, as of yet. The smell of old wet ashes and singed timber hung in the air more thickly as she came closer to it.

As she'd anticipated, there was a group of somewhat older boys lingering on the lot as if they owned it. A few girls, too, she noted, but none of them looked more than fourteen. Most of them squatted around a miserable-looking little fire, toasting what bits of food they had in the flames.

And they did look rough.

Most nits were dirty, of course, and dressed in tatters close to rags. But the crowd that lingered in the ashes of the lot went beyond that. They looked mean and cruel, ready for a fight or to perform some vicious prank. Many were natural bullies, she recognized, or too wild in nature to pursue honest work. They taunted each other mercilessly, and occasionally they feinted attacks against each other, all to prove who was the meanest among them. It was an appalling contrast to the gentle-natured teasing between herself and Atopol, she realized.

But they were the ones she sought, and she had to do this to complete the mission. Gatina closed her eyes and allowed her body to relax, willing herself to embrace a new image: that of a tough but skittish, quick-fingered orphan. She visualized her movements, committing them to muscle memory as she stretched her shoulders a bit. She knew she could be quick but realized that alone would not be enough if she got into a scrap. Boys like that liked to pick fights, she knew, even with girls, and she had to be ready to respond in a convincing way, she knew. And she had to be impressive – like a feral kitten, lightning fast, seeking the prey and striking, and then skittering back into the shadows. She remembered her acrobatic training and swordplay, and she visualized herself completing complicated routines on the beams her mother had taught her to balance upon back home. She felt her body twitch with the memory of those moves as she came closer to the burned-out lot.

She looked down at her tattered clothing. It was far from the finery she had worn on the journey here, but it was perfect for this assignment. Dirt and blood, coal and ash streaked the torn skirt. Her feet were bare and filthy, caked in dried street dirt. Her dyed hair, now greasy, hung over her face like a veil. She felt like a monster from one of the children's fables in the Cysgodol Hall library.

But she was ready. Wishing she could really call the shadows forth to provide cover, Gatina eased forward to the edge of the children before her.

"Hey!" called one of them, as she walked by. She had hoped to escape their notice, but she also recognized an opportunity.

"Hey, yourself!" she said, instead of ignoring the boy.

"What you have in that bag?" he asked, slyly.

"None of your concern!" she shouted back.

The boy laughed. Another took notice and leaned over the burnt timber that used to be a doorframe to gawk at her.

"Tiny little thing, you are," he commented. "What's your name?"

"Lissa the Mouse," she said, grudgingly, as she came to a halt in front of them.

"Why they call you that?" the first boy asked.

Gatina made a fateful decision. She whipped out the little blade she carried and pointed it at him. "Because I'm so timid," she said, coolly. The boys were well out of range, but they appreciated her boldness, and laughed.

"What are your names?" she asked, as she put the knife blade away.

"I'm Bikamay, this is Naxer," the first boy chuckled. "Haven't seen you around, before."

"I hang out by the broken fountain," she revealed. "With the younger nits. Just looking to do a few jobs, scrounge a bit," she said, casually. "Is there a problem with that?" Gatina asked, pointedly.

"As long as you stay out of our way," Naxer warned, arrogantly. "We're the kings of this part of town. Don't cross us!"

"I heard that there was coin to be had around here," she said, skeptically.

"If there was, we'd have it," Bikamay said, shaking his head. "Couple of odd jobs a week, maybe, for a bit of leftover garbage, but not much coin."

"I'll see for myself," Gatina said, resolutely. "Can I stand by your fire for a bit?" she asked, trying not to sound desperate. "My feet are cold."

Both boys wore shoes, though they were grossly too large, mismatched, and filled with holes. They glanced at each other, then shrugged. "Go ahead," Bikamay decided. "A little one like you won't take up much room. Just stay out of the way."

Once admitted within the lot, she tried to blend in with the other children as she made her way toward the fire. They barely noticed her. As she warmed her feet, she listened to the banter between the boys and tried to figure out the hierarchy among them.

The leader, the oldest, appeared to be Attie's age, and bossy. Not just bossy, but cruel. He lorded his status over the others, telling them what to do and threatening a beating with every other word. He was overconfident, arrogant and argumentative, and Gatina figured most of the others listened to him simply because they feared challenging his authority. They called him Racer, for some reason.

This should be easy, Gatina thought, after listening to Racer's boasts for a while. Then she self-corrected, hearing her mother's voice in her head, reminding her that she did not know all she needed to yet in this situation. She could verbally whip Atopol in an argument. Racer's ruthlessness became all too clear soon after she arrived, when two boys of about thirteen or fourteen entered the lot, carrying an unconscious man.

"We found him behind the *Hammer and Rose*, passed out in the privy!" one of the boys, who was carrying the man's feet, said excitedly as they came closer to the fire.

"What's he got?" asked Racer.

"Let's find out!" the one carrying his head said, unceremoniously dumping the unconscious man into the sooty ground. The stench of cheap spirits emanated from him like a cloud.

Gatina reluctantly followed the others' examples, bending down and helping another nit remove one of the man's boots, not realizing the orphan would fight her for the shoe the moment it came off of his feet.

"'Tis mine. I saw it first!" the girl, easily a year older than her, hissed, her eyes ablaze and her face contorted into a threatening scowl.

Gatina knew she could not back down. She held on to the well-worn boot and shoved the girl, hard, in her shoulder, knocking her off-balance and onto her back. She glared at Gatina, from where she was sprawled. Gatina had won the boot, and the girl's respect and that of the others who had previously looked up to her, she figured. She ran with it.

"*Mine,*" she said firmly, and cradled the stinky boot to her chest. Of course, it was no treasure, nor would it fit her and what good was one boot, she wondered, but she had claimed it. The group pulled away from the man, leaving him without clothing, save his undergarments. His boots, knife and his purse were now other people's property. Gatina went along in their throng, though she was shamed to rob a man in such a way. It was against the codes, unless – like now – it was necessary for the greater mission.

"The little mouse knows how to fight!" Bikamay laughed, approvingly. "Although to fight over *one* boot is a bit stupid."

Racer looked at her thoughtfully, as if noticing her for the first time.

"Nay, give up the boot to Pudding," he decided. "And you, give up the other one. It is stupid to fight over it."

"But I won it!" Gatina whined.

"Now you just lost it," explained Racer, as if he was a lawbrother. "Pudding's been around for weeks. You're *new*. She gets the boots. *Both* of them. That's the rules," he pronounced with authority.

With a great display of reluctance, Gatina did just that. The girl glared at her, but took the boot from her, and then its mate from another boy, and gleefully crammed them on her tiny feet. Triumphantly, she looked around at everyone as if she'd just been crowned a duchess. Nor did she seem to hold a grudge against her, since she had won out. But Gatina guessed she would be a lot more loyal to Racer, after the decision.

"Does this happen often?" she asked the girl, after the drunk was carried back to the street to be dumped in some alley.

"About every night," Pudding admitted. "Not so much in the daytime, unless we find someone who fell asleep like that. The time between dusk and early dawn is the best time for this sort of thing. You just wait until they're *good* and drunk, and they can't defend themselves. Serves them right for being stupid!" she said, viciously.

Stupid was the nits' favorite term for anyone they stole or begged from, she'd noticed. She realized that they considered themselves smart, despite their low station. Perhaps some of them were, she considered. But it was often a means of cheering themselves up from their desperation.

The group had robbed four more men before the sun was up, Gatina discovered. Indeed, they were all too willing to recount their robberies, detailing each victim and clearly enjoying the thrill in the hunt. Clearly, they did not feel the slightest bit bad for leaving these men bare. They had, after all, set their own paths, the gang explained. If they were stupid, then they deserved to lose their money and their possessions. Stupidity, she quickly learned, was also the primary excuse that the destitute nits used to justify their thefts. It was so far removed from the complicated codes on the matter held by House Furtius that she was more than a little appalled. Theft was an art, after all. The nits in the burned-out lot made it an industry, a trade, a sport. She took the distinction to heart.

Gatina knew that she could not judge them, just observe and learn. After all, she had participated in the looting herself. She had justified it as part of the mission, for the good of House Furtius and for Alshar. But it still strained her conscience that she had done so. She followed their example. Divvy up the loot; keep the best for themselves; then she found out that the nits were not entirely without scrutiny.

About noon one of the butchers strolled by and stopped for a moment at the burned-out doorway, where he conferred with Racer. Gatina managed to wander over so that she was close enough to overhear.

"So what was the take last night, Racer?" asked the butcher.

"Four, and one this morning," the boy beamed with pride. "Got a nice bit of coin, really. Here's yours," he added, as he pushed a handful into the man's hand.

"Good lad, good lad," the man smiled. "Master Hanik will be happy with that."

"When is he gonna have a real job for me?" Racer asked, his voice nearly a whine.

"You're getting there, lad," the butcher assured him. "Put a couple more pounds on you, you might be worth a damn. Don't worry, we look out for ours. We'll have plenty of opportunities, soon. Our crew is always looking for bright lads like yourself."

"You keep saying that, but I'm still sleeping in a sodding ash-heap!" Racer declared, his nostrils flaring.

"Don't worry, lad," soothed the butcher, as he added the coins to his purse. "With things unstable at the palace, Hanik says there'll be plenty of work, soon. If you don't mind thumping a few heads that need thumping."

"I can fight," Racer assured him.

"Robbing drunks and bullying nits isn't real fighting," the butcher said, shaking his head. "You've done good, here, lad," he admitted, looking around at the squalid camp. "You keep them here, and your tribute's been good. You run errands well. But fighting? Fighting, real fighting, that's different. Are you cut out for that?" he challenged.

"I can fight!" assured Racer, defiantly puffing up his chest. "I'm sick of running errands for pennies!"

"Just be patient, lad," the butcher said, frowning. "Master Hanik will ask me for a recommendation, eventually, and I'll say your name. Then you're in," he insisted, soothingly. "Providing you survive. One job leads to another. It's the way of the world. Remember Jorny? He came from here, and look where he is, now? Got his own flat, now. Silver in his purse. We pull a lot of lads from this crew. Just be patient. We've got a package to go this afternoon, if you're interested. Just a penny, but it's something," he said, encouragingly.

"I make more than that robbing drunks," the boy said, sullenly.

"I'll do it!" Gatina said, speaking before she could stop yourself.

"What?" Racer asked, startled that she'd been listening.

"Didn't see you there," the butcher said, likewise startled.

"I'll take your errand, if there's coin in it," she proposed. "I'll take it anywhere you want."

"Now, now, that's been Racer's job – that's why he got his name," the butcher said, fondly. "Speedy one, he. Or, at least he was," he added, with a sudden frown. "Maybe it is time we looked at new talent, since you want to make your way in the world, lad."

"Go ahead," the boy said, sullenly. "It's boring work."

"It's coin!" argued Gatina. "It's better than having no coin!"

"I can't argue with that philosophy," agreed the butcher with a chuckle. "I'm Flerian, little girl. What's your name?"

"Lissa the Mouse," she said, after an anxious moment.

"Can she be trusted?" the butcher asked Racer.

"I don't know! She's new! She hangs out with the broken fountain nits, normally. But she did listen, when I told her the rules," he conceded. "She's as good as anyone, for what you need."

"If there's coin in it for me, I'll do whatever it takes," she assured the gangster. "If I can carry it, I'll deliver it. I'm honest. Ask Goody Gavine, the tinker's wife!" she said, pointing to the shop. That was a risk, she knew; Flerian might not like the dour woman.

The butcher looked her up and down, then shrugged. "Fine, then. It isn't that heavy. But if you fail us, you don't see sunrise, understand?" he asked, his tone suddenly becoming dark. "Plenty of deep canals around here. And no one notices how many bones we send to the renderer!"

"I just want my coin," she insisted, dismissive of the threat. "I'll be there. The shop around the corner? I'll be there," she promised.

"Enjoy the working world," sneered Racer, shaking his head.

"At the third bell," the butcher said. "My name is Flerian," he reminded her. "If they give you trouble, just say my name. They'll let you in."

"I'll be there," Lissa the Mouse nodded. While Gatina the Kitten roared inside.

She was in.

"I find it interesting that the Brotherhood of the Rat has just as many rules as we do. I suppose it makes sense, and in a way we are practicing the same trade. The difference I see is that their code is designed to be enforced with the threat of violence, while ours invokes our sense of duty and tradition to keep us to the Rules. They depend on the fear of the Rats' retribution for any transgression. We trust in the great shame that would arise for violating our code. We also, in general, smell much better. Myself, lamentably, temporarily excluded. Blessed Darkness, I want a bath."

– *Gatina's Heist Journal*

CHAPTER NINE
INTO THE RAT'S DEN

"So, you're the new girl Flerian hired?" asked the delivery boy at the door of the shop. He was missing some teeth. Gatina nodded.

"Good thing you're on time," he said. "Flerian hates it when you're late," he said, ominously. "I'll take you up."

He led her past the wide tables where the carcasses were butchered. It was startling, to see the many cleavers and knives swiftly carve them into different cuts and dump them into baskets. The pile of waste that gathered on the floor at the feet of each butcher was a gory horror. Flies darted in and out of the open windows with impunity. And the smell was appalling.

The back stairs provided some relief from the smell, at least. The second floor was more office and storeroom than butchery, though there were strings of sausages and sausage skins hanging from the beams to dry. Flerian was waiting for her, smoking a short, squat pipe and sorting through parchment.

"You showed up on time," he nodded. "Good. Let me tell you what you're doing: You are to take this bag," he said, indicating a small leather satchel, "to an address I give you. Here are the rules: You do not talk to anyone on the way there. You do not stop to eat, drink, or take a leak. You do not open the bag. You do not take anything from the bag. You go directly there, and then come directly back with the receipt. You must arrive before the fourth bell. Failure to do so breaks the rules. On that return trip, you also do not stop to talk, eat, drink, or piss. You are expressly forbidden from having any encounter with a member of the City Watch. If someone tries to take the bag from you, you fight like hell. If they do take the bag from you, it's on you. You must tell us at once. Not tomorrow, not next week, not when the bleeding stops, you crawl yourself right back here and tell me at once. Can you follow these rules?" he asked her, directly, his eyes forming a penetrating stare. Gatina could tell he had recited the rules to many, over the years, the way he attacked the words.

"Of course, Master Flerian," she nodded.

"For this effort, you will be paid one penny. No more, no less; one penny. You must never speak of this task to anyone, or it breaks the rules. Failure to abide by these rules means you will disappear into a canal or something equally tragic. Do you understand what I am saying?" he demanded, quietly, his level gaze enough to almost unnerve her.

"Absolutely," she nodded, realizing that the penalty for failure was literally her life. These men did not care about one orphan. No one did. The only way Lissa the Mouse survived this was by doing exactly what they wanted.

"I'm not playing around!" Flerian exploded. "This is important! You get paid when I get the receipt. Take this to the warehouse on Blue Fountain Street, in Old Falasport, the one in the middle of the street with the sign of the gluepot. Big red sign. Can't miss it. Ask for Cleon," he said. "He'll take you up." Flerian looked hard at her. "Am I clear?"

"Blue Fountain Street, middle warehouse, sign of the red gluepot," Gatina repeated. "One question?"

Flerian looked taken aback. "Was I unclear?" he asked, skeptically.

"No, Master Flerian," she said, looking down. "I was just wondering if I could borrow a basket? This satchel attracts attention. No one looks twice at a girl carrying a basket. Or wonders what's inside," she explained. "I look less conspicuous that way."

"Hmph," Flerian grunted. "That's right. Good point. I'll get you a basket. I'll tell you how to get there. And then you get to the warehouse. Be back by the fourth bell, or you're done," he said, simply.

Gatina was glad she'd thought of the basket. The bag was heavier than it appeared, and it would have been a burden to carry the mile and a half she had to cross.

She could tell it was not meat – it was far too heavy. Nor was she that naïve. Indeed, she could feel the metal within the bag, and it felt bright and sparkly. Like gold and silver. A lot of it.

Gatina wasn't certain why Flerian was so concerned about security, even for this much coin. By her estimation it was at least sixty or seventy ounces, and entrusting that to a Rat Orphan instead of one of his men seemed riskier to her.

But, then, she tried to apply some perspective on the matter. As her mother had explained, the Brotherhood of the Rat was just a business enterprise, first and foremost. Business meant commerce, and commerce was money flowing from one person to another. Regardless of where that coin came from, it needed to be tracked and tabulated. Someone had to keep records, and keep possession of it. Even gangsters needed accountants, her mother had said.

And if those monies were illicitly gained, she realized, then stopping and searching a man carrying them could lead to arrests for corruption. She knew such things happened, at least under Duke Lenguin. Entrusting the coin to a nit, like Lissa the Mouse, attracted less attention than a member of the gang. And it would bring less recrimination back to the Brotherhood.

The way to the warehouse wasn't terribly long, but this far from the well-planned center of the city, the roads were more chaotic and difficult to follow. Even with Flerian's instruction, she started to get worried as she hustled through the streets to make her appointment. The warehouse was only a few hundred yards from the wharfs along the river port, and she could smell water in the air long before she spotted her destination.

Thankfully, she arrived with minutes to spare.

The warehouse was, indeed, just as the gangster had described it, bearing a red gluepot on its sign. It was a dark and decrepit old building, its tile roof was chipped and broken and the beams that supported the great roof were dark with age. Most of the windows on the second and third story were closed, and there were only a few wagons waiting to be loaded.

She saw one young man of around twenty standing in front of the building, slouched against the side of the wall.

"You must be Cleon," she said, as she approached him.

"Yeah, who's asking?" he asked, suspiciously.

"Flerian sent me," she said, simply.

"Right. Where's Racer?" he asked, not moving from his position.

"He had other things to do," Gatina shrugged. Just then another young girl approached. Another nit, Gatina decided, but not one she'd met.

"Hey, Cleon," she said, just as the temple bells rang three times.

"Just in time, Navala," the man said, shaking his head.

"I'm always on time," she shot back. She glanced at Gatina. "New girl?" she asked.

"New girl," he agreed, finally standing. He led them up to the first landing, in a darkened staircase, to a door.

"Since you're new," Cleon lectured, "here are the rules. Don't forget them. Do as I do and do not speak," Cleon instructed both girls. "That is, if you both want to leave with me. Gavin is . . . *creepy*. Even if Gavin asks you a question, do not speak any more than you need to. Do not let him touch you, if you can help it. Keep your eyes to yourself. Don't give Gavin any reason to keep you here or separate you from me. Leave the bag, get your receipt, and get out," he ordered. He lifted his tunic and showed them both a long, deadly-looking dagger. "I will keep you safe, but only if you are with me. Wander off, and I can't vouch for your safety." He lowered his tunic and pounded on the door three times. A guard wordlessly let them in, when he saw who it was, and they climbed another flight of stairs.

Once they reached the third floor warehouse, a second guard met them at the door. He wasn't as nice as the first. That is, he had a slimy, obsequious air about him.

"And what have we here, Cleon? Bringing us more treasure?" he reached out to touch Gatina's hair; she recoiled from his touch.

"That's Flerian's new girl, you moron," Cleon complained. "Leave her alone."

The man leered and laughed. "It's just a couple of nits, Cleon. Nothing to worry about." He extended his hand again.

Before it could touch her hair, Gatina whipped out her tiny blade and pressed it to his wrist.

"Ow!" he yelled, drawing his hand back. He stared at the mark on his wrist a moment, then reached out and casually slapped Gatina across the face. "Never do that again, my lovely," he warned, his eyes slitted.

"Don't give me a reason to, then," Gatina growled, her face stinging painfully as she put her blade away. Cleon stepped in front of him and hefted the basket up.

"Business," was all he said.

"Fine," the guard said, with a shrug. "Gavin is upstairs. Go on in." He opened the door and as she passed him, Gatina smelled stale spirits on his breath and odor on his body. She shuddered at the thought of what might happen to her if she found herself alone with this man.

The trio climbed the stairs, Gatina memorizing the number of steps to reach the top and absorbing as much information as possible about the place without actually looking nosy. Once at the top of the worn wooden steps, they crossed a wooden catwalk over the vast warehouse below to the opposite side of the building. The walkway led to a heavy door with an impressive brass lock. As large as it was, she knew she could easily pick it, based on what her mother had taught her about the craft. Nonetheless, it was an impressive piece of work, designed to withstand a determined assault.

She looked down and saw barrels and crates stacked nearly as high as the catwalk. Perhaps some of it was legitimate fare – she could smell the kegs and kegs of glue that was clearly the warehouse's main function. But there was far more than barrels of glue below. It was packed with crates, bales of cotton and wool, chests, and bags of all descriptions. No doubt all secured without the customary payment of the Duke's taxes. She assumed each contained smuggled goods and guessed untaxed wine was in the casks.

Cleon made a fist and pounded the door three times. On the third thud, the door was opened by a short, fat, balding man with a long fringe of hair around his ears.

"Ah, Cleon, come in, boy. We have been waiting on you. What treasures do you have for me today?" His tone was solicitous but not friendly. There was nothing behind his eyes to lead Gatina to believe him to be either genuine or kind. This man was a gangster, she realized. His every gaze was one of appraisal.

"My lord, we bring two baskets of merchandise today," Cleon began, before the Rat interrupted him.

"And who is this?" He grabbed Navala by her waist and pulled her against him. She let out a surprised shriek, her fists against his chest. She quickly turned her head away as the man tried to force a kiss on her mouth. Instead, he licked her face. Gatina saw the look of fear, felt it in the air.

"Enough!" Cleon complained. "That's Mandar's girl, and this is Hanik's. Flerian sent her," he explained. "They don't attract as much attention as boys do."

"And we're more reliable," Gatina said, evenly, as Navala wiped her cheek with her sleeve, a look of disgust on her face.

The portly man grunted and pushed himself into her threateningly before releasing her and shoving her toward Cleon, taking the basket from her hand as he did so. Gatina stepped closer to Cleon, too. Gavin looked at the trio, nodded, and continued as though nothing had happened.

He dumped the first basket onto a wide, smooth desk and used a long dagger to sort through the loot. "I see jewels, coins, daggers and a lot of nice clothing. About ninety, ninety-one silver's worth from Mandar. Not too bad. Hanik's bag?" he asked. Gatina placed it on the table, trying not to get too close to the man.

Gatina peered through the hair covering her face, raising her head to watch as he sorted through the stolen items. While he no doubt expected her eyes were on him and his accounting, she was using the time to observe elsewhere.

She looked beyond Gavin, to the cabinets built into the wall behind him. There were six cabinets, from floor to ceiling, heavy wood bound with iron. Each had its own lock made of steel and copper. She committed that to memory. She could hear Gavin's fat leg bump against a drawer in the desk, and realized there was probably more than one drawer. The desk was six feet long and at least three feet wide, large enough to hold shipping maps.

"Seventy-two, and change, I'd say. A tidy couple of days' work, for Hanik, but not great. Tell him to do better, next time," he growled as he wrote out receipts on two scraps of parchment and handed them to each of them. Gatina didn't even look at it. Lissa the Mouse could not read.

Cleon did not argue. Instead, he returned the two baskets and led Gatina and Navala out.

Gatina continued to pay attention to everything around her as she descended the creaking staircase; she counted the number of Rats she saw, two in the office, one at the door and seven downstairs. She stretched out her senses, and was rewarded.

She heard water – and smelled it. She slowed her descent slightly and strained her perceptions to see where it was coming from. It had to be underneath the building, of course, even though the river was two blocks away. It could be a sewer, she knew, but it sounded like a lot of water, not a trickle. A canal, perhaps?

The warehouse was also larger than it looked from the outside, Gatina realized; the place extended behind the buildings next to it and back further than she would have guessed. It was only used for storage, like all such places, but with a canal underneath it, there also was a ground level for access to the river . . . without anyone seeing what came in or out. Good for smuggling.

Gatina had a great desire to investigate it at night, under the cover of darkness, maybe even walk the perimeter and establish the access points, as her mother had taught her. But that would be up to her mother to decide. She'd made it clear that the Kitten was to follow orders and not do anything rash.

That made the desire to explore the mysterious warehouse all the stronger.

"What a disgusting animal!" Navala said, as they finally exited the building. "I can't believe he . . . he *licked* me!" she said, with a shudder.

"He's been known to do far worse," Cleon assured her, sympathetically. "I wouldn't advise crossing him. Or any of the Brothers," he added. "Just do your job, keep your mouths shut and collect your pay. You'll get along fine." It was more than a suggestion, it was a command.

Wordlessly, Gatina departed and started the long walk back to the butcher's shop. She lingered just long enough to memorize the placement of the windows in the upper stories and orient them with what she knew of the interior. When she rounded the corner, she took a glance at the parchment in her hand. It read, merely, HANIK 76 d. 4 p. GAVIN, with the date. Then there was a scrawl under the receipt that said DO BETTER! Hardly a secret message, she knew. Then she quickened her pace and hurried back to Flerian.

The butcher was waiting for her, it seemed, smoking a pipe outside the front of the shop. Another wagon was being unloaded – mutton, this time. His eyes widened appreciatively, when he caught sight of her.

"That was fast – as fast as Racer," he admitted. "Still several minutes before the fourth bell." He took the scrap of parchment from her and glanced at it with a grunt. "Well, if Racer wants to advance, he'll earn his chance," he said, shaking his head. "We need more coming in. Tell him that, when you go back. Oh, and here," he said, dropping two tiny coins into her palm. "Bonus for quick work on your first day. And just keep the basket."

Gatina stared at the two small mostly-round slips, and could feel that they were silver, not copper. She was not impressed at the pay for the effort; Lissa the Mouse, however, was astonished, and she made a show of it.

"Racer was getting silver pennies?" she asked, both outraged and impressed. "Not copper?"

"The price for keeping his mouth shut," Flerian agreed. "About lots of things. Like how much he was getting paid. See that you do likewise. Oh, and come back in three days," he added. "Probably have another opportunity for you. Bring the basket."

Lissa the Mouse closed her hand over the precious coins and nodded, before she slunk away. Only, instead of returning directly to the burned-out lot, she stopped at a baker's stall and got a full loaf of bread with her newly earned money, then purchased a dozen apples with the change, and she still had two copper pennies left. She tore the bread in half, putting away one part in the basket with the apples, under her bundle, before she arrived.

"Who's hungry?" she asked, triumphantly, when she approached the small fire. Unsurprisingly, there were several who leapt to their feet at the sight of it. She took a bite, herself, before letting the others tear the loaf into bits and devour it. She spotted Racer on the other side of the fire, and in a flash of inspiration, made her way over to him.

"Thanks for letting me do that," she said, simply. "Here, take this: I feel like I owe you." She dumped the two remaining copper pennies in his hand.

"If you want to do the stupid work, that's for you," he said with a shrug as he pocketed the pennies. "I'm moving up in the world, though!"

"About that," Gatina said, her eyes narrowing, "Flerian sent me a message. He wants you to increase your business, for a couple of nights. I got the feeling that if you do, he might have something bigger for you."

"I'll see what I can do," Racer agreed, grimly. "Thanks, Lissa."

She nodded, and began to slink away, mouse-like. That's what Lissa would do, after all. Gatina did not want to linger with the Rat Orphans, as she began to call them in her head, lest she be recruited to conduct their illicit "business" herself. Thieving was a high art, according to her family's code. Robbing drunks was distasteful.

She felt a great deal of relief and excitement, after she left. She had completed her mission, after all. She had infiltrated the Brotherhood of the Rat, in some small way. That was a success she could be proud of. And she'd done it without getting caught. She stopped at the broken fountain, on her way, and saw her younger friends still haunting it, with a few new faces. She was gratified when Marga saw her and waved.

"Lissa! Where have you been?" she demanded, clearly happy to see her.

"Scrounging, as usual," Gatina sighed. "But with some success – who wants to eat?" she asked, for the second time. The younger children were far more appreciative of her generosity than the Rat Orphans. While the bread was quickly gone, there were enough apples for everyone to have two. That was as much as a feast, to the poor children.

"I was worried," Marga admitted, in a whisper, while the others were eating. "I haven't seen you all day."

"Mice like me have to scrounge a lot – especially if we're to feed our friends," she replied, with a smile. "Don't worry about me, Marga."

"Of course I'm going to worry about – hey! No fighting!" she said, suddenly, when one of the boys tried to take Twopenny's apple from him. "You both have enough!" she chided them.

Gatina sat with the others until dusk, when the City Watch would begin clearing the streets of nits as well as they could. She departed and made her convoluted path back to the family's townhouse just as darkness fell. She wasn't a bit tired, though. Indeed, she felt invigorated by the danger and the challenge of today's mission. She could only guess what awaited her tomorrow.

"What is not known cannot be revealed."

– Rule of House Furtius

CHAPTER TEN
A RUCKUS ON PARCHMENT STREET

"The warehouse is at least thirty paces deep," Gatina dutifully reported, once she returned to the townhouse, "the front is only twelve paces wide, including the big door, but once you go back ten paces it opens up on either side. Three stories," she recalled. "The office is on the third, accessed by a catwalk, where Gavin can watch everything from above..."

She droned on and on with every little detail she could remember from her journey into the den of Rats while Cousin Onnelik took notes on one sheet of parchment and sketched the plan of the warehouse on another. Her mother interrupted her periodically to ask questions, or for a better description, or for clarification. Every name and every detail of Gatina's infiltration of the warehouse was taken down in the notes in Onnelik's neat, precise hand. And then they did the same for the butchery.

"Common thievery and robbery are the bread and butter of the Brotherhood of the Rat," her mother commented, disapprovingly, as Onnelik sanded the pages of his notes dry. "Often they get others, like that Racer fellow, to do the dirty work – and take the risk – while they get most of the reward. In return, they offer limited protection, and a market to fence the stolen merchandise. But their protection only extends so far, for anyone who is not a sworn Brother. They see the nits and the orphans as . . . disposable."

"That's what they told me," agreed Gatina, grimly. "It was horrible, Mother!" she sighed, shaking her head. "I never knew that there were such evil men in the world!"

"They are men worth stealing from," Minnureal agreed. "But that is not our goal, this time."

"What is our goal?" Gatina asked, curious.

"We have many, but the less you know of them, the better. What you do not know, you cannot reveal," she quoted. "But you did well, Kitten. Indeed, you gave us more information than we were looking for. And a lot quicker than I anticipated."

"Yes, a delightful amount," Onnelik agreed. "Quite enough for our purposes. I'll go take these to my study to be copied, and I will prepare one to be sent to Shadow," he said, as he gathered up his notes. "Minny, what would you have our Kitten do, now? With her alias, I mean?" he asked, thoughtfully.

Her mother studied her, and then cupped her cheek. "If you are willing, Kitten, I would have you maintain Lissa the Mouse for a few more days," she proposed. "It could be quite useful to know a bit more about their operation, before we finish the mission. Who the bosses are, who they speak to, that sort of thing. And it would be good to get even closer to the organization and gain their trust. But only if you are willing," she said, frowning.

"Of course I am!" Gatina agreed. "It's fun . . . if depressing, sometimes, to see how the nits suffer."

"Orphans never enjoy an easy life," her mother said, thoughtfully. "Those who live on the street are doubly cursed. Alas, not all the alms in the world will succeed in raising their station. All too many die before they reach adulthood. Many more are horribly exploited – not just by the Brotherhood, but by the corrupt. But it is the Brotherhood who reaps the harvest of such bitter lives. The meanest, cruelest of them are taken into the gang, and then used to continue the cycle."

"I just want to help my friends," Gatina sighed.

"Of course you do, Kitten," her mother soothed. "It's a credit to your compassion. Believe it or not, that is my goal, as well. But, for now, we must use them to achieve other goals. My family has always sought to raise the stations of the poor, since the Magelords came to Alshar. But that can happen best and for the most when we are governed by wise and trustworthy men."

With that thought ringing in her ears, Gatina went upstairs to bed. The goose down filled tick suddenly felt uncomfortably comfortable, after she thought about how her friends were sleeping.

"SOMETHING BOTHERING YOU?" MARGA ASKED, THE NEXT AFTERNOON. Gatina's late night reporting of her work to her mother had kept her in bed until late morning, but she'd managed to return to the broken fountain by noon. The streets were filled with workmen and artisans, shopkeepers and carters, vendors and serving women all on their errands. But there was a subtle difference, Gatina noticed. Whereas for the last few days the crowds had been casual and unconcerned, today there was whispering, and furtive glances around before bending their heads together to gossip.

"Just thinking about doing something stupid," Gatina answered, honestly. "Say, why do you think everyone's so . . . so . . ."

"Nervous?" Liddy supplied. The dark-haired girl shrugged. "I don't know. Probably that news from the palace."

"What news?" Gatina demanded.

"A bunch of counts arrested a bunch of ministers and officials," reported Toscar, authoritatively. "They're replacing them with new ones. There might be some beheadings. I heard it from the stableboy at the *Three Stars*."

"Are they, now?" Gatina nodded.

"What does it matter?" asked Gan. The youngest boy scowled at the crowd. "Nothing's going to change. Ever."

"It's just . . . interesting," Gatina observed.

"There's nothing remotely interesting about the government. Just look how they sic the City Watch on us! Although, the alms are better over at the Palace Quarter, it's said. But the adult beggars hate having us nits over there, so best to avoid it," she said, matter-of-factly. The City Watch was the biggest nemesis to the street orphans, Gatina had learned. She had quickly copied her friends who hid or contrived to be elsewhere when the local Watchmen patrolled the area. If they caught you, they would beat you or worse. The adult beggars were almost as bad. The only way to contend with them, if they took after you, was to run away or get as many nits together as possible and threaten a fight. Life was hard, on the streets of Falas, Gatina reflected.

"Well, that's kind of interesting," Toscar muttered, a few moments later. Instead of the City Watch rounding the corner, a line of men in armor, two abreast and a dozen ranks deep, was led by a banner-bearing knight on a horse.

People moved out of the way at the sight, regardless of rank or station. The soldiers marched past the fountain without giving it a second glance, headed toward the southern portion of the city. The banner, Gatina saw, was a bright blue flag bearing a golden anchor crossed with a spear, surrounded by golden cowrie shells. The children gawked at them, along with everyone else. It was clear that they were moving with purpose, too, not merely taking a stroll. In Gatina's estimation, those soldiers were up to something.

In a moment, she saw what their mission was. They halted at the end of the street, in front of a moderately pleasant residence, and four soldiers knocked on the door. When it opened, they burst in and grabbed the goodwife and continued to search and scour the house. Everyone on the street who watched murmured angrily at the violence, and a few even squeaked when, a few minutes later, two men and three more women were thrown into the street. The remaining soldiers quickly bound their hands with rope, despite their cries of protests. One of the men yelled angrily at them, until he was punched so hard with a mailed fist his nose exploded in blood. They were all led away by most of the men, but two remained behind to guard the residence.

"Who was that?" wondered Gan, aloud.

"I don't know, but they sure pissed off someone!" Toscar said, excitedly, as he shook his head.

"He was a scribe," Twopenny said, quietly. "I ran a few errands for him. He worked at the palace. Nice family," he added.

"A scribe? Just got arrested?" Marga gasped. "Why would they do that?"

"There's trouble at the palace," Liddy sighed. "That's never good news, my gran always said."

Falas was an odd city, Gatina had decided, even before the murders of the Duke and Duchess. She knew that her father preferred to venture to the summer capital, Vorone, even though it was hundreds of miles farther from their home. He said Vorone was more peaceful and relaxed compared to the main capital. Here, in Falas, she realized, everything was in constant motion. There were hundreds of thousands who lived inside its vast borders. And the more people there were, the more people were needed.

The city boasted butchers, both legal and Rat-backed, artisans, cheesemakers, winemakers, tea blenders, cooks, bakers, taverners and innkeepers, stablemen, scribes, counting men, priests and priestesses, teachers, seamstresses … so many different vocations, and all their families. There were thousands of common laborers who trudged to work at dawn, their shovels over their shoulders, and didn't return home until dusk. There were carters and merchants and bargemen and shipwrights and foresters and fowlers. There were minstrels and actors and singers who worked for grand theaters and operas. And there were lords and ladies who patronized them all.

It was far, far different than life in the countryside. Back in Solic Village, the closest to Cysgodol Hall, there were mostly peasants, a few artisans, and then the manor lords. Occasionally a monk or a nun. But things essentially stopped when the blessed darkness came at nightfall. Here, in Falas, dusk just heralded a different kind of activity. But the motion never stopped.

From what she had seen, there were also a large number of folk who didn't seem to do anything in particular, that she could see. There was a large class of people who had come to Falas – students, travelers, petty nobility with aspirations of fortune – and just never left. Yet they did seem to have position – or at least an income. Gatina wondered if they did not work, how did they live, unless it was off family money.

The soldiers' rough behavior drew her focus back to the arrest of the scribe. Clerks and scribes documented every detail of city life – codes, rules, laws, debts, and payments. Sister Karia had explained that to her, during their lessons. It stood to reason that those same clerks also knew intimate details about the Palace, including royal appointments and officials. And money. There were thousands of clerks in the employ of the Palace, temples, coin houses, and, Gatina assumed, the Brotherhood of the Rat. She wondered if most of the clerks also had families, like this man did, as she watched Twopenny's former employer and his family be led away from their home. What would become of them, now, she asked herself.

"Well, it wasn't good news for that scribe," agreed Toscar. "Fellows, I'm thinking we need to go someplace else for a while," he suggested. "With this sort of business going on, people are likely to be skittish with their alms."

There was a general note of agreement, and Gatina said her goodbyes to her friends . . . before walking toward the river.

She didn't know why she was returning to the warehouse, but her feet were taking her there as she watched the people around her. There was alarm in the air – not panic, but people were on edge, she could tell. It was little things: the way they glanced at each other. How they held themselves as they went about their business. Everyone was feeling some sort of pressure, now, she noted.

She was so involved in her observations that she nearly stumbled right into the street near the warehouse, which wouldn't do at all. She didn't want the Rats to see her and recognize her.

Instead, she hugged the opposite side of the street. She found a bit of a blind spot, behind the water trough next to the livery stable on the corner. It gave her a reasonable view of the door to the red gluepot warehouse and the entire street in front of it. She made herself as small as a mouse, in the narrow space, and set herself to observing everything.

She noted the position of the sewers she knew led to the underground canal; the upper windows, and how close they were to the lower roofs of the buildings next to them; the positions of the chimneys of those shops; the number of men she figured worked for the Brotherhood of the Rat who lingered around the front of the place. Mentally, Gatina traced several routes into the building. It wasn't exactly impregnable, if one was willing to climb or crawl through a sewer.

When she decided she'd seen enough, she quietly retreated back toward the neighborhood she had become more familiar with. Twice she saw City Watchmen looking anxiously at the streets they were responsible for patrolling, and twice she saw other soldiers guarding residences or offices. Yes, she was convinced, something was happening at the palace. If her mother didn't know about it already, she would want to be informed of it.

Gatina changed course before she made it to the broken fountain, and headed toward the townhouse, instead.

"They arrested the entire family of a scribe who lives over on Parchment Street, near the old marketplace," she dutifully reported to Onnelik, once she'd snuck in through the rear of the place. Her cousin was having a quiet cup of tea and reading a book, when she surprised him in his kitchen. "I made a quick trip through town; there are more soldiers stationed here and there." She described the heraldry she saw the men carry.

"Ah, yes, those are Vichetral's men," Onnelik sighed. "Anchor, spear and shells, on a field of sky blue. Vassals of his, but they bear his arms on this mission."

"Why is he arresting people?" Gatina asked.

"He is consolidating his position," explained Onnelik with a sigh. "He is removing anyone who might challenge the legitimacy of this council he's assembling. Them and their families. Duke Lenguin quite shrewdly ensured that the government at the palace was well-staffed with his loyalists. Now that he's dead, and his biggest rival is taking power, they are all in danger."

"Shouldn't we tell Mother?" Gatina asked.

"She's out, at the moment, meeting a contact," Onnelik said, shaking his head. "But I will inform her at once, when she returns. There is much happening," he muttered, as he peered out the kitchen window. There was a troubled tone in Onnelik's voice.

"I'll go back out and see what I can learn," Gatina offered.

"No!" Onnelik said, sharply. "I don't think your mother would want that, if things are becoming unstable on the streets. People get hurt, in such times. Even little nits like your Lissa the Mouse," he warned. "Nobody cares what happens to a couple of nits, when there is revolution and rebellion in the air."

Gatina sighed, but she had to agree with her cousin, despite the fact that she could keep herself safe. She knew how to hide better than Atopol, but she recalled how casually the soldiers had beaten the scribe. And her mother might have news, she reasoned. So, she contented herself with some bread and cheese and a cup of tea with Onnelik.

Her cousin was surprisingly forthcoming, when it came to the politics of the city; he had lived in Falas all his life. Gatina heard a dozen different names and their positions in the city and the palace, and tried to commit them to memory, as well as their associations. Some were power-hungry, like the counts of Rhemes and Roen, or any number of Sea Lords. Others were considered good leaders and honest officials, members of the court who had been loyal to the old duke. Some were his friends, others his professional colleagues. He feared that many of them were already arrested or worse.

The cook had already arrived to prepare the evening meal by the time her mother returned, right at dusk.

Lady Minnureal looked very different than usual, Gatina saw, as she was dressed in a very rich-looking burgundy gown with a light, hooded mantle that obscured her face and hair. Her shoes were elegant and clearly expensive. From what Gatina had learned about social class in Falas, she was dressed appropriately as one of the high-status nobles of the city. The kind who haunted the Palace Quarter and the Temple Quarter estates.

"At last!" Minnureal sighed, once the door was shut and she stripped off her mantle. "There are soldiers everywhere, between here and the docks! They've sealed them off," she added to Onnelik, who came to hang up her cloak. "They sent an entire company to the river. No one leaves Falas without a pass signed by the palace, now," she said, frowning.

"I've seen arrests, today," agreed Gatina. "A scribe from the palace and his family. Lots of soldiers patrolling the streets. Even the City Watchmen are nervous."

"They should be," her mother agreed, as she sank onto a couch. "Their captain was arrested this morning. Along with the captain of the Palace Guard. And Sir Standaly, the Lord Mayor, who is the brother of the Prime Minister. All men who were appointed because of their accountability and their loyalty to Duke Lenguin," she said, sadly. "Good men, from good families. Now their families are at risk, too."

"Did Shadow have any good news?" Onnelik asked, worriedly, as he poured them both a glass of wine.

"Not enough," her mother said, shaking her head. "Vichetral is moving too fast for much to be done. He is silencing opposition before they even know he is among them. He has been planning for this sort of opportunity for a long time – he must!" she insisted to herself. "Worse, Baron Jenerard is strutting around the palace like he's the bloody duke, now. He's already been appointed an advisor to the ruling council. That means the Brotherhood will have some say over the government, now."

"Like getting the City Watch to leave them alone as they steal everyone blind?" Gatina asked.

"No, they won't quite go that far, Kitten," Minnureal soothed. "The merchants would never stand for that. But they won't be nearly as aggressive in pursuing them, now. And if they are caught, you can wager that Jenerard will use his influence to aid them. No, the Brotherhood stands to gain much more than a lax City Watch from Jenerard's appointment," she predicted. "That much Shadow was able to tell me. Once the council firmly establishes power, there will be certain changes in policy in the new government. Taxes, for one; who is taxed and how much. Trade regulations, of course, favoring those that Jenerard and the Brotherhood have interest in. But the worst thing is that they will likely bring slavery back to Alshar," she warned, a dire tone to her voice.

"*Slavery?*" Onnelik asked, in disbelief.

"Oh, it will be a few months, but soon we'll see edicts from the council that will relax Duke Lenguin's laws against the practice. And piracy," she added. "He'll make it legal, again, for pirate crews to sell their wares on the docks of Enultramar. There is no business too dirty for the Brotherhood to wallow in!" she said, her voice filled with disgust. "My family fought against such policies from the Narasi for decades, and the Sea Lords before them. Lenguin was the first duke in generations who returned to the laws against slavery the Magocracy employed."

"Surely something can be done?" Onnelik asked, worriedly. "The ducal court could—"

"Most of the ducal court is stranded in Vorone, in the Summer Capital," she reminded him. "And in the middle of an active war. Most of their deputies are now under arrest or dismissed. They have no power in Falas, with the duke and duchess dead. They can't call the banners and summon an army to retake Falas, nor would Vichetral allow them to so much as set foot in the south. The roads are closed against them. They are powerless," she pronounced, sadly.

"So what do we do?" Onnelik asked, anxiously. "What does Shadow say?"

"We do the best we can, with what we have, no matter how hopeless it appears," Minnureal answered, taking a deep sip from her cup. "We keep the ember of rebellion alive in Lenguin's memory. We protect Anguin and his sisters, and we work to see him restored to his father's coronet. And we build a network of allies who feel the same as we," she announced. "House Furtius is committed to this, now. Vichetral would destroy us simply for having a close relationship with the duke. We must not allow ourselves to be destroyed, and we must work to build some sort of resistance to the counts usurping the duchy."

Minnureal sounded weary and almost hopeless, and Gatina could see why. She envisioned the kind of force it would require to counter all of those soldiers. Her house was not a militant one. They did not raise knights; they raised magi and thieves.

"Will that really make any difference, Minny?" Onnelik asked, as he refilled both of their cups.

"Whether it will or not, it is the only sensible plan," her mother proposed. "We may not be able to overthrow Vichetral directly, but we can prepare for the day in which we will. And avoid capture while we do it. Shadow is sending agents out this very night, to learn more. There are some he hopes can be rescued, or at least contacted to discover what they know. He says he has a contact at the palace dungeon, where they are being kept," she informed them.

"That's something, I suppose," Onnelik conceded, as he stared at his cup. "Somehow I just know this is going to interfere with the start of the theater season," he mused, glumly.

Gatina filled her mother in on her day's work, though she didn't quite admit that she'd returned to the warehouse. She had a feeling her mistress wouldn't approve.

"That does sound foreboding," her mother agreed, when she was done. "Good work, reading the streets like that," she added. "That's an important part of Blue Magic, actually. Reading someone's emotions is one thing, but reading the emotions of a crowd, or a street, or an audience is something else, again. People behave in groups very differently than when they are on their own. Being able to tell when the mood of a crowd shifts can keep you from being in a bad spot in the middle of a riot, or a panic. Or let you know when it's time to leave. If you know this well enough, you can use just a bit of magic and sometimes direct the entire crowd. There's a whole body of Blue Magic on those sorts of spells. You'll learn them one day, Darkness willing."

Gatina tossed and turned once she went to bed, that night, after dinner. The scene on the street replayed itself in her memory over and over. The hopelessness in her mother's voice haunted her ears. The alarm her friends experienced at the ruckus on Parchment Street made her shiver. She kept trying to relax and let her mind slip into unconsciousness, but every time she opened her eyes, the night sky out the window seemed to beckon to her.

Darkness. Her family's patron. The blessed darkness that concealed and protected.

A little after the temple bells rang the midnight chime, Gatina slipped out of her bed. Instead of donning the ragged dress of Lissa the Mouse, she pulled her black leggings and tunic out of her press. Her working blacks, as her mother called them.

Gatina the Kitten was going out for the night.

"Strategy and tactics are husband and wife. Strategy requires planning. Tactics require observation. A lack of observation can ruin the most carefully contrived plan."

– Rule of House Furtius

CHAPTER ELEVEN
WHISPERS IN THE DARK

The cobbled streets of Falas were dark and deserted, at this late hour. Only the City Watch, tired lamplighters, and a few artisans whose workday began at midnight were out and about as Gatina skulked her way through the streets. Hiding from them was easy. Falas had almost no public lanterns on most streets, and where they did occur they were rarely lit at so late an hour. As she encountered the occasional passerby or watchman, slipping into the shadows until they passed by was easy.

Soon she came to the now-familiar street on which the gluepot warehouse loomed. It seemed far more formidable and foreboding at night, she realized; the big gaping windows at the top, meant to admit light and the occasional breeze to the warehouse, appeared as sinister eyes on the face of the building. The doors at the street level were closed and locked, of course. They were also likely guarded from within, she reasoned, if the Rats were cautious and smart.

Yet she could see glimmers of light reflecting through the open windows on the upper floor. Someone was working tonight, she saw. While the rest of the city slept, the Brotherhood of the Rat was busy. Night was when rats worked, after all.

Night was also when cats went out to prowl.

Gatina hugged the shadows cautiously as she approached the door.

Her feet made no sound, as she placed them as her mother had taught her. She reached out her senses to detect anyone who might be watching – Mother had proven to her that even people without *rajira* could sense when someone was watching you. The street seemed completely empty, however, and she began to slink through the shadows with more confidence.

When she came to the edge of the doorway, she could hear the guard on the other side. So that entrance was out. Instead, she sighted a few handholds in the bricks and beams that surrounded the doorway, and she began to climb. It wasn't difficult, she found. The masons who had constructed the building had not been adept, and there were plenty of places for her fingers and toes to gain purchase. In moments, she was well above street level, near the top of the second story.

Heights had never bothered Gatina – she knew, intellectually, that she could fall, but she did not take the fear seriously. Like her brother, she was at home in the heights. It helped that their parents encouraged climbing trees at a young age, much against common wisdom. She and Atopol had not only climbed every tree on their country estate, they had also frequently scaled the manor house and outbuildings. It was a part of their training she genuinely enjoyed, like swordplay.

Gatina found even better purchase the higher up she went, as the architecture changed from brick to post and beam. Pulling herself up the big wooden beams that supported the roof was even easier, and soon she found herself on the third story. A glance down at the street below demonstrated that there was still no witness to her ascent. She took a moment to rest her arms and legs, and plot her route through the darkness.

Her plan was simple: break into Gavin the Rat's office and steal whatever money she could find. Then give it to her friends, the street orphans. And do it without getting caught . . . by Gavin, his Rats, or, more importantly, her mother.

It wasn't a well-thought-out plan, Gatina knew, but it had the merit of being simple. Gavin was sitting on top of a pile of silver from the Brotherhood's pilfering; it seemed only right to pilfer a little of it back, and give it to the people who needed it most. Sure, it was dangerous, and probably not the wisest plan, but Gatina felt compelled to do . . . *something*. The suffering she'd seen, the abject poverty her friends were forced to contend with, was just too overwhelming. The corruption the Brotherhood represented was abominable. Their exploitation of the nits made her ill to consider. She had to fix it, or at least try to help.

She found purchase inside the big window, the great wooden shutter wedged open to admit some light, and the river breeze to cool the vast warehouse and steal away the fumes from the barrels of glue below. On the other side of the cavernous expanse was the catwalk that led to Gavin's office. Thankfully, the massive wooden beams and trusses that supported the catwalk and office structure gave her a direct route to them. With a final glance into the darkness below, she took a quick breath and began crossing the great expanse, one careful foothold at a time.

It was easy, she reasoned. The beams of the trusses were sturdy, and it was so dark below her that she didn't feel the slightest hint of vertigo as she moved from one to another. Not that she had ever experienced vertigo, but she had been taught about it.

It was when she was slightly more than half-way across that she realized something. She was not alone, up among the trusses.

Gatina froze. She didn't know how she knew, but there was a stirring in the air, or a noise, or something else that told her that there was someone or something also dancing up here on the trusses. She held her breath and stretched out her hearing, alert for any hint that she was correct. She vowed not to move a muscle until she was sure.

It took several minutes of listening before she heard the slightest creak of wood on the other side of the warehouse, nearer to the office. Whatever it was – whoever it was – that was sneaking across apparently hadn't been alerted to her own presence in the rafters. They were continuing toward the office almost as quietly as she was.

Darkness! she swore in her head. *Who else is trying to rob Gavin tonight?*

She suppressed the desire to sigh heavily, as it would likely give her away. If it wasn't just her imagination, she argued with herself. It was, after all, a very creaky warehouse, and there were constant squeaks in the structure every time the wind blew. She might be imagining the entire thing. She didn't think so. But she was too involved to quit, now.

Instead, she continued her journey through the trusses, making a point to be even more careful not to make a sound. The lanterns within the office provided a point of focus for her, and allowed her to mark how close she was to her destination. But she also kept a mental focus on the other thief scuttling through the darkness.

Soon, she was on the rafter next to the catwalk railing. Instead of swinging herself over and proceeding normally, she used the side of the thing to scuttle along the beams toward her goal. She recalled how squeaky the planks in the catwalk had been, when Lissa the Mouse was making her deposit. No doubt they served as an alarm, warning Gavin if anyone was approaching the office. She was happy to bypass them, even if it meant dangling uncomfortably over the yawning darkness, below.

She was half-way down the bottom of the catwalk when she heard voices from the office. As soon as she pulled herself up against one of the trusses closest to the interior window, she could even make out individual words.

Her heart sank – she'd hoped Gavin was alone, counting his money and making evil plans by himself, like gangsters were supposed to do. But he had company, tonight.

It took a few moments to get into position to hear what was being said, but she found that hanging off of one supporting beam got her ear in just the right position to listen to the words being spoken, not just the sound of voices.

". . . we're always happy to help out our friends at the palace, my lord," Gavin was saying in an obsequious voice. "Anything we can do to assist the government in this stressful time is our pleasure."

"If this was a purely governmental matter," the other voice said, tersely, "I would not be here, Gavin. This is a favor that our Brothers can do for the Count, a favor that we can call in handsomely at some point. It's good to have those in power beholden to the Brotherhood. It portends an alliance with the new regime. An alliance that is greatly to our benefit," he insisted.

"We did all right under the old regime," argued Gavin, as he puttered around the office. Gatina could hear his footsteps creaking. "Wine, m'lord? Not the local stuff, this is a good Bikavar. Took it off a barge as tribute," he boasted.

"Of course," murmured the other man. "The opportunities available to the Brotherhood with the new regime could open up vast new chances to profit, Gavin," he lectured. "More than just having a few lawbrothers, magistrates and City Watch act favorably toward us, we will have access to the corridors of the palace, itself. And a government that needs our help to keep order and see its policies fulfilled. Without too much scrutiny," he added, knowingly.

Gatina did not know who the other man was, but he spoke with an arrogance and precision that she guessed made him a courtier.

"Oh, I understand, m'lord," Gavin's raspy voice agreed. "I just don't see how it benefits us . . . directly," he said, pointedly. "I suppose that it depends upon just what kind of favor the Count needs from us."

"Nothing you haven't done before," the other man snapped. "You take people out of the city every week, according to the word in the nests."

"Aye, we have a bit of trade for labor," Gavin agreed. "Someone who won't be missed, might go missing. Sometimes they end up on a galley in the bay. Sometimes they end up working a manor farm in the Great Vale. Depends on what the market requires," he said, trying all the world to sound like a normal businessman.

"The point is, you can move people out of the city without the Watch knowing," the other man said, irritated. "That is what I require of you."

"How many people and for what jobs?" Gavin asked. "Some skilled labor takes time to find. Warm bodies I can get you in a day or two."

"I don't need you to *procure* me people, I just need to move people," the stranger declared. "A few dozen, perhaps two score. Maybe more. But soon."

"From here to where?" Gavin asked.

"We'll need to secure a barge," the other man said. "But we need them to leave without any witnesses, so you will have to get them to that barge. After that, they go downriver to an estate in the coastlands. Secretly," he added, with emphasis.

"Why so secret, m'lord?" asked Gavin, sharply.

"Because there would be riots if we were discovered before they were moved," the other man said, testily. Clearly, he was not used to being questioned. "They are the families of certain courtiers who have become... problematic. The Count feels if they are quietly removed to a more remote location, they can serve as hostages for certain officials' good behavior," he supplied. "Few will take a stand against the new regime if they know their wives and children will suffer as a result."

"Ah, lovely man, the Count is," Gavin chuckled. "Are things really that tense, at the palace?"

"More than you know," admitted the other man. "There will be executions, shortly. Not many, at first, but he's hoping it won't take very many to get the others to fall into line. But we are committed to supporting him. For his opponents blame me, and the Brotherhood, for assassinating Duchess Enora," he said gravely.

"So you're the Rat who did in the duchess?" Gavin asked, his voice filled with both surprise and new respect.

"No, actually, she was a friend of mine, not to mention a generous mark," admitted the other man. "But someone used a Rat's Tail to kill her in Vorone, and then blamed the act on me. I had to flee as soon as she was found dead. Now we *have* to back the Count, for the loyalists to the old regime want to hang me out of hand."

"Well, as long as we can take a profit on the opportunity, I suppose it doesn't matter which head wears the coronet," Gavin said, philosophically. "We are making a profit on this, aren't we?" he added, suddenly. "I have expenses to meet..."

"Of course we will," chided the other man. "But it's not about the profit in the near term. There are much larger forces at work, here, Gavin. Fortunes will be made. And a lot of people are going to die. The Count intends to avoid civil war, but he needs help to do so. Our help. As a member of the Council of State, I'm calling on you to cooperate. Even if it means taking a loss," he added, darkly.

"Ah, the Council! Why didn't you say so, Brother?" Gavin said, his voice suddenly far more respectful. "If this comes from the Council, then I suppose it's my duty to help. For an ounce of silver apiece," he continued. "That will get them out of the city and to the barge of your selection with no witnesses. And no rumors."

"A steep price, but then the Count told me money was no object. He's taken control of the ducal treasury," he added, knowingly. "Funds are not a problem."

"Then two ounces of silver a head, and I'll see you get a third of it as commission, m'lord," Gavin proposed. "Seeing as how someone else is paying it. Out of our taxes," he added, amused. "I'd be upset with the expenditure, if I paid my proper taxes."

"You'll be upset with the result if you don't ensure this goes off without trouble, Gavin," warned the other man. "As a member of the Council, I can guarantee that. So keep your greed modest, for the moment. The time for greed will come later. For now, we must help the Count establish his government. And avoid civil war."

"No one wins in a civil war," Gavin agreed. "Bad for business."

"Exactly. I am so glad you understand. Now, three nights hence, we'll be bringing the hostages in by closed wagons. If you can see to their removal, I'll pay you on the spot for each one. On the morrow I will secure a barge for the journey, and send word which one to make for, when your men come to the river. But above all there must be no whisper of this, to anyone! Some of the people we're transporting are very important. Their discovery would likely raise a cry, and that is something the Count does not want. He wants happy little courtiers, singing the praises of His Excellency in court and terrified for the lives of their loved ones."

"We can do that," Gavin agreed. "I've got my own little dock, down under this place. Goes right out to the river. Takes an hour each way," he boasted. "But I can only take ten at a time. Boat won't hold more than that."

"All right, we'll bring them through slowly," sighed the other man, rising. "There shouldn't be more than forty or so, in this batch. But there might be more, later," he promised.

"We shall be happy to accommodate you, m'lord . . . and His Excellency, the Count. I look forward to meeting him some day."

"Don't," snapped the other man. "I am the representative of the

Brotherhood to the court. The Count doesn't need to see any more of our organization than he has. It's better for these things to be conducted in secret. Indeed, that's why he's coming to me for this favor in the first place."

"I understand, m'lord," Gavin sighed. "Let me walk you down. The stairs are tricky, at night," he cautioned.

"Thank you," muttered the other man. "Damned near broke my ankle, coming up here. And your wine is . . . poor," he added. "Try to steal a better vintage, next time I visit," he ordered.

Gatina hurried to conceal herself behind a post as she heard creaking, and then the door to the office opening. The light from Gavin's lantern was too dim for her to make out the face of the visitor, as the gangster led him across the groaning catwalk and down the stairs.

But he had thoughtfully left his office door unlocked, open, and unguarded, Gatina noted, as the men descended the staircase.

As soon as she was certain they were out of earshot, she swung herself back over to the catwalk, and then sprinted across as lightly as a kitten. In seconds she was in the office.

While there was a fair amount of clutter in the place, she knew where she was going. It took her only moments to locate the box on the shelf she knew contained Gavin's treasury, at least the money he'd collected from Lissa the Mouse two days ago. It wasn't even locked, she realized, as she slid it open. The silver was already arranged in neat little bags, likely to aid in accounting, she figured. She quickly pilfered five of the little bags, each sitting heavily inside her pouch, before she turned to flee.

And nearly ran into her brother.

"Aw, Kitten," Atopol whispered, shaking his head sadly on the other side of Gavin's desk. "What are you up to?"

"Depend, then, on others to inform and educate you when you cannot observe for yourself. Powerful men oft forget to conceal their secrets from their servants, and thus can useful intelligence be gleaned. Cultivate contacts who may have such information to inform your vocation. For the eyes of the cowherd or chambermaid see as well as count and countess, and the ears of many a common tradesman hear useful tales not meant for them."

– from **The Shield of Darkness**

CHAPTER TWELVE
A RECKONING OF SHADOWS

"Cat!" Gatina whispered in shock, using Atopol's name-of-art automatically. He was, after all, dressed in the same matte black clothing as she was, the kind that allowed you to disappear in the shadows. That included a hood that concealed his white hair. But she recognized Atopol at once. "What are you doing here?"

"I'm spying," he said, with a shrug. "You?"

"I'm stealing," she said, holding up one of the little bags with a grin.

"Nice work," Atopol nodded. "But I don't think this is the place for a reunion. Meet me on the roof? Last chimney over, before the inn," he instructed. "We need to have a little chat."

Gatina nodded, knowing that Atopol was correct. Gavin would return from below in moments, and she didn't want to be caught here. Or even suspected. She followed the silent shape of her brother's cloak as he nimbly sprang over the catwalk railing and onto a truss beam. Gatina selected the next beam down the catwalk and followed suit. Soon both brother and sister were making their way back over the warehouse floor though the rafters, moving more quickly and with less concern about alerting anyone. Exits were usually like that, her mother had told her.

She made the window in half the time that she'd crossed originally, as a result, and long before Gavin waddled his way back up the creaky stairs. By the time she found the chimney that Atopol had mentioned as a meeting place, Atopol was already waiting for her.

"Well, well, Kitten made her first heist!" he chuckled, as she knelt next to him in the shelter of the brick chimney. "How did you score?"

"Five bags of silver, probably twenty ounces each," she said, proudly. She knew enough not to jingle the bags. The sound of such clinking could be distinctive and heard over long distances.

"Well done," Atopol nodded. "Mother sent you?"

"Ah, well, not . . . not exactly," Gatina stumbled. "This is more of a . . . a midnight stroll," she admitted, guiltily.

"A stroll that ends on a rooftop and makes stops at a gangster's treasury?" Atopol asked, skeptically.

"Well, I was just scouting the place out, at first, but when the chance arose . . . well, we are thieves, aren't we?" she asked, defensively. "If anyone deserves to be stolen from, it's that monster. He licked a girl's face, right in front of me," she reported. "Just to be disgusting and frighten her. Say . . . why are you here?" she asked, suspiciously.

"I'm on a mission for Shadow," Atopol said, proudly. "I was able to get close enough to hear Baron Jenerard speak to that Rat."

"Gavin," Gatina supplied. "His name is Gavin."

"Right, didn't know that," Atopol admitted. "I've been shadowing Baron Jenerard since he left the palace at dusk, to see who he was meeting with. I followed him here. Shadow said it might be one of the places he would go. He said the upper windows were unbarred and unguarded if I needed to get inside."

"Yes, I've been the one scouting this place," she reported. "Gavin is a mid-level gangster who controls the river-front districts. Local Rats report and pay tribute to him."

"I just wish I'd gotten close enough to overhear what they were saying," Atopol grumbled. "The last stretch of truss was rotting and creaky. By the time I'd moved around it, all they were talking about was silver and hostages. Then he left."

"Slowpoke!" Gatina said, rolling her eyes. "I was close enough to hear just about everything," she boasted. "I didn't know who the other Rat was, but I knew Gavin, already. The hostages are actually the wives and children of court officials that are feared to be disloyal to the Count. That must be Vichetral," she added.

"Do you know any other counts usurping the ducal palace and arresting everyone in sight?" he pointed out. "Baron Jenerard has been a close advisor to His Excellency. But you were lucky to hear all that."

"I heard more than that," she continued. "Three nights from now, Jenerard will be sending enclosed wagons to the warehouse, full of hostages. Then Gavin will take them down into the sewers, where he has a secret canal that leads to the river. His boat can only take ten at a time, plus the polemen, but he can get them out beyond the docks and meet with a barge without anyone in the city suspecting."

"Smugglers," Atopol nodded. "Of course."

"Well, they're going to be smuggling about forty loyalists out to a barge that Jenerard is planning to hire, tomorrow, perhaps more. In three days' time. Then they are going to be taken downriver to some secluded estate, where they will be kept as hostages. If anyone in the court makes a fuss, then their families pay the price," she said, grimly.

"That's not playing fair," Atopol chided. "Shadow says a lot of the ministers and officials that Vichetral didn't arrest at once were whispering about an uprising. This would put a stop to that," he agreed. "Shadow will want to know about this, at once! Thanks, Kitten," he said, with genuine gratitude. "That gives us a lot more about their plan than I was able to get."

"Kittens are curious," she shrugged. "And I did get a lot of silver out of it."

"About that . . ." Atopol frowned. "You know that Mother is not going to be happy about this little midnight stroll?"

"I was thinking she didn't need to know," Gatina said, searching her brother's eyes with her own. "Just like Shadow doesn't need to know that I was here. I was just trying to help out some friends. Gavin had some silver that he didn't need, and they need silver they don't have. I didn't take it all," she pointed out. "In fact, he probably won't even notice, for a while. And I can help a lot of people with this," she said, patting her pouch.

"Maybe," Atopol said, his frown refusing to leave. "Maybe you did something foolish that gets us caught. What then? And how are you going to suddenly enrich your friends? And when did you start having friends?" he demanded.

"It's been a busy week," she dismissed. "Don't worry about it. I won't get us caught."

"I hope not," her brother sighed. "This has been a busy week. There is a lot going on. A lot of violent things. There was nearly a riot at the palace gate, today. Vichetral's men control it now. The head of the Palace Guard is in the dungeons, with a dozen others the Count suspects of resisting his rule. Things are going to get ugly in Falas, soon," he warned. "The last thing we need is a reckless kitten upsetting things. You could have gotten caught. You might get hurt, Gatina," he pleaded. "Do be careful!"

"I'm always careful," she lied. "But the same goes for you. I stole some coin, but you were there in the rafters, too, Cat. You could have fallen or gotten caught just as much as I could have. It's just a dangerous time."

"All right," he conceded, with a brotherly sigh. "I suppose you wouldn't listen to me, anyway. I'll take this news to Shadow. You go hide that silver. Especially from Mother. She will be upset if she thinks you've been stealing without permission. Which you were," he pointed out. "Be careful how you spend it, too," he added, as he pulled his cowl over his hair. "That sort of money is likely to attract attention in the wrong places, if you aren't careful."

"I'm always careful," she repeated. It was no truer the second time. That earned her an eye roll as her brother slunk away. "Darkness protect you!" she whispered, as he slipped over the edge of the roof.

"Shadows hide you!" he replied, and then was gone.

The trip home was uneventful, though Gatina took her brother's words to heart and sought to move without being discovered. The hour was late enough so that even the worst drunkards had long stumbled home. Only the City Watch still roamed the streets. By the time she made it back to the townhouse, the first light in the east was starting to glimmer over the skyline. Gatina yawned as she hid her loot in the bowels of the woodpile out back, and then returned through her window to her bed.

My first heist, she realized, as she was finally starting to fall asleep after the night's excitement. *My first actual heist! I'm a real thief now!* she assured herself, as she drifted off to sleep.

THERE WERE NO RECRIMINATIONS THE NEXT MORNING FOR HER OUTING. Indeed, Cousin Onnelik did not rouse her from bed until late in the morning, feeling that she had been exhausted by her recent days' work. He was a kind soul, Gatina knew, and she was glad she was related to him. He resembled her father enough in face and voice that he was a comfort for her. He'd even had the cook leave her some porridge over the fire before she left for the market.

"Where's Mother?" she asked him, between hungry bites at the kitchen table.

"She had business elsewhere, today," he said, in a tone that told Gatina she would get no more from him on the subject. "She left instructions for you to continue your street work. She still wants you to keep infiltrating the local Rat's nests. But avoid trouble, at all cost. I'll keep taking your reports until she returns."

"I will," she agreed. "Any new word from the palace?" she asked, hoping for news. Hearing about Atopol's work had intrigued her further.

"Alas, just more pronouncements about days of mourning, and temple services for Their Graces, and a few edicts," he sighed. "Count Vichetral's banner flies near the gates, and his men guard them. I heard as much from the milkmaid this morning."

"The milkmaid?" Gatina asked. "Is that a code name?"

"No, no, Artessia is an actual milkmaid," Onnelik chuckled. "Some of my best sources are common folk, like that. Servants and artisans always gossip, and they go places and see things others do not. Artessia sells milk to the houses on the far end of the Processional, to a wealthy family who lives across from the palace. Their stableboy hears everything that happens near the palace gates. And he has a crush on Maid Artessia, so he tells her everything. And she tells it to me," he supplied.

"Interesting," Gatina nodded. She knew from personal experience the kinds of things people saw when they were almost invisible. The nits witnessed lots of things as they tossed around, looking for alms or work. Unfortunately, Gatina had found, their tendency to exaggerate or lie to make themselves important – or for the pure joy of lying – made them unreliable about most things. "Tell me, this Shadow person, the one she reports to, is he to be trusted?" she wondered. She had never been told about the man to whom her mother was passing along information. Secrets were secrets, she knew. But kittens were curious.

The question took Onnelik by surprise. "Shadow? Why yes, yes, he can be trusted," he assured her. "Your mother places a lot of stock in his leadership. He's terribly well-informed. And he has the interests of the duchy in mind, of that I have no doubt, and the welfare of the ducal house. Yes, I would say that Shadow is to be trusted."

"Would he help people, if he had a chance?" she asked.

The question puzzled Onnelik. "Well, I suppose so, but that isn't his focus at the moment, I'd wager. He's trying to keep the duchy from sliding into either tyranny or civil war, and that's a demanding task," he assured her.

"That's true," Gatina sighed, finishing her last bite of porridge. "I guess I'll go put on my costume. The kids will be gathering in the broken fountain, soon."

"Yes, best you not break your alias if you don't have to," Onnelik agreed, as he took her bowl. "Anything and everything you can find out, my dear. We need to know it all, if we're to be effective."

Gatina went upstairs to change, and Lissa the Mouse returned. Not just her appearance had changed; Gatina found that her entire demeanor and mindset changed, as well, as she became Lissa. By the time she nodded to Onnelik, dirtied her face with some ash from the fire, and ducked outside the back door, she was Lissa the Mouse in her mind, not just in her features.

She paused only long enough to check on her stolen horde in the woodpile. It was still there, all five bags, at least a hundred silver pennies. Enough to buy a small house, or more, she knew. But if she just showed up and started handing out silver at the fountain, that would attract far too much attention. Worse, if her friends were known to have money, they wouldn't keep it very long. The streets of Falas were brutal, and a nit had only what money they could hide or fight for.

It was a problem, she knew. But it was a good problem to have, she decided. She still had her solitary silver penny from the other day, if she needed to buy any food. That, at least, wouldn't attract much attention.

The crowds were thinner and meaner, today, she saw, as she finally made it to the broken fountain. There were at least ten other children there, milling about, playing, shoving each other, and exchanging outrageous lies. Liddy and Marga were in their accustomed spot, on the edge of the upper portion of the fountain, where they could see a little better. As usual, the crowd was ignoring the knot of nits infecting the place.

Only, Gatina decided, as she sat down next to Marga, the crowd was ignoring the orphans harder, somehow, today. There was some nervous energy in the air, as the artisans and townsfolk hurried on their errands. She studied faces and how the crowds moved. People were upset, some angry. There was no particular reason that she could tell. No one was screaming or making a fuss. But the people passing by the fountain were possessed by some anxious excitement, and it made the plight of the orphans even more ignorable, somehow.

"Hard day," Marga said, glancing up at the overcast sky. "Not one slim copper, from this bunch. Of course, with such a crowd here, it's hard to attract proper attention!" she said, a little loudly, as she looked around at the milling of nits in the fountain. "Trygg's grace, it's annoying when everyone hears you got a good spot!"

"It's your fault, actually, Lissa," Liddy said, smirking. "Word got around that you always have food. So this lot showed up today. Not that anyone was throwing alms before then," she added. "People are scared."

"More soldiers marched by, just before you got here," agreed Marga.

"Well, no food today," Gatina said, a little guiltily. "But maybe later, when some of these fellows move along. I won't have enough for them all!"

"Where did you get money?" Liddy demanded.

"I've been scrounging," Gatina said, defensively. "A little sweeping, a little carrying and fetching."

"That's why you have porridge on your neck," Marga said, pointing out a spot under her ear. "Where did you get porridge?"

"I found a cook who's too lazy to fetch her own wood," Gatina said. "I got the leftover porridge the pigs were to get. It wasn't bad," she added.

"You're getting good at this," Liddy approved. "You aren't half as scrawny as most of us."

"No one minds feeding a mouse a crumb or two," she dismissed. "I work hard. And I never turn down a good opportunity to make a penny."

"Easier to beg than to work," sneered Toscar, arrogantly. "You just find the right old bag, the grandmotherly type, and you come on all pitiful," he said, dramatically affecting a miserable disposition. "You just tell them you haven't eaten in days, and your poor father was a mariner, lost at sea, and your mother was eaten by Sea Folk, and if you don't get a morsel you'll die, and for Trygg's Grace will you please help an orphan out of a tight spot?" he said, tears forming in his eyes. Then his manner changed again. "You get them right after a temple service and they're good for a couple of bits."

"Or you do a bit of honest scrubbing and earn your coin!" Liddy sneered.

"Begging's easier," Toscar insisted, as he daringly walked around the highest edge of the fountain. "A lot easier on your knees, too. Hey – it's Charcoal!" he said, suddenly catching sight of someone in the crowd.

"Charcoal?" Gatina asked in confusion.

"Oh, you *gotta* know Charcoal," Toscar said, admiringly. "He's one of Racer's fellows from up the street. At the burned-out lot," he explained. "The big kids."

That immediately got Gatina's attention. Indeed, a moment later a scrawny boy of maybe twelve slid through the crowd like a cat. He was, perhaps, grubbier than other nits, but Gatina didn't see why he was called Charcoal. He was, however, a familiar face, one of the many older children who'd been hanging around the ruined building. But she hadn't caught his name.

"Hey, Charcoal!" announced Toscar. "Where you been?"

"Working," the boy said, with exaggerated seriousness. "Making real coin. Not begging," he added, arrogantly, as he surveyed the crowded fountain.

"Doing what?" demanded Twopenny.

"Important things," the boy assured. "For important people. Like running errands."

"What kind of errands?" prompted Twopenny.

"Like finding little girls for people," he said. "Which one of you nits is Lissa the Mouse?" he asked.

"I find my condition frustrating: a thief admonished about stealing! My brother's sage wisdom on the subject may well prove correct . . . but I'll never tell him that. I simply want to help my friends with the talents my Mistress and blessed Darkness have bequeathed to me. I don't see how stealing from criminals is wrong, but I do understand how it might appear to be greed or foolishness, when it is merely altruism. It was my First Heist! I should be able to do what I want with the loot!"

– *Gatina's Heist Journal*

CHAPTER THIRTEEN
AN UNUSUAL ERRAND

"Why?" asked Liddy, suspiciously. "What's she done?"

"Racer wants to talk to her," Charcoal said. "Sent me to fetch her. Said she hung out here."

"What's Racer want with her?" demanded Marga.

"He needs a seamstress, and she's got a great reputation and good references?" Charcoal supplied, sarcastically. "I don't get paid to ask questions. The man wants to see her. Said she should bring her basket. Which one of you nits is she?"

"I'm Lissa," Gatina said, before her friends could get into trouble with the older boy. "I remember Racer. From the other day. Don't worry," she urged Marga and Liddy. "I'll be alright."

"You know *Racer?*" Toscar asked, in disbelief.

"He's not one of the nice ones, Lissa!" warned Marga.

"*How* do you know Racer?" asked Liddy, confused.

"Only in passing," Gatina dismissed. "The briefest of acquaintances. I'll be back," she assured.

"Come with me," Charcoal ordered, and then led her in a winding path through the crowd. Soon they were headed for the burned-out lot, the street less crowded.

"So what's Racer want with me?" she asked.

"I told you, I don't know. But he told me to find you. So I found you," he answered, tersely. "You'll know in a minute."

Gatina sighed, but kept plodding away across the cobbles until they came to the lot. The miserable fire was still burning, though there were fewer of the Rat Orphans around, today, than usual, she noticed. But one of them was Racer, holding court among a few of the bigger boys.

"What do you need, Racer?" Gatina asked, before he could speak.

"Flerian wants to see you," the boy grunted. "Right away."

"Why?" she asked, confused.

"Probably because he has another job, stupid," Racer suggested. "Don't keep him waiting. He hates it when you're late. It breaks the rules."

Gatina nodded. More accurately, Lissa the Mouse nodded. Lissa was shrewd, in Gatina's mind, so she acted the part. She left the lot without another word and hurried to Hanik's Butchery. She had to go inside to see Flerian, where the man was cutting thick chunks of lamb from the bone.

"Hey, it's the Mouse!" Flerian said, cheerfully. "And in good time. How have you been, Lissa?"

"Hungry," she shrugged. "What do you need? Did I do something wrong?" she asked, suspiciously.

"No, no, Hanik had something come up, and needs something taken somewhere without anyone knowing about it," Flerian said, his cleaver coming down hard on the mutton. "You up for that?"

"Depends on where it goes," she shrugged again. "I'm not walking to Enultramar."

That made the butcher laugh. "No, no, it's in town. Nice part of town, too. Hanik needs a letter delivered to someone. Business," he said, with another hack of his cleaver.

"All right," nodded Gatina. "What's a letter?"

That made Flerian laugh, too. "A message on parchment. Only, it's a long message. Never mind. You can't read, anyway. You're perfect. But if it doesn't get there, you go in the canal," he said, with an especially vicious chop.

"What's it pay?" she demanded.

"Same as last time," Flerian said. "But only when you get back. Same rules as last time, too."

"All right," she agreed. "Where is it?"

"Hanik will be down in a minute. Just sit here and be quiet," he said, nodding to a short stool.

Gatina took a seat without comment, and just watched the gangster brutally chop the mutton into smaller gobbets. He maintained a conversation with the other three butchers in the gory room, each working on a different sort of livestock. Gatina was both appalled and fascinated at the casual way they went about their business. She was even more fascinated by the conversation. Much of what they were discussing, in vaguely coded language, was gossip about their real business – not butchery, but their business for the Brotherhood.

As well off as they were doing, compared to many in Falas, they complained bitterly about an increase in their workload. They spoke of threatening people and demanding money, of gambling and other vices they administered and profited in. Indeed, they bragged about how brutal they were to their fellow shopkeepers, who apparently paid a premium price to avoid their displeasure. They did it without coming out and admitting it, but by using innuendo and double meanings, as well as a volume of unique slang, so that Gatina had to guess at most of what they spoke of.

But Gatina was a very good guesser. She learned a lot about Hanik's business.

Nearly half an hour had passed before the older gangster, Hanik, descended the stairs, a folded letter in his hands.

"Hey, Flerian, where's that nit?" he asked his fellow.

"She's right there," grunted the butcher, nodding at Lissa. Gatina nodded and stood.

"Oh, didn't see you," Hanik admitted.

"People don't see a mouse," Gatina shrugged.

"Good," the master butcher agreed. "Don't let anyone see you with *this*," he said, indicating the letter. "And gods help you if anyone reads it, 'cause you'll need it. I need you to take this in your little basket over to Cordwainers Street. You know where that is?"

"No," admitted Gatina.

"It's easy, it's down Parchment to Archer Street, take a left, then across the Processional to a circle with a fountain with a bull in it, and then go south on Cordwainers. Nice neighborhood, near the palace," he supplied. "The kind with fancy gardens and statues and such. Look for the third house down from the wineshop with the red awning. House has a green door and a brass dog on the front step. Go around to the back and tell the cook you need to see the lady. That you're from the butcher's. When you see the lady, give her this," he said, thrusting the letter under her nose. "Let her read it. Then get her answer. It's a yes or no answer," he said, emphasizing the point. "There are no other answers but yes or no. Understand?"

"Yes," Gatina nodded.

"Good, make sure she understands, too," Hanik agreed, handing over the letter. Gatina put it in her basket without looking at it. "You remember where to go?"

Gatina considered a moment. "Down Parchment to a left on Archer, cross the Processional to a circle, down Cordwainers to the third house past the wineshop, green door, brass dog, go to the kitchen, tell the cook, meet the lady, read the letter, yes or no," she reported, from memory.

"Good girl," grunted Hanik. "And don't stop for no one. Anyone stops you and reads that, it's the canal for you. Or worse," he said, just as Flerian hacked a thick sheep's bone in half.

"It would be more believable if I had some sausages," Gatina said, before she left.

"What?" asked Hanik, confused.

"If I need to explain why I'm in that nice neighborhood, if I had some sausages I could say I was delivering them," she explained. "That's believable."

Hanik considered, then grunted. "Flerian, give her some sausages," he decided. "Kid is right. But if you get nicked, those sausages came from Holman's Butchery, over on Canal Street. I don't like Holman," he added, unnecessarily.

"I won't get stopped," Gatina assured. "No one sees a mouse."

"Good girl," Flerian said, placing a string of raw sausages hastily wrapped in a rag into her basket. "Now hurry. And hurry back."

Gatina nodded to both men before setting off with purpose. She followed the directions Hanik gave her explicitly . . . but paused briefly when another column of soldiers pushed their way through the crowd. She had to – everyone stopped and stared. The soldiers had grim expressions on their faces, no doubt going to some duty that was apt to get violent.

But Gatina took the distraction to quickly pull the letter out of the basket, while the crowd pressed close, and open it. Hanik had not sealed it, trusting to her illiteracy. But thanks to Sister Karia, Gatina's command of the art allowed her to read it in a glance.

MY LADY, it read in a careful scrawl, *If You Persuade Your Brother To Halt His Efforts To Bring His Men To Falas, I Will Reduce Your Debt By Half. If You Fail, I Will Double It. A Simple Yes Or No Will Suffice. My Regards To Your Husband And Child. H.*

There was a simple sketch of a butcher's cleaver next to the initial. Gatina folded the parchment and pushed it back under the sausages before she continued on, after the soldiers marched past.

Gatina's head spun on the remainder of her journey. While the note could have several meanings, the implication was clear: whoever this poor woman was, Hanik had some hold over her due to a debt. Considering the wealth of the neighborhood she came to, she didn't think the debt regarded the normal butcher's account for even the gentry of the town. The meaning was clear: she must do this thing, or risk her reputation, her fortune, and perhaps even her family. No, Gatina decided, it was definitely her family at risk. Hanik would not have mentioned them, otherwise.

She found the house easily enough, just down from the wineshop, a brass statuette of a dog on the front step. The tasteful display of heraldry on the outside denoted both wealth and a high status, though both could be faked, as she'd learned. She made her way to the back and caught the attention of the cook, who was snapping beans into a bowl in the scant sunshine.

"I'm here to speak with the lady of the hall," Gatina said, carefully, as she approached the old woman. At first the matron scowled, but Gatina forced a gaze that would allow no dismissal. She'd seen her mother do that, too. "Summon her. I bear a message for her hand only."

The cook wordlessly put aside her beans and hurried inside. It took several minutes for the lady of the hall to emerge.

To her surprise, the woman was young, only a few years older than herself. She was well-dressed, her gown falling to her feet and her slippers matching the fabric. She was wearing far more jewelry than an artisan's wife. She looked surprised and a bit scared to see Gatina.

"It's from the butcher," she said, thrusting the note at her. The noblewoman took it and fumbled it open. It took her a bit longer to read it than Gatina had taken, but when she looked up from it, Gatina could tell that she'd read it in its entirety. And understood it.

"Yes, or no?" she asked, evenly. The way a representative of a gangster would ask.

"Y-yes, yes, tell him yes!" the woman said fearfully. "I'll do it at once!"

Gatina nodded, then turned and left without another word.

She stopped briefly at the wineshop and asked the boy carrying casks and bottles who lived at the address.

"Oh, that's Lord Relnaman's house," the boy informed her. "He's a nice fellow, for a noble. Good customer. He's some sort of official at the palace."

"And his wife?" she probed.

"Lady Isadra? She's very nice," he assured her. "Relnaman just married her, last year. She just had a baby. She's some sister to a baron up-country, I hear. Not a big wine drinker," he added, shaking his head.

"Thanks!" Gatina said and kept going.

She thought about the matter the whole way back to Hanik's butchery. She paused again, when she got to the broken fountain, and distributed the sausages in her basket before she returned, but she arrived in plenty of time to avoid the butcher's ire.

"She said 'yes'," she told him, herself, as the shop prepared to close for the afternoon. "Where's my money?"

"She said yes?" the gangster boss repeated almost surprised. "Of course she did. You made good time, kid," he praised. "Pay the girl, Flerian."

"Come by at noon, tomorrow, if you want another job," Flerian added, as he dropped two silver pennies into her dirty palm. She grasped them eagerly – just as Lissa the Mouse would do – thanked him and ran off.

She was glad that she'd given away the sausages beforehand, for she did not want to tarry with her friends when she had news to share. She did not even know, exactly, what the note had meant, but it seemed important enough to Hanik to be important to her mother. She took a more complex route through the streets to get back to her cousin's neighborhood, to ensure she hadn't been followed, but she arrived well before dark.

"She's the youngest sister of Baron Antremin of Larethin, a prosperous fief to the south of Falas," Onnelik explained, after she duly reported her findings to him. Her mother had returned midafternoon and was glad to hear the news. But she was uneasy about its implications.

"Baron Antremin is one of the six or seven barons in County Falas who oppose Count Vichetral's usurpation of power," she said, sighing. "Shadow has had agents rallying them to ride to the capital and defend it. Vichetral is not their count, after all – they're sworn to Duke Lenguin as Count of Falas. Between them they could raise ten thousand men in a day's time. If they have the political will to do so. If they don't," she warned, "Vichetral's men from Rhemes will reinforce him, and he will never be dislodged from the capital."

"So how is this butcher playing a role in this?" Onnelik asked, confused.

"The Brotherhood is leaning on all who they have control over," her mother explained. "If Lady Isadra convinces her older brother to keep his men at home, that will help undermine any resistance to the Count's rule. No doubt other relatives of the barons will be squeezed the same way," she said, troubled.

"But why would she listen to a butcher?" asked Gatina.

"Because she owes him a debt, most likely, Kitten," explained Minnureal. "People borrow money for all sorts of reasons. Most temples and money-lenders require a good reason to incur a debt. Purchasing property, perhaps, or buying a ship. The Brotherhood lends it to all, regardless of their reasons. But they charge a high price to do so, and will not hesitate to threaten violence to collect." She frowned. "This is bad news. And we've had too much of that, this week."

"We may not be able to prevent him from taking up the rule of the duchy, my dear," Onnelik said, gently. "He was prepared for this moment. He has strong allies. His opponents were taken by surprise. No one of senior rank is standing to oppose him," he reasoned. "Any baron who does would risk his men and potential retaliation. That could lead to civil war, or worse, brutal oppression."

"I know, I know," her mother said, shaking her head sadly. "It may well be that the best we can do is preserve those that we can, and await a change of circumstances."

"What about magic?" suggested Gatina, as she picked at a chicken wing the cook had prepared for her. "He has no defense against that, I'd imagine."

"If there was a way to bring magic to bear, we would," her mother promised. "Indeed, we are. But magic is not the answer to everything, you will find, Kitten. It's not even the answer to most things. It is but a useful tool in the pursuit of our goals. Alas, things are moving too quickly, now, and we were unprepared for this. All we can do is keep to the blessed shadows and plan for the future."

It disturbed Gatina to hear her mother take such an attitude of defeat to the matter. Her mother was never pessimistic about most things. Yet the dread in her tone and the slouch of her shoulders spoke volumes.

"So Shadow had no good news today, either?" Onnelik prompted, his manner similar. No one wanted to face an usurper who promised to be a brutal tyrant, it seemed.

"Some," her mother admitted. "We have learned how Vichetral plans on kidnapping some of the families of the palace officials and holding them hostage to their good behavior. An ugly business," she condemned. "Innocents should never be harmed in politics. Which is why they are, all too often. Shadow is planning to counter their operation," she revealed, a pleased little smile on her lips. "Of course, you should know all about that already, Kitten. Seeing how you were the one who got close enough to listen to their plans. And then steal from them. All *without* my permission!"

"Blessings of Fortune are well and good, but they don't ease our existence. We forge our own future with cunning, craft, and the aid of Darkness."

– *Kiera the Great's Heist Journal,*
from **The Shield of Darkness**

CHAPTER FOURTEEN
THE STREETS OF FALAS

GATINA HAD NEVER TAKEN SO UGLY A SCOLDING SINCE SHE BECAME HER mother's apprentice. Part lecture and part recrimination about her failure, Minnureal chewed Gatina's ears for hours over her unauthorized heist. Upon her mother's direction, she had to go out to the woodpile and retrieve the five bags of silver and give them into her mother's custody. Onnelik wisely withdrew to his study to allow his cousin's wife to chastise her charge in privacy.

"I just cannot believe that you would sneak out and raid that Rat's den without my express permission!" she raged, in the parlor. "You could have been killed, you could have fallen, you could have been discovered and risked us all!"

"It's a good thing I did," countered Gatina, impertinently. "Else we'd never know about the hostages and Baron Jenerard. Cat didn't get close enough," she reminded her, doing her best to not sound argumentative.

"Do not change the subject, Apprentice!" her mother snapped. "The danger was bad enough, but you *disobeyed* me," she pronounced. "And for what? Silver? A measly hundred ounces of silver?" she asked, appalled. "Not even worth the effort! What were you trying to do?" she pleaded.

"Just trying to help my friends!" Gatina said, defensively. "They're starving, out on the streets!"

"There are thousands and thousands of nits starving on the streets, Kitten. We cannot save them all," her mother said, crossly.

"No, but we can save the ones who are *my* friends," Gatina said. "I took that silver to do that."

"And imperiled us and all we work for!" insisted her mother, flinging her hands in the air. "Do you have any idea how many lives are at stake, right now? Our entire House is at risk. We *have* to be careful, Kitten, more careful than we've ever been before. We might face the magistrate, if we are captured on a heist, but if we are found spying against Count Vichetral and his allies, it will be a summary execution and no questions asked!" she pointed out, angrily. "Never, *ever* disobey my orders again!"

"I was just following the codes!" Gatina said, in her own defense. "The ones you taught me."

She quickly picked up the cards her family used for teaching, and flipped through them until she found the one she wanted – ironically, just under the one called SECRECY. She held it out for her mother to see. OPPORTUNITY, it read, and displayed a hand finding a coin on the ground. "I saw an opportunity, and I took it. Like I was instructed to!"

Minnureal began to renew her lecture, but then stopped herself. That surprised Gatina – she fully expected to get her ears chewed for sassiness. What came out, instead, was surprising, too.

"Perhaps you are right, Kitten," she sighed, staring at the card and then at her daughter. "In different times, perhaps I would have been justified in my anger over this. But these are challenging times, and the rules may have to be different, now," she admitted, as if defeated. "Just as Onnelik is right: we may not be able to prevent Vichetral and the likes of Jenerard taking power. Neither situation is pleasing to me," she admitted, "but both are true just the same. You are going to be impetuous. It is in your nature. That's what kittens do. And we may be ruled for a time by a tyrant. And there is little I can do to change either circumstance."

Gatina put the card away guiltily. While she had reduced her mother's wrath, somewhat, it had been at the cost of admitting her defeat. She didn't like the way her victory felt.

"I wasn't trying to create trouble, Mistress," she said, sincerely. "I just saw a chance to . . . to . . ."

"To steal something away from evil men and give it to your friends," Minnureal finished, throwing up her hand in the air, resigned. "I understand the impulse, Kitten. Trust me, I do. And I bear some of the responsibility for that, for I am the one who put you in the path of danger . . . and created an irresistible opportunity for my curious kitten.

"It's hard, doing what we do," she said, simply. "Being other people most of the time is confusing, even to those of us who have done it for years. That's one reason why we have these codes. To help us keep our minds straight. As well as to keep us from being caught. I have to admit, you did well, under the circumstances," she said, fixing her daughter with a sharp stare. "But that is not an excuse for wayward apprentices to ignore the wishes of their mistresses!"

"I wasn't trying to, and I won't in the future, I promise!" Gatina replied.

"Did you know that *Shadow* was observing Cat that night?" she asked, pointedly.

"Shadow?" Gatina said, her attention rapt. "*He* was watching?"

"He's everywhere you don't expect him to be," Minnureal said, her eyes narrowing. "He *saw* you. Just once, but he saw you."

"I didn't get caught," Gatina reminded her. "And I got away with the loot."

"Yes, yes you did," her mother said, glancing at the five bags of silver. "Your first heist. Usually, that occasion is well-planned in consultation with your Mistress. But there is a certain amount of promise in what you did. Here," she said, opening one of the bags and digging out a thick silver piece. She handed it to Gatina. "I will take the rest in trust on your behalf, and perhaps eventually we will find a way to help your friends with it, as you intended.

"But everyone in House Furtius keeps a trophy of their first heist. It's tradition. Keep it with your journal," she instructed. "Perhaps it will serve to remind you of this lecture, in the future."

"Oh, I don't see myself ever forgetting this," Gatina said, staring at the coin. "Never."

Gatina sat up in her room, late into the night, playing with her mother's cards. There were, indeed, different games you could play with them, she knew, but the games were of secondary importance. To the Blue Magi, such cards were useful for other things, it was said. They suggested paths and plans to those who knew them well and knew how to use them. They weren't for foretelling the future or gambling, they were for offering insights on your very thoughts. If you knew how to use them.

Gatina was reflecting on the worsening situation on the streets, the plight of her friends, the evil of the Brotherhood and men like Vichetral, and the hopelessness of it all. For some reason, their using Lady Isadra's debt against her in such a way appalled Gatina as unbearably unfair, and she could not let the matter go. So she turned to the cards, shuffling them and then laying them out in simple patterns.

For a time she found some wisdom in them, and then their complexly-painted images seemed to mock her. She didn't feel as if she knew them well enough to understand their meaning, and that was frustrating. But, then, she had to admit that there might be no way out of the situation.

Men like Vichetral would always seek power and do anything to gain it. The histories that Sister Karia had assigned her were full of such tales. Men like Hanik and Gavin and Baron Jenerard would always seek advantage and money. Children like Marga and Toscar would always be hungry and homeless. Women like Lady Isadra would always be vulnerable to being victimized. There seemed no end to the suffering in the world, and Gatina was furious with herself for not finding a way to end it.

She knew how silly that sounded, when she thought about it. She was only eleven, after all, and hadn't even come into her *rajira*. But she also knew that there had to be a way, at least a way through the current crisis. She knew she could find one, if she tried hard enough. Alas, the cards held no more counsel than the silver coin she had placed on her journal. She went to bed that night staring at both of them.

The next day she became Lissa the Mouse again and went forth with her basket just after dawn. Her friends weren't there, yet, and so she contented herself with watching the street wake up while she waited.

"So what did Racer want with you?" Marga asked, suspiciously, when she arrived an hour later. "He didn't try to . . . to *kiss* you, did he?" she added, uncomfortably.

"No, no, he had a job for me. Just an errand, I promise," she pledged.

"Why *you*?" Marga asked.

"Why not?" Gatina countered. "I'm good at errands. I follow directions. I can be fast."

"Maybe, but why you? And why would you want to do that sort of thing? For them?" Marga demanded.

"The coin is good!" Gatina defended. "Good enough to feed us, isn't it?" She held up a loaf of warm bread she had picked up that morning.

"Be careful, Lissa," Marga urged, biting her lip as she eyed the bread and then her friend. "Those boys are trouble. Don't let them get *you* into trouble."

"I'll be as careful as a mouse," she promised, earning her another skeptical look from her friend. "But I'll also be generous. It *is* good coin, and it's not hard work. But at least it's work."

"I know, I shouldn't judge you," Marga sighed. "You have to eat. I understand. I just worry. I've heard stories."

Gatina watched two City Watchmen nearest her spot on the fountain, where she sat and slowly nibbled at her share of the bread. She was listening to Marga explain explicitly why she should not get involved with the Rat Orphans, again, along with a few lurid stories about people she knew who had and regretted it. She wondered if that might become a problem to Marga, but shook it off. Instead, she just nodded her agreement to do so while knowing that she would not avoid the Rat Orphans. They were the entire reason she was Lissa the Mouse in the first place.

She watched the pair of watchmen closely. They didn't look

bored for a change, or even mean. They looked worried. That disturbed Gatina. For the most part, the City Watch left the nits alone, Marga had assured her. It was only if they were up to no good – stealing and getting caught, vandalizing, or creating a nuisance for merchants or common folk – that the nits even came into their awareness.

"They're more concerned with the adult beggars and the drunks because they cause more trouble," Marga had told her. "They don't see us as worth the effort. We're small and we're disposable." Gatina understood immediately what she meant. Nits were invisible. And the canal was deep.

The City Watch of Falas, according to Cousin Onnelik, was at once a valued organization designed to provide order and law from the palace to the people – of all classes. Their charge was to keep people safe and their property secure. They were to intervene in domestic disturbances, mitigate arguments before they came to blows, bring footpads and belligerent drunks before the city's magistrates, and alert their superiors to suspicious activity.

But while the job had a certain status, the men who watched for danger in the city were not paid well, and a little bit of coin could encourage them to look the other way. That was a benefit, when you were a well-connected thief, Gatina knew. Corrupt and bribable officials could often get a thief into or out of some places.

That petty corruption was useful to House Furtius, but it also made the men who guarded the city less than honest in other ways. Some were ridiculously crooked in how they administered the laws that they were sworn to uphold. The quality of men recruited to the ranks was not equal, Onnelik had warned. Some watchmen were altruistic and genuine and wanted to help their fellows; but others, he strongly cautioned, were not kind at all.

A certain type of man, he'd lectured, would abuse his position of authority cruelly, and would hurt someone just to see the discomfort it would bring. The latter kind of man was no better than a Rat. Onnelik also warned her that there was no way to truly determine which type of man was which until it may be too late. That was one message Gatina had heeded carefully. She had done her very best to be invisible to the eyes of the Watch.

The two watchmen were young – a few years older than Attie, she guessed. She wished she knew magic so that she could listen into what they said, but she learned a lot just by observing them.

When they first walked down the street, checking on each shopkeeper and moving foot traffic along, they seemed to her to be friendly. But once they arrived at the roundabout, they began to argue.

From her seat, she could only make out random words, and only if one of them spoke loudly. But their body language revealed tension. They ignored the nits and focused on their argument until one screamed *"It's for both of us!"* loudly enough to attract attention.

Heads turned; not only the nits, but the passersby suddenly stared at the argument. One watchman's face turned red, before reluctantly nodding and offering something to his fellow. It was food, she saw – a couple of pies. It was time for luncheon, and she guessed they were hungry. But from the way the pie vendor glared at them from behind his cart, Gatina suspected that they hadn't paid for the pies.

"And they call us thieves!" sneered Gan, shaking his head.

"That pie man is a friend of mine," Twopenny growled. "Well, he gives me a crust that's fallen off sometimes. Mevon's a good fellow. Just got his journeyman's certificate, but he has to rent a cart because he's not related to anyone at a bakery. He works hard, and just barely pays his rent. I can't believe that they just took it, like that!"

"Who's the pie man going to report them to?" Toscar pointed out. "The Watch Captain is in the dungeon, from what I hear."

"That isn't right," frowned Liddy. "Drinking a little ale on the sly is one thing, but that was outright theft! From the Watch, of all people!"

"You're right," grunted Twopenny. "I think someone should mention it to them."

"Oh no, Twopenny, what are you doing?" Marga said, distressed, as he jumped down from the fountain and approached the two men, after they stopped arguing. Twopenny's palm was outstretched and he asked for a bit of the pies.

The taller of the two ignored him. The shorter did not. Instead, he stalked over to Twopenny and began to angrily berate him. Loudly. Loudly enough to draw the attention of bystanders, again.

"No, no, *no*," Marga said to herself, worriedly. "You don't just go up to the City Watch! That's begging for trouble! This is bad."

"Twopenny is a bold fellow," nodded Toscar, nervously.

"He's going to find himself in front of a magistrate, if he's too bold," warned Liddy.

Gatina watched as the shorter watchman slapped Twopenny firmly across the face, sending him spinning back so that he stumbled and fell. The crowd parted to avoid his touch, like the dirty little boy was not worth their compassion.

But then she quickly realized that the bystanders moved to avoid the *watchman,* not Twopenny. Some gasped at the rough treatment of a child – even a nit. The folk of Falas obviously expected better behavior out of their public servants.

But the watchman didn't seem to care. The man's face was beet red, he was so enraged and intent on his harassment of her friend. Ignoring the disapproval of the townsfolk, he began to kick and stomp at Twopenny, who quickly crab-walked away from the watchman before he could grab at him.

But the watchman kept coming, shouting at the boy far more than the offense deserved. He tried to kick him several times with his heavy boots. He was so intent that he did not see a priestess approach, a nun devoted to Ifnia, by the color of her habit.

Like most clergy, the coinsisters and coinbrothers of Ifnia were allowed to beg for alms in the streets, gates, and markets of the city, Gatina knew. But instead of merely carrying a begging bowl, they carried a pouch of pennies and a pouch of dice. A laborer could try his luck to win up to three pennies, dicing with the clergy of the goddess of luck.

It was traditional to tip the clergy one of the pennies, if you won all three rounds, because you also got a token good for entrance to the temple. Win or lose, they came away with a special blessing for good fortune and an invitation to the temple and higher stakes. Ifnites were a popular sect, especially in the poorer parts of town where luck was thin.

But many a fellow had gotten his lunch paid for or took home a bit of coin. Most lost their pennies to the temple.

This coinsister did not look particularly cheerful, as she confronted the Watchmen. She was angry at what she'd witnessed.

Twopenny rolled behind her, clinging to her robe as he peeked at the watchman. The priestess finally put an end to it, loudly shaming both watchmen in the process, and she helped Twopenny get to his feet. The angry man glared at the nit, who dusted himself off and glared back, as the nun asked to see if he'd been injured. Then she, too, glared at the two Watchmen, and escorted Twopenny back to the broken fountain.

It was clear that the belligerent man wanted to pursue the matter, but the crowd and his fellow were clearly on the side of the nun. They might be corrupt, but they knew better than to confront a member of the clergy. No sane watchman wanted to start an argument with a coinsister.

"All Twopenny did was ask for food!" Marga told the priestess, as she helped him back to his customary place. "He didn't threaten the men."

"And it was food they'd stolen!" Twopenny agreed, angrily, as he rubbed his bruised face. "From my friend Mevon! All I did was point that out, and then ask for a bite!"

"I can't believe the Watch would behave so poorly," the mature nun grumbled, glancing and glaring at the two as they continued their patrol. "It's the times we live in, children," she said, turning back to them. "Ever since the Duke died, life has been rolling threes and eights in this town!" she complained. "No respect, anymore. Folk are scared," she warned. "Stealing, and beating a defenseless child! It's outrageous!"

"What can you do, Sister?" shrugged Toscar. "Their captain is in the dungeon. And a magistrate isn't going to listen to a poor fellow like Mevon – let alone a nit. Life's a gamble," he said, philosophically, clearly trying to impress her with his worldly wisdom.

"Of course it is!" the coinsister agreed, fiercely. "But the rules should be fixed! If a watchman wants to wheedle a discount with a merchant on his patrols, that's one thing. If one of you nits is acting up or stealing, then maybe a beating would be preferable to the magistrate's bench. But to act like a thug, not an officer of the Watch, in front of the public they're supposed to be on watch for?" she fumed, shaking her head. "No respect!"

"Why is everyone so . . . tense, Sister?" Liddy asked nervously, but politely.

"More chaos at the palace, most likely," the nun sighed. "Vichetral of Rhemes is trying to be duke when there's already a lawful heir. Bold and ugly, he is. Fortune won't favor him for long, if he lets things get this bad," she warned. "When there's trouble in the palace, there's soon trouble on the streets. Only Our Lady's favor can save us from that fate, and I don't see good odds for that. My abbess is livid with what she's hearing! Arrests, people getting sacked, all manner of chaos. Folk are jumpy. Scared. The divination dice have been rolling dark numbers. Nothing good will come of it. I'm glad you're alright, boy," she said, looking at Twopenny. "Your name is Twopenny?" she added, amused. "That's a lucky name!"

"Yes, Sister, on account of how much I earn in a day begging," he said, smartly. Gatina had heard him explain his name a half-dozen ways, no two of them alike. "Not that I'm trying to undercut the clergy, understand," he added, slyly.

"A boy needs to eat," she agreed, with a sigh, and tossed him a penny from her pouch. He caught it deftly in his fist.

"How about a token, and I'll try to double this at the temple?" Twopenny asked, cocking his head.

"Perhaps . . . in five years," she smirked. The temple of Fortune would not cater to the prayers of children by tradition. "How about you buy some lunch and say a few prayers for the city? But if you come by the temple tomorrow, I'll see if there isn't a chore or two that's worth a meal. Blessings of Fortune be on you, children. But don't depend on that . . . be careful. The streets aren't feeling lucky, this week."

"Only the fool fights the darkness, the tides, or the winds of the storm; make your efforts fruitful and to purpose, and when the twilight inevitably breaks, be away from harm and well into shadow."

– from Lord Tyrusal's Heist Journal,
as relayed in **The Shield of Darkness**

CHAPTER FIFTEEN
OCCUPATION

When she explained what had happened at the fountain to her mother and Onnelik that night, they both nodded thoughtfully.

"The coinsister is right," her cousin agreed. "They're often good judges of how the people are feeling. They see all sorts of folk, from peasants and stableboys to lords of the realm. But you have to understand that some in the City Watch didn't care about right and wrong, despite the oaths they take. The watchmen have been known to use their power as a means to bully those they are meant to protect. These nits have no one to stand up for them, save the clergy, and most of the temples ignore the problem – even hers. It was good timing that the sister came along when she did, lest your friend find himself in a worse way."

"But all he did was ask for food," Gatina protested. Before she could add her own thoughts about how unfair the situation was, Lady Minnureal spoke.

"My Kitten, I believe what Cousin Onnelik means to say is that oftentimes, thanks to their authority, the City Watch sometimes view themselves in positions higher than those they serve. Even those who are usually restrained in using their authority are encouraged to abuse it, when the political situation is uncertain. Power is shifting in the city, and that means everyone's futures are uncertain, even the watchmen's. Those who are already corrupt are tempted to even more graft, while those fellows who might hold them to account keep silent out of fear and insecurity. If things in the palace come to a head, they will have to choose sides . . . and if they choose poorly, they lose their livelihoods or even their lives."

"That doesn't stop some from taking sides," Onnelik said, ominously. "One of my informants says that Vichetral is appointing one of his vassals over the Watch in a few weeks. A Rhemesman," he added.

Gatina had soaked up enough politics to know how contentious such an appointment would be. The folk of Falas were naturally suspicious of the lords of Rhemes, across the river. "Some in the Watch are already scrambling for position, in that case. Some are aiding Vichetral's effort with quiet threats."

"They won't stay quiet much longer," her mother said, grimly. "From what Shadow has said, that type of behavior will be on the rise as Vichetral takes power. He is marshaling support wherever he can: among the temples, the nobility, the burghers, the merchants, and the City Watch. Jenerard and his Rats embrace the use of force to keep the common folk in line. Vichetral is not finding a lot of the support he seeks, but there are always men in the Watch who care very little about tradition and the law they're sworn to serve. Power and money are their motivation."

"Exactly, Minnie," Onnelik said. "Darkness and obfuscation are the best defenses, in such times. Be very careful, always, Kitten," her cousin advised. "Keep your eyes open and do not let your guard down."

"I'll be fine. In fact, I have another job for Hanik tomorrow, at noon. I'll come by afterward just so you can see I'm not drowned in a canal somewhere."

The next day, Gatina arose before dawn and got to the butchery well before noon, quietly haunting the street until it was near time to go in. Flerian greeted her by name, and had her wait while he fetched the parcel from Hanik.

"Same rules as last time," the butcher instructed, handing her the parcel. "Get there by the first bell. Be back here with the receipt by the second," he reminded her. "We're going early, this week. Gavin is having some kind of fit, or something," he shrugged.

"I'll be back by the second bell," she promised, before settling the heavy load in the basket and covering it with a rag. Then she was off to the gluepot warehouse.

She found her way there even more easily, this trip. Just as last time, Cleon was waiting outside . . . although this time he was sporting a black eye.

"What happened?" she asked, abruptly, when she saw it.

"Boss came up short with the money," the gangster admitted, gruffly. "A *lot* short. I warned you about him," he said, shaking his head. "Probably just a mistake with the books, but he's swearing over a hundred silver just up and walked out of his office."

"That doesn't seem likely," Gatina said, sympathetically. "This place is a fortress!" she lied. Indeed, she could see at least three or four ways an enterprising thief could get in, besides the route she'd chosen.

"That's what I told him," agreed Cleon. "So now he thinks it might be one of us who took it. As if we were that crazy as to steal from Gavin. Hey, there's Mandar's girl. Just on time, too," he noted, as the temple bell struck a single time.

Cleon once again led the girls up the creepy, creaking stairs to the office. Gatina reflected that it was much easier to walk across the catwalk than crawl under it, dangling from the bottom, but she found having both experiences very interesting. Only this time, Gavin was not in a jovial enough mood to attempt to lick anyone's face. Indeed, the gangster looked exceedingly grumpy. And dangerous.

"Sixty-one and two copper, for Mandar," he declared, shaking his head as he made out the receipt. "That's low." A moment later he unwrapped Gatina's bundle. "Eighty-two and five!" he said, nodding appreciatively. "Tell Hanik good work. Let's see that again, next time!" he wrote the second receipt out and then handed one to each girl. But as they tried to take them, he stopped, and fixed both girls with a penetrating stare.

"You have any idea about some money that might have wandered out of my office, girls?" he asked, sharply.

"What money?" Gatina asked. "I get a penny for delivery. That's the only money I've gotten."

"What's this about?" demanded Navala, angrily. "We didn't take anything!"

"Gavin, enough!" Cleon barked. "You can't accuse everyone you see of stealing from you! You know they didn't take it! They're just a couple of stupid nits! Leave them be!"

The gangster growled and glared at the girls one last time, but he let go of the receipts. Gatina folded hers into the basket and then followed Navala downstairs. Cleon stayed behind, presumably to argue with his boss over the missing money again.

"What a grouch!" Navala muttered.

"At least there wasn't any licking, this time," Gatina shuddered. "But he was plenty mad. I wonder what happened to that money? Cleon thinks he just put the wrong numbers into the books and made a mistake."

"It isn't good to talk about such things," Navala said, over her shoulder. "Not with these folk. The less you know, the better. The less you say, the better still."

"I know," Gatina agreed, guiltily. "I'm just curious." As she plodded down the stairs, she spotted something that she hadn't seen from the catwalk. In another part of the warehouse, just out of sight from the higher angle, she saw a single door being obscured by a few bolts of sailcloth. From her sketch of the building, there shouldn't be a door there. There was a tailor shop on the other side of the wall, she recalled. There was no reason for a door to be there. Those walls were thick stone and brick, she knew. Gavin wouldn't have allowed the access to his warehouse.

Unless the door *didn't* go through. It might lead *down*, she realized. Down to the secret canal. It would be easy enough for a couple of men to move the bolts of cloth, and then, she imagined, a narrow stairwell leading below. It wouldn't even pierce the thick wall, she estimated. It would be an easy access to the secret dock Gavin had referenced.

Gatina immediately jerked her head back to focus in front of her – not a bad idea, considering the rickety nature of the stairs. She dutifully followed Navala, trying her best to look like timid, determined Lissa the Mouse.

"See you in a few days," she mumbled to the other girl, before hurrying back to the butcher's shop with her receipt. She was careful, as she walked quickly through the cobbled streets. There was a certain caution still lingering in the air, she noted. The people who shuffled about their business after the luncheon hour looked worried and anxious, she noted as her bare feet propelled her toward Hanik's shop.

She saw why, a few blocks from the warehouse. Soldiers had set up a checkpoint, where they were stopping and questioning all who were trying to cross the Processional. Not City Watch. Soldiers in mail and carrying swords and spears, wearing light blue livery.

There were eight of them, blocking the street. A cart had been placed to constrict the flow of traffic, and while four of them stood menacingly around the edges of the checkpoint, spears in hand and swords at the ready, the other four questioned everyone who wanted to get from one side of the street to the other about their business.

Gatina almost turned around and tried to find another route – she could not be late, she knew. But she also realized that doing so would attract more attention than if she meekly submitted to their questions. She dutifully got into line behind the other subdued townspeople, making sure to quietly hide Hanik's receipt where the soldiers would not dare to seek it.

"What's your business, here?" demanded the Ancient in charge, as he dismissed the goodwife in front of her.

"I'm running errands for Hanik the Butcher," she said, proudly. "He sent me with a delivery of sausages, and I must return for my next one," she added, brusquely.

"Hanik the butcher?" the Ancient asked, as if she'd used one of the Sea Folk's strange names. "Never heard of him!"

"His shop is over off of Parchment Street," she explained, annoyed. "And he owes me a copper for this. If you keep me from getting it . . ."

"Count Vichetral has declared that there will be no unnecessary travel in Falas," the Ancient boomed, arrogantly. "It's to quell civil unrest," he declared.

"What's this 'civil unrest'?" demanded Gatina – or, more properly, the nit Lissa the Mouse.

"The people getting unruly," the Ancient sneered.

"Well, keeping the people from doing their business, that might make them unruly, don't you think?" snapped Lissa. "You're keeping me from a copper!"

"And how is that entirely necessary?" chuckled the square-jawed Ancient.

"You want to know?" Lissa asked, her eyebrow cocked. "Let me whisper..."

She waited until the Ancient grudgingly leaned down and allowed her to whisper into his ear behind her cupped hand.

"Baron Jenerard is involved," she said cryptically, but insistently. She followed the admission with a steely glare in the older man's face, as if she had authority from the mysterious noble.

The Ancient did a double-take, until he recognized that the nit in front of him might be more than she appeared. After all, there were few who would invoke the name of Jenerard without knowledge of his newfound position at the palace. Or his involvement with Vichetral's ascendency.

"The Palace Rat?" grunted the Ancient. "Alright, pass. *Pass!*" he insisted, pushing Gatina through the checkpoint with a firm hand on her shoulders. Before she'd taken two steps, he was already interrogating the confused cobbler behind her in a loud tone of voice.

Gatina walked away with determination, proud of the strategy she'd come up with on the spur of the moment. Using Jenerard's name in such a situation was dangerous, she realized. She'd taken a risk in bluffing her way through the checkpoint.

But she'd succeeded, she'd realized. She'd fooled not just an adult, but a soldier in charge of finding dissidents working against Vichetral's attempt at grabbing power.

That thought gave her the energy to skulk back to Hanik's arriving just before the second bell.

"Here!" she said, thrusting the receipt at Flerian. "You didn't say there would be soldiers!" she said, accusingly.

"Soldiers?" Flerian asked, rubbing his shaven jaw. "Where?"

"On the Processional," Gatina related, indignantly. "They were stopping everyone and questioning them. I had to come up with a story to get through. They didn't want me to go," she added.

"Then why'd they let you?" Flerian asked, puzzled.

"Because I'm really sodding good at coming up with stories!" she said, impatiently. "The whole bloody town is getting locked down," she groused. "What happens next time, when they don't believe my tale of a sickly old aunt?"

"Good question," Flerian admitted, perplexed. But he took the receipt, and glanced at it before tucking it away. "How many soldiers?" he asked, after a pause.

"Eight," she said, without hesitation. "All spearmen, but they had swords. And in the livery of the Count Vichetral," she added. "He a friend of yours?"

"He likes sausages, I hear," Flerian said, fumbling in his purse for her payment. "Three silver pennies, today. For your trouble," he added, apologetically, as he dropped the tiny coins into her waiting palm. "Check in again in a day or so," he ordered. "I don't know what the soldiers mean, but business has to go on."

"Thanks," she said, grudgingly, as she eyed the coins before closing her dirty fingers greedily around them. "Be careful going home tonight," she warned, suddenly. "Those fellows didn't look like they were playing around." Then she spun around on her heel and headed back out into the street.

"Thanks!" called Flerian. "Two days! Or be at the fountain if I need you before," he added.

"If they let me," she shrugged, without turning around. "Bloody soldiers!"

Gatina didn't try to return to the broken fountain and see her friends. She had too much to report to her mother and Onnelik. If Vichetral was taking control of the streets, they needed to know, she reasoned. And they needed to know about the concealed door, and probable staircase to the sewers. She carefully returned to Onnelik's townhouse using back alleys and lanes to avoid the major streets. As a result, it took her nearly twice as long to get back, just before dark.

"There's a curfew, now, orders from the palace," Onnelik said, as he dabbed at her face with a towel in the kitchen, wiping away the street grime. She would use soot and dirt again in the morning to return as Lissa, but for now, she was Gatina. At least for a few hours. "Another few thousand of Vichetral's men arrived today," he murmured. "He's extending his control beyond the palace, and into the entire city!"

"I know," Gatina said, impatiently enduring the man's attempt to wipe some of the dirt from her brow. "I got stopped by them, today. Checkpoint on the Processional. Rude, they were," she snorted.

"Of course they were, they're conducting an occupation," sighed Onnelik, finally giving up on her face. "You don't occupy a palace with nice and pleasant military forces. And you don't occupy a palace unless you occupy the entire city. The entire point is to make sure the population knows that they are being controlled. Bullies!" he fumed, shaking his head. "They're nothing but bullies with swords."

"Where is Mother? Mistress?" Gatina corrected.

"She's . . . on another mission," Onnelik said softly. "Hopefully she'll be back by midnight. Why?"

"I just have a few ideas," admitted Gatina.

"This is not the time for ideas, Kitten," Onnelik clucked. "This is a very dangerous time for us all."

"Which is why I'm having ideas," Gatina reasoned.

"Shadow is the man with the ideas," the counterfeiter argued. "He knows far more than we do. Doing anything without his blessing—"

"It's about Lady Isadra, and her brother the baron, and those hostages," Gatina explained.

"That is not your concern, Kitten," chided Onnelik, gently. "You have a very limited role in things, right now. A dangerous role, but limited. I caution you against doing anything . . . rash."

"I wouldn't do anything any other kitten wouldn't do," argued Gatina, crossly.

"That's what I'm afraid of," Onnelik said, dryly. "Look, my dear. I applaud your bravery and your professionalism – indeed, you are perhaps the most promising student I've seen in either House in all my life," he admitted. "You seem made for this sort of work.

"That being said," he continued, as he threw a few logs on the kitchen fire and filled the tea kettle from the urn in the corner, "this is not a mere training exercise, anymore. Real lives are at stake. There were nine executions in front of the palace this morning," he related, his face growing pale. "Good men, honest ministers and officials of Duke Lenguin who happen to not approve of Count Vichetral's assumption of power. Nine!" Onnelik said, more to himself than to her. "Vichetral is making no pretense of legitimacy, beyond his constant public mourning of Lenguin and Enora, and his constant blame of Castal for their deaths. He has made it clear that he plans on seizing control of all of Alshar, from Enultramar to Vorone, and anyone who stands against him will pay a price."

"That is not his right!" declared Gatina, her nostrils flaring.

"Of course not, my dear," Onnelik said, gently, leaning against the wall next to the stove, a concerned expression on his face. "And that's why we do what we do. But that doesn't mean he won't do it. Alas, Alshar's history is filled with tyrants who usurp power. Occasionally, it has been a good thing. But mostly it has led to suffering, when the rightful duke has been overcome by such men. Your family knows this, Kitten. We fight against it. But not at the expense of our lives, if we can help it. Martyrs are noble, it is said . . . but they rarely accomplish anything useful."

The common-sense explanation took Gatina aback; after her rough treatment at the checkpoint, and the rough manner in which Vichetral's soldiers had behaved, she wanted nothing more than to strike a blow for justice.

Yet she understood Onnelik's perspective more than she wanted to admit. The armored soldiers that now marched through Falas' streets were one expression of the Count's newfound power. The Brotherhood's cooperation was another. She had learned all too well how much the latter had control over the lives of the people of Falas. She had no doubt that, if ordered, the former could wreak havoc on the common folk of the city and terrorize them into compliance with the Count's seizure of power.

"Perhaps," she sighed, unwilling to entirely accept his pronouncement. "But perhaps we'll see what kittens can accomplish."

"The world can change in an instant. A spark can become a blaze or a raindrop a torrent. A dog may bark and call unexpected attention, or a twig may break at an inconvenient moment. Fortune fouls the best of us at the worst of times. The Craft of the House is to avoid unnecessary entanglements, when they are foreseen. The Art of the House is to reply to Ifnia's dubious grace with cunning and initiative."

– *from* **The Shield of Darkness**

CHAPTER SIXTEEN
THE BROKEN FOUNTAIN RIOT

"Well, we have a little bit more information on what's going on in the palace," Minnureal sighed, when she finally returned that evening. It had been a difficult journey across town, she reported, because of Count Vichetral's ordered curfew for the city. She'd had to dodge soldiers the entire way home, just as Gatina had. "Shadow was able to get another operative into the palace, a very good one. They tell us that arrests are going to start happening tonight – entire families. Which means the first few hundred prisoners will be taken out in the next few days."

"He's moving quickly," observed Onnelik, shaking his head. "And he is very certain of himself."

"Baron Jenerard has already secured a barge large enough to receive them. And we've identified the exact estate to which they will be transported and held. But they will have to use their underground port; there have already been two riots along the docks as people object to the Count's rule," she said, grimly. "Small ones, and they were put down quickly, but people got hurt."

"I thought the Brotherhood controlled the docks," frowned Onnelik.

"They control *some* of the docks, a few warehouses, and many of the stevedores," her mother corrected. "Most are controlled by legitimate companies, temples, Coastlords and trading houses. Those are where the riots happened. As the news about Lenguin and Vichetral's new council gets out, more and more people are rejecting it."

"Enough more?" asked Onnelik, pointedly.

"Alas, no, we don't think so," sighed Minnureal. "Vichetral has the support of Leod, Count of Roen. Even though he's a cousin to Lenguin. He has troops on the way down the river to support Vichetral, and the few barons who might have stood against them in provincial Falas are unorganized. Many are wary of the uncertain politics of the time," she explained. "Others are being manipulated to hold their peace. While he enjoys many other faults, Vichetral is skillful at dismantling his opposition."

"So what does that mean for the prisoners?" asked Gatina, curiously.

"We don't know, yet," her mother admitted. "The original plan was to take them upriver and hide them in the countryside, if we were able to rescue them. But Count Leod's army will make that difficult. We need to find someplace closer . . . and downriver. We need a friendly estate, someone who will not reveal where they are hidden. We're searching, but it's difficult to know who to trust. But as of now, the plan is to go along with the rescue."

"What will we be doing?" Gatina asked, imagining a sudden attack on the warehouse, with swords and knives.

"As for you, *you* will stay home," insisted her mother. "This is not the kind of operation a first-year apprentice thief is useful in. I must not reveal any details, but there are many others involved, now. Count Vichetral has many enemies, and already they are coming together against him. But after your last night-time activities, I need to know where you are, and that you are safe, while all this is happening."

"Is Cat going to be staying home and staying safe?" Gatina challenged, indignantly.

"That is none of your concern," her mother said, her eyes narrowing. "Kitten, there is much happening, right now, and things could go horribly wrong at any moment. I have a great deal to worry about. I do not need to worry about you. Nor need you worry about your brother.

Trust that I would not risk either of you for anything, if it can be helped."

"I'll behave," Gatina promised. "I just wanted to know."

"Of course you did," sighed her mother. "But what you don't know, you can't tell. Other people's lives depend on that," she reminded her. "Discretion."

Gatina nodded . . . but she also felt left out, after all she had done. She suspected that Atopol would not be staying home. They would be using him in some capacity, she was sure. Even though he was older and more experienced and had actually gotten his *rajira*, she resented that.

"Is there no one who will stand against the Count?" asked Onnelik, exasperated. "Vichetral will take us back a century! You know what kind of man he is."

"Who could stand against him?" asked Gatina.

"Anguin, Lenguin's son, is duke by right," Minnureal reminded her. "But he is a prisoner in Castal. Vichetral knows Rard and Grendine are pressuring the boy to swear allegiance and fealty to them as King and Queen. And he knows that he would rather rule a duchy in truth than be a mere count under a puppet duke and a foreign king. Vichetral's attempting to justify his rule with nationalism. Our agent has learned he plans to begin issuing a series of edicts to that effect. Thereafter, any who take issue with his control of the duchy will be deemed traitors . . . with the usual penalties for treason," she said, grimly. "All the more reason why discretion is essential, now."

"Will he crown himself duke?" Onnelik asked, with a wince.

"I haven't heard, but it's doubtful, from what I know," her mother said. "As long as Anguin lives, even in exile, Vichetral would be a usurper in name, as well as in fact. His legitimacy as a self-appointed steward of the realm is tenuous enough. To take the coronet and proclaim himself duke while Anguin still lives would, indeed, inspire an uprising against him."

"I fear for the boy, then," sighed Onnelik. "But we can do nothing about that. These prisoners, however, we may have a chance to save. If we can find them some safe location. What about your estate in the east?" he asked.

"It is not large enough, nor do we suffer outsiders there," her mother said, shaking her head. "Much the same problem with the other old Coastlord families. We've clung to the cities and allowed the Narasi to hold the countryside. With certain exceptions. And many of those would side with Vichetral against Castal, once he frames it that way."

"Leaving Lenguin's loyalists at his mercy," sighed Onnelik. "Minny, this cannot stand!"

"It must be endured," she countered. "We have no other choice."

THE NEXT MORNING THE STREETS OF FALAS WERE QUIET – BUT NOT peaceful. The common folk went about their business as they could, filing through more checkpoints and watching as yet more soldiers detained and arrested those thought too loyal to the late duke, or thought to be too much against Count Vichetral. Gatina knew her mother probably would not want her out wandering in such conditions, but she neglected to ask her, before she slipped out.

Disguised as a nit she had more freedom to move through the streets than a noblewoman. Indeed, she saw the well-dressed nobility was especially singled out by Vichetral's soldiers for inspection, while the poorer artisans were waved through the checkpoints with only a glance. So was she, as she made her way to the broken fountain. Indeed, the soldiers didn't even look at her as she walked back through where they were stationed.

But when she arrived, she discovered that the haunt of her friends was occupied by soldiers. Four big men in chainmail hauberks, wearing surcoats bearing Count Vichetral's device, were standing guard at the intersection around the fountain while a dozen more raided a nearby townhouse.

Concerned, Gatina searched the area for her friends. She found all of them had fled, save Marga, who was doing a credible job of unobtrusively watching the matter unfold from the shelter of a fruit vendor's shop. The vendor had wisely closed his store and covered his wares with a blanket before disappearing inside. He didn't even bother to shoo away Marga, so worried he was about the arrest.

"What's happening?" Gatina asked her, as she squatted next to her friend.

"They're going after a counting man, this time," Marga frowned. "He doesn't even work in the palace, like the scribe they arrested. Only, he has a big family," she said, nodding toward the brick house. Like the other residences on the street, it had a narrow presentation but went back deeply and was three stories high. "He works for a lawbrother, they say."

"A counting man?" asked Gatina. "What does he do?"

"He counts things," shrugged Marga. "Mostly money, I imagine. They keep track of who owns how much of what."

"Why would someone want to arrest a counting man?" Gatina asked.

Marga shrugged again. "There are plenty of people who want to arrest them. Or beat them. I guess it depends on who you owe money to. Oh, look! They're *resisting!*" she said, excitedly.

Indeed, a commotion was erupting at the townhouse, as a soldier was kicked through the door and back into the street by four large men who had cudgels in their hands. Windows opened, above, and several women and boys began shouting down at the soldiers. A few more men emerged behind the artisans and stood bravely in front of the door.

"It appears that the counting man doesn't want to be arrested," observed Gatina, as some of the neighbors came out of their homes at the noise.

"Or his family doesn't," Marga agreed. "Let's hope the family of carters next door doesn't get involved," she said, indicating the wider house nearby. "They're big men, too, and there are a lot of them."

Gatina could not make out what was being said, there was so much shouting between the artisans and the soldiers. The Ancient trying to make the arrest was waving around a scroll of parchment, screaming, while the family shouted and jeered in return. The other soldiers held their spears threateningly, but the artisans did not look like they were willing to back down.

When the Ancient finally ordered his men forward against them to get through the door, a crowd had begun to gather behind them. Mostly just curious, Gatina could watch some rumor get passed about the incident as if it was a bottle of wine, from one onlooker to another. Whatever was being said angered most who heard it, and within moments there was a growing buzz of murmuring in the crowd.

"Uh, oh, the carters have arrived," Marga grunted, nodding toward the building next door. A stream of large men poured out into the street bearing axes, knives, and staves, and immediately menaced the soldiers who were threatening their neighbors. Calls for the City Watch were yelled.

"I don't think the Watch will get involved," Marga predicted. "Not against soldiers."

"Would you want to get into the middle of that argument?" snorted Gatina.

That's when things turned truly ugly. As the soldiers continued to try to press their way into the counting man's home, someone in the crowd threw a rock that rang off of the iron helmet of one of the soldiers from behind. At about the same time, the women on the second floor began flinging pots and pans, crockery and sticks of firewood down on the heads of the soldiers. In reply, the soldiers began striking at the resisting artisans with the butts of their spears.

That was too much for the carters, apparently. With a scream of defiance their leader swung a cudgel at the head of a soldier, and then all was chaos.

Gatina was shocked by how quickly the scene turned violent, going from angry protest to a violent mob. Vicious fighting broke out everywhere, as the soldiers struggled to defend themselves against the townspeople. In seconds, Gatina saw the first bloody face appear; then, like spring blossoms, they began to appear everywhere. The soldiers were using the sharp end of their spears, now, and some had drawn swords.

"It's a riot!" Marga screamed over the tumult in amazement. More townspeople were arriving, now, men who worked in the shops and workshops along the street and heard the shouts and noise. A lot of men, men who had spent days fearful of the occupation and angry at Vichetral's usurpation, Gatina realized. And some women, too, she discovered, when a large washerwoman was suddenly flaying about with her washtub, screaming angrily.

"We need to stay put," Gatina advised her friend as fear and excitement rose in her. "If we step one foot out there, we'll be swept away like a river!"

"Let's hope no one notices us," Marga agreed, reaching up and stealing a few apples from the rack, above. She handed one to Gatina. "Besides, I wouldn't know which way to run," she confessed.

Gatina nodded in agreement as she bit into the apple and watched the explosion of violence.

There were hundreds of people on the street, now, and the soldiers seemed surrounded. One of them was frantically sounding a horn, she saw, as two of his mates kept the crowd at bay with spear and sword. The mob seemed a screaming, wrathful creature of its own, now, Gatina observed, wide-eyed. They proved it, a few moments later, when a mounted knight attempted to lead another squadron of soldiers into the fray. He was knocked off his horse by a flung frying pan a moment later. From the other direction, a steady stream of townsfolk was arriving to assist their neighbors, or were just curious about the commotion . . . and then became swept up in it.

It was hypnotic to watch the riot unfold in front of them. Seeing normal, civilized folk suddenly fight so viciously was surprising, especially against armed and armored soldiers. But then, she reasoned, the people had been fearful and angry for days, now. She watched as one group of soldiers tried to get around the crowd, and instead get pinned against the buildings by the swirling madness.

That group got close to where she and Marga were hiding and she was anxious, for a moment, that the fight would spill over into them. They weren't more than ten feet away, on the other side of the stall, when the last soldier of the squadron fell, his spear shaft breaking in half under him as he was beaten with a plank of wood. The crowd moved on, once the man was down, his face bloodied, but one lad of twelve or thirteen was gleefully jumping up and down on his armored back.

The noise was too loud, now, for the girls to speak to each other without shouting. More soldiers were arriving at the end of the street, but the mob still outnumbered them dramatically. At a horn call, however, Gatina watched them take formation and begin driving the crowd back at the point of their spears, while other soldiers grabbed those who got too close to their lines and threw them to the ground. The mob moved back and compressed against itself. But the townspeople did not run.

A hail of cobblestones and firewood flew from them against the soldiers, instead, and someone had brought out a trestle tabletop to use as a shield against them. For a tense moment it looked like the soldiers would be overwhelmed, until they reformed their ranks.

The four soldiers guarding the fountain were long gone, of course, and someone had pulled a two-wheeled cart next to it to form a barricade of sorts. Four horn calls from the other streets announced the arrival of more troops from other directions. Someone was ringing the bells of a temple wildly to add to the noise. Men were manning the barricade, some bearing swords or spears they had captured in the brawl, others wielding axes and shovels or long knives.

Gatina could not imagine who was organizing them – it didn't seem anyone was. People were just deciding it was the right time to revolt against the soldiers occupying their city and interrupting their commerce. Many of those people were now lying on the ground, their faces and hands covered with blood.

"I don't think this is going to be a safe place for much longer!" Marga yelled.

"I know!" Gatina agreed. "But which way do we go?"

Before Marga could answer, a portly man with a bloody smock and sword in his hand rushed by, caught sight of the fallen soldier, and began to move on him menacingly.

"Hey!" Marga called, angrily, as she scrambled to her feet and lurched to interpose herself between the man and the wounded soldier. "He's already down!"

"Shut up, nit!" the man sneered at her, as he turned toward the girls. "It's a bloody riot! Off with you, before you get some of this!" he said, hoisting his captured blade triumphantly.

"Leave us alone!" Gatina screamed, placing herself in front of Marga. "He's wounded! There's plenty of soldiers over there to fight!"

With a mindless cry, the man instead turned his fury on the two girls, backhanding Marga with his left hand while he swung at Gatina crudely with his sword. It was a weak strike, she thought to herself, critically. He'd never held a sword in his life, she was certain. Moving out of the way was simple.

So was picking up the shard of the soldier's broken spear shaft. It was heavier than the practice swords she'd used in the country, but about the same length. The next time the man threw a lazy attack at her, the thick wood blocked the blade resolutely.

His eyes went wide, and his fat shaven face contorted into a snarl as he confronted Gatina. He struck at her again, this time with more strength, but it was the same clumsy attack from the same angle as before. Gatina smiled to herself as she blocked it easily, and then quickly flicked her makeshift weapon in a lunge – first at his wrist, and then across his brow. The first shot flung his stolen blade out of his hand. The second sent him tumbling to the flagstones.

It was odd, striking a man in earnest for the first time. It gave Gatina a feeling of power. And of fear.

"We've got to get out of here, Lissa!" screamed Marga, grabbing her hand. Her bottom lip was bruised and bloody where the rioter had struck her. Gatina nodded, and took a moment to see if there was any further danger to them, and then dropped the stick.

"I need to do something," she said, resisting her friend's grip. She knelt and listened to the soldier's chest – his heart was still beating, she could see, and though his face was caked in dirt and blood, he was still breathing through bloody nostrils. He was alive.

He was also unconscious, Gatina noted. And entirely unable to protect his purse. It took but a few moments to separate it from his belt. Then, pausing only to grab her basket, Gatina let Marga pull her into the street and past the fountain that was fast becoming a barricade.

It was a timely retreat, they realized, for a moment later the distant horns sounded again, and the sound of horses' hooves could be heard over the din. A lot of horses.

"To the canal," suggested Marga, pulling her in the direction of the dirty drainage ditch. "We can hide under the bridge!"

Gatina nodded and ran with her friend through the remainder of the crowd, until they could tumble down the narrow bank and slide into the small space under the bridge just as the first horsemen arrived, above. It wasn't much of a bridge, but it was blessed darkness when she needed to hide. The horsemen were more soldiers, of course. Likely called to quell the disturbance and rescue their fellows. There seemed to be no end to them, and they were loud. But they eventually passed.

"That ... that ... " Gatina said, her lungs heaving for breath.

"That was a bloody *riot*," Marga nodded, gravely, her eyes wide with shock. "A real riot ..."

"We could have been killed," Gatina realized.

"We nearly were," reminded Marga, turning to face her friend in the shadows. "How in two hells did you ... how did you do that ..."

"What?" Gatina said, defensively. "I just hit him with a stick!"

"You didn't 'just hit him with a stick,' Lissa. You bested him and you did it so fast I barely saw it!" accused Marga. "I'm happy you did, don't mistake me," she said, pulling her half-eaten apple out from her dress and taking a bite. "But Lissa ... you're more lion than mouse! Where did you learn that?"

"I just did it," she shrugged, annoyed. She realized that any explanation she gave would only risk more questions.

"And what did you do to that soldier?" she asked.

"Made sure that he was still alive," shrugged Gatina. "And relieved him of his coin purse," she added, pulling the little bag out of her basket. "He didn't seem to be using it, so ..."

"Lissa!" Marga said, surprised. "You *didn't!*"

"A lot of things are going to go missing in this riot, I think," she shrugged. "A purse is a small price to pay for saving his life against that . . . that ..."

"He was a brute and a coward," Marga assured her. "You don't hurt people who are already wounded. I wish you'd stopped to get his purse, too."

"You were rushing me," complained Gatina. "How is your lip?"

"It stings," the other girl admitted, as she continued chewing her stolen apple. "How much did you get?" she asked, interested.

Gatina spilled the coins into her palm and was disappointed. Four silver pennies, a single ounce coin, and nine copper pennies, as well as some iron slugs. Hardly a fortune.

"Trygg's Grace!" Marga swore, staring at the money in the shadows. "That's a lot!"

"Here," Gatina said, taking the big ounce coin for herself, and dumping the rest of the money into her friend's dirty palm. "Take it. Hide it," she emphasized.

"But I didn't earn this," Marga said, frowning. "I didn't even help you steal it!"

"You're my friend," Gatina shrugged. "I'd feel bad if I spent it all on myself. You can buy food for weeks, with that," she pointed out. "Or a new cap. Or—"

"Or a gown for the midsummer ball, at the palace," her friend said, sarcastically. "Really, Lissa, this is a lot of money! Not enough for a gown, but . . ."

"This is worth far more," she said, holding out the big coin. "But it is easier for me to hide. And this way, if either of us are caught, gods forbid, neither will have the right amount of money," she pointed out.

"It just seems like a lot," grumbled Marga. But the girl began hiding it in her smock and her bundle. "What are you going to do, now?"

"Get away from this riot," snorted Gatina. "You should, too," she advised. "Go find a shrine or temple, or a friendly hayloft, and stay put until this passes. It will pass," she insisted. "Just stay out of sight until it's over."

"Where are you going?" asked Marga, curious.

"Me? I'm going to find a wineshop," Gatina said, suddenly filled with resolve.

"Sometimes opportunities present themselves in the oddest of situations, I've noticed. It is said by the House that blessed Darkness guides our fate, yet I cannot help but wonder if such occasions are the work of Fortune, not Fate."

– *Gatina's Heist Journal*

CHAPTER SEVENTEEN
LADY ISADRA

Gatina found herself walking toward Lady Isadra's house, but she didn't know why. It was in the opposite direction of the riot, which made it a favorable direction, but she could not figure out why her feet had decided to take her there. Most of the traffic was headed in the other direction, toward the commotion. Including more soldiers, she saw, on foot and on horseback. A lot more.

Steadfastly, she kept moving forward, her head down, and tried to escape anyone's notice. That was pretty easy, until she got to the Processional. She had to alter her route by several blocks to get around another mob that seemed to be forming. She didn't want any part of that. One riot a day was quite enough.

The streets on the other side of the Processional were quiet, quieter than the first time she'd been here. People seemed to sense the mood on the street and were keeping inside. That was good, for Gatina's purposes. She didn't want many witnesses. But she noted that the wineshop was closed up, as was the chandler's stall next door. She passed by, wondering about the nice boy who'd given her information, last time. She hoped he was safe, and not out in the crowd, somewhere.

Lady Isadra's home was right where she remembered it. She slunk down the alleyway next to it and found herself back in the garden.

Instead of knocking for the attention of the cook, she climbed the cherry tree in the garden and waited.

Because she didn't have the faintest idea of why she was there.

Somehow, she knew, Lady Isadra was important. She was certain of it. She just didn't know why. She was indebted to Hanik the Butcher, her new husband worked at the palace, she had a new baby, she was the sister of a baron, she was newly come to Falas . . . Gatina ran through every fact she had about the woman, but nothing suggested itself. It was frustrating, she reflected, to be so compelled about something but without understanding why.

It was actually peaceful, up in the cherry tree, though she could hear the murmur of the crowd far away. This would be a decent place to hide, she decided. It overhung the roof of the woodshed, it was gloriously shady, and she had an excellent view of the back of the house and the garden below with little chance of being spotted.

That observation proved itself an hour later, when she was surprised to see Lady Isadra, herself, emerge from the back of the house with her new baby in her arms. The lady had apparently chosen to take some afternoon sunshine, it appeared, as she settled into a garden chair next to a little stone table. Gatina waited and watched for a while, until Lady Isadra pulled out a little book and began reading aloud.

Sighing to herself in frustration, Gatina wondered which card in her mother's deck was appropriate, for the moment. Each of the trump cards represented thoughtful action, in one way or another. In the end, Gatina fell back on OPPORTUNITY, and decided to act.

She let herself fall from the cherry tree as gracefully as possible, her basket in her hand. She landed without injury in the soft turf below, then stood to greet the startled noblewoman.

"You!" Lady Isadra said, her eyes wide with surprise and worry. "Tell the butcher I did as he asked!" she insisted, hurriedly.

"He knew you would," nodded Gatina. "I'm actually not working for him today."

"You're not?" asked the woman, confused, as she clutched her baby to her.

"No, not today. Today I'm working for myself," Gatina explained, and approached the table. "I got curious when I came here the other day. So I wanted to come by and . . . I guess I came by to talk to you."

"Talk to me? Goddess, why would you want to talk to me?" she demanded.

"You seem like a nice woman," Gatina shrugged. "I know the butcher's note disturbed you. I felt sorry for you."

"That's an unusual perspective to hear from a gangster's nit," Lady Isadra sniffed.

"Like I said, I'm not working for him, today. Today, I'm working for myself. And I wanted to talk to you. If you're feeling talkative. Maybe ask you a few things."

"If you're looking for money, I have very little," she sniffed.

"No, just conversation," assured Gatina. "Like, how much do you owe the butcher?"

"Now? After what I've done? Only forty ounces of silver, and some change," she admitted. "I would think you'd know that."

"Gangsters are notorious for not giving out details of their business," Gatina pointed out, taking a seat in the other chair. "I didn't even know about your account, until that day. Forty ounces? You borrowed eighty ounces of silver from Hanik?"

"I borrowed a hundred, but managed to pay back twenty, in the last year," she explained.

"Why?" asked Gatina. "I thought all you nobles were rich?"

"Are we?" she laughed, humorlessly. "Perhaps by some standards. I borrowed the money to pay for a gift for my lord husband. He loves to ride, and so I bought him a charger," she explained. "A very expensive charger."

"You spent a hundred ounces of silver on a *horse*?" asked Gatina, in disbelief.

"He's a quite magnificent horse," Lady Isadra said, defensively. "He loves riding it. I spent my own money on a new saddle and tack for it, but the horse was more than I had. I heard from one of my neighbors how to get a quiet loan at easy terms – a loan that would not cause gossip, lest I did not repay it. The terms seemed reasonable enough but . . . well, I've had to scrape the money from the household accounts. Or ask my brother or sisters for money to repay it. That was . . ."

"You didn't want to cause a scandal," nodded Gatina. "I understand. And you did do that thing Hanik wanted to do. So your debt is cut in half."

"Yes, though it shames me to have done it," she said, her cheeks turning red. "My brother is a proud supporter of Duke Lenguin. Or was," she corrected, sadly. "He and my family have always been stalwarts of the ducal house. And he hates Count Vichetral, after all he has done over the years to undermine the Duke."

"Tell me more about this brother of yours," Gatina persuaded.

"My brother? Antremin? He is the baron of Larethin, like our father before him."

"Larethin . . . is that where you grew up?" Gatina prompted.

"Aye, on the baronial estate. A beautiful place," she said, clearly homesick. "Larethin is a grand place. Fifteen domains, almost seventy estates, and nearly thirty villages! So big and abundant and friendly. Not at all like the city."

Gatina thought for a moment. "My lady, do you think your brother would remain loyal to the memory of his late duke?" she prompted. "And perhaps take action to support his son, in exile?"

"He was about to ride to Falas with two thousand men to do that very thing, until my letter dissuaded him," she admitted. "Hence my great shame. Everyone is upset about dear Duke Lenguin's death. To have that . . . that tyrant move into the palace and start arresting people is horrible!" she moaned.

"Say that not too loudly, my lady," counseled Gatina. "Indeed, incautious words may imperil you and your family, in these times."

Isadra's eyes narrowed. "You don't speak like a nit. Or a gangster," she accused.

"I'm a very complex and complicated person, my lady," Gatina dismissed. "But we now live in times where your politics being known could prove deadly. Keep your family's allegiance to the ducal house quiet, or you will gather attention."

"Perhaps you are right," the young woman said, biting her lip. "It just infuriates me..."

"Many are frustrated, my lady," agreed Gatina. "But not all moves should be made in the open. Tell me . . . do you think your brother, the baron, would consider such a course?"

"What do you mean?" Isadra asked, sharply.

Gatina bit her own lip, wondering how much she dared trust the young noblewoman with. Not too much, she knew, but she had to tell her enough to engage her.

"There are others who share you and your brother's loyalties to the ducal house," she said, her voice just above a whisper. "Attacking Vichetral in Falas would be foolish . . . for the Count of Roen rides south with an army in support of the Count. He will be here in days. Long before a sufficient army could be raised to counter it."

"The Count of Roen? Rides for Falas?" the woman asked, surprised. "But Leod is Lenguin's cousin!"

"I can only tell you what intelligence I have heard," Gatina said, carefully . . . clearly implying that she had overheard something at the butcher's shop. "But your letter may have saved your brother from a traitor's death. Better he save his strength, for now, and bide his time. It shall be known who is loyal, and who is not.

"In the meantime, there are those who need to escape Vichetral's grasp – men and women who remain loyal and are in danger here in the city. Would your brother possibly consider concealing some of these against persecution?" she proposed, boldly.

"What?" the woman asked, confused.

"Could your brother be persuaded to hide some loyalists from Vichetral's men?" she repeated, quietly but more insistently. "Deep within his big, beautiful, prosperous barony? If his sweet sister should ask it?" Gatina asked.

"I . . . I don't know," she said, shaking her head. "Perhaps. I could write to him, if any message can be sent. But . . ."

"Would it speed my lady's hand if the silver needed to pay off your debt was provided?" Gatina asked, abandoning all pretense of being a simple, penniless, ignorant nit.

"You . . . you could pay off my debt?" the lady asked in disbelief.

"I can arrange for it to happen," Gatina nodded. "If it would encourage you to ask your brother."

"That . . . that is an interesting proposition," Lady Isadra agreed, swallowing hard. "I suppose I could ask," she sighed.

"If my lady consents to write to him, I will ensure your debt is repaid. You will have nothing more to do with the butcher. Until your husband's very expensive horse dies," she added with a smile.

"That damn horse," she laughed, despite herself. "I swear to Trygg he loves it more than me or the baby. He was so pleased, but I wished I never got it for him."

"People do strange things for love," shrugged Gatina.

"And nits do strange things for the memories of dead dukes," Lady Isadra pointed out, giving Gatina a searching stare.

"As I said, my lady, I live a complicated life," Gatina said, standing. "I will be back tomorrow. To read the letter you will send."

"You . . . *read?*" she asked in surprise.

"Complicated," Gatina repeated, with a bow, before heading up the lane toward the street. "Very complicated."

IT WAS ALMOST TWILIGHT – AND TIME FOR CURFEW – WHEN GATINA slipped back into Onnelik's townhouse. She was surprised to see her mother pacing the kitchen, clearly waiting for her.

"Gatina!" she declared, surprised, when she came in the back door. "Where in Darkness have you been?"

"Hiding," Gatina said. "Occasionally running. There was a riot, today."

"There were five riots today, across the city," her mother corrected. "I was worried sick when you didn't come home for supper!"

"I had to be careful," Gatina reminded her. "I was working."

"Working? Working on what?" Minnureal demanded.

"I was working to find someplace those prisoners can go and hide, once they are rescued," she explained as she poured herself a cup of apple cider from the jug. The sweet, tangy juice seemed to energize her. "I found one, I think."

"You . . . found one?" her mother asked, skeptically.

"Yes. The Barony of Larethin," she supplied, "ruled by Baron Antremin. The brother of Lady Isadra. The one who Hanik threatened into writing to dissuade her brother from riding on the city."

"You . . . Gatina, didn't I forbid you from going back there?" she demanded.

"No, you said nothing about Lady Isadra," Gatina reminded her. "I didn't steal from any Brothers of the Rat, though. Just an unconscious soldier. I had to, to keep my alias intact," she defended.

"I . . . well, *Darkness and Shadows!*" her mother swore. "This barony is downriver? And ruled by a loyalist?"

"He's no friend to Vichetral, at least," considered Gatina, between sips. "I checked, on my way back. Larethin is south of here, and it's fifty miles inland from the river. It's large enough to hide hundreds from Vichetral, if the baron is willing. His sister will be writing to him tomorrow. I will go by and ensure that she does. I hope it reaches him in time."

"It will, I think," sighed her mother. "I received a message from Shadow. The riots have delayed when the prisoners are to be moved by a few days, according to our agent in the palace. I'm afraid we're going to be living like this a little longer," she said, apologetically. "But if your solution to our problem works, then we will be fleeing the city, soon after."

"What?" Gatina asked, surprised.

"Falas will be too 'warm' for us, for a while, Kitten," explained her mother. "If we pull this off, Vichetral's men – and the Brotherhood – will be searching everywhere for the thieves who stole their hostages. I'm afraid you'll have to abandon Lissa the Mouse. Shadow has me working on a plan for our extraction even now. That may have to change, now that we have a possible destination for our loot."

Gatina didn't know how to feel about that. Marga and Liddy and the others were the closest things to real friends she had. But she also knew that she could not be Lissa the Mouse forever. Nor did she crave the life of an orphan. Continuing to associate with them when she might be hunted by the Count would put them in danger.

That made her feel bad, for the simple reason that she wanted to care for her friends, somehow, and save them from an ignoble death on the streets.

"There is one thing," she remembered. "I'm going to need some of that silver I stole back. In fact, I think I'm going to need it all back."

"Darkness protects us. You need know only what is deemed essential to play your role."

– Rule of House Furtius

CHAPTER EIGHTEEN
CODES AND CIPHERS

"I HAVE WRITTEN IT, JUST AS YOU HAVE BID," LADY ISADRA SAID, HANDING A scrap of well-cut parchment to Gatina. "A poor cousin of mine who lives in the city has agreed to ride to Larethin and deliver it to my brother, personally."

"Can he be trusted?" Gatina asked, suspiciously.

"With my life," she assured, nodding. "He is poor, a petty official with the town, but he is proud of his kinship with me and my brother and has a great affection for us both. He tells me he has a way into and out of the city. He will bear back the answer by the fastest horse he can find. I trust him at his word."

"For your sake, I hope you are correct, my lady," Gatina murmured. "You feel he will accept our proposal?"

"My brother will grant me any boon I ask," she agreed. "If it discomfits his political opponents, all the more so. I have done as you asked. Shall you convince Hanik to retire my debt?"

"No, you will," Gatina said, drawing a shabby little sack out of her basket. It was heavy with silver. "This is the exact amount you owe the butcher. Pay him yourself and tell him you want no further commerce with him. Mention me not," she added, warningly.

"I will not," she promised. "Is it . . . is it really that simple?" she asked, confused.

"It is a start," Gatina shrugged. "If he holds none of your debt, he has no further business with you. Therefore, no hold over you. But be careful, my lady. Men like Hanik are untrustworthy by nature. Once you begin to do business with them, they will want more. But I can't imagine he would have much use for you, now."

"I shall do it today," she sighed, relieved. "I want this strife to be done with. Every day I contend with the terror of the hold that man has over me. It was affecting my health. I was so foolish to deal with him to begin with!"

"Now you have conquered foolishness with wisdom," Gatina said. "My . . . mistress says that debt is a prison. Debts to men like Hanik are heavy shackles to bear."

"How did you come by this?" Isadra asked, suddenly, as she hefted the bag. "And what do I tell the butcher when he asks the same question?"

"I found it . . . in the shadows," Gatina said, mysteriously. "You can tell him that you sold some jewelry to a friend." Then she took out a second bag. "To repay me, I ask for your assistance, one last time. This is a like amount of silver. But I want you to spend it to a purpose."

"On what?" Isadra asked, even more suspiciously. "I will not be part of any criminal enterprise! That would imperil my husband's position at the palace!"

"This is nothing of the sort," assured Gatina. "Quite the contrary. I want you to give it to a priestess as alms. A special offering in thanks for the joy of your new baby. With instructions. But not just any priestess. A Trygite nun. I will give you her address."

GATINA STAYED CLOSE TO THE TOWNHOUSE, THE NEXT DAY, AS THERE were more disturbances flaring up in the city. Additional soldiers were arriving from across the river, increasing the tension that could be felt on the streets. For once Gatina did not mind staying in, even if it meant more lessons.

Instead of her mother, however, she sat with Onnelik and practiced her writing and learned about codes. She didn't mind the lessons. She liked Cousin Onnelik and found him full of valuable information about their family, its interests and city life. The scribe's gentle manner, quick mind, and vast knowledge of detail on many subjects made him as good a teacher as her tutor, Sister Karia.

"There are all manner of secrets our families have developed over the centuries," he explained. "Even during the Magocracy, when our people first came to Alshar, we each had our codes to conceal important knowledge and protect it from our enemies. Some are held in common amongst many of the old Magelord families. Some are known only within a family. It is an institution that has proven valuable, over the years. Particularly after the Narasi invasion, when the Censorate began policing the magi. And the Narasi began their rule over all Alshar."

"What is a code?" Gatina asked, innocently.

"It is just a secret way of communicating information," explained Onnelik. "It can be in writing, through symbols or by some other subtle means. All that is required is that both parties know the symbolism, know what it means and know where to look. This one, for example," he said, as he unrolled a scroll. "This is the code known as the *katkea*. It is one of the old codes from the Empire that almost all Magelord families use."

"It looks like leaves," Gatina observed.

"As it was supposed to," Onnelik agreed. "Indeed, this code was used in drawings or decorations. This code often served as a kind of title for other codes. Many of the old magical manuscripts have beautifully illustrated pages that seem no more than an exercise in artistic expression . . . unless you understood them to be vehicles for coded messages.

"Using the *katkea*, magi could leave instructions or provide important information, often concerning the accompanying text. If you didn't know about the code, then the text reads one way. A book on farming, perhaps, or even elementary magic. But by recognizing and understanding the *katkea*, the pictures often explained to those who read them properly just which secrets were hidden in the text, and by what code it was concealed. It proved particularly valuable when the Censorate began confiscating forbidden books of magic. The wise among us encoded them in other works, and concealed the knowledge with *katkea*. Priceless works were spared, as a result."

"So it's a code for telling you about other codes," Gatina said, trying to understand.

"Yes, and therefore it's vital that a young mage – or any young woman of the Coastlord families – knows it. Lest she miss something important, one day."

"Wait!" she said, as she realized something. "I've seen these leaf patterns . . . on Mother's cards!"

"Yes, there are many codes within the cards," he smiled. "Once you know the *katkea* and a few other codes, some interesting things will be revealed. Indeed, the cards themselves are a kind of code. But the key to them is understanding," he said, cryptically.

"Understanding what?" she asked, confused.

"Understanding where they came from, who made them, and what they meant at the time. Like all codes, the one who wrote it and the one who reads it must both know the same symbol. That is the key to their meaning. Your mother's cards are a reflection of her, and it is quite possible she has added her own messages in their creation. Perhaps by codes you will never be aware of. Now, let's do a few practice sentences and translate them into *katkea*."

They spent all day poring through books from Onnelik's library, seeking to recognize *katkea* and other codes.

There were several, she discovered, beyond basic *katkea*. There were simple replacement codes, where letters became numbers and then letters, again. There were ciphers. There was *Ubikas*, which was a symbolic code used to indicate location; there was one known as *Threading the Needle* that was used in embroidery patterns and public signs; and there were several different methods that concealed knowledge in books.

Though she did not master all of them, she was fascinated by how often she'd passed right by the coded messages and did not notice them.

She was so enrapt in discovering the secrets already in her possession that she nearly forgot about the disquiet in the streets.

While he was teaching her about codes, Onnelik also worked on a commission of his own: Shadow had ordered some forged orders written up and sealed, and Onnelik had taken the task.

"That's what I'm best known for, in the families," he admitted, as he finished one set of orders and prepared a fresh parchment leaf. "I didn't have *rajira*, but I was always a neat copyist. I had a talent for it. Often the old families need forged papers for one thing or another. So I started doing them this service, among others. We all help out, in our way," he reflected. "Well, most of us. There are a few ne'er-do-wells, I suppose, but most of us like to be useful. And it can be lucrative," he added, as he took up his pen and began. "The secret is to have the personality of the man who is supposed to be writing it firmly in mind. Military, political, statesman or scoundrel, a man's personality comes out in the words he chooses and the way he writes them."

"What is that one you're doing?" she asked, curious.

"Ordinarily, I wouldn't tell you for security's sake, but these are just a few general passes that allow the bearer to be out after curfew. The kind of thing that the sergeant of the palace guard might issue, or the lieutenant of one of the City Watch troops. Indeed, that will be his seal upon them," he said, as he carefully wrote the pass. "I have a whole collection of forged seals. In some cases they're exact copies. Quite proud of that. But, in general, you should try not to rely overmuch on forgeries. They can be unreliable. Especially where the magi are involved."

"Are there others in the family like you?" she asked, curious.

"Oh, my, yes," he chuckled. "It goes back to the history of the Coastlord houses, when we ruled the old Magocracy, and then the Narasi conquered us and brought those awful Censors. We've taken these precautions since then. As I said, we all have a part to play."

"Like what?" Gatina asked, genuinely curious. She knew only a small proportion of Coastlords (or any people, really) were gifted with *rajira* and could learn to practice magic. Under the Bans on Magic, they were denied their nobility as a result, and either became practicing adepts, little better than village spellmongers, or concealed their Talent and avoided the Censors. Most of the Coastlord houses had a few clandestine wizards among them.

But that left an awful lot of non-Talented people, she realized.

"In some cases, literally, some of us have a taste for the theater, for instance, like Huguenin once did, while others are content to live as the quiet, country gentry they are . . . until a favor is needed. Some run safe houses, others act as a business front, if we need one. Magi and mundane alike, we all have secret skills to aid the families. You have a second cousin who is a genius locksmith, for instance. Another owns a vineyard where it is very convenient to hide things – and he can be trusted to do so. A cousin of mine – on the other side of the family – is a lawbrother and magistrate who can be quite helpful, if we need it. My mother kept the family records hidden away inside a crypt – the real records, not the ones the Censorate and the tax collectors see. One of your great-uncles is the abbot of a Saganite monastery – quite a beautiful library, there," he said, recalling it fondly. "Palomar Abbey is a lovely place for advanced studies."

"Studies in what? Thieving?" she asked, eagerly.

"Oh, skills far beyond simple thieving," he assured. "It could be magic, science, astronomy, medicine, forgeries," he said, indicating the second pass he had completed. "There is no telling what one of the families might need, to survive – first the damn Narasi and their Censorate, then the Black Duke, and now the Five Counts," he sighed. "But places like that monastery were established to aid in our efforts. And kept secret," he reminded her. "The important thing is to protect the families. It is our mutual duty to one another, woven over centuries. Not everyone is privy to our particular side of the old magical nobility, but everyone suspects it's there."

"How do I know if I meet someone who is . . . involved?" she asked.

Onnelik smiled. "If everything goes smoothly in an operation, then you shouldn't need to know, unless you are told you do. But emergencies arise," he admitted. "There are certain codes that might reveal one of our secret friends.

"If you suspect someone you meet is . . . involved, then tell them this, exactly: *'I've always had a fondness for good . . . porridge,'*" he said, pausing deliberately. "That little pause between 'good' and 'porridge' is the key. As is using the word 'fondness.' Without that pause, someone is trying to trick you into revealing yourself. Most of those in our little circle understand this code as a sign of distress. If they reply, once again, exactly, *'My grandmother's porridge was hearty and . . . delicious,'* again with the pause, then they are your ally." He made her repeat the two phrases over and over again until she knew them precisely.

"That's enough for tonight," Onnelik said, rubbing his eyes. "Let's see what cook left for supper, and then off to bed. Perhaps after a brandy," he considered. "Your mother is due back by midnight. We should know more, then," he promised. "And no more sneaking out the window!" he added, as he rose. "What is it with you Furtiusi thieves and windows? It's almost as if you have something against doors. Your father is the same way. He likes to appear and disappear mysteriously. He's nearly given me my death of fright, more than once."

"I wonder where Father is, and what he's doing," Gatina sighed. "I miss him. And Atopol," she added, "but mostly him."

"He's got his own tasks set for him," Onnelik assured. "Shadow is a stern taskmaster, and lets none of our talents go to waste. With this much at stake, you can wager that he's neck-deep in some contorted plot. But if anyone can thrive in that kind of work it's Hance. He's got more nerve than any man I ever knew. Smart as a lawfather, too," he added, with admiration.

It made Gatina proud to hear of her father spoken of in that way. It gave her something to aspire to, for one thing, but it also pleased her that her father was seen as such a figure, even by his kin. But she did wonder what task Shadow had put him to. Indeed, she fell asleep thinking about that very thing.

GATINA AWOKE AT THE SOUND OF THE KITCHEN DOOR OPENING. THEN SHE heard the tell-tale footsteps she instinctively knew as her mother's. Despite what Onnelik had said about her family, Minnureal had chosen to return to the townhouse in a conventional manner. She began stripping off her hat and wig almost immediately, revealing a very tired-looking face underneath.

"You're back safely!" Gatina said, as she flung herself downstairs.

"No riots, this time," her mother said. "But military checkpoints are going up all over town. They're restricting movement between quarters of the city, now. I do hope Onnelik finished those passes," she said to herself.

"He did, I saw them," Gatina assured her. "Tea? I think the fire is still hot."

"Thank you," her mother said, sinking into a chair. "Between the heat and the damp, my throat is aching. I never liked Falas in the summer," she said. "It's slightly better, after dark, but it won't be tolerable until mid-autumn. Well, we received our orders," she said, as Gatina put a few small sticks into the iron stove. "Shadow is informed that they will finally move the hostages tomorrow night. Our man at the palace is doing very well at getting us good information. So we must prepare."

"Prepare, how?" Gatina asked, as she scooped tea into the strainer.

"I have a list of things to do, tomorrow, that will prepare us for our escape from Falas. Shadow has requested that you make one last appearance as Lissa the Mouse, to handle two small but important tasks, tomorrow. Then you can wash that color out of your pretty hair and leave the life of a nit behind you. I'll have your clothing and wig picked out by morning," she promised.

"What am I to do?" she asked, eagerly.

"First, you must visit Lady Isadra, and see if she's heard the word from her brother. Then, return to Hanik the Butcher," her mother informed her. "Tell him you aren't going to be able to work for him anymore after this run. Explain that you discovered you may have an aunt in Tracton who owns an inn who might take you in. Tell your little friends that, too. Tell him that the riot scared you and you want to get out of town, and with this run you'll have enough to get upriver."

"And then?" she prompted.

"And then you are to take Hanik's bag . . . and you *disappear*. That is, you'll come back here and we'll restore you to your beautiful looks and proper attire. You'll be done with Lissa, then. You'll become Maid Murel, of House Comalas, daughter of Lady Minwess of Dastine. Temporary aliases, but enough to get us through the checkpoints and out of town. I'll have Onnelik draw up the proper credentials. We will be leaving as soon as this mission is done. Perhaps before," she decided.

"Before the mission is done?" Gatina asked, confused, as she poured the boiling water into the pot to warm it, before dumping it out and adding the tea strainer.

"Our part of it will be complete before midnight," her mother reminded her. "We just need to do our tasks and get out of town. It's much safer to do so before what we've done is discovered. Especially when the Rats will be seeking Lissa the Mouse and their stolen money all the way over in Tracton. It's a crossroads market town, and it has a dozen inns. Misdirection," she explained. "When they tie you to the rescue, they will be seeking a dirty orphan girl in the wrong town, not a well-dressed country maid and her mother headed east in a coach. Or whatever transport I can arrange."

That made sense, Gatina could see, as she poured the water into the pot. The last thing she wanted to see was her friends hurt because Hanik was seeking her. If Lissa the Mouse had to disappear, then she was glad she could do one last service for her friends at the water fountain. But, she wondered, why would they tie her to the rescue?

"What happens to the stolen money?" she asked, as she prepared two cups.

Her mother shrugged. "Keep it. It's nothing. You steal it, you keep it. Retain nothing that can identify you as Lissa, but the coins you may keep. Perhaps hide a little away, for emergencies. Emergencies can always happen," she reminded her.

"I can think of a few things I could spend it on," she agreed. "Mistress, why would they tie *me* to the rescue?"

Minnureal sighed. "It's part of the plan. You and your Lissa alias are but one of many of Shadow's operatives in Falas. Each is doing their part and playing their role. And some of those parts include subverting others' work to confuse and mislead our enemies." She sipped her tea, eyes on Gatina.

"I think I understand," Gatina said. She realized she wasn't the only one involved. Attie was there, and her parents and the palace operative and even Onnelik had his part. There were undoubtedly many more people working on this effort – perhaps dozens. People she didn't know, or even know about. It just hadn't occurred to her how large this plan actually was until now. She had been caught up in her part of the conspiracy.

"Just one more thing," her mother added, tiredly. "Don't deviate from the plan. In order for it to work, the Rats *must* believe that Lissa the Mouse is the one responsible for the information that allowed the rescue. There are lives at stake. They must believe it is Lissa . . . and then she must disappear . . . *forever.*"

"You have a duty to your House, and your House has a duty to you, whether you are blessed with rajira or no. Magic is the tool of our House, but those without find a way to their duty, just as the magi serve in their way. Nor is every man forged by the gods to be a thief, yet still may serve the House in myriad ways. The House has an obligation to educate, succor and sustain every member therein. The Blessed Darkness covers us all. Only thus can the House survive."

– from **The Shield of Darkness**

CHAPTER NINETEEN
LISSA'S LAST RUN

IT FELT ODD, DRESSING AS LISSA AND KNOWING IT WAS THE LAST TIME, Gatina reflected as she prepared herself the next morning. She applied some fresh grime to her face, realizing that she was getting good at such disguises. She would almost miss it. There was something comforting about the grime. The smell of her hair and the cold of the hard cobbles under her feet she wouldn't miss, but she would miss the subterfuge of portraying Lissa the Mouse. It was like being invisible.

She stopped and purchased some buns from an early-rising cart vendor, as she shuffled toward the fountain one last time. She used some of the money she'd taken from the fallen soldier, figuring it was best to spend it quickly. Any nit who had too much coin on them would become a target.

For once it was the boys who'd arrived at the fountain first, pushing and shoving each other playfully, enjoying the cool morning before things got warm and the streets got crowded.

"Lissa the Mouse! What cheese have you brought for us today?" Gan asked, eagerly.

"She's always got food," nodded Toscar, grinning. "She's so nice!"

"I didn't disappoint," she agreed, breaking the buns in half and presenting each boy with one. That left plenty for Marga and Liddy, when they arrived. Perhaps even more. "I got a discount for buying so many," she added. "And because they weren't quite done baking, yet. They're doughy in the middle."

"It's bread! Where did you get money? Where were you, yesterday?" demanded Toscar, his mouth full of bread. Twopenny was scarfing it down greedily as well.

"Scrounging," she shrugged. "There were riots. People needed help cleaning up. Besides, I've been saving. I may go up to Tracton. I heard I may have an aunt who works at an inn, there."

"She'd take you in?" Toscar asked, through his mouthful.

Gatina shrugged. "I can only ask. She can only say no. It's worth the risk."

"An inn is better than this," Twopenny agreed, nodding. "Tracton? Where's that?"

"In the north, upriver. It's a crossroads. Market town. Lots of inns, up there," she explained.

"Never been there. We'll miss you," Toscar said, sincerely. "And the food."

"We'll likely starve to death without you," agreed Twopenny, somberly.

"You'll starve of laziness," she teased. "Where are the girls?"

"Haven't seen 'em," Twopenny shrugged. "They might have jobs in the morning. Or got kidnapped by bandits. Snatched away by a dragon. Or something interesting."

"But they probably found jobs," Toscar agreed. "They're always working! They barely beg, anymore. They make us look bad!"

"You make yourselves look bad," Gatina lectured. "If I leave these buns with you, will you ensure they get to the girls?"

"We are entirely trustworthy," assured Toscar, with great solemnity.

"He'll eat half of them, before they get here," predicted Twopenny. "Let *me* watch them."

Gatina groaned. "You know I'll ask them about it, later!" she reminded them.

"We'll watch them," Toscar sighed. "And we'll watch each other. We'll still get to smell them, at least."

"Thank you," Gatina sighed. "I have an errand or two to run, but I'll probably be back this afternoon, sometime."

"Bring more food!" suggested Twopenny, cheerfully, as she started off across town.

The way to Lady Isadra's home was becoming familiar to her, now. She was starting to notice little changes, like where a barricade for a checkpoint had been hastily abandoned, or where a cart had been pushed in front of a broken door to block it. She saw broken crockery and random rocks littering the street. Even the nicer areas of town had seen some trouble, she realized.

Like the last time, she approached the back door and then quietly knocked. The cook recognized her, and silently nodded her inside. Lady Isadra was sitting in the kitchen feeding her baby.

"I was wondering when I'd see you again," she said, quietly.

"Have you heard from your brother, my lady?" she asked, peering at the baby.

"I have. My cousin came in last night, after curfew. He brought a response from my brother. He assures me he is willing to give secret refuge to those in question," she answered. "If they disembark at a place called Greenwall Landing on the eastern bank, he will have men there to guide them to his lands. He has a remote estate he can lodge them at, for now, where they can hide from Count Vichetral."

"Good," nodded Gatina. "Thank you, my lady."

"Thank you," Isadra said, after a pause. "I paid the butcher's bill, yesterday. He was quite surprised. I told him I sold some jewelry. And that we'd have no further business."

"Good," Gatina agreed. "Try not to have dealings with such people in the future, my lady. This town is corrupt, it is said, and everyone who lives here gets corrupted, eventually. Avoid that, as long as you can," she warned. It was the sort of thing her mother would say, she realized.

"I do wish we could move back to the countryside," Isadra sighed. "But as long as the palace is in turmoil, my husband dares not lose his position. There were more executions, yesterday, in front of the palace!" she whispered.

"Nine, to be exact. Do be careful, my lady," Gatina urged, as she turned to leave. "Oh, and did you make my bequest?"

"Bequest? That's a big word for a . . . a . . ."

"Nits, they call us," Gatina pointed out. "I heard it from a priest, once. Did you?"

"Yes, I found the nun you told me to, and asked her to do as you requested. I gave her all that money."

"If I give you more, can you do the same thing?" Gatina prompted.

"I can," Isadra agreed, reluctantly. "In truth, I just wish this business was over and done with!"

"It's unlikely that you'll see me again, after today," soothed Gatina. "But it's important that she has the resources she needs."

Gatina stopped back by the broken fountain on her way to Hanik's to see if the girls had shown up. Liddy was there, sitting between Twopenny and Toscar, but there was no sign of Marga.

"Where's Marga?" Gatina asked. "I haven't seen her since the riot."

"Which one?" complained Twopenny.

"The one two days ago, right here. Have you?" she demanded.

"No," admitted Toscar. "I thought she might have a job."

"She might," Liddy agreed, hesitantly. "But I don't know. I haven't seen her, either."

"If she's smart, she slept in," Twopenny said, wisely. "We get up too early. It's not good for our health."

"Keep an eye out for her," Gatina suggested. In truth, she didn't want to disappear without saying goodbye to her friend. But she was starting to get worried about her. Nits disappeared all the time – "fell into a canal" was the idiom they used for a sudden disappearance. Sometimes it was nothing. Sometimes they were, indeed, found drowned in a canal, or they got sick. Sometimes they just . . . vanished. And nobody cared, save for a few friends on the street.

"We will, we like Marga," assured Toscar. "If she doesn't turn up soon, we'll look for her."

"I'm sure it's nothing," Liddy said, uncertainly.

"She's a smart girl," Gatina agreed. "I'm sure she's fine. But keep your eye out," she repeated. "We have to stick together." She felt bad saying such a thing, right before she was about to abandon her friends, but it was the sort of thing Lissa the Mouse would say. "I've got to go to a job, now," she said. "You did get that bun I left for you, didn't you?"

"Yes, but only because these two threatened to punch each other if they ate it, first," she complained.

"And because we like Liddy," reminded Toscar. "We wouldn't do that to her."

Gatina said her good-byes casually, knowing that they might, indeed, be final, if all went to plan. She made her way over the Hanik's near the appointed hour, and walked right in, basket in hand.

"You're early," accused Flerian, who was helping Mils dismantle a side of mutton. It was gruesome work. "He's not ready, yet."

"I'll wait," she sighed, climbing onto the stool. "It's getting too hot outside, anyway. Did you see the riot?"

The two men glanced at each other. "Oh, we saw plenty enough," chuckled Flerian. "Great big bust-up it was, too. A lot of heads got busted. Got a couple of licks in, myself," he said, proudly.

"I just hid and waited it out," Gatina said. "It was very exciting, at first, but then it got terribly violent. I hated it," she declared, sullenly. "Saw some heads getting bashed in, myself. Ugly."

"Six killed, the City Watch says," grunted Mils, the youngest of the butcher's apprentices. "Bloody day."

"Twelve executed in front of the palace," Flerian pointed out. "Very bloody day."

"Who got executed?" Gatina asked. She knew the number was nine, not twelve. Shadow was rarely wrong.

"Traitors, troublemakers, political enemies, the usual lot. Vichetral's declared himself the 'protector of the realm' and is taking action to secure the government. What kind of title is that?" he demanded.

"As long as he rules well, who cares?" Mils shrugged.

"I just don't want to ever go through that again," Gatina assured them. "I might leave the city. I heard I have an aunt in Tracton, works at an inn. Might take me in."

Flerian whistled. "Tracton's near thirty miles upriver, lass. That's a long walk."

"I could get a ride," she protested. "At least part of the way. It's out of the city, isn't it? Too bloody dangerous, here!"

"The road is just as dangerous or more, for a girl your age," Flerian assured her. "Best you stick someplace where you have friends to watch over you. This mess out in the streets will pass. Vichetral will set things to rights, and then we'll have peace again. Good times are coming," he said, encouraged. "Right man in the palace, everything else will be fine."

"Is the runner girl here?" called Hanik, from the office above.

"Yeah, is the bag ready?" Flerian called back.

"Send her up," Hanik ordered gruffly from the stairwell.

With a nod, Flerian encouraged her to climb the narrow stairs. She bounded up quickly, but quietly, automatically noting which steps creaked and which didn't.

"You got here early," Hanik noted, as she entered his office.

"Didn't know if you'd need me early or not," she said, defensively. "There was a riot or two," she reminded him. "I was trying to be flexible."

"Right," Hanik grunted, sitting down at his table. He pushed the bag of loot over to her. "Same as last time," he said with a sigh, and then scratched his belly. "Don't tarry anywhere. It's dangerous out there. Oh," he said, before he dismissed her. "You know that lady across the Processional I sent a message to?"

"Yeah?" Gatina shrugged.

"She came in and paid her entire bill off, yesterday," he said, considering her. "Did she mention anything about that when you were there?"

"She said she was going to sell some jewelry," Gatina reported. "She looked like she had some, if you know what I mean. Snooty sort of lady," she said, wrinkling her nose.

"It's just . . . unusual," Hanik said, staring at her. "Most of my clients take a while to pay me back. A little every week or so."

"She didn't look like she enjoyed being in your debt," Gatina replied. "Especially after you asked her that question. It shook her."

"She's the nervous sort," agreed Hanik with a sigh. "Those petty nobles are always tricky. Not the best sort of client to have. They get all sorts of ideas about talking to the City Watch, or the magistrate, or their lawbrother, or the Duke himself. That makes problems," he said, knowingly. "But her paying out her debt causes problems, too."

"Better off without her, then," nodded Gatina. "Are we done? I don't want to be late."

"Scamper off, little mouse," grunted Hanik, dismissively. "And watch out for Gavin," he added, suddenly. "He still hasn't found that missing money. It's making him insane. He might be inclined to do something . . . unpredictable."

She nodded as she concealed the bag in the basket and headed down the stairs. Darkness willing, this would be the last time she would be in the butcher shop. And she was quite relieved that she wouldn't have to face the creepy gangster, Gavin, again.

She wasn't more than a block away from the butcher's shop when she noticed something: there was a certain tense feeling in the street, all of a sudden. People were walking quickly on their errands, the street carts that usually plied the side-streets were absent, and a few knots of artisans were beginning to form, their angry mutters loud enough for Gatina to hear from across the street.

It was the feeling of expectation like that which arose before a storm, she realized. She'd come to recognize it more clearly, since the day she was caught in the riot. The overcast sky seemed to reflect the mood of Falas, as she trudged determinedly toward the warehouse, heavy basket in hand. She was not ready to cut out with the loot, just yet – there were Rats near the shop watching, she knew, even if she couldn't see them. She had decided not to depart her usual route until after she crossed West Canal Street, a broader thoroughfare that ended Hanik's territory.

But as she came to West Canal Street, the tension in the air became acute. There were shouts in the distance that she could hear over the usual din of the city. Angry shouts. In unison. People were chanting. She couldn't tell where, exactly, but the rise and fall in their pitch and volume gave her some idea of how many were gathered, out of her line of sight, and how close they were. It made her ill at ease and nervous.

She had just come to the intersection of Inkmaker's Street and West Canal Street when it became apparent that this was not merely a spontaneous riot, the result of some unpopular neighborhood arrest. There was more purpose and less chaos to the commotion than a mere riot.

"What's all that noise?" complained an old woman waiting next to her for the traffic to pass so that they could cross. "Trygg's grace, I can't go to the bloody grocer's without an insurrection breaking out!"

"You didn't hear, Auntie?" asked an artisan, shaking his head sourly. "It was released this morning at the palace. Count Vichetral has ordered another raft of executions. Starting with the Prime Minister," he said, darkly.

"What?" the old woman asked, in disbelief. "He's going after old Count Venn? How'd that happen?" she demanded.

Gatina stopped, the news startling her. She listened carefully, as the artisan explained the disquiet in the streets.

"Announced this morning at the palace, it was," the man said, with authority beyond his station. "Just came from there – well, at the farrier's shop, across the way. Heard some whispers, there – it all happened last night," he said.

Gatina saw that he was a man who enjoyed delivering news, the worse, the better. "Seems a lot of the senior clergy released Count Venn from house arrest – Lawfather Mithus, Birthmother Angine, Landfather Moress, Skyfather Benfane, and more than twenty others. Then old Venn led them to confront Vichetral," he related, darkly. "In the middle of a meeting of his council. Spoke out about his lack of authority, about how he has no right to dictate policy in place of the rightful duke, and how he should quit the capital and return to his own lands."

"Aye, he should!" the old woman said, sourly. "Naught has been right, since the Duke and Duchess died. It's got worse, since that wicked count came here!"

"Count Vichetral didn't see it like that," the artisan said, shaking his head sadly. "He said that he had written to the Duke of Castal and demanded the young heir's return – as well as the return of Gilmora, and sovereignty over Farise! Then he had all of them arrested, on the spot, and taken to the dungeons. Accused them of treason against the council. They're to die at sunset – the nobles by steel, the clergy by rope. All of them," he said, grimly.

"All of them? The Birthmother, too? And the Lawfather?" the old woman asked, shocked.

"Every last one who stood with Count Venn," the man assured. "No appeals. No mercy for their holy orders."

"That's outrageous!" the old woman nearly shouted. "The people won't stand for it!"

"They aren't," the artisan agreed, nodding toward the growing noise on the other side of the Processional. "Some are taking it right hard."

Gatina's mind raced as she realized the implications of the news. In her short time in Falas, she'd noted the city's respect for the clergy, particularly the temples of Trygg, Luin, and Orvatas. They were essential for operating hundreds of important services the people of the city depended upon, from schools and libraries to orphanages and poor houses. They controlled the great hospital, near the palace, she knew, and the birthing and dying chambers in their temples. The clergy controlled the civil courts, and they were often involved in criminal courts. The senior members of the clergy frequently presided over almsgiving and other charitable works, and they supported arts and culture. Some were truly beloved, among the Falasi.

Not to mention the general respect that the Prime Minister, Count Venn of Darlake, held, she knew. He had calmly steered the affairs of Alshar since before her parents were born, and folk had generally prospered under his administration, from what she'd learned in her time in the city.

If Count Vichetral was willing to risk open rebellion, Gatina realized, then he was one step away from deposing young Anguin altogether and declaring himself Duke of Alshar. And that, she knew, would be disastrous. That would be civil war or worse.

She was still distracted by the idea of Duke Vichetral when the other side of the intersection was suddenly filled with a crowd of people. Angry people. Many carried staves or flags or banners, but they were pushing down the street like a wave. They weren't rioters, she realized, as she watched the crowd seethe its way into the intersection to block it. They were protesters. They were furious.

And they were headed right for her.

"If we must fight, we fight to win. Winning often means getting away without getting caught."

– from **The Shield of Darkness**

CHAPTER TWENTY
AN UNEXPECTED PROBLEM

GATINA AND THE OTHER BYSTANDERS WATCHED IN GROWING HORROR AS the crowd across the street purposefully pushed into the intersection, forcing the long line of carts to stop altogether. In moments, the entire crossroads was filled from side to side with milling, angry bodies, until they were pushing out in all directions. There were hundreds of angry people, Gatina could see, perhaps nearly a thousand. And there were more joining in all the time, too, as word of the executions spread. In moments she saw both the artisan and the old woman amongst the crowd, shouting slogans and chanting *"Spare their lives! Spare their lives!"*

This was different from the riot, she knew at once. The riot had been a fight that had attracted a crowd. This was a crowd in search of a fight. They had purpose, direction, she saw, and they had leaders: there were several who had taken advantage of the numbers of people involved and had elevated themselves enough to give a speech, shout slogans, or lead the chants. They weren't fighting yet, but it was clear that they were being charged up to do so.

In moments, Gatina was being pressed from all sides by the angry mob. She suppressed the desire to panic, as she stumbled to keep from being knocked down, relying on her training to nimbly avoid the press of humanity – even if it meant stepping on the occasional boot instep.

While she danced her way toward the edge of the street, where it was presumably safer, her mind raced about how this affected the timing of her plan. By the time she made it to the safety of a wall, she'd realized that the demonstration was actually the perfect distraction she needed. There was no way she could make her way across the crowd to the warehouse, after all. And the few City Watchmen on the edges of the disturbance were keeping their distance, this time. The number of people who had spilled out onto the streets of Falas was just too large for them to contend with.

While the riot had been confined to one neighborhood, Gatina could see that the demonstration had attracted hundreds and hundreds from across the social sphere of the capital. Maids and artisans milled about next to clergymen and shopkeepers. There were folk from the nobility rubbing shoulders with bondsmen. There were black-clad clerks shouting in unison with angry street sweepers. It was as if all of Falas had erupted into the street at the news of the pending executions.

A few fights had already broken out, on the edges of the demonstration. That suited Gatina just fine. She quickly tucked the heavy bag under her dress and threw her empty basket on the ground.

Then she stepped on it, hard enough to break the willow fibers and crush it out of shape. But it was still recognizable. Hanik and his men would know it to be her basket. To be sure, she left a few of her other simple possessions behind in it, all save her money and her little knife.

Satisfied, she made certain that the bulge in her clothing wasn't obvious before she began to make her way through the streets away from the demonstration. She knew that Count Vichetral would not – could not – allow such a protest to reach the palace, lest it undermine his seized authority. She wondered when he would send in his troops to confront the angry protesters, and then wondered just how bloody a confrontation it would become.

She tried not to look too hurried, as she walked through the streets away from the crowd – and the warehouse. There were plenty of people hurrying through the streets now, some actually running toward the protest, eager to join it. Others were running away, out of fear or a sense of duty to inform someone of the gathering. No one noticed her as her dirty bare feet plodded along the cobbles. And no one noticed the bulge under her dress.

It took her nearly half an hour to find her way near Lady Isadra's townhouse. While no one had yet confronted the protestors, the City Watch was positioning barricades around the protest, she noted, as she slipped into a lane she knew was unlikely to be guarded. It was between and behind a boarded-up spellmonger's shop and a tailor's shop, and deserted.

She considered breaking into one of the shops, but then spied a better way to ensure her privacy. Making certain no one was watching her, she shimmied up the stone corner of a spellmonger's shop until she found purchase on the chimney. In moments she was on the roof, above the streets, and safe.

Gatina wasted no time in finding a secure spot on the roof and opening up the bag she'd carried for Hanik. Within, wrapped in a layer of relatively clean butcher's cloth, was a pile of coin, a pretty scarlet silk scarf, five earrings, three finger rings, and six necklaces of varying quality. Gatina quickly counted out the money, then estimated what the jewelry and scarf would go for, if one wanted to sell it quickly.

"Only forty-seven silver?" she summed, out loud to herself. "You're going to have to do better, Hanik!" she said, mocking Gavin's manner and voice. After a moment's thought, she bundled all the jewelry in the scarf and stuffed it into the bag. Then she found a loose brick in the chimney – no difficult task, considering how much in disrepair the thing was. The owner couldn't have been a very good spellmonger, she decided.

Once she'd concealed the jewelry and replaced the brick, she gathered the coin in the butcher's cloth until it made a considerably smaller package – and much easier to hide about her person.

Gatina paused to look out over the city from her vantage. She could hear the muted roar of the protest in the distance, and feel the level of anxiety it was producing in the city. That made her errand all the more urgent, she realized. It was only a matter of time until the rumble of thunder the protest represented would turn into a storm, and it was a storm she did not want to be caught in.

Quickly, she descended the chimney and continued on her way, more confident, now that she wasn't lugging a bag of stolen loot around under her dress. She had to skirt two more City Watch barricades, but they weren't concerned with nits, at the moment. Indeed, they were being issued crossbows and pikes from one of the City Watch's many carts, she saw with alarm. That made her hurry even more.

By the time she came to Lady Isadra's street, Cordwainers Street, she was starting to feel relieved. She could give the silver to the noblewoman, she figured, and she would in turn give it to the priestess. And then Gatina could make her way to Onnelik's, remove Lissa the Mouse from her hair, once and for all, and get out of the city. That prospect suddenly had a great deal more appeal to her. All of this chaos throughout the city was not to her liking.

She nearly skidded to a halt as she approached Isadra's house, however, and paused in front of the wineshop. There were three horses outside of the place, one of them occupied by a soldier who held the reins of the other two steeds and watched the street. Gatina's eyes opened wide at the sight of the open front door of the townhouse.

"Bad bit of business, there," the wineshop boy said, coming out into the street and wiping his hands on a dirty rag. "They showed up an hour ago."

"Why?" Gatina asked, her heart sinking.

"Don't know," the boy shrugged. "Can't be good, though," he said, shaking his head. "Taxes, maybe? Only they're soldiers, not bailiffs. Those fellows don't mess around. Look like the ones living in the palace, now," he added. "I seen them up there, when I make deliveries. They order a lot," he added.

"Maybe it's her husband," she suggested. "Maybe something has happened to him."

"Well, if he's to be executed, he's going to have to wait," the boy said, with dark humor. "Word is it's the Prime Minister's turn, today, along with a mess of clergymen. It's got folks mad," he added, informatively.

"It's going to get folks killed," Gatina agreed. "I think I'll find another way around," she announced, studying the soldier. His crossbow was not cocked, but she knew it wouldn't take him long to do so, and that cavalry sword was quite long enough to reach her neck from horseback. And he looked rather alert, too, in the saddle, unlike some of the City Watchmen she'd gotten used to studying.

"Good luck," the wineshop boy wished her, as she turned around and began to go the other way. She waited until she was half a block away and out of sight of both soldier and wineshop boy before she dove into an alley. Her mind working furiously, Gatina walked to the next street over and found the house she was seeking – the one directly behind Lady Isadra's.

While the open windows and smoking chimney indicated someone was home, Gatina didn't hesitate. She leapt over the short wall into the garden, then scaled the timbered wall until she reached the roof. Then she made her way nimbly across until she was within reach of the cherry tree that was between the two houses, the same one she'd climbed the second time she'd come here.

Climbing a cherry tree from the top, down, proved more difficult than she'd imagined; Gatina had a few anxious moments as she leapt from the roof, her hands grabbing the wrong branch – and one that was far thinner than the bough she'd sought. But she swung her legs quickly around the correct branch and carefully pulled herself to sit on the heavier limb, before pausing to catch her breath.

She could peer through the leaves and see the back garden and kitchen door easily enough. The garden was empty and the door was open, she noted, the old cook absent from her duties. And she could hear voices from inside – not well enough to make out what they were saying, but there were clearly voices. Gatina silently cursed not having her *rajira*, yet – there were spells for that sort of thing, she knew.

Instead, she decided to get closer to overhear what was being said. Her heart pounded as she quietly descended the tree and crept over to the back door. The woodshed and privy gave her some cover, but there didn't seem to be anyone in the kitchen to see her. The voices were coming from deeper in the house.

She carefully, silently made her way to the doorway, squeezing into the tiny space next to it. She pressed her ear against it, just as she had when she and Atopol had spied on their parents, at the country house. It took a few moments to adjust, but soon she could hear what was being said inside. Mostly.

"... been here for an hour, now, and I still don't understand what this is all about!" Lady Isadra was saying, fear and anger in her voice.

"And I've told you, my lady, that your name and this address was given to us by our watch commander," explained a patient but stern male voice. "This warrant says that you are a 'person of interest' to the ruling Council. It is my duty to carry out the orders of that Council."

"But I still don't know *why!*" Isadra insisted, her voice tense with emotion. "My husband works at the palace!" she pointed out.

"So you've told us, repeatedly," the man's voice replied, tiredly.

Gatina's eyes were wide as she listened. Why in the name of blessed Darkness was the Council of Counts interested in the wife of a minor palace official? That didn't make sense.

"I was given no further information from the Ancient," the soldier continued, "merely these instructions: to allow you to pack one bag for you and your child, and then to take you and a young girl – a street orphan, no name known – by this warrant – if found in your presence and convey the three of you to the collection site. So if you will finish packing your bag, we can leave as soon as the carriage arrives."

Gatina's blood froze when she heard the word "street orphan" – that could only mean her! How did the Council know about *her*? It had to be some spy for the Brotherhood of the Rat informing them – *but how did they know?* Too much about this did not make sense. But then things got even more compelling.

"I told you – repeatedly – that I've never set eyes on this girl in my life!" Lady Isadra insisted. "She was just lingering around my house when you barged in!"

"Which is exactly what you would say if she was your accomplice," a second male voice said, coldly. "Yet there she was, staring intently at your door, as if she was waiting for some signal."

"I wasn't waiting for a signal!" a new voice – and one she recognized, to her horror – insisted, angrily. "I was just waiting for my mates! Some of them do a bit of chore work in this neighborhood! I just thought she had a pretty house! I got nothing to do with all this!"

It was Marga's voice. Gatina's heart sank.

Gatina didn't know how Marga had come here, but she could guess: she'd followed Gatina, maybe after the riot. Why she'd done it was a mystery. She'd probably been curious about where she was disappearing to, all the time. But there she was, clearly ensnared in this mess. They'd mistaken Marga for Gatina – for Lissa the Mouse, more appropriately.

"You shut your mouth, nit!" warned the second man. "This discussion is among your betters!"

"That will all be settled out when we arrive at the collection site," the first man said, in a reasonable tone. "The carriage will be here momentarily. I'm sure if there is nothing substantial to the Council's suspicions, then you will all be allowed to go free. Now, finish packing up, and we'll wait out front."

"You're not taking me anywhere!" Marga insisted, angrily. "I didn't do anything!"

"It doesn't matter if you did or didn't," the first man dismissed. "It only matters that I bring you in. You were the only nit found near her house, so you'll be going in, too."

"What are they planning on doing to us?" Isadra asked, fearfully. Her baby started crying.

"I don't know," the first soldier admitted. "Depends on what you did. Or what they think you did. And no use lying about it – they got them Censors in the palace, now, helping out the Council. They'll use a magic spell to see if you're lying or not. If you are . . . well, the palace executioner might have a bit more work. Or it might merely be prison for a few years," the man said, nonchalantly. "Depends on their mood, I suppose. Not my job to know that. My job is to bring you in."

"What if I was able to . . . to . . . pay you to look the other way?" Lady Isadra asked, desperately. "I don't have much, but—"

"Pay us?" snorted the second man. "My lady, any money you might have is forfeit to the Council, if you're guilty. You know how many times someone's tried to bribe us? Won't work," he said, a sneer in his voice. "Because we don't want to provide more work for the palace executioner. The man's dreadfully overworked as it is," he said, with a harsh laugh. "Besides, once you're gone, we can look around this place properly and pretty much take whatever we like. Perquisites of the job."

"You wouldn't dare!" Lady Isadra said, angrily.

"Won't be anyone around to stop us," admitted the first man. "You do have some nice things, here . . ."

"You leave my things alone! *My husband works at the palace!*" she reminded them, shrilly.

"Yeah, and so do we," the second man said. "My superior is Count Vichetral. Who's his?"

"None of this would be happening if the Duke was here!" Isadra said, bitterly.

"But he's dead, isn't he?" the first man asked. "So that's how the world turns. Count Vichetral is in charge, now. And we take *his* orders. And his pay. Is your bag packed?" he asked, his patience starting to run out, if his voice was any indication.

"I don't know! I don't know what I'm packing for! All of this is so confusing! I—"

"Hey there!" someone behind Gatina called. The third soldier.

Startled, Gatina whipped around and saw the man standing next to the clothes-drying pole, pointing at her accusingly. "Oy! I think we got another one!" he shouted to his fellows inside.

Gatina was frightened. She'd been so intent on listening to the conversation inside that she'd neglected to keep watch behind her. In moments, the kitchen door opened fully, revealing one of the soldiers inside.

"Who's this, then?" the man said – the second man from inside, she could tell by his voice. The unreasonable one. He was tall, with a well-trimmed beard and beady eyes. He reached out and tried to grab Gatina by the shoulder.

By reflex, Gatina dodged out of the way, causing the soldier to curse.

"You two were taking all year to get them out, so I came back here to take a crap," the third soldier explained, triumphantly. "That's when I saw her, ear pressed on the door!" He moved closer, using the clothes-drying pole to block her in as she twisted around and stared at first one soldier, then the other. There was no easy way out of this, she realized.

But she was not going to get caught, she vowed. Her mother – her mistress – would be mortified. Her brother would never let her hear the end of it. If she wasn't executed, she reminded herself. But that was the unbreakable family rule: Furtiusi didn't get caught.

So she wouldn't.

"Shadows hide you. Darkness bless you. Secrets bind you. Family guide you."

– Rule of House Furtius

CHAPTER TWENTY-ONE
THE MOUSE NO MORE

"I was looking for work," Gatina protested, backing away from the kitchen door. It appeared that she was trapped between the two soldiers, but neither of them had drawn weapons. They didn't think she was any danger to them than ... a kitten, she realized. "Sometimes these rich ladies need some help, for a penny or a bowl of soup," she said, emphasizing the Falas accent she'd picked up in her time among the nits. Both soldiers had the western accent associated with the counties on the other side of the river.

"You were *listening!*" accused the man slowly crossing the yard. He was doing a very good job blocking her from running past him and into the street. Thankfully, the street wasn't where she wanted to go.

"I saw you big hairy fellows giving the lady a hard time," explained Gatina. "I was just wondering what—"

Before she finished the sentence, Gatina sprang – but not at the men, or even the narrow space between the soldier in the yard and the lane, beyond, where they might have suspected she would go.

Instead, she leapt at the drying pole, capturing it in both hands as high as she could. She used the momentum of her leap to swing her legs around, and snapped them straight just in time to hit the soldier in the yard with both feet, squarely in the face.

She wasn't trying to kill the man, or even hurt him. But the force of her small body, swung around the pole, gave her feet just enough momentum, when they encountered his face, to knock the soldier off his feet. He sprawled to the ground as Gatina continued her arc . . . but not toward the lane, where the second soldier was already heading.

Instead, when her bare feet hit the ground she sprinted toward the big tree at the back of the garden. In seconds she was twenty feet in the air above the men, who were still trying to recover. In a few moments more she made the leap to the roof of the house in the rear, and was soon dropping over the eaves and into the lane beyond. There were two walls and a fence between her and the soldiers. They would have no real idea which side of the building she descended.

Gatina only continued running for about half a block, until she could duck into a narrow alley between an apothecary's shop and a block of flats. She took several turns through the streets, after that, almost at random. She wanted to put as much distance between her and the soldiers as possible.

Her mind raced and her heart pounded as she slowed her pace to a walk and tried to blend into the neighborhood she was now in. It wasn't as affluent as Lady Isadra's, which gave Gatina a better chance of escaping notice as she shuffled along the narrower streets. There were still angry people headed for the Processional, where the mutter of the distant crowd could be heard over the din of normal city life. But no one took notice of her, and there was no sign of soldiers in this unimportant section of Falas. While that was a relief, it also gave her time to catch up on her regrets.

Isadra was arrested. *Darkness*, she swore to herself. Marga was arrested, merely for being in the wrong place at the wrong time. And it was her fault, she realized. Somehow, she had called attention to the young noblewoman, and then Marga had grown suspicious and had followed her, after the riot. Her heart ached as she recognized just how badly things had gone wrong. She had no idea about the "collection site," where it was and what its purpose was, but there was little hope she could effect a rescue by herself.

It was bad enough she had run away and abandoned both of them to the soldiers, after getting them arrested in the first place. She could not bear to think of their fates, should no one act on their behalf. Yet, if she brought the situation to her mother – on the same day of an important operation – not only did she risk the wrath of her mistress for doing something so stupid, she also could embroil more innocents in this mess.

But she also knew she could not conceal this from her mother, as much as she wanted to. If there was any way to help her friends, it would have to come from her family, not her alone. She just didn't know enough, she admitted to herself, and she did not have the resources to help on her own.

Gatina started to realize that this game she was playing was dangerous. Very dangerous.

The words of caution and restraint that her mother had patiently instructed her with over the last several months all came tumbling back into her mind. Each seemed a harsh rebuke, now, and she hung her head in shame as she turned her direction towards the Tower of Sorcery, Onnelik's neighborhood. She could do no more out on the street, she knew. She had to go home, confess her stupidity, take her punishment, and strip away every trace of Lissa the Mouse. Perhaps her mother would be merciful. Perhaps her mother would have some idea about how to help.

But with the entire city on the edge of madness, Gatina had a sinking feeling that her mother would force her to abandon them. There was just too much at stake, she knew. Even Isadra's baby was not worth the life of a hundred innocent hostages, in the cold equations of the moment.

Gatina took the most circuitous route back to Onnelik's house and avoided the streets she'd grown familiar with, as often as possible. It was late afternoon by the time she finally came to the back door of the forger's house. She slunk in the back door, defeated and in tears.

"What's wrong, Kitten?" Onnelik asked, frowning, when he saw her tearstained face. "Were you hurt?"

"No, I'm fine," she assured him as she collapsed into a wooden chair.

"I was in a riot – no, a *demonstration* – for a little bit, but I slipped away before things got ugly."

"The executions at the palace," he nodded, gravely. "I heard. Even some of my neighbors are angry enough to go protest. I fear it will only bring them grief for doing so," he sighed.

"There's enough grief already," she said, dejectedly. "I accomplished my mission," she reported. "But I . . . I . . . Onnelik, I did something . . . *ill-advised*," she said, choosing her words carefully. Then she began telling him what had happened.

She didn't want to, of course, and she had considered keeping the matter to herself to spare the consequences she knew she deserved. But as soon as the words began to flow, they would not stop. She confessed everything, from how she'd helped Isadra get out of debt with Hanik to her plan to help her friends to Marga's suspicions to the near-disastrous brush with capture by the soldiers. By the time she was done with the story, tears were streaming down her filthy face and splashing on her dress.

"Oh, Kitten!" the forger said, shaking his head sadly. "That is a bit of bad luck. But you cannot blame yourself," he insisted. "This was not your doing. This is the result of Vichetral's attempt to seize power.

"Yes, you were likely spied upon, by someone. And your friend's actions were unfortunate. But you and your friend were just reacting to the situation; you are not its author. Many, many people are being swept up in this chaos. All we can do is make the best decisions we can with the options we have available. And it's likely to no avail, sadly enough.

"It appears that none of the other powers in Alshar will stand against Vichetral. Once the Prime Minister is dead, he will have no rival. Even our rescue plan is unlikely to do much beyond save a few souls from immediate danger. Ultimately, we will have to endure the rule of this Council, with Vichetral the duke in all but name. Do you want my opinion of where you went wrong?" he offered, gently.

Gatina swallowed, wiped away her tears with her hand, and took a deep breath.

"Not really, but I guess I won't learn anything if you don't," she sighed, resigned.

"You erred in having Lady Isadra pay off her debt," he explained. "Oh, the intent was noble and compassionate," he admitted. "Anyone under the thumb of the Brotherhood of the Rat is to be pitied. But in doing so, you drew attention to her. Consider it from their perspective," he suggested.

"*Their* perspective?" she asked, confused and a little appalled.

"Yes, it's always best to view a situation from your adversary's perspective, if you can. It allows you to discover their motives, their strengths, their weaknesses, and often gives you insight into how they will react to a given situation," he advised. "In this case, there is an alliance between Count Vichetral's Council, a political organization, and the Brotherhood of the Rat, a criminal enterprise. Vichetral needs to control the palace and the reins of government, while effectively silencing any opposition that might evolve."

"That's us," Gatina realized.

"Yes, Kitten, we are in opposition to the Count. As are many in the duchy. Some protest in the streets, as you saw today, while others preach against him, while still others prepare their forces to confront him militarily, and then we're busy opposing him by stealing from him and spying on him.

"But that's where the Brotherhood comes in," he continued. "Vichetral knows how corrupt the ducal court is, and the government in general. That is true even under the reign of dukes like Lenguin, I'm afraid. The Brotherhood is part of that corruption. With their alliance, Vichetral is using that as leverage against his opposition in the palace. Which is how they got Isadra to persuade her brother not to march on the city."

"But I paid her debt!" Gatina protested. "They shouldn't have any more hold over her!"

"Ah, but her brother was not Lady Isadra's only use, to them," he pointed out. "Her husband works at the palace – a minor official, but an important one. No one who would lead a rebellion, but perhaps one who would undermine Count Vichetral's affairs as he takes over the duchy. Replacing the entire apparatus of the government overnight would lead to utter chaos, Vichetral knows. For now, he needs those minor officials to cooperate, not only to keep the duchy functioning in the transition to his rule, but to legitimize it. To ensure Isadra's husband's compliance with his policies, and keep him from joining the opposition, Vichetral and the Brotherhood were planning on using the leverage of Isadra's debt to control him.

"But now that leverage is gone," he reminded her. "When you removed it, they had to find another means to establish it. It also drew attention to Isadra, and, unfortunately, to you, and your friend Marga. Had you left things alone, Lady Isadra would still be suffering under her debt to the Rats, but she would be doing so safely at home. Now her fate is unknown."

"I really messed this up," she said, starting to weep again.

"Perhaps," Onnelik shrugged. "Perhaps not. Isadra is not the only one enduring such scrutiny, right now. Indeed, it's happening all over Falas, all over the duchy. As is the rise of the opposition, from the clergy to the navies to the merchants, to the petty nobility. Where he cannot use his soldiers to enforce his rule, he can use the Brotherhood. I expect him to ally with one of the prominent Sea Lords, next," he predicted. "But this error should inform you that the best of intentions does not guarantee the result; indeed, often the very best intentions lead to the *worst* possible consequences. Blame it on the fickle nature of the gods, if you like, or the weakness of man or the perversities of fate, but that is often how the world works."

"So, I should have just left her to suffer being extorted," Gatina said, dully.

"If you had, she'd merely be extorted, in all likelihood. Or, perhaps, she would have suffered the same fate anyway, as the situation progressed. Or, even more unlikely, something much worse could have happened to her – we'll never know. All we know is that you did what you did, and this has been the result. All else is unhelpful conjecture and painful guilt."

"So what do I do, Onnelik?" Gatina asked, miserably.

"Do? My dear, look what happened when you *did* something last time," he chided. "Sometimes doing nothing is the best thing to do. So *do nothing*, for the moment. For there is nothing much you can do. Well, I take that back," he clucked. "The one thing you can do right now is take a bath and wash that horrible stain out of your hair. You've made it clear that your Lissa alias has to disappear. She's attracted too much attention. It's time for the Mouse to become the Kitten, again. For good. And then the Kitten becomes this petty noble girl for a few days, until you get to the safe house.

"But your work here in Falas is done, for good or ill. It's time to wash away the grime, pack your things, and prepare to go. Soon," he urged. "Your mother will be returning shortly, and the sooner you can escape, the better."

"What about you?" Gatina asked, suddenly concerned.

The man smiled. "Oh, Falas is my home. There are places to hide, here, if I need to. But some of us need to stay behind and be in place to observe Vichetral. Just as some of us need to prepare for a protracted struggle against the Count. We will need both, in the days to come. It isn't widely known yet, but I've been told that Rard, Duke of Castal, is preparing to declare himself king over Alshar and Remere. When news of that is well-known, that will only add fuel to the fire, on both sides. Indeed, some may change sides. It's best to prepare for all contingencies.

"Now, off to bathe," he instructed. "I'll put some water on to heat, while you dig the tub out of the closet under the stairs. I've also got the potion Huguenin left to remove the dye from your hair. A little soap and hot water will do wonders to sustain you, Kitten. By the time your mother gets back, you'll be a new girl. Literally."

GATINA DID FEEL BETTER AFTER SCRUBBING THE WEEKS OF DIRT AND GRIME off of her grateful skin, not to mention removing the poor-smelling dye from her hair. Dressing in proper shoes and clothes was refreshing. She was Gatina the Kitten, again.

But none of it really made her feel better about Marga and Lady Isadra. In fact, being clean, fed, and safe made her feel even worse about what had transpired. She spent the time waiting for her mother to return by filling out the account in her heist journal, with Onnelik's encouragement. She didn't really feel like recording her failure, but she had to agree that a mistake unlearned from was foolishness.

Surprisingly, writing a quick page detailing the event did make her feel better in ways the bath did not. She had to be more objective, for one thing. She had to acknowledge that she hadn't done anything specifically disastrous . . . just disastrous enough. She finished the entry by outlining the areas where she had gone wrong, what she would have done differently, and how this would affect her future actions in a similar situation. It was a little humiliating to do so, but it gave her something to focus on while she waited for her mother and the inevitable lecture.

Surprisingly, Minnureal did not arrive before she was done, though she was scheduled to do so. That was troubling, but then there was a lot going on in the city, she reasoned. There were plenty of reasons why she might have gotten delayed.

In the meantime, she practiced her new alias, after she tried on the wig her mother had left for her. She began by saying the name over and over, out loud, so it came easily and naturally to her tongue: "Maid Murel of House Comalas, daughter of Lady Minwess of Dastine!"

She said it with some authority, pride, and entitlement. She'd witnessed how girls of the nobility acted, while she was trying to beg from them, and the mannerisms came easy to her. She adjusted her accent a few times, trying to overlay the Falas accent she had learned over the accent of the country nobility.

Likewise she adjusted her movements. Lissa the Mouse shuffled, unseen among the crowds. Maid Murel of House Comalas was the proud daughter of a distinguished – if not terribly important – line of Coastlords, and would not be disrespected. She was arrogant in her class, Gatina decided. She was vapid. She prided herself on her knowledge of obscure family history and dance and the arranged marriage her parents would inevitably provide for her in the future. She was a braggart, bossy, and insulting to those of lower station. The kind who would never throw a half-penny to a nit, no matter how pitiful they looked.

Maid Murel wasn't a terribly likable person, Gatina decided, and that was the point. If you were confronted with an obnoxious, entitled little girl who thought the world was hers to command, you really wouldn't want to spend more time with her than was necessary, Gatina reasoned. They were trying to leave the city, after all. Anything that sped them on their way was a good thing.

Finally, the front door banged shut, startling Gatina. She peered down the stairs and saw her mother – looking very different from normal. She wore a noblewoman's gown in burgundy, with black embroidery along the hem and collar, as well as a matching hat that was aggressively ostentatious, as was the style. Her face was made up with so many cosmetics, and done so masterfully, that Gatina would have been hard pressed to recognize her in public.

"I'm late," she announced, as soon as the door was shut behind her. She made a point of latching it. "There have been problems. The plans have changed."

"What? Why?" asked Onnelik, coming from his study.

"Because the protests in front of the palace are getting rougher. People are bringing weapons. When the first priest was hung, they attacked the gate. In reprisal, Count Vichetral ordered every entrance to the city sealed and the port closed. Including the one we were to escape through," she said, tiredly.

"So the plan has been called off?" Onnelik asked.

"The plan has been changed, again," corrected Minnureal. "Shadow sent me word: they're going ahead with the rescue, despite the protests. In fact, it becomes even more important, now. Vichetral's men have arrested hundreds. He wants them sent away from Falas quickly, before they can be seized by the mob. That would spark a true rebellion, not just street protests. An insurrection against his rule would lead to far more deaths."

"That's not good," frowned Onnelik.

"No, it is not," agreed Minnureal, taking off her hat. She caught sight of Gatina for the first time. "And who is this charming young lady?"

"Maid Murel of House Comalas, daughter of Lady Minwess of Dastine," Gatina replied, haughtily, with a sniff at the end. She curtseyed to emphasize her risen station.

"Well done, Kitten," her mother praised. "A little work on the make-up, and refresh the eye-color spell, and you don't even look like the same species as Lissa the Mouse. Which is good. The protests swept through the warehouse district already. They're likely looking for you, now."

"I know," sighed Gatina. "I pray that our story convinced them. But I have reason to think it has not. Mistress, I'm afraid I have something to tell you..."

"Darkness mayhap obscure even our own vision and deceive us into ruin, if we are inattentive. The difference between what may seem and what is lies on the edge of a sword. Employ discernment in all matters. Find the truth in each situation."

– Rule of House Furtius

CHAPTER TWENTY-TWO
SHADOW BLADE

"Gatina, what were you *thinking?*" her mother asked, exasperated, after Gatina explained what she had done, why she had done it, and the consequences that had evolved.

"I was just trying to help my friends," Gatina defended, guiltily. "I know why – *now* – I should have resisted the urge."

"You should have listened to my commands!" her mother said, sharply. "Really, Apprentice, we had words about this!"

"I didn't steal anything else," Gatina said, sullenly. "That's what those words were about," she reminded her.

"You were almost caught," Minnureal said, her eyes narrowing.

"But I wasn't, Mistress," Gatina pointed out. "In fact it was an excellent test of my skills," she said, falling back on her education. "I was able to evade three grown men – armed and trained soldiers – by using the element of surprise and superior leverage. And then disappear into the streets without detection," she defended.

"That is not the point, Apprentice!" her mother said, sternly.

"Does this affect the plan?" Onnelik asked, concerned.

"The plan is already in the chamber pot, thanks to this demonstration. Unfortunately, our people weren't able to save the Prime Minister.

I saw him executed with my own eyes," she reported, sadly. "As well as most of the senior clergy."

"Aren't the temples up in arms over that?" Gatina asked.

"Who do you think inspired the protests?" she asked, throwing a hand up in the air. "That wasn't our operation. The temples organized them. But once the clergy saw their leaders swing on the gallows, many of them had second thoughts about protesting further. Of course, by that time the damage was done.

"When the Prime Minister met the headsman's axe, the people were furious. They charged the palace gates, and even gained the walls until they were pushed back. Hundreds were hurt. Dozens died. Vichetral called in reinforcements from Rhemes, set his forces on the protests, and he has threatened more executions. He closed all the city gates and the port. It's going to be impossible to slip through, now."

"That does complicate things," nodded Onnelik. "Of course you are welcome to stay here as long as you like," he offered. "It's been fun, having company."

"We appreciate the offer, Cousin," sighed Minnureal, pouring herself a glass of wine from the cupboard. "But I don't know how much longer we can escape Vichetral's notice. Shadow has orchestrated several successful operations in a very short time. The Counts have found their plans and plots have not gone as easily as they thought they would, as a result. Messages have been altered, or have gone undelivered. Messengers have been replaced. It will only be a matter of time before they discover the conspiracy and start looking for those behind it."

"Conspiracy?" Gatina asked, curious.

"That is what we are, Kitten," Onnelik confirmed.

"I thought we were thieves?" she replied, confused.

"Oh, House Furtius are thieves, thieves of the highest order," agreed Minnureal. "But we are not alone in this struggle. A conspiracy of other Coastlord houses and even some in the Great Vale and the Great Bay are working to resist Vichetral. Perhaps even overthrow him, one day. Shadow is helping organize and run it, for now. Conspiracies thrive in darkness, and Darkness is the patron of our house," she reminded her.

"We are well suited to the task. But it also puts us in danger," she reminded her.

"We cannot tolerate problems like Lady Isadra. She is but one woman, and we are concerned with the lives of thousands. Your friend, too, sadly. We must take the utmost care in our conspiracy's security even before Vichetral realizes its existence," her mother said.

"There must be something we can do for them," Gatina said, shaking her head.

"That is not our concern," Minnureal snapped. "Now that our exit from the city is delayed, we have had to alter our plan. Shadow's agents are spreading rumors amongst the protesters that the prisoners are being kept in secret locations – which is true – and providing a few of those locations. He's hoping to put pressure on Vichetral not to delay the prisoner transfer, in fear of the population striking a few of them and rescuing them."

"So, what is our role?" Gatina asked.

"As Maid Murel and Lady Minwess are prohibited from fleeing the city, Shadow wants us to help provide surveillance to cover the operation. We're to visit the river port, tonight after curfew."

"After curfew?" Onnelik asked, surprised. "Aren't Maid Murel and Lady Minwess going to attract attention, being out after curfew?"

"We won't be dressed so flamboyantly," her mother said, shaking her head. "We'll be more elegantly dressed – in black. We'll be wearing our working clothes, tonight. In fact . . ." she said, digging around in the big bag she had carried in, "while I met with Shadow I stopped and picked up something for you, Kitten." She rummaged around for a moment longer and then brought out a sword.

Gatina caught her breath. It was only about twenty inches long, in its matte-black scabbard, and the hilt and pommel had been darkened, but there was no denying that it was a sword.

"With things as bad as they are in the city, it has been decided that we will be armed," Minnureal announced. "This is a . . . well, it's a kind of practice blade, though it is sharp enough. It was the smallest I could find in the arsenal, but it should be within your capabilities to wield – but only in your own defense," she insisted. "I pray to the concealing

Darkness that you have no need to draw it at all. If you do, wound and run away – we are not warriors. Indeed, you shouldn't have the need.

"Our task is more observational in nature than confrontational. We're to keep lookout over the spot where the secret tunnel empties into the river. There are additional patrols, due to the protests and riots. If we see anyone coming, we're to warn the others, is all. At the very most, we'll be in a position to offer a distraction, before we withdraw into darkness. The last thing this plan needs is interruption. Two extra pairs of eyes on the docks should help."

"What *is* the rest of the plan?" Gatina asked, eagerly.

"Secret," emphasized her mother. "We have our part. Others have theirs. What you do not know you cannot tell," she reminded her.

"I can be trusted!" Gatina protested.

"No one can be trusted not to reveal something under torture – and neither your age nor your sex would keep Vichetral's men from putting the question to you. It's not a matter of trust, Kitten, it's a matter of security. The only way we can protect the conspiracy is by keeping everyone's job in their own purse. The less we each know about the entirety, the more secure everyone is."

Gatina frowned, but she picked up the sword. It was light in her hand, even with the scabbard. The hilt was wrapped in black suede, and seemed to stick to her palm when she grasped it. The guard was just barely wider than the blade, a smooth, darkened disc of steel set on its edge. The pommel was a small but heavy ball of steel, ground smooth and then blackened with some alchemical process, Gatina guessed.

"Draw it," encouraged her mother. "Don't ever take a blade on a heist that you haven't practiced with."

"It's a real sword," Gatina breathed, as she slid it from the scabbard. It made no noise as she drew it. The blade was thin, elegantly shaped, coming to a slender point like a needle. It, too, was darkened. Only the gleaming edge reflected the lamplight.

"It's not a stick," agreed her mother with a sigh of resignation. "It's not a wooden practice sword. It's as sharp as a razor and strong enough to parry a heavier blade. Note the sharpened point – it's designed for stabbing, not slashing. If you do draw it, poke, don't swing. And then run like six hells into the darkness. If we get separated, do not return here – go to the teashop Onnelik took us to when we first arrived."

"I know where that is," nodded Gatina.

"This is not how I wanted to present you with your first shadow blade," Minnureal admitted. "You have barely begun your swordplay training. But I will not take my daughter on an operation undefended," she said, firmly. "Someday, you'll have a real shadow blade made to your specifications."

"What is a shadow blade?" she asked, curious.

"The signature weapon of House Furtius, and expert thieves in general," Onnelik supplied. "For those with *rajira*, it is often akin to a mageblade, like the warmagi use. Some have powerful enchantments woven into the steel and laid upon them when they are constructed. Distracting cantrips, concealment spells, spells of silence, that sort of thing.

"But it is designed for stealth, not power. A weapon of defense and utility, not attack. Most of them are constructed to the specifications of the thief who will use it. They do not reflect light – even the edge is darkened. They will not clink, when you carry them. The blade of a master thief."

"It's lovely," Gatina said, as she studied the sword.

"It is no toy, Kitten," her mother reminded her, sternly.

"I swear I will not treat it as such, Mistress," she agreed, sheathing it again. It was silent, as it slid into the scabbard. She started strapping it to the belt at her waist.

"No, Kitten, not at your hip," her mother corrected. "Over your shoulder. Else it could entangle your legs and trip you, if you're, say, dangling from a rooftop or rolling under a door," she reminded her. "I brought a harness you can use," she said, removing a black leather belt from her bag. "It's a little big, but if—"

"I can help with that," Onnelik said, taking it from her. "I have the equipment to alter it to fit Kitten. Where are you going to be stationed, tonight?"

"I'll be on top of the House of Marus warehouse," her mother answered. "Gatina will be on the ground level, in front of Gamon the Shipwright's office."

"I have plans for both, in my files," the forger agreed.

"I knew you would. Afterward, we will retire and lay low, to see how soon it takes Vichetral to figure out his hostages have escaped. We should be able to leave soon after, when his attention is elsewhere. If there aren't any more unexpected protests and sudden riots."

"Running a conspiracy in the midst of political turmoil is a challenge," agreed Onnelik. "Still, it has to be more fun than robbing jewel merchants and goldsmiths."

"Goldsmiths don't torture you to death, if they catch you," corrected Minnureal. "While I appreciate the challenge, I dislike the danger. But the stakes couldn't be higher. The entire duchy is at stake. If we rescue these people, we will have the basis for a legitimate resistance movement on which to base our next steps. If we don't, we'll struggle for years to build one. Vichetral cannot extend his direct control to the rest of the duchy until he conquers Falas. The more we can slow him down here, the longer we have to establish the networks and facilities we will need."

"Can't he just be . . . assassinated?" Onnelik asked, saying the word with distaste.

"We are not assassins," her mother said, shaking her head. "And though there are plenty who would be willing to take that role, Vichetral is well-aware of that. He is extremely well-guarded and suspicious of everyone at the palace. Even Baron Jenerard is searched, before he is allowed an audience, now. Nor would that stop the rebellious Council – though Vichetral has limited membership to five, for the sake of simplicity, there are a score of high nobles who would be willing to fill the power vacuum, out of a sense of ambition or greed or duty. Some of them could prove worse than Count Vichetral. No, killing him would not defeat him, I suppose you could say. Not without someone to replace him. At least, that's Shadow's opinion."

"Well, I wouldn't want to second-guess him," agreed Onnelik. "Still, let's keep that in the back of our minds . . ."

"Shadow thinks the best course is to retrieve Anguin from Castal, somehow. But there are many problems with that plan, yet. We just don't know enough. The situation is too fluid, and there are too many powerful players in the game. Our goal is to survive, develop our resources and try to keep the duchy from falling into full civil war. That's the best we can manage, for now."

"But for how long can we manage that? With a tyrant in control?" challenged Onnelik.

"As long as we have to," sighed her mother. "Our ancestors held out under the reign of the Black Duke for nearly twenty-five years. We can do no less."

Gatina stared at the shadow blade for a long time, as her mother and Onnelik discussed politics, the news of the day, and the horrible executions in front of the palace.

As names of nobles and ministers of the past flew around her, she started to realize just how serious things were. The thing before her was a weapon – not a toy. It could kill. It could hurt. It could save her life or take someone else's. In all of the stories she'd read, such weapons had held a mythic quality to them. The heroes and villains who fought each other used their fabled blades like props in the story.

But this sword was real . . . and it was intended for her hand. That was a heady responsibility, she realized. Stealing things was fun, in a way, as was sneaking through the darkness, and she did enjoy the boisterous swordplay she and her mother had practiced in the country garden with wooden swords. But the presence of a real blade, intended to harm someone, brought a greater seriousness to her shadow play.

Part of her mind saw it as acknowledgement of her maturity, and that made her feel far more grown-up. Part of her mind saw it as an effective end to her childhood, and it rebelled against the notion.

But there was no going back, now. She had a duty to her family, she knew, and a responsibility to her friends. Just thinking about Marga being corralled in some makeshift gaol, at the mercy of soldiers and magistrates, gave Gatina resolve. Part of her wanted to pick up the sword and go marching into the city to find her. Part of her wanted to throw the thing into the nearest canal and go find some stupid kid's game to play.

"If we can't get out of the city," her mother was telling Onnelik, when she finally tore her eyes from the dark blade, "then we will have to move to another location – we cannot endanger you, here. We can go to another safe house."

"Oh, don't be silly," dismissed the forger. "My neighbors already think you're my country cousins – which you are. There shouldn't be any questions about that. I'm well-trusted in the community," he smiled. "Any watchman or soldier who asked about me and my guests would hear about how respectable I am."

"No one is beyond suspicion, according to Vichetral's men," she reminded him. "But then things are very fluid, right now. A lot could change, depending on how tonight's rescue operation goes. We should prepare for every contingency. Now, let's go over the plan . . . do you have any maps of the port?"

"I wouldn't be very good at my job if I didn't," chuckled Onnelik, rising. "I think I have just the one, in my study. Then I'll get to work on Kitten's harness."

"Now you should go upstairs and change," Minnureal said, turning her attention back to Gatina. She reached out and touched her white hair. "You do look so very pretty and grown-up in that gown," she sighed. "But it's not exactly the fashion for midnight skulking. It's time you wore your working blacks," she said. "Including the hood and mask. There's no moon, tonight. It should be perfect for our purposes. But one flash of white hair, and you'll be too easy to identify."

"Yes, Mistress," she said, standing . . . and gingerly picking up the shadow blade and her discarded wig. The moment she did so, she knew she was committed. She grasped the hilt even more firmly. "I won't disappoint you, I promise."

"To think all our House does is steal mistakes our purpose and insults our pride. For Darkness has blessed us with our skills and our power, and mere theft, alone, is poor recompense to our patroness. We pursue our blessed vocation to enrich mankind, more than ourselves in honor of the Darkness. Our House must employ our arts with cunning and craft for higher purpose than mere gain. Darkness demands her due. This House steals away injustice and rewards wickedness with loss, it torments tyrants with insecurity and blesses the righteous with unexpected gain. Only thus do we honor our patroness and elevate ourselves above common thugs through our Art."

– The Institutions of Kiera the Great,
from **The Shield of Darkness**

CHAPTER TWENTY-THREE
THE DOCKS

THE GREAT DOCKS THAT RAN ALONG THE NORTHERN SIDE OF FALAS, ON the Mandros River, were a vast neighborhood of wood planks and well-traveled streets. The first four blocks between the docks and the rest of the city were filled with warehouses storing goods destined for down-river destinations or coming in from the upriver estates of the Great Vale. Scores of barges arrived and departed from the riverport every day, Gatina knew. She'd spent a few hours as Lissa the Mouse watching the activity. There were even nits she knew who lingered around the docks searching for a few quick coins for running errands or bearing messages. Porters and stevedores and carters and merchants were constantly moving from boat to warehouse and back again, calling out orders and shouting at each other over the merchandise that flowed through the port like the river itself. The docks, she knew, were a noisy and crowded place.

But that was during the day. At night, most barges were tied up at the banks for fear of running afoul of floating debris or overshooting their destinations in the dark. At night, the workingmen went home, and apart from a few rough inns and taverns that catered to the port's visitors, the actual docks were fairly silent. Only the lap of the river on its banks, slapping against mooring poles and dock supports, and the occasional call of a night bird filled the silence. With the curfew, not even the regular Port Watch was patrolling the boats tied up there.

Nor was it entirely in darkness. The Portmaster's spire, just north of the Tower of Sorcery, kept a lamp burning at its peak to alert any barges that might be passing that this was, indeed, Falas. But apart from that, there were few lanterns along the long stretch of cobbles and planks. What few there were cast long shadows . . . the kind that it was easy to hide in, her mother pointed out as they skulked through the empty streets. Especially with the rising mists.

They had spent an hour going over Onnelik's maps and deciding on their placement, before they left, near midnight. They had also covered all the contingencies in case things went wrong. Her mother had given her a special black candle before they departed Onnelik's house.

"It's a normal candle enchanted to burn thrice as brightly as a normal one," she'd told her, as she presented it. "The light should be bright enough to penetrate the fog. After half a minute, the flame turns bright green. You ignite it with an enchantment that even the non-Talented can use. That's very expensive, so don't use it if you don't have to. But if you see my signal, a green magelight, then light it on the dock where it can be seen from the river," she instructed. "Or if things just go to six hells. That will let our fellows know that something is amiss, and they can take steps accordingly."

"How do I know if things have gone to six hells?" Gatina asked.

"I think it will be obvious," her mother smiled. "But we're here to ensure it doesn't go to seven."

Her smile comforted Gatina, and reduced the anxiety that was making her heart flutter in her chest. She realized that she wasn't even that nervous about running into a stray Brother of the Rat or soldiers. She was worried about being on a mission with her Mistress for the first time, under her critical eye. Darkness would not protect her from that scrutiny.

"The river mist will help, as well," Minnureal said, quietly. Both wore normal cloaks over their working blacks, so as to appear, well, *normal*. Their soft leather shoes made no noise as they moved. "Of course, it will also obscure our view, so it is best that you keep your ears open, as well as your eyes. They will have to make at least five or six trips. When you think the last boat has passed, then give me a sign and head back to our meeting spot. I'll be able to see you with magesight. Other than that, just count and watch for my signal."

Gatina nodded, but did not answer. Family doctrine demanded as little speech as possible, when working.

Minnureal was to climb to the top floor of a modest warehouse, near the secret canal's exit, where she could watch the street in both directions with magesight, while Gatina was to conceal herself much closer to the hidden exit, on the dock which hung over and hid the ancient tunnel's entrance. There were actually two, Shadow had informed them: one on the upriver side, to enter the canal, and one downriver.

As they came to that point, Minnureal gave Gatina a pat on the shoulder and a single nod, and then slipped off toward the warehouse.

Gatina nodded back, swallowed nervously, and then made her way to the entrance of the dock. *Move as quiet as a shadow, as silent as a breeze*, her mother's voice filled her mind. Only this time it was not practice. It was work. And her mother was watching.

She left the dark green cloak in a folded pile behind one of the piers, out of casual sight, before she found a good spot behind a barrel to observe the space where the boat would likely exit. She settled into as comfortable a position as possible before freezing into place.

Freezing was something that had taken Gatina a long time to master. To be utterly still, not moving a muscle, was difficult for any young girl, and Gatina was more active than most. But countless hours in the countryside estate spent doing just that had allowed the energetic girl the practice she needed to do it now. Being as still as a statue was vital, her mother had often warned her, as the eye sees movement before it recognizes shapes. Merely shifting your weight while trying to be still was enough to alert even a casual observer to your presence. She slowed her breathing and allowed the discipline of stillness to take control of her body.

Only her eyes moved, darting from one part of the dark, swirling waters under the dock to another. With no moon and an overcast sky, she did not even have starlight to rely on for guidance. It took a while, minutes, for her eyes to adjust to see anything of consequence. But neither could any witnesses who might have been lurking see her behind the barrel. Darkness and shadow concealed her.

It was nearly an hour before she heard the first out-of-place splash echo from under the dock, as well as the distant sound of voices. In moments, a small punt emerged from below, crowded with people. Two Rats were in the boat, one poling the punt with a long pole at the front and the other sitting in the back, glaring balefully at the frightened prisoners between them. There were eleven, Gatina counted, all looking confused and anxious as they left the city as hostages. Many were children, she noted, well-dressed and squirmy in their captivity.

A snatch of conversation wafted up from the water as they passed by.

". . . railing around like that over a couple of hundred silver? It's unprofessional," the man poling the boat was saying. "He even accused Cleon – *Cleon!* Never a more honest Brother, and he goes and accuses Cleon! One of these days he's going to end up with a Tail in his ear," he predicted.

"Mayhap he'll settle down now that he's got that nit he's been looking for," grumbled the other man. "Saw her come in with the second crowd. She's up in his office, now. She'll be in the river by morning, no doubt. He's like to have sport with her, if she stole – hey! *No talking!* Or I'll poke you in the gut and throw you over the side!" he growled at one of the children who was trying to whisper to his mother.

Before they could continue the revealing conversation, the punt passed beyond Gatina's ability to easily overhear. A few moments after that the boat disappeared entirely in the river mists.

But she had heard enough. The man they were speaking of could only be Gavin, the master of the warehouse and sinister gangster chief. And the nit was likely Marga – it *had* to be Marga, she reasoned. She nearly shuddered at the thought of her innocent friend in the hands of the vile Rat. It wouldn't matter to him, Gatina suspected, that she wasn't Lissa the Mouse – Gavin seemed like the kind of man who would take out his petty grievances on any convenient subject, if the true object of his ire was unavailable.

That disturbed Gatina far more than the thought of Marga being under arrest. Her sense of guilt deepened over her friend's likely fate. Nits disappeared all the time, after all. A girl like Marga washing up on shore would not raise an eyebrow among the City Watch – especially not when the entire city was in chaos.

It didn't take long for the boat to return. The barge must be fairly close, Gatina reasoned. Half an hour passed before the boat emerged once again, another load of prisoners crowded into the shallow bottom. This time the two Rats were discussing some girl they both admired, and in very unsavory terms. Gatina got the impression that they were doing it for the cowing effect it had on their terrified hostages. Indeed, from what she could see of their faces, their eyes were wide with fear as they were ferried to an uncertain fate.

Gatina was wondering when the actual rescue would happen. No doubt the mysterious Shadow would be moving his forces into position, now, she reasoned. Of course, they would probably want to wait for the last of them to be gathered on the barge when they struck. No doubt she'd hear the attack from her position – or at least she hoped so. As it was, she felt helpless seeing one boatload after another of terrified prisoners go into the mists. If something went wrong, then all of those people would be doomed to suffer Vichetral's retribution if their loved ones at the palace displeased him.

The punt returned farther upriver, she knew from Onnelik's map, and twice she thought she saw it come back through the fog. A few moments after each sighting it returned through the exit, filled with people. She had still yet to hear the noise of an attack on the darkened barge. But she did overhear a few more snatches of conversation between the Rats as they worked, some of which was useful.

Six times the boat emerged from under the dock – and on the sixth, she saw something that made her want to shout. Lady Isadra, holding her infant close to her, was among the poor souls caught in Vichetral's scheming. She didn't shout, of course – her training in stillness had included the suppression of her reflexes, when she was in that mindset. Indeed, a spider walked across her hand as she crouched, and she made no move to swipe at it – even though she was not fond of spiders.

But seeing Lady Isadra and her baby alive gave Gatina some hope, as well as increasing her anxiety about the rescue. It made sense for Vichetral and the Rats to include her among the hostages, when she contemplated the matter. With her in his custody, both her husband at the palace and her brother, the baron, would be under his control in exchange for her life. None of that would have happened if Gatina hadn't interfered, she knew. Isadra would still be in the thrall of Hanik the Butcher, but she would still be safe at home with her child.

Or would she? Gatina had learned enough overhearing her mother's conversations with Onnelik about palace politics to know that it might not have mattered to Count Vichetral whether Isadra was being extorted. He may well have had her arrested, anyway, due to her husband's position. There was no way to know. That was frustrating to Gatina, but she was starting to understand that such things as rebellions and seizing political power were brutal occasions. Plenty of innocent people got caught up in them, regardless of whether they were involved. She thought of all of the citizens who'd gotten trapped in the riots in the last few weeks – how many of them had done nothing more than be in the wrong place at the wrong time?

Her thoughts were interrupted by the return of the boat a seventh and final time. It was only half-full of prisoners, now, mostly men who had their hands bound behind them and blindfolds over their eyes.

". . . last of the night, so he says. Dawn's coming," the Rat poling the boat yawned. "Then we just got to take care of that nit, and it's off to bed."

"Good thing, too – that barge is near full," agreed the guard. "Why'd they get such a small one?"

"Our regular lads are all down at the Bay, right now. They had to hire one," explained the poleman. "Cost a couple of pretty pennies, too, to rent the old wreck, I hear. Nasty business, this," he grunted, as he put his back into propelling the punt forward.

"It's better than moving untaxed wine," chuckled the guard. "We don't have to carry this lot. Of course, we do get to sample the wine . . ."

As soon as the boat passed out of sight, Gatina finally moved. She resisted the urge to stretch, as she stood, and once she was certain there was no one on the dock or the street that served it, she made a sign with her thumb, holding it up in the air for her hidden mother to see, signifying the last boat had passed. A moment later there was a tiny light on the top of the warehouse that flashed three times, as her mother signaled their people on the river. Then Gatina retrieved her green cloak, and slunk off into the shadows.

The operation was done – at least her part of it. She paused behind a pile of empty crates to sling her cloak over her shoulders, and tried to listen for the sounds of attack and struggle on the river. She heard none. She even saw the barge, as the fog briefly lifted, a long dark shape on the river. But she did not see any other boats than the punt, which was coming back to shore.

Did something go wrong? she wondered, as she fastened the cloak and watched until the mists concealed the barge again. Perhaps Shadow's attackers were swimming their way to the barge, she figured. She and her brother could both swim. Or perhaps they would take it once it was underway, further downriver, beyond the help of Vichetral's forces in Falas. Either way, she was worried that her mother's signal had somehow gone unanswered.

She was about to stand and plot her route home when it occurred to her . . . her part of the mission was done. And while she was resigned to let other people in the conspiracy effect a rescue of the hostages, she was otherwise free.

And Marga was still in danger. If not dead already.

That stung Gatina, deeply. Not even the prospect of saving Lady Isadra and her baby made up for what had happened to her friend. No one would come to rescue her. She was an unseen orphan. Only her fellow nits would wonder about her, and then forget about her. No one would try to free her. Not unless Gatina did it, herself. She had no idea how she could possibly do that, but her heart compelled her to consider it.

She was considering how to get to the gluepot warehouse with so many checkpoints between here and there when the punt emerged from the mists, making its way to the entrance of the sewer . . . and it occurred to Gatina that she had a far more direct route to the warehouse available for her. She could go in with the Rats.

She didn't allow herself to talk herself out of the insanely foolish idea. Marga was in danger, and if there was even a chance that Gatina could save her, then she had to try. She knew her mother would be furious with her, and that the punishment would be severe – if she survived. Usually breaking into an adversary's lair when you know it was filled with his men was a stupid idea. A good thief waited until no one was around.

But she wasn't stealing, she was rescuing, she rationalized in her mind. In seconds she let the cloak slip back to the ground, and then she made her way silently to the edge of the dock, where the punt was returning. She saw enough to know that both Rats were facing forward . . . so the moment the boat passed, she adjusted her mask, held her breath and stepped off the dock, falling eight feet into the river, feet first.

She was worried about the splash she may have made, as her body reacted to the shock of the cold and not-terribly-clean water. But this close to the docks, the river made all sorts of noise, she reasoned. The tired Rats might have noticed it, but she was counting on their relaxed state, after finishing their grim night's work.

Indeed, when her head finally came out of the water in the darkness, and her hearing cleared, they were grumbling about the approach of dawn and breakfast, not stealthy witnesses sneaking up on them. When Gatina was certain that they hadn't noticed her, she quietly swam to the back of the punt, and grabbed it.

That put her in the unpleasant position of being directly beneath the guard's gassy hindquarters, but it also allowed her to both listen in more carefully and let the Rats lead her directly back to the warehouse's hidden door.

". . . way I hear it, Nagal is pushing to get his own territory," gossiped the guard. "He's been working for the Tanner for three years, now, and he thinks he's ready."

"Not if Gavin has anything to say about it. He's over the Tanner, you know. He's not fond of Nagal," the poleman warned.

"Well, you can't always be happy who you have to work with," the guard said, emitting another noxious cloud from his hindquarters as Gatina clung to the boat.

"And Gavin won't live forever," admitted the poleman. "Not the way he acts. If he was gone, Nagal could move up."

"You aren't thinking of challenging Gavin, are you?" asked the guard, surprised, as they made their way through the forest of wooden piers supporting the dock, above. It was even darker down here than on the dock, Gatina noted. She could barely see anything.

"Me?" the poleman asked, surprised. "By the Maiden, no! I'm not that ambitious," he said, with a hint of pride. "I'm just saying that with all this ruckus in the street, one more body turning up isn't like to be noticed."

"Mandar would notice," the guard said, shaking his head.

"What's he gonna do, if he don't know who did it?" countered the poleman. "He's got a business to run. He'd get over Gavin's early demise pretty quick."

"Don't let anyone hear you talk like that," growled the guard. "'specially Gavin. He's excitable. Ugh, finally here," he grunted, as the punt entered a small opening in the bank: the entrance to the sewer. The river current helped push the boat through into a much narrower passage. Indeed, Gatina's soft boots were finally able to touch bottom . . . although she carefully avoided doing so, after the first time. The bottom was squishy in ways she didn't want to think about. She continued to let the boat pull her along, as it made its way through the twists and turns of the old sewer, listening to the Rats gossip about assassinations and such until there was suddenly light above her. Someone had lit a lamp in the tunnel. And then the punt came to a halt.

There was a little landing, about ten feet wide, that had a lantern on the wall and a stairway of stone leading up.

"Quitting time!" the guard said, with one last – and particularly heinous – fart before he stood in the boat and disembarked, while the poleman tied the craft up to an iron ring on the wall. "Glad that's over. Thought I'd have to poke that one little brat and feed him to the river, when he wouldn't shut up."

"That's why I don't have kids," the poleman said, shaking his head distastefully as he placed his pole against the wall of the sewer. "Noisy buggers, kids."

"Oh, mine aren't so bad," the guard said, as he blew out the lantern and headed up the stairs. The poleman followed. "Gotta knock 'em around, every now and again, but they stay quiet, after . . ."

Gatina waited until she couldn't hear them anymore before she pulled herself out of the filthy water and onto the landing. She took a moment to catch her breath and collect her thoughts.

This was, she knew, an incredibly stupid idea, she chided herself. This could easily get her killed. Or worse, caught. Mother would be angry, even if she was successful. She might even stop training her. It wasn't too late to leave, she knew. The punt was right there, ready to go. She could untie it and just drift along with the current, until she came out under the dock. Then she would be free to head to the meeting point.

But then Marga would likely die in the clutches of the vile Gavin. That thought stiffened Gatina's resolve. She could not permit that, not because of something she did. She made a fateful decision.

I'm committed, Gatina announced to herself, as she crept up the stairs. *For good or ill, by Darkness, I am committed!*

"Plan your mission. Know your objective. Doing both will save you time and disappointment. But when opportunity unexpectedly rises, react decisively and without hesitation. Such moments are gifts of the blessed Darkness."

– Rule of House Furtius

CHAPTER TWENTY-FOUR
ESCAPE!

At the top of the stairs, Gatina discovered a larger room, where it was clear the hostages had been held. It was thankfully empty, now. It was lit by a single taper in a lamp that provided enough illumination to make a quick examination. There were coils of rope, a pile of bags, and minor bits of clothing that had been discarded while they were waiting. Though the stench of fear still lingered in the musty air, the stains on the walls indicated that the chamber had witnessed far more gruesome things than mere kidnapping. She could barely detect it, considering the smelly state of her working blacks, but it was distinctive and it reminded her of Hanik's shop, the pungent smell of blood cutting through the stink of the water that clung to her clothing.

A door led to a second flight of stairs, which led to another door – one that had a convenient peep hole, likely to keep watch before allowing access to the smuggler's den. Gatina scanned the warehouse on the other side of the door through the hole, but there was little to see in the darkness. So she listened carefully for a few moments, until she was satisfied there was no one on the other side of the door.

She opened it a crack just to double check, ready to flee back down the stairs in an instant . . . but there was no one on the other side. She glanced around, ensuring there were no witnesses, then dove into the shadows.

Gatina scanned the rafters lurking in the darkness above her for a few moments, until she found her hiding place. She needed some way other than the rickety, creaky stairs to find her way up to Gavin's office, where Marga was likely being kept. She knew she had to work quickly – dawn would be breaking, soon, and even a pale sky would complicate her infiltration. Darkness was her cloak, but it was slipping.

She remembered the first time she had been here at night, the evening she'd stolen Gavin's money and run into her brother. She wished the Darkness would produce him again. She could use his help. Atopol would know how to approach this. But for all she knew, he was part of a boarding party taking control of the barge. No, she was in this alone.

She decided to try scaling the wall nearest the overhead office, instead. A stack of crates and barrels of glue made ascending the first half of the wall easy. The poorly-mortared bricks may have been too challenging for an adult to climb, but Gatina's nimble young fingers were small enough and strong enough to pull herself up, especially with her special gloves. Her boots found toeholds, even while wet, and she managed to grasp the lowest rafter of the roof mere moments after she had begun.

She smiled to herself, under her mask, as she dangled over the warehouse. She loved climbing.

As she'd done before, she started climbing along the rafters, hand over hand, getting more confident as she got closer to the office. And, as had happened before, she heard voices.

"... not my problem!" Gavin's gruff voice was insisting, loudly, as she came close enough to make out the words. "I paid him what I said I would. He gets the rest when I hear that he has made the trip."

"That was before he saw who he was hauling," said a dull voice that nonetheless sounded familiar. "Half of the court's families are on that barge, now. We thought we were hauling serfs or something, not nobility. That attracts *attention*," the other voice said, with an odd lilt. "My master wants something for the additional risk."

"Bah!" Gavin snarled. "He charged me twice the normal rate as it is!" he objected.

"This time of year, most traffic is already down river," the other voice said. "There are limited resources. Thus, our prices are higher. Especially for this kind of work. Especially for our silence," he said, with special meaning.

"Silence from who?" Gavin laughed. "You gonna run to the Duke? That's going to be inconvenient, at the moment. The Prime Minister? The Lawfather? Both grow cold while their heads decorate the palace gate. I got friends at the palace. Who you gonna tell?" he sneered.

"We figure that there are some who might be interested in that information," the other man shot back. "Folks from all over—" he said, and then his voice got muffled by someone crying. "Hey, will you keep her quiet?" the man asked, his voice irritated.

"Hey!" Gavin shouted. "We're trying to do business here! You in a hurry to fall into a canal? Cry quieter. Shut up!" he barked.

"What's with her?" the second man asked.

"Another business matter. Someone sent me the wrong goods. A friend of hers stole from me. None of your concern. By tomorrow, it won't be of anyone's concern. She'll stay quiet, won't you, honeycake? Else things could go much rougher than planned. Anyway, I wouldn't go around singing about this job," Gavin warned. "That might be dangerous for your captain."

"Which is why he wants to be compensated. Things are very unstable, right now. That makes a businessman like Master Gamard uneasy. Silver helps ease his troubled mind."

"Oh, does it?" Gavin challenged. "A man who works the Mandros has to know who I represent."

"Oh, we know," the other voice said. "We aren't scared of you lot. The rivermen talk. Nothing gets down river or up, without us. You wouldn't want to tarnish that reputation, now, would you? Especially for such a small sum, over such a delicate matter?"

Gatina couldn't believe it – *he was trying to extort the Brotherhood of the Rat!* Usually, as she'd learned, it was the other way around.

There was a long pause. Gatina eagerly moved forward through the creaking rafters to get a better vantage point from which to listen. She couldn't quite place where she knew that voice from, but she was certain she knew it.

"Your master is firm about this?" Gavin finally asked, his voice resigned.

Gatina finally managed to mount the rafter, instead of just hanging onto it. The change in perspective allowed her to look through the window of the office that looked out over the warehouse floor, so the gangster could keep an eye on his wares. Though the light was dim, she could just make out the stranger in the chair. Behind him, she saw Marga, her hands tied, squatting in the corner like a sack of potatoes.

"Exceptionally," the other man said. He said it in just the right way that it triggered Gatina's memory of where she knew the voice.

It was her brother, Atopol.

She nearly broke discipline and gasped, when she realized it. Her own brother was trying to extort Gavin, in disguise!

With horror, Gatina realized that she was intruding on another part of the complex rescue operation. Shadow, whoever he was, had contrived to get Atopol in Gavin's office, for some reason. She did not know why, or what the purpose of his mission was.

The light was just bright enough for her to make out his face – and even in the shadows, she could tell it was transformed. He wore a dark wig that gave his hair a bowl-shaped cut. There was a scar she knew Atopol didn't have on his cheek. His eyes looked blurry, and his chin seemed in need of a shave. And there was a gap between his teeth. He looked nothing like Atopol. He looked like a bargeman.

But it was Atopol's voice coming out of his mouth.

"I'll give him another thirty silver, not a penny more," Gavin sighed. "This whole bloody thing is costing me out of my own purse, now," he grumbled.

"It's uncertain times," Atopol shrugged. "Half now and half when it's done?" he proposed.

Gatina suddenly felt the wood under her feet start to give. It was a terrifying and entirely unexpected feeling, but as she tried to shift her weight, she remembered Atopol warning about some rotten boards in this section. Indeed, she felt the entire beam start to splinter under her weight. Desperately, she retreated across the straining timber to the corner of the office, placing her just outside of Gavin's window – far too close to the gangster for her comfort.

But then if she was going to rescue Marga, she was going to have to get a lot closer. Stifling her panic, she clung to the exterior of the office and tried to come up with a plan. Some sort of distraction that would get Gavin to leave the office, and leave Marga alone for long enough for Gatina to get to her. She realized the irony of not having a plan, or a backup plan. Especially after her Mistress's many lectures.

It occurred to her that Atopol's mission might be imperiled by that sort of thing. She could, indeed, be messing it up by interfering with the gangster in any way. She glanced down at the warehouse floor, below her. The sky outside was growing pale. The blessing of Darkness was receding. But now she could see the crates, barrels, sacks and piles more clearly. She scanned them all, desperately looking for something that she could use to draw the Rat out of his nest. Perhaps if she rigged a stack of boxes to fall, for instance . . .

"I'll just go and fetch your coin," Gavin sighed, getting up and heading for the office door. "Wait here. And don't talk to the girl. She's a liar, anyways."

The movement drew Gatina's eyes back to the interior of the office, as Gavin got up from his chair. That confused her – she knew he kept his coin in his office, where it was safe from all but the most daring of thieves. Why would he get up to get it, when it was right there?

As he crossed in front of the window, Gatina discovered with horror what motivated the man. There was a . . . *feeling*, the feeling she got when she sensed metal, coming from his left hand. She didn't see anything there, in the gloom, but she was sure she felt something there. Something iron, perhaps. And something long.

While she didn't know what it was, she could guess. And once Gavin went to the office door, he would be directly behind her brother. The way he was slouched, he would be in the perfect position to strike at his neck, from behind.

Gavin was about to stab her brother.

Gatina didn't think. She reacted. Just as Gavin was pretending to open the door, he turned and revealed a long, sharp piece of iron in his left hand. A Rat's Tail, Gatina recognized, the favorite weapon of the Brotherhood. He was moving cautiously, but as Marga's tearful eyes lit up in recognition of what was about to occur, Gatina flung herself through the window and into the office, as fast as she could.

"No!" she shouted, through her mask, as she rolled over the little table and into the middle of the small room. Atopol sprung up, surprised, which spoiled Gavin's aim – and revealed what he was holding to them all.

"Hey!" Atopol said, angrily, as he stared at the naked blade in the gangster's hand.

"Who in four hells are *you*?" barked Gavin, angrily. Realizing his intended target had discovered his attempt on his life, the gangster shifted his weight and moved the Rat's Tail from one hand to the other.

"What do you think you're doing?" demanded Atopol, still in character. "You was going to shank me!"

"We'll discuss that later!" Gavin demanded. "Who is this? He with you?" The blade wavered threateningly in the air. In the small space, it would only take a few steps to reach either of them.

"No!" Atopol said, surprised. "I thought he was with you!"

"I'm with *her*," Gatina said, gesturing toward Marga.

"This is going to really get bloody," Gavin said, tiredly. "It's already been a long night." With a sigh, he moved toward Gatina, raising the blade to strike.

He didn't get the chance. Atopol slammed his shoulder into the man as he took his second step, which pushed him into the corner.

But Gavin had not risen through the violent ranks of the Brotherhood without knowing how to fight. He slammed his fist into Atopol's side as he kicked out at Gatina a moment later. He moved fast, far faster than his misshapen body would suggest he could.

But Gatina could move fast, too. In a blink, she had drawn the shadow blade from over her shoulder, and as Gavin spun to attack once again, it was suddenly near his throat. He froze.

"Looks to me like you're the one who might get bloody, Master

Gavin," Atopol drawled, as he staggered to straighten himself. "This fellow looks like he means business!"

Gatina was gratified that the blade she held did not shake in her hand, as it hovered inches from the gangster's neck. He did not drop the Rat's Tail, but he did lower it a few inches, and held his hands farther from his body.

"Let's not be hasty," he said, in a tone of voice she assumed he thought was calming. Gatina didn't feel particularly calm. Indeed, she expected the Rat to try something. It was, she decided, in his nature.

"*Let her go!*" Gatina commanded, pitching her voice low and adding a gravelly element that she hoped disguised her sex as she nodded toward Marga, who stared at the scene, enrapt.

"What, *her?*" Gavin asked, surprised. "You came for the *nit?*"

"Her name is Marga, and she has powerful friends," Gatina said, maintaining her gravelly voice, as she took a half-step forward. "They sent me to fetch her!"

"Take her," shrugged the Rat, staring at the point of her dark blade. "She's no use to me. Once she tells me where her little friend went," he added.

"I'm not telling you anything, you monster!" Marga shouted.

"Untie her," Gatina commanded her brother. To her surprise, he held his hands up and shook his head.

"This is really none of my concern," Atopol protested. Gatina blinked, under her mask, then flicked her blade at her brother.

"Untie her," she repeated. Surprised at the sword suddenly pointed in his direction, Atopol shrugged.

"Only because you kept this fellow from sticking me," he conceded. "Thanks for that, by the way, boy."

"A pleasure," Gatina grunted, in her gravelly voice.

"You know you won't get away with this," Gavin said, his eyes narrowing. "In a few minutes my men will start coming in for the day's work. You won't be able to get out of the building."

"There is no building that can keep me out, much less in," Gatina boasted, returning the blade toward the Rat while Atopol quickly untied Marga. The girl rubbed her wrists where the ropes had chafed. She nodded her thanks to Atopol, who had stepped away from her, and then glared at her captor.

"You have no idea who you're messing with, boy," Gavin growled.

"The Brotherhood of the Rat," Gatina spat back. "Criminals of the lowest order. I know precisely who I am messing with." The admission caught Gavin by surprise.

"Look, this has been a very long day," Gavin said with a sigh, lowering his Rat's Tail. "Ordinarily, I'd gut you slowly for far less than this, but I'm tired, and—"

In the midst of his sentence, Gavin suddenly sprung at Marga and pulled her close to his chest. The point of his blade pressed dangerously against her throat. He grinned at Gatina triumphantly.

"Drop that sword, boy, or I'll open her veins right here in front of you!" he commanded, his voice menacing.

Instead, Gatina quickly lunged at him, the point of her blade jabbing at his right eye. Reflexively he raised his right hand – the one with the Rat's Tail in it – to protect his eyes. Which he did – at the cost of getting his palm stabbed by her shadow blade.

It wasn't a serious wound, but it was enough to allow Marga to twist away from the gangster, kicking him in the shin for good measure. Gavin howled in pain and nearly dropped the Rat's Tail – but managed to switch it to his vacant left hand, instead. He swung wildly at Gatina with the spike of iron, and for a few moments there was a struggle. She parried his strike and twisted to the side, sliding past him. He spun to strike again when Marga rammed him from behind.

The girl's mass wasn't sufficient to knock him over, but it did make him stumble. Just enough for Gatina to bring the pommel of her blade down on his left wrist, hard. The Rat's Tail tumbled to the floor, where Atopol's heavy boot came down to cover it.

Gatina knew she had to end this. She was about to grab Marga's hand and flee, when Atopol's other boot came up and kicked Gavin squarely in the face . . . hard. The Rat collapsed, unconscious, on his own office floor. Just to be certain, Atopol kicked him again. He grunted, but didn't stir.

"He's out," Atopol assured.

Gatina's chest heaved as she stared at the fallen gangster. She felt like kicking him, herself, but she knew that would be petty and unladylike of her. Perhaps she'd do it as they were leaving.

"What are you doing here?" Atopol asked her. "And why do you smell so bad?"

"I came to save her," she said, sheathing her blade awkwardly on her back. "No one else was going to. What are you doing here?"

"Keeping Gavin in his office until after dawn," he shrugged. "It looks like I was successful."

"So it does," she nodded toward the unconscious Rat.

"Who in three hells are you people?" Marga demanded, eyes wide, as she heaved for breath herself.

Atopol looked at Gatina searchingly, then shrugged. "You came to rescue her. I'll leave it to you to explain."

"I'll explain when we're out of here," she said, moving toward Gavin's disorderly desk.

"What are you doing?" her brother asked.

"It doesn't seem right to leave without stealing something," Gatina reasoned, popping open the cupboards she knew contained Gavin's loot. She found plenty to choose from, but contented herself with a few more small bags of silver. She turned and tossed one to Marga, who caught it automatically.

"Compensation," she explained. She took two more of the bags and tucked them into her pouch. It was far easier to carry there than under a dress, she decided.

"We don't have time for this," Atopol warned, peering out the window. "The sun's up, and Gavin said his workmen will be here soon."

"I'm done," Gatina nodded. "And I have a way out where we don't have to go past Cleon. All right, let's go," she said, heading for the office door. On the way out, she did kick Gavin. She didn't mind not being ladylike in this circumstance. Not one bit.

"Keep close secret our ways and our hidden lairs and refuges; for these are the fruits of centuries of toil and forethought, the treasury of our House, and should not be revealed lightly. Tell only your most trusted servants and allies of them, and thus take them into your household. For our Art requires many allies and safe houses, to be performed in fullness, and Darkness demands our trustful discernment ere it permits its secrets to be pierced."

– from **The Shield of Darkness**

CHAPTER TWENTY-FIVE
SAFE HOUSE

Gatina led them down the creaky stairs to the main warehouse floor, which was still empty of other Rats. Quietly, they opened the concealed door and shut it behind them. The chamber was dark when they entered. While that suited Gatina's sense of aesthetics, it also troubled her, suddenly.

"There was a taper burning down here, when I came up," she whispered to her brother. "Someone's been down here!"

"Are you sure?" he asked, in a murmur.

"Positive," she assured him. Indeed, it was as if she could feel someone else had passed through here recently. She was about to draw her sword when her intuition was proven correct – because Cleon lumbered into the room from the bottom stairs, carrying a lantern. There was a club in his hand.

"Hey!" he bellowed in surprise, as his lamp revealed them.

"Uh, we're looking for the privy," Atopol explained. It was clear the moment he said it that Cleon didn't believe that because the big Rat began to raise his club.

Gatina almost drew her shadow blade again – but her hands had another idea. She grabbed the black candle her fingers had brushed against in her pouch when she'd put away the stolen silver – the enchanted one. Quickly she spoke the word her mother said would activate the spell as she jabbed it in Cleon's face.

It obligingly lit into a brilliant burst of flame – bright enough to nearly blind her for a moment. That close to Cleon's eyes, it was painfully bright. He dropped both club and lantern, and clutched at his face.

"Run!" she yelled, as she pushed past the Rat. Atopol pushed Marga ahead of him, and all three tumbled down the stairs to the small landing and the secret canal.

The punt was still there. Gatina drew her sword and slashed at the rope. It took two strikes to slice through it. By that time, Atopol was in the boat with the pole, and Marga was reluctantly following.

"This is how you got in?" her brother asked.

"Yes, and how they got out," she explained, as she pushed off into the current.

"That explains how you smell," Atopol sniffed.

Gatina ignored the jibe as they drifted through the ancient sewer. Rats – real rats, not the criminal variety – skittered along the walls, as they rounded a corner. A bright spot of light in the gloom proved to be the opening, where a sliver of dawn's light promised escape.

"Who are you people?" Marga demanded, again.

"I'm a humble bargeman," Atopol said, with a shrug.

"I don't believe that," Marga said, skeptically.

"You shouldn't. He's far from humble," Gatina agreed. "I came to rescue you. Why does my name matter?"

"I'm curious, that way," Marga said, flatly. "I mean, thank you," she added, sullenly. "I do thank you. But I want to know who you are."

Gatina sighed, glanced again at her brother, and then took off her mask. She couldn't very well wear it in public, in the daylight, anyway.

"I am Maid Murel, of House Comalas, daughter of Lady Minwess of Dastine," she announced, shaking her white hair free of the cowl. "And no, that's not my real name either, but it is the name I'm using. The name I used to use was—"

"Lissa the Mouse!" Marga said, shocked. *"You're Lissa!"*

"Not anymore," Gatina said, twisting her lip. "But I was, for a few weeks. Now I'm Maid Murel. And this is . . . my brother," she admitted. That made Atopol roll his eyes. Clearly, he thought she'd said too much.

"Discretion," he reminded her, warningly.

"We just saved her *life*," Gatina replied. "She deserves to know at least a bit of the truth. I trust her," she emphasized. That earned her a reluctant shrug from Atopol, difficult to do while you're poling a punt under a dock.

"We are . . . well, that's complicated. But we do things . . . like this . . . sometimes."

"I knew something was fishy about you," Marga nodded, her eyes narrowing. "You . . . always had food. A bit of coin. And the way you fought that man in the riot—"

"You fought in a riot?" Atopol asked, with a mixture of surprise and respect.

"Just a little bit," she said, uncomfortably. "We – I was sent to infiltrate the Brotherhood of the Rat by pretending to be a nit. That's really all you need to know – or should know. Anything else I tell you might put you into danger."

"You think I'm not in danger, now?" Marga asked, as they came to the edge of the dock. Dawn had painted the sky a dull gray, and other colors were starting to appear.

"Hold, here," Gatina commanded her brother. He nodded and grabbed one of the piers, halting the boat's progress.

"Brother, be a dear and climb up the dock and get my cloak, would you?" Gatina asked. "I can't very well walk through the street looking like this," she said, indicating her working blacks. He nodded, and obliged her. As his feet disappeared from sight, Gatina turned back to her friend.

"I was going to—" she began.

"You lied to us!" Marga accused her, unexpectedly. "You lied to me!"

"What?" Gatina asked.

"You lied to me!" Marga repeated.

"Well . . . yeah," Gatina admitted. "That's kind of what you do when you adopt an alias. Pretend to be someone else. You lie about who you really are. And I'm sorry I had to do that but . . . I had to do that. I had to get into the Brotherhood of the Rat's trust, and pretending to be a nit was the only way I could do it."

"I guess you couldn't say you were Maid Murel and expect that they'd invite you in," admitted Marga with a sigh, after she thought about that. "I just . . . I don't like it when my friends lie to me."

"I can appreciate that," Gatina agreed. "For what it is worth, I really do like you. Enough to rescue you from gangsters in the middle of the night."

"I . . . well, yes, there is that," Marga nodded. "I'm sorry. Thank you again, for that. I don't think I could have done that. For what it is worth, I really do like you, too. Well, I liked Lissa. I just met you," she pointed out.

"I'll tell you a secret," Gatina decided. "While my brother is gone. He wouldn't like me saying this, but my . . . my secret name is Kitten. The Kitten of . . . Night," she decided. "If I ever need to contact you, I'll try to use that name."

"Why would you need to contact me . . . oh," Marga realized. "I guess . . . I guess we won't be seeing much of each other, will we?"

"We just broke into a gangster's den, wounded two of them, and stole money from them . . . for the second time. The Brotherhood is going to be out for blood. That's another reason why Lissa the Mouse needs to disappear. They're looking for her, not Maid Murel. Or the Kitten of Night. And I need to disappear, at least for a while. Our work here is done, for now. And no, I can't talk about it," she added, apologetically. "Let's say that it probably pissed off more than just a few gangsters. So being in Falas is dangerous, at the moment."

"Being in Falas is always dangerous," Marga said, shaking her head. "Aren't they going to be looking for me, too, now?" she asked, anxiously.

"Uh . . . I'm working on that. But you might want to use a new name for a while, yourself," she said, reluctantly.

"Great," Marga sighed. "The one thing I own . . ."

"It's just temporary," Gatina said, as Atopol slipped back over the side of the dock and into the punt with her dark green cloak. . . all without making the slightest noise.

"Here," he said, tossing it to her and picking up the pole. "Now it just looks like I'm a bargeman ferrying passengers. Where to?"

"Can you get us close to the Tower of Sorcery?" she asked.

"Close enough to walk to it," Atopol agreed, as he pushed the boat out into the daylight. The mists were starting to clear in the light of the dawn, and the river looked peaceful.

It didn't take long for them to find a small dock near the looming tower, and soon Marga and Gatina were climbing stairs up to the street. Atopol waved goodbye, before pushing back out into the river.

"Where's he going?" Marga asked.

"He's—"

"Wait, I'd be better off not knowing," Marga said, shaking her head. "Right?"

"Right," sighed Gatina. "Sorry."

"No, no, I'm getting used to it. I go try to see what my best friend is up to, because she disappeared after a riot and I was worried, only to find her talking with some high-born lady. And then I get arrested and questioned by soldiers all day. And then we're sent to this awful old warehouse, and I'm sold – sold! – by the soldiers to that . . . that monster! Do you know what he did to me? *He licked my face!*" she said, as they came to the street level.

"Yeah, he does that," Gatina sighed. "Did you say best friend?"

"It was disgusting! And yes. Then he asks me about my best friend, who I haven't seen, and who I'm worried about, and then he tells me he's going to torture me and dump me in the river if I don't talk, when I know he's going to do that even if I do talk!"

"See why it's best you don't know these things?" Gatina asked.

"Do you think he would have not tortured me because I didn't know?" Marga shot back.

"No," admitted Gatina. "But you couldn't tell something you don't know," she pointed out.

"Yes, that's quite the comfort," Marga snorted, sarcastically.

"I live a complicated life," Gatina said, a little frustrated.

"So it seems!" Marga said. She stopped, suddenly. "Where did you learn to use a sword like that?"

"It was my first time," Gatina admitted. "With a real sword, that is. I practice a lot."

"Anything else that would surprise me?" Marga demanded.

"Lots," agreed Gatina, apologetically.

"Like the fact that you're a thief? And your brother probably is, too?"

"I . . . we're more spies than thieves, at the moment," Gatina explained. "But . . . things sometimes get stolen. This time, I stole you. How did you figure it out?"

"Right," nodded Marga. "That was the only thing that made sense. You – Lissa the Mouse – was a strange girl, even for a nit. Little things. The way you talked, I guess, and the way you moved. I guess I always knew something was . . . off about Lissa."

"I expect I need to work on my disguises," Gatina grumbled.

"Oh, no one else suspected. Maybe Liddy, but she's more trusting than I am. Why are you a thief, Murel? Lissa? Whoever you are?"

"It's . . . complicated. A family thing. A legacy. It's just what I do. What we do. Anyway, try to forget you ever knew it. Well, after this," she sighed, as she continued walking. Marga followed her. "We'd better get off the street before we run into a patrol and have to explain what we're doing."

"Where are we going?" Marga asked, hesitantly.

"To get yelled at. I have a safe house near here. Only, it's not safe from hearing what my mother has to say about all of this."

"Is she – wait, I don't want to know," Marga said, firmly.

"That's the spirit," Gatina grinned, pulling the hood of her cloak up to hide her distinctive white hair. "You just keep not wanting to know things, and you'll be fine."

"Your life is, indeed, complicated," Marga said, shaking her head.

"It's about to get a lot more so," Gatina nodded.

"MOTHER, BEFORE YOU GET UPSET, I CAN EXPLAIN," GATINA SAID. SHE HAD returned from her mission, and she had brought Marga with her. To the safe house. In the middle of a crisis. Without her permission. There would be nine hells to pay, she knew. "First, this is my friend, Marga. Marga, this is my mother, Lady Minwess of Dastine," she said, alerting her mother to how much she had told the girl – and how much she hadn't.

"I expect you will," her mother said, looking back and forth between the two girls. "And I assure you, Murel, I am far, far beyond being upset!"

"I took the initiative to go back and rescue Marga from the Rats," she said, boldly. "I know it was wrong to do so without your permission. And then bring her here. But I didn't have any other place to take her, and they'll be looking for her, now."

"Murel, you try my patience like a drunken uncle," her mother glared at her. "Did we not have words about this? Twice?" she demanded.

"Yes, we did," Gatina said, uncomfortably. "I fully expect to face the consequences for this. But she's my friend," she emphasized. "I had to save her."

"Of course," Lady Minnureal said, smoothly. "And we will have yet more words about this, in private. For now," she sighed, looking from her dirt-streaked, sewer-stained daughter to the other filthy girl, "we have more pressing priorities. I'll have Onnelik prepare a bath . . . for both of you. And a bite to eat. Then we will decide what to do with you."

"There was a sewer," Gatina muttered.

"Of course there was," Minnureal said, shaking her head.

"She was very brave," Marga said, for the first time. "She really was!"

"Of course she was," Minnureal said, flashing the orphan girl a quick smile. "Murel is my daughter. Now, head up to your room and pick out some clothes for your guest to wear," she instructed. "I'm going to speak to our cousin, and then send word to your father that you're alive."

"You . . . *live* here?" Marga whispered, as Gatina led her up the stairs.

"Just for a few weeks. We have a place in the countryside," she said, keeping her answers vague. "This is the house of one of my cousins who is letting us stay here."

"Is he a . . . ?" Marga asked.

"No," Gatina said, shaking her head.

"Does he know?"

"Yes. But don't talk about it," she urged. "You aren't supposed to know."

"Right. You have your own room?" she asked, as Gatina opened the door.

"For the moment. It's pretty small."

"It's a room!" Marga pointed out, accusingly. "Not a hayloft or under a bridge! How big does it need to be?"

"When we get back home I suspect I'll be sleeping in the chicken coop, after this. I wasn't really supposed to rescue you," she informed her friend, as she dropped her cloak onto the bed.

"So I gathered. But your mother didn't hit you. She seems nice," she said, cautiously, as she looked around the little chamber Gatina had been sleeping in. "This . . . this is . . . you're . . . you're rich," she finally said.

"Rich?" Gatina asked, in surprise. "Well, by comparison, perhaps."

"You eat every day," Marga accused. "You have nice clothes. A nice house. Another in the countryside. Your mother is a noblewoman, whoever she really is, and you're thieves."

"It's more complicated than that," Gatina said. "But yes, money can be easy to come by, if you know what you're doing. We've invested it well."

"I can't believe my best friend is a rich noblewoman thief," Marga said, shaking her head. "This is just . . . weird. Complicated," she agreed.

"Did you mean that?" Gatina asked, suddenly.

"Mean what?" Marga asked, confused.

"About being my best friend? Even after I lied to you?" she asked, wondering if she really wanted to know the answer to that.

"Of course I did," Marga said, with another snort. "Why wouldn't I? I said I liked you."

"I just never had a best friend, before," admitted Gatina, as she started stripping off her filthy working clothes. She emptied her pouch on the table, including the two bags of silver. Marga reluctantly put her bag on the bed and began taking her own ill-fitting dress off.

"There aren't thief parties, where you come from?" she asked, sarcastically.

"It's a remarkably small social circle," chuckled Gatina. "And I'm just starting out. What color do you like?" she asked.

"What?" Marga asked, still confused.

"What color do you like?" she repeated. "I've got a dark red dress that is nice, and a yellow one that should fit you. But if you're more partial to blue, there's this dress I brought that just didn't look good on me. But I think it would look exceptional on you," she proposed.

"I . . . I never had a dress before. Not one that wasn't half rags. Much less more than one. And yes, I'm partial to blue."

"I thought you would be, for some reason. It's not fancy or anything—"

"Did you not see what I wore to . . . well, every day for the last year?" the orphan asked, rolling her eyes. "I'm very grateful for anything you give me," she assured. "I was thankful even when it was half a pie you had to keep Twopenny from eating. Especially for you coming to rescue me when I thought . . . when I thought the worst was about to happen."

"You're very welcome," Gatina said, sincerely. "You're my best friend, after all."

"And you're mine," Marga agreed. "My pretty, rich, noble best friend. Who's rich."

"Now you are, a bit," she said, nodding to the little bag of silver. "It's not much, but it should come in handy."

"Depending on what happens to me," Marga agreed. "Thanks for that, too. How did you know where his money was?"

"Because I was working as a runner for the Brotherhood," Gatina explained, as she handed Marga a towel. "That's the second time I stole from Gavin."

"No one deserves it more. He was awful."

"More than you know. He licked one of the other runners, once. And he smells . . . well, like a rat. I enjoyed stealing from him. It was my first heist," she revealed, with a grin. "Only I wasn't supposed to, and I got in a lot of trouble for that."

"More than . . . more than you're going to get for coming for me?" asked Marga, guiltily.

"We'll see after our bath," Gatina sighed. "But don't feel bad about it.

I don't," she said, realizing that it was true the moment she said it. "Your life was at stake. I couldn't let that happen. So you were my second heist. Also unauthorized."

"It sounds like you're developing a habit," Marga observed.

"I'm afraid that's what my mother will think, too," admitted Gatina.

"The House consists of all true-born heirs of Kiera the Great and her children, legitimate or no; for those conceived in Darkness should be retained and protected by the House in some manner, and enlisted into its service. The bastards of our House offer the promise of Talent both arcane and mundane and should be taken into service as cadet lines. Further, the House contains the allies and servants of the House, for our blessed vocation requires many willing hands and closed mouths to succeed. Trust not lightly, but when the Darkness sends the worthy to our attention, retain them in good faith. Darkness demands the House reward them for good service, protect them from harm and retribution, and ensure their prosperity; but also to repay disobedience with ire, disloyalty with dismissal, and betrayal with vengeance."

– *Institutions of Kiera the Great,*
from **The Shield of Darkness**

CHAPTER TWENTY-SIX

A RECKONING

"This is my second bath this week," Gatina said, pleased, as she soaked in the big copper pot.

"This is my first bath in . . . this is my first bath," Marga revealed, as Minnureal poured more water from the kettle into the washtub they'd brought in to serve as a second bath. "Thank you, my lady."

"The soap is lovely. It's made with goats' milk and rosewater," she informed the orphan girl. "I encourage you to use it . . . thoroughly," she said. "If anyone is searching for you, they're looking for a girl with a dirty face. Not a little girl with a clean, shining face. You're quite pretty, under all of that dirt," she complimented.

"Thank you, my lady," Marga said, self-consciously. "Am I?"

"I have every confidence," Gatina's mother agreed with a matronly smile. "But I hope you will excuse me speaking to my daughter, for a moment, while you bathe. There are things I need to know. Such as . . . how much does Marga know? And please be candid. And discrete."

"I'm getting used to Murel being vague and obscure," shrugged Marga, as she started to scrub. "I find I don't mind so much, my lady."

"She knows I was Lissa, and that I was doing things. Things that involved the Brotherhood, which she also knows about," Gatina reported, as she scrubbed under her nails. She did not want one trace of the sewer water to remain. "She knows our names. She knows they aren't our real names. And she knows that she's in danger from the Brotherhood, now. She's also very grateful for me rescuing her. I trust her, Mother," she said. "She won't tell anyone anything."

"This is a severe breach of our protocols, Murel," her mother chided with a disapproving frown.

"I know, Mother, but I couldn't help it. She knows that she doesn't want to know anything that could put her in further danger."

"Well . . . then I suppose we will have to do something to protect her," she sighed.

"I can just go back to the streets," Marga objected. "Really, just let me disappear."

"I think we can find a better solution than that," Minnureal frowned. "Besides, even with as little as you know, I would feel better if I knew you were protected. For our sake, as much as yours. I hope you understand."

"Whatever you think is best, my lady," agreed Marga. "Considering they were going to kill me and throw me in the canal, I count myself fortunate to be in any situation."

"Agreed," Minnureal nodded. "Murel, I've sent word to your father and others. We'll see if we can figure something out."

"Mother, I have an idea," Gatina said, hesitantly. "Before all of this . . . mess began, I had given some silver to Lady Isadra, to donate to Birthsister Karia, at her temple."

"Generosity is noble," her mother admitted. "But I assume you had purpose?"

"I wanted her to start an orphanage. For my friends," she proposed. "With what I took from Gavin tonight – sorry, last night," she said, as the sunshine poured through the window, "that should be enough to purchase some place. Or at least rent a house. Then they'd be safer," she insisted. "Sister Karia could take care of them, teach them to read and write like she did me, and . . . and . . ."

"Give them a home, of sorts," sighed her mother. "You remind me so much of your grandmother, sometimes. That is not a bad idea, actually," she agreed, reluctantly. "It might help our . . . activities to have someplace like a temple orphanage in town. Let me think on it and consult . . . other people. If nothing else, you've given me an idea to solve our short-term problem. You, my dear," she said, turning back toward Marga, "must disappear for a while. I think I have an idea of how to do that. Let me go prepare some messages."

"Uh, did that . . . other thing, the big thing, work out?" Gatina asked, not wanting to give away any details.

"I will know soon," she promised.

"Oh, there was one more thing," Gatina said, as her mother turned to go. "We ran into my brother, at Gavin's warehouse."

"You did?" Minnureal asked, surprised.

"You didn't know?" Gatina asked, with equal surprise.

"No, I didn't," she said, with a tired sigh. "Your brother. You're certain?"

"He helped us escape. He was in disguise," she reported.

"That's . . . very interesting. No, I was not aware. You see, there are things *I* don't need to know," she said, pointedly. "I am content with not knowing them, and trusting those who do. Perhaps you should meditate on that while I fetch more hot water, Daughter."

"I think I will, Mother," Gatina agreed.

"See? She isn't mad," Marga said, optimistically.

"Oh, no, she's furious. She's very angry. My family hides that sort of thing well, to outsiders. But she's pissed. At me. This is going to be bad, when she has time for it."

"Maybe she'll forget about it," suggested Marga.

"I wouldn't wager on that. Not an iron penny," assured Gatina. "But, for now, she's focused on you. Thanks for that."

"That's what best friends are for, I guess. She won't sell you into slavery or anything, will she?"

"No, but she might marry me off to somebody awful, just to teach me a lesson. No, probably not," she decided. "Maybe a convent. She might put me in a convent."

"At least the food will be . . . well, at least you'll have food," Marga said. Ecclesiastical fare was rumored to be plentiful, but not terribly good to anyone who wasn't a street orphan.

They speculated idly about Gatina's possible consequences until Minnureal came back ten minutes later.

"I just received a message. That thing you were asking about? It went perfectly," she said. "They are all safe, now."

"Really? Lady Isadra is safe?" Minnureal swatted at Gatina's ear. "Oh, I mean, they're all safe?"

"I was arrested with her," Marga explained. "She was nice to me, even if she didn't know me."

"She and her baby are safe, now. And that is all you need to know," Minnureal added.

Gatina felt a great sense of relief wash over her. She hadn't realized how much she'd been concerned for the naïve noblewoman who had been caught up in events far beyond her control. The idea that she was safely on her way to her brother's barony was comforting, after all she'd been through. At least she would be with family.

"Now, the two of you get out of those tubs, dry off, and take a nap. I'll wake you for luncheon. Our cousin should be back with news by then, and we'll discuss what we shall do with you."

Gatina was happy for the chance to sleep. She had been running on adrenaline and excitement since the night before, and her body was exhausted. Marga was likewise fatigued, and fell asleep next to her mid-sentence. When her mother did come to wake them, she barely felt like she'd rested.

Onnelik had returned from the market where he had met some of his contacts. He looked concerned, as they ate in the kitchen. Her mother also looked disturbed, but she was better at hiding it.

"The protests are continuing," he reported. "Smaller, today, but there are still hundreds making speeches and railing against the Count. But I confirmed that our operation was a success – the palace was in an uproar this morning, apparently. And there were no injuries among our people. All are accounted for, now. The order is to stay in place until the city settles down a bit. The gates are still closed, as is the port. That doesn't mean that we don't have some means, but with as much scrutiny and chaos as there is in the streets, it is just too dangerous to make an attempt to flee, just yet. There are armies in the field, now, some under

Vichetral's banner, and some against. Some have yet to declare. We've been told to carry on as normal and avoid suspicion until it's deemed safe to leave."

"Reasonable," her mother frowned. "Frustrating, but reasonable. And my son?"

"Safe and accounted for," Onnelik smiled.

"Good," she said, simply.

"There's more," Onnelik continued with a sigh. "There's to be a council tonight. The one we've been waiting for. You are required to attend, of course, for House Sardanz," he informed her. "There has been news from Castal."

"What sort of news?" her mother asked, even more concerned.

"We will learn tonight at the council. In the usual place," he added.

"So we will," she sighed. "Kitten, go fetch Marga and get yourselves dressed. We are going to brave the streets this afternoon. Dress for temple. Marga will have to portray your handmaiden, I'm afraid."

Gatina shrugged. "It's work. She won't mind."

THE STREETS PROVED LESS DEADLY, TODAY, AT LEAST IN THIS neighborhood. There were no coaches for hire, however, so the three of them were forced to walk. Marga made certain to walk deferentially behind Gatina, as a maidservant would, and they were only stopped and questioned twice by the roving patrols of soldiers. Both times Gatina's mother expertly talked her way through the checkpoints.

"No one questions a woman and her daughter on their way to the temple of Trygg," she explained to the girls, quietly, after she'd persuaded the second checkpoint to allow them to pass. "Men are so squeamish about such things.

"She really is going to put you away in a convent!" whispered Marga, shocked.

Gatina didn't respond because she did not know what to say. She had a suspicion of where they were heading. There were several temples and shrines to the All-Mother scattered throughout the city. When she saw a familiar clocktower, she realized which one they were headed to. The noble-looking dome of the sanctuary loomed over the other buildings as they approached. It wasn't the central temple of Trygg, where the senior Birthmothers commanded, it was a subsidiary temple. Still, it was grand, the result of generations of thoughtful gifts by rich and poor alike to support the Holy Mother's sacred work through her birthsisters.

But it was also the temporary home of Birthsister Karia, Gatina knew.

Once inside, it took a few moments to convince the novitiate on duty to summon the nun, but a silver coin encouraged her speed after she showed them to the parlor. Soon the familiar-looking clergywoman glided into the room and embraced both mother and daughter. Without using their names, Gatina noted, until Minnureal called her Murel. Sister Karia did not miss a beat.

"Blessed sister, I have a boon to ask," Minnureal revealed, when the nun had led them to the beautiful courtyard of the cloister.

"Anything that is in my power and within my vows," Sister Karia assured.

"I have heard that you have been recently given a bequest," she began.

That surprised the nun. "How did you know, my lady?"

"It is my business to know. I would like to add to that bequest – actually, my daughter would," she said, giving Gatina a matronly stare.

Wordlessly, Gatina presented the two bags of silver. She'd counted it already. Nearly fifty more ounces of silver.

"This is to further the original bequest," Minnureal explained. "My daughter is anxious to see an orphanage opened under your care, where a number of street orphans might find succor and solace . . . and perhaps a lick of education. This young lady," she said, gently guiding Marga toward the nun by her shoulders, "is to be your first charge. She will show you where the other children can be found. But until such a place may be built or acquired, I wish for her to be lodged here, and entered as a novitiate of Trygg. Under her sacred name, whatever she chooses that to be, after mediation."

"I'm going to *what?*" Marga asked in disbelief. "I don't wanna be a nun!"

"Many girls enter the novitiate cloister, my dear," explained Sister Karia kindly. "The temple provides a good education for them. Only a few of those go on to take their vows and enter holy orders in earnest. Most find good professions, or marry."

"More importantly, a cloister offers protection – and a new name. As well as room and board, and a course of study," Minnureal added.

"It is not arduous, I assure you," Sister Karia nodded. "She is . . . pursued, then?"

"Yes, by rodents," Minnureal agreed. "A new name, a clean face, and a sister's habit would go far to protect her. We will, of course, pay for her upkeep. By the time you are ready to open the orphanage, the search for her should have ended, and she can resume her normal life, I believe."

"That is . . . I shall do as you ask, my lady," Sister Karia assured, studying Marga carefully.

"I happen to know of a burned-out lot that might sell cheaply. Marga knows where it is," Gatina added, nudging her wide-eyed friend as she suffered the gaze of the nun.

"She's bright? Bright enough to learn how to read?" she asked Gatina.

"Oh, yes," she nodded. "And write, I have no doubt, Sister."

"I'm going to . . . learn to *read?*" Marga asked, confused.

"And sew and paint and cook and a great many other things," Sister Karia nodded. "If I am to build this orphanage, I will need plenty of help. Such things do not happen in a day, and even silver does not buy time and patience. If you can succeed as a novitiate, by the time we are ready for your friends, you'll be ready to help them learn these things, too."

"I am nimble with a needle," Marga said.

"And, in return, perhaps you can assist us in some of our other endeavors," Minnureal said, meaningfully. "Provided you maintain your discretion," she added.

"My lady, you have earned my trust," Marga said, politely. "Though I don't even know your real name. I . . . I hope to earn yours," she said, uncomfortably. "But I still don't understand why you are doing this . . . why are you spending all of this coin on just me?"

"Why not you?" Gatina said. "You're used to being invisible and despised. All nits are. That doesn't mean they aren't worthy of consideration. I think you're worthy of investing in, Marga."

"I'm just not used to someone being that nice to me, I guess," Marga said, still uncomfortable. "Not without asking something in return. Usually something unpleasant."

"Wait until you endure lessons with Sister Karia," Gatina said, glancing at the nun. "And all we ask in return is your discretion and your cooperation, in the future."

"I will look after her, I promise, my lady," Sister Karia assured Minnureal. "And I would not let down a friend of yours, my dear girl," she added to Gatina.

The girls' farewells were tearful, after all they had been through, but as Sister Karia led Marga away to enroll her as a novitiate with the temple, Minnureal sighed, made the holy sign of Trygg, and then led Gatina back out into the street, which was not busy.

"Do you feel better, Kitten, now that your friend is safe?" she asked, as they walked side by side.

"Yes, of course, Mother. Thank you," she said, sincerely. "And perhaps my other friends will have . . . have a home. Or at least a chance at one."

"That was nobly done, Kitten, but I must caution you with some wisdom: you cannot steal enough in a thousand lifetimes to secure such a benefit for all the world's poor. And you will go mad if you try. We help those who cross our path, as best we can, and according to their own worthiness . . . and usefulness."

"I . . . I thought you would be angrier about this than you are," Gatina confessed, as they walked.

"Oh, I am still plenty angry," her mother agreed. "But your heart was in the right place, even if your brain was being shortsighted. And such encounters do serve us. Would it surprise you to know that Sister Karia enjoys her position and status as a holy sister partially due to my doing? She was not too far from Marga's condition when we met. Once she proved her trustworthiness, assisting her to a better life was an investment that paid our family richly. And she is but one of many. All Furtiusi develop networks of friends and associates who know how to keep their mouths closed and give us what aid they can, when called upon." Her mother glanced at Gatina. "I don't fault your impulse, but I do find flaws in your execution," she said.

"Sorry, while we were running from gangsters there wasn't a lot of time for finesse," Gatina grumbled.

"Of course not," sighed her mother. "Plans change. Which is why we change our plans. But there is always a plan," she reminded her. They watched as a column of soldiers in full armor marched by. "This was not the world I planned for you, Kitten, but it is the world we find ourselves in, now. All we can do is find the best way for us to live in it. Unfortunately, that means that instead of allowing you a proper girlhood, we have to ask you to be of use to the family prematurely."

"Oh, I am eager for that, Mother," Gatina nodded, enthusiastically.

"Far too eager," frowned her mother. "Still, you have shown great skill and reasoning, while you were doing foolish things. More importantly, you didn't get caught, and you managed all to complete these tasks without a shred of *rajira*," she praised. "I don't know what the future holds for you, my love, but I can assume from this episode that it will involve greatness.

"As for your future – and mine – we must figure that out for ourselves. It is time you were introduced to some of the deeper mysteries of our family . . . and our conspiracy. It is time for you to go to the House of Shadow."

"What's the House of Shadow?" Gatina asked.

"You're about to find out," Minnureal said, as she led her into a tailor's shop.

"Among your safe houses, create especial lairs where the House can find repose, sanctuary, and a place from which to safely plan your heists. Make them as a Narasi knight makes his castle: a fortress of shadow concealed by the blessed Darkness. Make them an arsenal where the secret properties of our Craft may be safely stored. Make them an archive of the hidden knowledge of our House, far from the eyes of the mundane. Make them strongholds of arcane power from whence spells of concealment and protection may be cast. Conceal them with all of the manifestations of your art. Reveal them not to those outside the House, save for select cases and matters of extreme importance. Let these citadels of Darkness stand as unseen shadows amongst the cities of common men, hiding in their normal sight."

– from the Institution of Marella, Daughter of Kiera,
from **The Shield of Darkness**

CHAPTER TWENTY-SEVEN
THE HOUSE OF SHADOW

THE TAILOR'S SHOP SEEMED PRETTY ORDINARY, TO GATINA, WHEN SHE followed her mother inside the well-lit space.

There were two shop girls a few years older than Gatina sitting in the front, using the afternoon light to sew. They started to rise to greet them when Minnureal made a sign as she and Gatina passed. The girls nodded and went back to work, allowing her mother to lead her back to a fitting room.

On the walk to the fitting room, Gatina made note of the normal odds and ends one would find in a tailor's shop. The front of the shop displayed bolts of wool, from undyed to dyed, propped against the wall that ran the length of the shop. Measuring sticks were hung on the wall, everywhere. Baskets of thread in every color she could imagine were placed underneath the risers clients stood on for fittings.

Midway to the fitting rooms, they walked between two dressmakers' dummies showcasing the tailor's skills for both men and women, in what Gatina assumed to be the latest fashion trends, on display, though she hoped Mother had not planned to purchase such an outlandish ensemble for her to wear. The wimple itself was the only item she could see herself in, and that, to Gatina, was overdone. It looked like a honeycomb. Instead of blending in, this would cause attention, she thought, with its unusual design. *And what if bees thought so, too?* she wondered.

One of the many rules involved blending in, and she would stand out in it. The heavy silk cloak was a rich lavender, which she did like, but it did not seem to have much function to it. One small tear would shred it to pieces.

She thought back to the rafters at the gluepot warehouse. She could not begin to imagine making her way across those in a cloak like this one. It was pretty but she preferred her clothing to be far more functional. Her cloak was lightweight and could be used as a cover up; but, the fabric was also incredibly strong, so she could also use it as rope. The gown underneath the lavender cloak was a deeper shade of purple trimmed with the ivory color in the wimple. This gown was made for formal affairs. The shift peeking out underneath the dress featured that same honeycomb fabric treatment.

It was a pretty outfit, but Gatina could not imagine where she would wear it.

Gatina shook her head, garnering a tap from her mother as they made their way deeper into the shop. As they walked past a large sewing table, Gatina noticed a symbol carved into one of the table's beams. At first, she thought her eyes were tricking her, so she blinked, looked away and back. The carving was a small rose. Just like the rose painted on her great-grandmother's deck of cards. She would have to ask Mother about it, she decided.

At the fitting room's painted door, she noticed the cipher Cousin Onnelik had shown her during her lesson: *Threading the Needle*. It was disguised in the ornate decoration. But they went within too quickly for Gatina to puzzle out what it said.

"They know you?" Gatina whispered to her mother once they were inside the room, wondering how a simple hand gesture stopped the shop girls in their tracks.

"They know enough not to question me," Minnureal answered quietly, as she closed the door to the small chamber behind her. "A cousin of mine owns this shop."

"Our family owns a tailor shop?" Gatina asked, surprised.

"Who do you think made your working blacks? That's not the sort of thing you can stitch together out of homespun. Cousin Astus is an expert at such things. And no one can design a ball gown better than he – that darling gown with the honeycomb wimple and the violet cloak is one of his designs. But we aren't here for dresses, Kitten," she said, fumbling around behind a bolt of cloth that was leaning up against the back of the room. Gatina heard a click, and then was surprised when the wall slid away, revealing stairs descending into darkness. "This is one of seven entrances to the House of Shadow."

"What is the House of Shadow?" she asked, as her mother lit a taper.

"It is our main safehouse and headquarters in Falas," Minnureal supplied. "It was built by your great-grandfather, originally. That was at the beginning of the reign of the Black Duke, against whom he strived for most of his life. It is an ideal refuge in the middle of the capital. Over the years, we have entirely concealed it from view. It extends in many unlikely directions. Parts of it are known by others, but only those of our House knows all of its secrets."

"Why didn't we stay here, then?" Gatina asked.

"Because it was decided that it would be safer and more useful to stay with Onnelik. There are reasons for everything we do, Kitten. You need not understand them all, just yet. But we do everything with purpose." She descended the stairs, the taper throwing wild shadows across the secret stairwell. There was a chamber at the bottom that resembled a study. She continued across the room to another door, which revealed yet more stairs. "This is where I've been going, to collect information and report to the others. This is where we coordinate our efforts."

"It seems . . . big," Gatina agreed.

"The House of Shadow contains supplies, costumes, weapons, tools, everything we need. It amazed me, when your father brought me here to meet his parents. And it's a fortress, as strong as a castle in some ways. Yet entirely unknown to anyone who isn't familiar with its secrets." At the bottom of the stairs there was another door, which she unlocked with a key she took from her pouch.

Within was a long, wide hall that was packed with clothes of all descriptions. It made her mother's closet in the country look sparse, by comparison. "One of my favorite rooms," she added, as she brushed passed dresses and doublets, gowns and even suits of armor. "You can make yourself look like anyone, in here. That entire chest? Cosmetics. That door there leads to the shoe room – nearly a hundred and sixty pairs, in all sizes and colors – it's amazing! That door leads to the armory. And that is our jewelry room."

"Jewelry room?" Gatina asked, curious.

"Most of it is purely ornamental – we have a vault where the good stuff is," her mother explained. "But nothing sells someone on the reality of your costume like jewelry. And we've stolen an awful lot of it, over the years. It's a pretty impressive collection."

"Don't we sell stuff like that?" she asked, trying to absorb what she was seeing.

"Mostly. I'll teach you about fences someday. That's someone who sells stolen goods. But some things we steal to use, not sell." She opened a door at the end of the hall. That door led to another long passageway, and then to another door. Beyond that, however, was a chamber well-lit by lamps on the walls . . . which revealed some familiar faces.

Atopol was there, dressed in a black velvet doublet and hose, his dark mantle making him look very grown-up. His white hair was mussed, as usual, but he was not in disguise for a change. Not even his violet eyes were disguised. He grinned at her, as she emerged from the passageway.

But it was the other figure that made her squeal.

"Daddy!" she shouted, and flung herself at her father.

Hance embraced his daughter tightly, and kissed the top of her head. He looked tired, she decided when she looked up. Very tired. There were lines around his eyes that didn't used to be there, she noted. He, too, wore all black.

"I've missed you!" she burst out, as he hugged her.

"I've missed you, too," he admitted. "But your mother has kept me informed of what you have done for us, so far. I'm quite impressed. If it hadn't been for you, I don't know where we would have sent those hostages. So, how is your apprenticeship going so far, Kitten?" he asked.

"It's been eventful," she admitted with a grin. "Where have you been? What have you been doing? I've tried not to worry, but . . ."

"I've been here, there, and everywhere," he chuckled. "Most recently, I was on a barge ferrying a bunch of hostages downriver. I just got back a few hours ago, after I turned that responsibility over to someone I could trust."

"But . . . but I didn't hear any fighting on the river!" she said, confused. "How did you capture the barge?"

"That's because there was no fighting," Atopol explained. "There didn't need to be. It was our people on the barge to begin with. That's why I was at Gavin's warehouse, to distract him from checking too closely, too soon. We figured if someone from the barge came and demanded more money, that would reduce suspicion that it was a rescue – just another shady bargeman trying to get by."

"And for that he almost killed you," she reminded him.

"What?" Minnureal asked, sharply.

"It's . . . it's a long story, Mother," he said, swallowing uncomfortably. "The Rats are tough customers. You can't trust them at all. But Kitten burst in just in the nick of time, stabbed the Rat in the hand, and rescued us both."

"I only stabbed him a little," Gatina said, sheepishly. "But I did expend that magic candle, unfortunately, in the escape. Sorry about that."

"As long as it was useful, it was worth the expense," sighed her mother, who was giving her father significant parental looks. The kind of looks that usually meant a nice, long discussion would be had in the future. Clearly, Gatina saw, she wasn't terribly happy about Atopol being put in danger like that. "I was told none of our people were hurt or captured?"

"They didn't know anything was amiss until we were twenty miles downriver," her father said. "By that time it was too late. I hopped on a ferry going the other way and made it back late-morning. The former prisoners should be arriving at their new quarters by tomorrow, at the latest. Many of them could be very useful to our cause," he added. "But

I'm proud of both of you, Atopol and Gatina, for the work you've done. It has aided our effort in many unforeseen ways."

"Hopefully, Shadow approves, as well," Gatina sighed.

Atopol gave her a look. "Father *is* Shadow," he revealed with a guffaw. "You hadn't figured that out, yet?"

"What?" Gatina asked, confused, then embarrassed. "I thought he worked for Shadow, like Mother and me!"

"Which is all you would have said, if you were ever captured," her mother sighed. "That's what code names and secrets are for. Yes, your father is Shadow, leader of this conspiracy. Master Thinradel, the Court Wizard, gave him tacit permission to convene a secret council of enemies of Count Vichetral, those families loyal to Lenguin's line. He has spent months doing so. It has taken a lot of work to establish who might be loyal, and who might betray us. He's been speaking to some of the old Magelord houses and inviting them to participate for months now. His work the last few weeks in Falas is only part of what he has been doing."

"And much of that work has led to this night's emergency council," her father agreed. "Seven of the old Coastlord houses have agreed to work with us. Five have been able to send representatives to the Shadow Chamber tonight to hear our report."

"That's the chamber that we let other people know about," Atopol explained. "The only one. It's secure but separate from the rest of the House of Shadow."

"Are they Magelords or Coastlords?" Gatina asked, confused.

"Some are one or the other, some are both," reasoned Minnureal. "Each represents a family of hundreds. Some have powerful magi in them. But all trace their lineage to the Imperial Magocracy, as do we."

"And I have much to report to them, and much to discuss. We must agree on how to proceed," explained Hance. Or Shadow. Gatina's head spun, realizing that it was her father who was organizing this resistance, not merely participating in it. "Master Thinradel has sent us a message from Castal. I'm to read it to everyone at this evening's meeting. Including you two," he said to the apprentices. "It's time that you see some of what we're doing. But I encourage you not to speak, unless invited to do so. This is a very tense time, and we don't need any distractions."

"Who are these people?" Atopol asked, skeptically. "Can we trust them?"

"The original council was organized after the Narasi invasion," their mother explained. "When the Magocracy was overthrown, the Narasi Censorate was everywhere. We turned to each other during that dark time to preserve our Houses and their knowledge. That's when the protocols we use began. They were revived during the darkest times of the Black Duke's reign to conspire against him, when he again used the Censorate and his dark policies to suppress the Coastlords. But it hasn't been used since then. Our invitations referenced codes in books contained in their family libraries explaining them. If they have the proper passwords, they can be trusted. At least to be who they say they are. Some have already contributed to our cause."

"We will find out soon enough if they can be trusted against Vichetral," Hance added. "Indeed, in a way that is the purpose of calling this council. All of the families have a representative. This is the first time it has been convened in more than twenty years. I spoke to no one who was in Vichetral's employ, of course, but I'm expecting at least some support of our purpose among those I contacted. And I will warn any who consider betraying us, even if they reject the council," he added, in a darker tone. "We have a certain reputation, even among those houses who don't believe we really exist."

"You will need these," her mother said, handing Gatina and her brother each a mask she took from a chest. "I had them made for the occasion. We all go masked, in council, to protect our identities. It's tradition."

Atopol's was in the shape of a black cat, and obscured his face entirely. Gatina's was formed like a white kitten's face, and left her mouth uncovered. "Everyone is masked and uses a code name," she explained. "Only Shadow is certain who is who, under the masks. It keeps us from betraying each other."

"These are all old Magelord families, like ours," her father agreed, as they put on their masks. It felt odd, tying a kitten's face to her own, and

Atopol looked a little silly, but she could see the utility of them. "We used to have these clandestine meetings all the time back when we were defying the Narasi and the Censors, and then with the Black Duke. But Count Vichetral has made them stylish again." His own mask was a plain black void that concealed every part of his face, under the cowl he pulled over his head. Her mother's was shaped like the moon's face and, like her father's, covered her completely.

"It's an informal council," her mother said, as she straightened her own cowl. "Not all of them are magi, but all of them understand the seriousness of the situation and agreed to reconvene the council. It is a useful legacy from more troubled times. Our house is to lead, for the moment, so Shadow is to address them. But be wary – always assume that any one of them could betray us, or try to. It has happened before," she warned.

Gatina nodded, and then followed her parents down another long passageway, up some stairs, and through three separate doors. Atopol was behind her.

"You won't believe how much of a maze this place is," he whispered. "It's amazing! Secret doors, passageways, hidden stairways . . ."

"You've been here the entire time?" she whispered back.

"When I wasn't being a stableboy, a pompous young nobleman, or, most recently, a bargeman," he answered. "I only got lost once. The smell of bread drew me up toward another entrance, near a baker's shop."

They emerged into a circular chamber, neatly appointed and lit by oil lamps. There was a large table and many chairs, each with a distinctive design. Hance took the chair with a starry sky pattern on its back. Their mother took a seat with a watery chevron with three stars over it.

"So, where do we sit?" Atopol asked, looking around.

"Just stand behind us, keep silent, and look imposing," advised their father. "As I said, we have a reputation to uphold. Our white hair is telling, and the more of us in evidence, the more convincing we'll be. They'll be admitted in a moment. The protocol is to announce the house they represent and then announce their code names. Remember them," he urged. "They may come in handy later."

"I still don't know how we know we can trust them, Father," Atopol said.

"We will test their loyalty and discretion," he replied, as he removed a number of parchments from under his cloak. "Indeed, that is our purpose, at the moment. Any one of the Houses can call to convene the council, technically. But when our ancestors put this council together, they made House Furtius the guarantor of security. That's why Master Thinradel asked me to take this step."

"None of the other Houses know our true names or how many of us there are," agreed Minnureal, adjusting her mask. "The books we referenced were coded, but they explain – in part – what our house can do. We could be anyone, in any disguise. Most of them are barely aware our House even existed, until your father used the old protocols and invoked the council. Our shield is Darkness. Being mysterious and obscure is our best defense against betrayal, and the other Houses know it."

"Or they will learn," Hance agreed, firmly. "Bide. They are coming."

"Of necessity, the truth about our House must be shared with our kinsman and allies in other Houses. We dwell in Darkness, not in a vacuum. Our loyalty to our House includes loyalty to our lawful and worthy sovereigns and our fellow Coastlord Houses. For our legacy descends from the Magocracy and the power of the Magelords, before the Narasi invasion, the wisest of all folk. To fail to employ it on their behalf is a failure of our duty and dares to dishonor the Darkness. Yet such relations between Houses should be carefully controlled, concealed, contained, and encoded. Our reputation is to be cloaked in appropriate mystery, revealed only in part, and masked with all due discretion. Thus, do we manifest our power without exposing our House to discovery and menace."

– from **The Shield of Darkness**

CHAPTER TWENTY-EIGHT
THE CONSPIRACY OF SHADOWS

Sure enough, one of the narrow doors around the room opened, and a masked figure stumbled inside. The mask portrayed a dog, though not a terribly attractive one. The man under it had a beard more suited to a lion than a dog. But he bowed, when he saw Shadow and his family at the table.

"House Hegedus," the man announced, proudly. "The password is 'banner.' I am to be called Lord Hound."

"Lord Hound, you are accepted to our company," Hance nodded. "Please take your seat."

The next mask was a stylish white bird, worn by a small, thin woman in a burgundy cloak. She appeared high-born, though she wore no wimple or hat. She carried herself in a manner that spoke of temple training.

"I represent House Astutus," she said, her voice trembling. "I have heeded the call of the council. The password is 'vineyard.' I am to be known as Lady Gull."

"Lady Gull, you are accepted to our company," Minnureal agreed. "Take the seat of House Astutus."

Three more representatives arrived in quick order, two men and a woman, on behalf of Houses Salaines, Astucial, and Arcal. Their code names were Lord Ox, Lord Sky, and Lady Wind. When they were all seated, there were still chairs empty.

"Two other houses have expressed their participation, but they were not able to send representatives: Houses Falgerine and Carvial," announced Hance. "I am the representative of House Furtius, to be known as Lord Shadow. This is my wife, and representative of House Sardanz, Lady Moon," he said, as her mother stood and bowed. "We have invoked this council to address the current crisis. Duke Lenguin and Duchess Enora were killed, as I'm sure you have heard—"

"I had heard that His Grace died in battle," asked Lord Hound, confused.

"I assure you, my lord, His Grace survived the battle . . . but died overnight. It was claimed that his death was due to his wounds, but those wounds were minor. Sorcery was involved," Hance informed them.

"Who?" demanded Lady Gull. "It was said that Enora was assassinated by the Brotherhood of the Rat. Did they slay Lenguin, too?"

"No, it was likely done by the Castali," sighed Hance. "I looked into it myself. A shadowmage, most likely, who penetrated their Graces' security and blamed it on the Brotherhood. Not that they wouldn't do that sort of thing, if it suited their purpose."

"Perhaps this spellmonger everyone is talking about?" proposed Lord Ox, a big, portly man well-suited to his code name. "He is Castali, reportedly."

"I thought he was from the Wilderlands?" asked Lady Gull, confused.

"He was Castali by birth," answered Lady Wind, an older matron with a mask with a stylized cloud upon it. "He could easily have done it, from what I hear. He has irionite," she said, whispering the word.

"That may be," conceded Hance. "But we do not know enough, yet. I can tell you that the Court Wizard, Master Thinradel, who is known to many of you, has been keeping an eye on the man. As Duke Lenguin knighted the wizard himself, it would be an act of great betrayal to kill our duke. If so, we shall act accordingly," he said, menacingly.

Gatina had never heard her father use that tone of voice before, and it made the hairs on the back of her neck stand on end.

"Indeed," he continued, "I just today received a message from Master Thinradel – Magelord Thinradel, now. He is in Castal, and he is alert for our interests. It was he who suggested I convene this council," he added.

"Under the circumstances, I think that's wise, if regrettable," Lady Wind said, nodding slowly. "Not since the death of the Black Duke has Alshar been in such turmoil."

"I had no idea that this council even existed," confessed Lord Sky. "Not until I received the message that led me to a book in the family library. You say we've met before?"

Lady Wind shook her head. "I am so disappointed how some of the old Houses have neglected the education of their children. Since Lenguin took the coronet, we've all gotten lazy. Sloppy. Read your family histories," she urged Lord Sky. "You'll see the presence of the council at work, over the years. Some of us have always been on guard for the dangers that could menace us all. I am just glad that House Furtius has had the foresight to act so quickly."

"Act to do what, exactly?" Lord Hound asked. "Lenguin and Enora are dead. Their children are the captives of the Castali. Vichetral has taken control. He'll likely name himself Duke before the end of the year."

"Not while there are heirs to the coronet alive, captive or no," corrected Lady Gull.

"I really don't think he cares," pointed out Lord Sky. "Do you? He has executed half the senior clergy and a score of senior officials, since he's been here. Hundreds have been arrested. Armies are forming upriver and down. Ships in the bay have taken on weaponry, all at his command."

"Or opposed to his command," Lord Ox countered. "Half my county is ready to march against him. Alas, that is not many folk."

"There are many who would oppose Vichetral, but he opposes the Castali," Lady Gull reported. "As long as the Castali have the heirs, he's going to use that to support his legitimacy."

"As long as the heirs are in Castal, he feels entitled to do as he wishes," agreed Lord Hound. "You say that Thinradel is in Castal, watching the situation? He's a loyal Alshari, at least, if an insufferable prat on his best days. What says the Court Wizard, then?"

Hance cleared his throat and unrolled a sheet of parchment in front of him.

"This was written . . . about four weeks ago, in the Castali capital of Castabriel . . . where Thinradel reports witnessing the elevation of Duke Rard of Castal to claim the rank of King Rard of . . . Castalshar," he pronounced.

"King Rard?" scoffed Lady Wind. "What is this Castalshar?"

"The name of the united duchies of Alshar, Castal, and Remere," Minnureal explained. "Rard has . . . persuaded the Duke of Remere to agree to the union. In exchange for certain commercial concessions. So, too, does Duke Anguin. Rard had the Coronet Council recognize him as his father's heir. In part to secure his agreement to the union, no doubt."

"That's preposterous!" Lady Wind declared.

"From what we have heard, despite his captivity, the Duke – *our* Duke – favors this union as policy," Hance replied, tapping the parchment. "Thinradel reports that he spoke to the boy at length about it. He cites the success of the Farisian venture as evidence that uniting makes us more secure and prosperous. He is less certain about who, exactly, should bear the crown, but he is not in a position to be making any claims."

"I cannot fault his logic," Lord Ox said, nodding. "Shipping and commerce have blossomed, since Farise."

"I always said it was a bloody mistake to go in with the Castali on that," Lady Gull said, her eyes narrowing beneath her mask.

"But trade has flourished," Lord Ox continued. "Alshar's coffers were full."

"And now we lack a duke and duchess," pointed out Lord Hound. "There are more important things than coin, Lord Ox. The Castali slay our sovereigns, and then they claim sovereignty over us. That's a bitter draft to swallow."

"Vichetral is the antidote, then?" challenged Lady Gull. "The Duke and Duchess are dead. We can follow this Orphan Duke from his exile, or we can accept the Count of Rhemes ruling us all. I find that unpalatable. My House has opposed the House of Rhemes for a hundred years. I will not bow to him, now."

"Your House is filled with spellmongers and conjurers," dismissed Lord Hound. "Hardly a formidable adversary, you've made, or else we wouldn't be here. No, I do not prefer Vichetral. He's the nephew of the Black Duke, don't forget. He's as bad as the Narasi and the Sea Lords. But I do not see much alternative. Save open war."

"We would lose that war," Lord Ox assured him. "Despise Vichetral if you wish, but he is strong. His army in Rhemes is twice that of the Falas musters – if they would muster for anyone but the Duke. He has made alliance with the Count of Angarlan, and thus has a potent navy to control Enultramar Bay. Those two alone would be enough to dominate Alshar. Add in the strength of the Vale Lords he's recruited, and they would be impossible to defeat without outside assistance. His opposition is just not united."

"And why isn't it?" asked Hance. "Because this was an unexpected crisis, and we were caught unprepared. Now the heir is a hostage and prisoner, and our mutual foe seeks to rule. No, military strength will not defeat Vichetral," admitted her father. "Not without someone to rally our banner around. Yet I would not see our duchy conquered by Castal."

"And if Anguin does, indeed, favor this union?" asked Lady Sky, skeptically.

"There are considerations, to that," Lady Gull, said, thoughtfully. "King or no, Rard has overturned the Bans on Magic, and expelled the Royal Censorate of Magic from all his lands. From Vorone to Remere. And his wizards now work openly with irionite," she reported. "Those stones have not been used since the Magocracy. Not legally," she added. "This spellmonger . . . he has some, it is rumored."

"So does Thinradel," Hance revealed. "It is no rumor. He took an oath to the spellmonger, actually, to receive it, but receive it he did. Indeed, he favors the man, in his letter. Apparently, he and Grendine have been at odds, recently, and his support for Rard's bid for kingship has been in exchange for generous concessions to the magi. Ennoblement, for instance. Thinradel speaks highly of this . . . Minalan," he said, reading from the letter. "He was once a warmage who fought in Farise."

"For Castal," reminded Lady Wind.

"Regardless, he was in the assault on Orril Pratt's keep. Brave, at least. And politically astute enough to irritate Duchess Grendine, or rather, Queen Grendine."

"That does speak well of him," Minnureal said, with a sigh. "I see the advantages of what he has done, but he has put Rard and Grendine on the throne as a result. For the first time in four hundred years there is a king over Alshar."

"That is not entirely a bad idea, actually," Lord Ox said, cautiously. "Hear me out," he said, holding up his hand. "We all oppose Vichetral. He opposes Rard. If the Orphan Duke supports Rard as king, it gives us a possible ally against Vichetral."

"Vichetral controls the northern passes, now," Lady Gull reported. "There will be no help from Castal by land. Nor by sea."

"And if Rard did come to our aid, it would be to conquer Alshar in Castal's name. That's what Grendine will do," predicted Lady Wind. "I do so hate that woman!"

"The new Royal House, as distasteful as it is, is a distant problem," Hance insisted. "Count Vichetral is far closer and a far greater and more immediate danger to our houses. The allies he has assembled will be brutal in their oppression, especially if the Castali are the only alternative."

"So, what do you propose we do, Lord Shadow?" asked Lord Hound, his voice somewhat mocking.

"We marshal our strength," Hance proposed, after a thoughtful pause. "We support Anguin's right to the coronet. I was a personal friend of Duke Lenguin. I will see no other man than his son take sovereignty over Alshar."

"I concur," Lady Wind agreed. "Action now would be disastrous. But if we prepare properly, someday there will be an opportunity to strike. I care not whether Anguin or one of his sisters is installed, but Vichetral is unacceptable," the old woman pronounced.

"House Astutus agrees," Lady Gull nodded. "Now is not the time.

But if we work together, we can build toward the time, when it presents itself. I know Vichetral. He will beggar us all, for the sake of his vanity."

"I . . . I agree," sighed Lord Ox. "Commerce will be crippled, if Vichetral's policies are enacted. He wants to build a new navy to confront Castal, my sources tell me. He will tax us into ruin to pay for it. Twenty ships a year, he has proposed building. Warships! Do you know how expensive warships are? With the Wilderlands in Castali hands?" he complained.

"It is not his taxation I fear the most," Lord Hound offered. "It is his lax view on slavery. It is said he favors restoring the practice, recalling the glory days of the Sea Lords' slaving fleet."

"That would send the price of labor through the decks like an anchor," Lord Sky said, shaking his head. "Free men cannot compete with slaves. I stand with the council."

"The practice is abhorrent, but the Brotherhood of the Rat advocates for it endlessly," Minnureal said, her lip curled. "They will prosper if the fleets go out seeking slaves. And the people will suffer. Choose between the evils of Vichetral and the wickedness of Grendine? It galls me to say it, but my House supports organizing against the Council of Counts, against the day Anguin takes the coronet. But not as Rard's puppet," she declared.

"That is seven Houses," Hance nodded. "I shall inform the others of our decision. We will expand the network as we encounter other loyal elements. But we must proceed cautiously," he reminded them. "House Furtius was chosen to lead this council for a reason: we are adept at obfuscation and secret dealings. If there is no objection, we will contend with security. But I am open as to the next steps we take."

"Knowing who is with us, and who favors the Council of Counts would be a start," proposed Lady Wind. "The time has come to choose sides in Alshar."

"Agreed," Lord Hound said. "Assessing our strength is the first step. Knowing our enemy is the second. All of our enemies – in Castal, included."

"There are other allies we could call upon," suggested Lord Ox, thoughtfully. "In Farise, perhaps. Some of the old Houses remain there, even during the occupation."

"A Farisian contact would be welcome," Hance agreed.

"What about the Wilderlands?" asked Lady Gull. "That is part of Alshar, isn't it?"

"The part that isn't controlled by the Castali is controlled by the gurvani," Lord Hound said, shaking his head. "Vorone is ruled by a steward appointed by Rard. In Anguin's name, of course," he said, with a chuckle.

"There are those in Gilmora who would be willing to help," Lady Wind pointed out. "They're mostly Narasi, but I suppose we can't be too picky, under the circumstances."

"We will develop our alliances where we find them," agreed Minnureal. "We will define who our enemies are and what their strengths are. But we must proceed carefully, without exposing ourselves. Our council must remain the closest of secrets . . . is that understood?"

"I would be vexed to discover betrayal in our midst," agreed Lord Hound, with a growl. "It is not wise to vex me."

"I propose we name Lord Shadow as head of the council," Lady Gull proposed, "and Lord Hound as our... war leader? Sorry, I'm new to organizing a conspiracy."

"Master-at-arms, I believe is the term," Hance chuckled. "I have no objections to that. House Hegedus has produced many great warmagi over the years. I would propose we name Lady Gull our record keeper. I trust you have the resources for that?"

"If battles were fought with parchment, I have contrived a mighty army," she agreed. "We shall encode them, of course, but I shall keep the record."

"Then you shall be our archivist," agreed Minnureal. "And I recommend that we name Lord Ox as our treasurer and Lady Wind as our secretary. She will be in charge of communicating between the houses, for this conspiracy, if there is no objection."

"I can take that task," the woman agreed. "I write plenty of letters as it is."

"And what of me?" Lord Sky asked, curious.

"I was thinking of putting you in charge of recruitment, if you have a mind," Hance said. "You enjoy a certain amount of prestige, both within the Houses and out. You are trusted by both the high nobility and the petty lords. That would be in our favor."

"I will use what . . . prestige I have, I suppose," conceded Lord Sky. "I think you credit me with too much. But I do have a few fellows I think will be effective at this sort of thing. They aren't sneaky, like Furtius is, but they are capable enough, I'd say. And they hate Vichetral. They fought in the Five Barons War," he explained.

"Just how are we going to pay for all of this?" Lord Ox asked. "I am happy to keep the treasury for the conspiracy, but I cannot pay for it."

"Oh, we will find funding," smiled Hance. "Indeed, Vichetral and the Brotherhood and the other Counts will contribute, quite against their will. My house will see to that. We have a certain expertise in such matters. Any objections? Then it is settled," nodded Hance. "We all have our tasks. Soon, the city will open its gates again, and most of us can depart and see to our secret duties. I will send word about where and when we shall reconvene, and the means by which we shall communicate. Until then, be wary. These are unsettled times."

Each of the lords and ladies bowed as they departed, some through different doors. As the last one left, Hance let out a deep sigh.

"Well, that went much better than I expected," he said, taking off his mask. "I thought House Hegedus might balk at the proposal, but they are with us. And they do have many resources we can use."

"What about the clergy?" Minnureal asked, taking off her own mask. "Surely they are prime for some means of avenging the deaths of their prelates?"

"One step at a time, my love," Hance said. "We have to retreat from the fire, before we seek to add more fuel to it. We've laid the foundation. We've done what we can, on our own. Now we get a little more help. Next year, we'll get a little more. Eventually we'll be able to challenge Vichetral."

"Eventually," her mother said, shaking her head. "You did very well, my husband," she added. "I do think they are scared of you."

"As intended," he nodded. "Now, what shall we do with our cats?" he asked, glancing back at Atopol and Gatina. "They managed to stand there the entire time and not make a sound. What shall we do with them?"

"As soon as the gates are open and we can proceed, I think we need to accelerate their training even more. Cat needs his magic lessons. Kitten needs to round out her education. We're going to need both of them well-trained, if this is to succeed."

"A little seed money might be helpful, too," agreed Hance. "Lord Ox was right – this is going to be expensive. We need some coin to start out. Preferably at our foes' expense."

"Vichetral has a few estates near Falas," Minnureal pointed out. "I'm certain they have some things of value, there."

"Lightly guarded, too, with his men packed into the city," reasoned Hance. "Probably loaded with expensive items. Vichetral has extravagant tastes. So what do you think, children? Are you ready for your first family heist on our way to our country estate?"

"I find myself very enthusiastic," agreed Atopol.

"Me, as well. I like stealing things," Gatina agreed. "I think I could really get *very* good at it."

Sign up for updates to be notified of new releases in the Spellmonger world.

CONNECT WITH TERRY MANCOUR

Get updates
http://spellmongernewsletter.com/

Check out the Spellmonger series
https://spellmongerseries.com/

Join the Spellmonger Discord
https://discord.gg/68txXKR

Follow him on Amazon
https://www.amazon.com/Terry-Mancour/e/B004QTNFOO

Like his Facebook page
https://www.facebook.com/spellmongerseries/

CONNECT WITH EMILY BURCH HARRIS

Visit her website
https://emilyburchharris.com

Follow her on Amazon
https://www.amazon.com/Emily-Burch-Harris/e/B017Y87Q7U

Like her Facebook page

https://www.facebook.com/avalonschoice/

Follow her on Instagram
https://www.instagram.com/emilyburchharris

Follow her on Twitter
https://www.twitter.com/emilydbharris

ABOUT THE CREATORS

Terry Mancour is a *New York Times* Best-Selling Author who has written more than 30 books, under his own name and pseudonyms, including *Star Trek: The Next Generation #20*, *Spartacus*, the Spellmonger Series (12 books and growing), among other works.

He was born in Flint, Michigan in 1968 (according to his mother) and wisely relocated to North Carolina in 1978 where he embraced Southern culture and its dedication to compelling narratives and intriguing characterizations. He attended the University of North Carolina at Chapel Hill, where he majored in Religious Studies.

Emily Burch Harris grew up reading Nancy Drew and Susan Sand mysteries before diving into fantasy and horror novels. Born in Maryland and raised there, and in North Carolina and West Virginia, she has a knack for finding cold spots in rooms, legends about witches, lost objects, and folks who like to talk. She worked as a journalist before deciding fiction was far more fun than the stark reality of news. Emily and her husband have one son, two cats, two dogs, and a few fish. She is the editor and writing partner of Terry Mancour.

MORE TALES FROM THE WORLD OF SPELLMONGER

SPELLMONGER SERIES

Spellmonger, Book 1

Warmage, Book 2

The Spellmonger's Honeymoon: A Spellmonger Novella, Book 2.5

Magelord, Book 3

Knights Magi, Book 4

High Mage, Book 5

Journeymage, Book 6

Enchanter, Book 7

Court Wizard, Book 8

Shadowmage, Book 9

Necromancer, Book 10

Thaumaturge, Book 11

The Road to Sevendor: A Spellmonger Anthology, Book 11.5

Arcanist, Book 12

The Wizards of Sevendor, Book 12.5

Footwizard, Book 13

SPELLMONGER CADET SERIES

Hawkmaiden, Book 1

Hawklady, Book 2

Sky Rider, Book 3

SPELLMONGER: LEGACY AND SECRETS

Shadowplay, Book 1

Printed in the USA
CPSIA information can be obtained
at www.ICGtesting.com
LVHW040002250324
775403LV00024B/290